TOR PARANORMAL ROMANCE BOOKS BY JENNA BLACK

Watchers in the Night
Secrets in the Shadows
Shadows on the Soul

Shadows
on the Soul

Jenna Black

tor paranormal romance

A TOM DOHERTY ASSOCIATES BOOK
NEW YORK

This is a work of fiction. All of the characters, organizations, and events portrayed in this novel are either products of the author's imagination or are used fictitiously.

SHADOWS ON THE SOUL

Copyright © 2007 by Jenna Black

All rights reserved, including the right to reproduce this book, or portions thereof, in any form.

A Tor Book
Published by Tom Doherty Associates, LLC
175 Fifth Avenue
New York, NY 10010

www.tor.com

Tor® is a registered trademark of Tom Doherty Associates, LLC.

ISBN-13: 978-0-7653-5717-5
ISBN-10: 0-7653-5717-8

First Edition: September 2007

Printed in the United States of America

0 9 8 7 6 5 4 3 2 1

In loving memory of my mother-in-law, Lilian June Barlow, who served as a surrogate when my own mother passed away. I will miss you more than I can say.

Acknowledgments

Thanks to Cynthia Cooke, who critiqued this book without having read the first two Guardians of the Night books and reassured me that yes, it can stand on its own. Thanks to my husband, Dan, for not minding (too much) that I spend hours on end neglecting him shamelessly to write. Thanks to my editor, Anna Genoese, for allowing me the freedom to write the kind of stories I love. And thanks to my agent, Miriam Kriss, for everything she's done for me since she made that leap of faith and decided she could sell my books.

Shadows
on the Soul

1

GABRIEL GLIDED INTO THE Four Seasons Hotel bar in a cloud of glamour. He smiled as he imagined what the patrons would think if they caught a glimpse of his studded motorcycle boots and black leather. But tonight, as every night, he'd declined to dress for dinner.

He passed by a table where an amorous couple huddled close together, the besotted male oblivious to Gabriel's passing. The woman's eyebrows drew together and she shivered, sensing the passage of a dangerous predator even if she couldn't see him. He lingered, his nostrils flaring as he scented the air, but neither of them tempted him.

He'd held off feeding for the three days he'd been in Philadelphia, wanting to make a statement with his very first kill in his dear father's territory. The woman shivered again, and Gabriel realized she felt the chill of his rage. He reeled himself back in. For his revenge against the man who'd sired him and then tried to kill him, he would need to leash his rage and act with calculated precision. Which was why his first victim had to be perfect.

He could never defeat Eli in a fight. His father had been

an old and powerful vampire when Gabriel was born, and Gabriel would reach his five hundredth birthday this Christmas. But after careful thought, he'd realized he had the perfect weapon with which to torture the old man for as long as it pleased him.

Table after table he passed, considering, then discarding, one mortal after another—until he approached a woman who sat alone at a table for two. His nostrils stung as he picked up a familiar scent, acrid and yet cloyingly sweet all at once. He paused to focus his full attention on her.

He guessed her age at around thirty, and her appearance screamed Corporate America. An expensive pin-striped pantsuit clung to her curves—no doubt tailored, because off-the-rack clothes never looked so perfect. Hair of varying shades of blond framed her face in a rather severe pageboy, and her eyes held a look of intense concentration as she tapped away at her BlackBerry. A vodka martini sat neglected on the table before her.

Gabriel smiled. Now *here* was perfection. Female, pretty, with all the trappings of wealth and respectability. No doubt she was a pillar of her community. And yet, there was that scent, fighting its way through her expensive perfume . . .

He dropped his glamour enough to allow the woman to see him, then pulled up a chair uninvited.

She was so intent on her work that, for a full sixty seconds, she didn't notice him. He might have felt insulted if he were inclined to vanity. In his long-ago youth, his appearance had been quite pleasing to the ladies. But that was before Eli's sword had drawn the ugly scar across his cheek. He supposed he should be thankful the old man had lost his nerve at the last moment, or the sword would have sliced clean through his neck instead of slashing almost harmlessly across his face. But he *wasn't* thankful, and despite the fact that vampires weren't supposed to scar, the scar remained two centuries later, an ever-present reminder of his father's *love*.

When she finally noticed him, the woman started, her hazel eyes growing wide as she put the BlackBerry down.

She opened her mouth, no doubt to tell him he wasn't welcome at her table, but he reached out to her with his glamour and she froze in place with that startled look still on her face.

Gabriel smiled at her, but it wasn't a warm smile. Even through the glamour, she sensed the menace in that smile, for a hint of fear blended with her other scents. He rested an elbow on the table and leaned toward her.

"What is your name, pretty one?" he asked.

She blinked and swallowed hard. "M-margaret. Margaret McCall." The scent of fear sharpened as his glamour dragged the answer from her lips against her will.

He let his eyes drift from her face to her throat, where her pulse visibly drummed. His fangs descended, and he made no attempt to hide them. Margaret's face went pale, the pulse in her throat now leaping wildly. He could hear the beat of her racing heart as primal instincts warned her she was staring death in the face.

"You've been a very naughty girl, haven't you, Margaret?" he asked, tonguing one of the fangs.

"I-I don't know what you mean," she stammered.

He sensed her trying to look away, trying to break the hold of his glamour, but it was a futile effort. He breathed deep the scent of her, the fear and the perfume and the . . . other. The scent he liked to think of as corruption.

"I'm quite sure you do," he said. He pushed back his chair, then stood over her and offered his elbow like a gentleman. "Come along, my dear. Let's have a private little chat, shall we?"

A tiny whimper of fear escaped her throat, but she managed no more sound as his glamour forced her to her feet, forced her to take his elbow and allow him to lead her away from the illusory safety of the public bar.

"I'm going to kill you," he said conversationally as he guided her past the tables, then finally out the front door of the hotel. Fear rolled off her in waves, and he fought an unsavory urge to prolong it, to use that fear like a torturer's hot iron, not for any purpose but that it pleased him.

She was far from innocent, but she was still a mortal woman, and her crimes, whatever they were, could not compare to those of vampires, of Killers. Like himself. No, he felt no special urge to be merciful to her, but he would not torment her more than necessary. The most vicious of his torments were reserved for Killers, and there was only one of those—other than himself—in all of Philadelphia.

"Please—" the woman started, but he stopped her voice with a shake of his head.

"I cannot be bargained with. Nor can I be swayed to mercy." They were nearing a dark alley, the kind of place a woman like her was taught never to set foot in at night. "The only question is how much you will suffer as you die."

Her terror was a palpable force as they stepped into the alley to find it deserted. He pushed her up against a wall in a pool of shadow, grabbing her chin and forcing her head up so that she met his eyes.

"Confess to me the worst sin you have ever committed, and your death will be quick and painless. Lie to me, or refuse to tell me, and I will make it last, and you will feel every second of it."

Her heart galloped, and twin tears leaked from her eyes. Tremors shook her entire body. He watched the conflict that raged behind her eyes, saw her desperate desire to deny any wrongdoing. But no mortal could look into his eyes and doubt he meant what he said.

"I killed my daughter," she whispered, trying to look away but failing.

"Go on," he urged when it seemed that was all she would say. "Tell me all of it." His lips twisted into a sneer. "They say confession is good for the soul."

She swallowed hard. "I found out my husband was having an affair. He used to beat us both. I'd called the police on him once, so it was on record.

"I . . . I beat my daughter to death and said he did it. I didn't mean to kill her!" Her eyes pleaded for Gabriel to believe her.

He curled his lips away from his fangs. "You just meant to knock her around a little and then call the police on your husband?"

She nodded frantically. "Yes, yes, that's all—"

"You think that absolves you of sin?"

She didn't answer. He wasn't sure if it was fear or guilt that had stopped her tongue. Maybe both. He thought he sensed a shadow of misery on her soul, but perhaps he was projecting. If her crime made her miserable, then he was granting her mercy by killing her. He smiled to himself. Mercy, justice, and revenge all wrapped up in one pretty package.

The woman's fear spiked, but he reached out with his glamour and stilled the clamoring of her mind. Her eyes glazed, her jaw slackened, and her pulse slowed its frantic rush. At his mental urging, she turned her head to the side and exposed her throat. He brushed her hair out of the way, then lowered his head to just above her skin, breathing in deeply, drawing her bouquet of scents into his lungs.

Then, he sank his fangs into her flesh, pulling them out with a slashing motion until blood gushed from the wound. He sealed his mouth over the flow and drank deeply.

Five hundred years of kills hadn't diminished the flood of sensation that always overwhelmed him at the first taste. His head filled with power as his soul soared with giddy elation and his body hardened.

Then, he saw the memory he'd drawn to the surface, saw Margaret McCall in one of her pretty designer suits, wielding a frying pan like a weapon. Her eyes glowed with madness, and her fury slammed into him until the memory was as real as his own . . .

Betrayed. Again.

She'd believed every lie Frank had told her. Believed the anger management classes had his rage—and his fists— under control. Believed he'd been working late, even though she knew better, even though she'd caught him with that slut just last year.

She wanted to kill him, wanted to beat him as he'd beat

her, only *she* wouldn't stop. She wanted to see his head cave in under the weight of her blows. But he wasn't here, would probably never come back now that she'd caught him in his lies yet again.

She banged the frying pan against the counter, desperate for an outlet for her rage. The crash brought her six-year-old daughter running. And the rage crystallized within her, no longer a roaring, out-of-control blaze, but a cold, hard core of ice.

Gabriel wrenched his mind away, putting distance between them as that first rush of power cooled, became manageable. So much anger in her. Anger that had lived inside her all her life, that she'd never allowed herself to vent. Then one day, the anger had burst her skin and she'd welcomed it, embraced it, done things she'd always wanted to do but never dared.

Her blood flowed down his throat, her body now slack, only the press of his body against hers keeping her upright. He drank it all in, her blood, her life force, her soul. Drank until her essence had filled all the empty spaces inside him and all that was left of her was a hollow husk.

He sucked the last swallow of blood from her throat, then stepped back and allowed her body to crumple to the ground. Life and energy flowed through his veins, tingled in his extremities. His breath came short and quick, and his heart beat with renewed vigor.

He looked down at the dead woman and felt nothing but contempt for her. She thought herself a helpless victim of her own rage.

Gabriel snorted. She had no idea what true rage was. But *he* knew. It was rage that animated his body, that kept him alive and functioning from day to day. If *he* could control a rage so monstrous it felt like a separate living being within his body, then *she* certainly should have been able to control it. Instead, she'd taken it out on a six-year-old child and then absolved herself of the crime because life had treated her unfairly.

Gabriel bared his fangs in a snarl, feeling soiled by the woman's blood.

His kills were always like this. Unbridled euphoria when first he sank his fangs, then rampant disgust when his victim lay dead. And at these moments, when the kill was freshly finished, he wished he could be like other Killers. No one else he knew seemed to absorb so much of their victims. No one else felt and saw any of their victims' lives during the kill. From what he gathered, all they felt was the euphoria, the joy of the kill, each one identical—not individual human beings, with unique personalities. Just *food*.

Fury coursed through his veins, this time his own, not his victim's. He leaned his hands against the wall and closed his eyes, holding it in.

This was all Eli's fault! Eli had known when he'd bedded Gabriel's mother that it was possible for vampires to have children. True, he hadn't believed Camille was fertile, but he could have been more cautious.

Because of Eli's carelessness, Gabriel had never been human, was doomed always to be different from everyone around him. And then, after three hundred years of tolerating his Killer of a son, Eli had found God—or whatever the hell it was that happened to him—and decided all Killers must die.

Gabriel had made his life over as he took his place at his mother's side, the two of them ruling their adopted home of Baltimore for two centuries. Then Camille had shown that her own affections were as shallow as Eli's. Gabriel had put her in her place, but it was Eli who was the center of it all, who was the author of Gabriel's fate.

He knelt beside the dead woman and pulled a sheet of paper from his pocket. On it, he'd written a short but sweet note to his dear Da. He used a safety pin to attach the note to the woman's suit jacket. Then, he hauled her over his shoulder and carried her through the city streets, his glamour making them invisible to everyone they passed.

* * *

JEZEBEL BLINKED, AND FOUND herself lying on her back on the floor, staring up at a cream-colored ceiling. For an instant, she had no idea where she was, what had happened, why she was lying down. Then a familiar face hovered over her, looking down at her with concern.

"Are you all right?" Eli asked.

She blinked again, but wasn't sure how to answer the question. She felt . . . strange. And she still couldn't remember how she'd ended up on the floor.

"What happened?" she asked.

A furrow appeared between Eli's brows. "I was hoping you could tell me. One moment, you were sitting in that chair," he said, motioning, "the next moment, you bolted to your feet, took one step, then collapsed."

She shivered, suddenly cold. Intellectually, she realized Eli didn't know everything. But in the three months she'd been living under his care, she'd come to see him as the fount of all knowledge. She'd never persuaded him to tell her how long he'd been a vampire, but she knew it was a long, long time. He'd helped her through every step of her transition, always knowing just what she needed before she even guessed at it. He even *looked* the part of the wise old man, with his lined face, gray hair, and penetrating eyes.

If *he* didn't know what happened to her . . .

Eli put a hand gently under her shoulder. "Can you sit up if I help?"

There was only one way to find out.

She cautiously pushed herself up onto her elbows, Eli's hand hovering just short of touching her. She smothered a smile. He was way too knowing, understanding without having to be told that she'd prefer to sit up without his help if she could. Three months he'd known her, and already he understood her so much better than her family ever had.

Her throat tightened on the thought, and she shoved it viciously away. As far as she was concerned, her family was dead, her past buried. She'd started a new life when she'd been transformed, and she was determined to embrace it.

Her head swam a moment, then she steadied. Closing her eyes, taking in a deep breath, she tried to remember what had happened to her.

Her mind seemed reluctant to give up the memory, but she forced it to the surface. And her heart leapt into her throat.

She remembered fangs piercing a fragile throat. She remembered a rush of pleasure, like nothing she'd ever felt before. The taste of blood hot on her tongue, a woman's life draining away. And she remembered a bottomless pit of rage.

Jez put a hand to her throat and swallowed hard, fighting to keep the sudden surge of panic from showing on her face. That hadn't been *her* memory. She'd never bitten anyone, had only drunk lamb's blood, and that only when it was mixed with milk to make the task of feeding a nauseating necessity rather than a pleasure.

"Are you all right?" Eli asked again.

She nodded, not trusting her voice.

Gabriel. It had to be. He'd told her after he'd transformed her that their bond with each other might be different from the usual bond between a master and his fledgling. But he'd sent her away, sent her to Eli, only a month after she'd died and been reborn.

"I will give you time to adjust to the changes in your body and your mind," he'd said to her, looking her over with a proprietary eye. "And I will give you time to work your way into Eli's good graces. Then, when I am ready, I shall come to Philadelphia and call on you."

Gabriel scared the shit out of her, but she'd managed to look him in the eye and ask, "And what happens then?"

He'd smiled, an expression that didn't reach his chilly, gray-green eyes. "Then you will fulfill your half of our bargain."

She'd wanted to press for more information, but the look in those eyes persuaded her to hold her tongue.

In the months she'd lived in Philly, she'd tried her best

not to think about her bargain with her maker. He'd transformed her into a vampire to save her life, after she'd been gang-raped and fed on repeatedly by a flock of fledgling Killers. The memory of that horrendous trauma might have driven her mad, but Gabriel had done something to her memory, something to blunt the force of it. She knew what had happened to her, but thinking about it provoked no emotional response whatsoever. It was as if it had happened to someone else.

For protection from that memory, she'd have pledged her very soul. Perhaps she *had*.

"I think I'd like to go lie down for a while," she said, hoping Eli would just let her go home and be alone with her thoughts.

But having Eli understand her so well was a double-edged sword. He met her eyes, and she saw a hint of anger in his gaze, though his voice when he spoke was soft and gentle.

"You're hiding something from me, Jezebel."

She raised her chin a notch. Eli was a living, breathing lie detector, at least where she was concerned, so she didn't bother to lie. "I never promised you full disclosure. You said I could start here with a clean slate, and I intend to hold you to that."

He fixed her with that penetrating stare of his, his eyes eerily like Gabriel's. It took all her willpower not to look away like a guilty child.

Finally, he shrugged and offered her a hand up. She didn't think she was in any danger of collapsing again, but she let him help her anyway. He didn't let go immediately.

"When you're ready to talk to me, I'm ready to listen," he said.

Inwardly, she cringed. He'd been nothing but kind to her since the moment she'd met him. Gabriel had painted him as some kind of sanctimonious, holier-than-thou power monger, and she'd come to Philadelphia fully prepared to hate him and to enjoy whatever revenge Gabriel planned. It hadn't taken her long at all to see how distorted Gabriel's view was.

"Thanks, Eli," she said. Her voice was a bare whisper. She was afraid it would shake if she spoke out loud. She knew now she wouldn't enjoy Gabriel's revenge, and that she'd loathe whatever part she had to play in it. But she'd made a promise to her maker. He'd held up his end, and she'd be damned if she'd renege on hers.

But then, if she believed her family, she'd been damned from the moment she was conceived, so what did one more sin matter?

2

Camille stepped off the plane in the Charles de Gaulle Airport and tried to feel something. *Anything.*

She should be excited to return home after a four-hundred-year exile. Overwhelmed by the new experience of flying in an airplane. And downright terrified of her reception by the current *Seigneur* of the region, whoever that was.

Instead she felt nothing. Empty inside. Broken.

She followed the tide of mortals as they moved like sheep through the airport halls, and she was no different from them, a mindless animal at the mercy of those stronger than herself.

Her lips twisted in a mockery of a smile. There *was* some core of emotion in her, a well of bitterness she'd only just begun to tap. But was that emotion enough to sustain her immortal life?

Of course, that wouldn't matter if the *Seigneur* took exception to her arrival. If she could have contacted him and requested permission before coming, she'd have done so, but she hadn't the first idea how to go about locating him. Easier to boldly enter his territory and let *him* find *her.*

In reality, she wasn't sure it would be an unmitigated disaster if he killed her. Ever since that dreadful evening when Gabriel had revealed the extent of his powers, when she'd realized how devastatingly helpless she was in the face of her own son's anger, she hadn't been the same.

At first, she'd lived from day to day in a welter of fear, wondering if Gabriel would turn his ferocity on her. If he chose to kill her, it would not be a quick and merciful death, of that she was sure. But over the last few weeks, that fear had faded into numbness. When he'd left her nominally in charge of Baltimore while he went to Philadelphia to confront Eli, she'd known she couldn't stand to be there when he returned.

Glamour eased her through customs without need of identification, and she took a taxi to the Hôtel de Crillon. It was almost sunrise, and though she was easily old enough to walk in the daylight, exhaustion weighted her shoulders. Some of that was no doubt due to hunger.

Gabriel insisted she feed only on the mortals he brought her, and he made sure she was miserably hungry by the time he brought them. She could have fed the moment he left Baltimore, but she'd been too busy arranging her hasty trip. The cab driver would have made a perfect meal—young, quite attractive, and smart enough to be frightened of her from the moment she slid into his cab—but she was sure the *Seigneur* would frown upon her making a kill without his permission.

When she lay down to sleep on her sumptuous bed in the hotel's best suite, Camille thought she sensed a hint of contentment in her core.

She was home. And even if she died here, at least she would have seen her homeland one more time after Eli and Gabriel had robbed her of it.

Smiling faintly, she let her eyes drift closed and slept.

JEZ PACED THE LENGTH of her apartment, unable to sit still although her constant restless motion left her limbs sore and achy.

Ever since she'd left Eli's, she'd been waiting. She glanced at her watch and groaned. It was three in the morning, which meant she'd been pacing for almost four hours. For the millionth time, she forced herself to sit down.

Gabriel would either come to her, or he wouldn't. Worrying about it would do no good whatsoever. She took slow, deep breaths through her nose, closing her eyes and willing herself to calm.

Calm. Yeah, right!

After five minutes of keeping her ass in the chair, she sprang to her feet once more. She rooted through her purse until she found her pack of cigarettes, then lit one and took a long drag.

Her nose crinkled in disgust. Damn, these things smelled bad to a vampire nose! And the nicotine had about one tenth of the effect it had when she was mortal. But one tenth was better than nothing.

"And here I'd thought you'd given up that nasty habit."

Jez shrieked and whirled, the cigarette flying from her fingers. It would have landed on the couch—and possibly lit the thing on fire—except Gabriel's power stopped it in mid-air.

The cigarette rose until it was at her eye level, and the lit end collapsed in upon itself until it went out. A thin tendril of smoke snaked from the snuffed end; then the cigarette dropped harmlessly to the floor at her feet.

Jez stared at it, her heart thrumming in her throat. She knew full well that avoiding eye contact wouldn't protect her from her maker's glamour, and yet she never could resist trying.

As she kept her eyes pinned on the cigarette, Gabriel's silver-studded boots came into view. She reached out tentatively with her senses, but she couldn't "feel" him there like she could anyone else, vampire or mortal. Her vampire senses insisted she was alone in her apartment, despite what her eyes told her.

"I've had more enthusiastic greetings," he said, a hint of laughter in his voice.

She swallowed her fear and looked up at him. The sight of him was like a soft punch in the gut, stealing the air from her lungs.

Even with the scar that slashed across his left cheek, he was a treat for the eyes. The lines of his face were sharp, angular, made more so by his hair, which was a nearly white blond that he wore in stiff spikes. He had stopped aging the moment he reached adulthood, so he looked as if he might be the same age as Jez—maybe even younger. His eyes, though . . . They were not the eyes of a young man, not with that peculiarly flat, cold look to them.

His lips twisted into one of his nasty smiles, the look in his eyes not changing a bit.

Jez frowned. No one should be able to read any expression save menace from that face, and yet she knew there was pain behind the menace.

"If you wanted a more enthusiastic greeting," she said, "you could have tried coming to the door instead of sneaking up on me and scaring the shit out of me."

He shrugged and grinned. "More fun this way."

She sniffed. "If it's so much fun, then don't get pissy when I don't fling myself into your arms in welcome."

He blinked a couple of times. She knew for a fact that he wasn't used to anyone, mortal or vampire, talking back to him. But she'd been talking back to her elders ever since she went to live with her grandmother at age ten. She wasn't about to change her ways for Gabriel, or let him intimidate her.

At least, she mentally amended, she wouldn't let him intimidate her *too* much. She'd need a lobotomy not to be intimidated by him at all.

He pushed away whatever chagrin he might have felt and gave her his version of a friendly smile. "And if I'd come to your door, would you have flung yourself into my arms?"

She couldn't help laughing, a dry little chuckle. "I'm not really a throw-myself-into-a-guy's-arms type of person. No offense."

His smile looked a tad more genuine. "None taken." He looked her up and down, starting at her face and working his way down to her feet. He nodded his approval. "You look well."

She stifled any number of retorts. He had some sort of Pygmalion complex where she was concerned. He'd insisted she let her hair grow out to its natural blond instead of the jet-black dye job she'd had. He'd removed all her piercings, and had actually sliced the tattoo off her arm while she'd been unconscious during her transition from mortal to vampire. Considering his own wardrobe choices—which tended toward black leather and silver studs and chains—she didn't know why he was so fond of her demure new look. Her Gram would laugh herself sick to see Jezebel looking like a school teacher.

"Eli's been very good to me," she said, knowing just how that statement would be received.

Gabriel's eyes hardened. "I sincerely hope you aren't considering breaking our agreement."

There was no mistaking the threat in his voice. She spoke anyway. "You lied to me."

He looked both startled and offended. "I did not!"

"You made Eli seem like this wicked, evil old man who doesn't care about anyone. And he's not like that at all. He's—"

Gabriel moved so fast she didn't see his hand coming until it was wrapped around her throat. The grip was firm, but he wasn't choking her. Not yet, anyway.

He leaned into her, eyes boring into hers, freezing her so she couldn't move a single muscle. "Don't presume to tell me about my father," he said. His breath smelled like fresh blood. "I've known him for five hundred years. You've known him for three months. He is not the saint he paints himself to be."

Anger had tightened his fingers. If she were mortal, he might have left bruises on her throat. As it was, his grip was merely uncomfortable. His eyes held a hint of madness, the pupils night-dark in the center of those gray-green irises. His breath quickened, flooding her senses with the scent of his kill. She tasted that scent on the back of her tongue, and she recognized it.

She spoke without meaning to, her head reeling from the scent and taste of human blood. "Your breath tastes like the woman you killed this evening."

His eyes widened and his mouth dropped open. In a movement that was almost reflexive, he shoved her away from him. Hard.

A squeak escaped her lips as Jez suddenly found herself airborne, heading toward the wall at high speed. She closed her eyes and braced herself for the impact, but it never came.

Her breath coming short and ragged, she opened her eyes.

She hovered in the air, just slightly off the floor and about six inches from the wall Gabriel had flung her toward. She looked up and met his eyes, only to find that his impassive shield was back in place. He lowered her gently back to the floor, his power steadying her when her knees threatened to give.

"My apologies," he said in a very neutral voice. "You startled me."

She let out a shaky breath. "I guess we're even, then."

He raised his eyebrows.

She concentrated on her breathing, on slowing that frantic pulse. "You startled me when you snuck up on me," she explained. "Now, I've startled you. We're even." Although she hadn't nearly flung him into a wall in reaction to her surprise. She supposed that, considering Gabriel's nature, she was lucky he'd caught her before she hit.

His gaze pierced her. "No, we're not even, my dear. And I believe we have much to talk about."

He gestured toward her sofa. With a sigh of resignation, she brushed past him and sat down. She had a feeling this was going to be a long, uncomfortable conversation.

* * *

DRAKE WAS IN THE mood for some female companion-
ship, so after a brief evening patrol, he stopped by one of his
favorite haunts, a quirky little bar known as the Underground.
Located on Walnut Street, the bar was in a basement directly
below a terribly respectable antique dealership. An interesting contrast, though the establishments were rarely open at
the same hour.

Decorated in a London Underground motif, the bar billed
itself as a "pub," complete with dartboards and a wide selec-
tion of imported ales and beers. But it was the bar's strangely
diverse clientele that Drake found so appealing.

No one looked out of place here. Descending into the
smoky darkness, Drake saw college-age, just barely legal
kids, yuppies in business attire only slightly modified for a
night out, punks who would have usually hung out almost
exclusively on South Street, and everything in between.
There was almost a sense of magic in the place that made it
into a true melting pot. Of course, as a vampire and a Killer,
Drake was just as much an outsider here as he was anywhere else.

The weather had finally grown too warm for his trademark black leather pants and jacket, but the moment he
stepped inside, he felt feminine eyes locking onto him. He
wore faded denim jeans that fit snugly, but comfortably, and
a plain white T-shirt, but even without the leathers he had no
difficulty attracting feminine attention. He cultivated a refined bad-boy look that seemed nearly irresistible to the opposite sex, and he enjoyed the attention. He made his way
through the crowd toward the bar, ordering an exotic beer
that he wouldn't drink.

By the time the bartender popped the lid off the bottle
and set it in front of him, a busty brunette had sidled up to
the bar beside him. He smiled faintly as she feigned indif-
ference, ordering her own beer and keeping her eyes focused on the mirror behind the bar. Rarely did he have to
make the first move in a place like this.

He took a furtive look at her out of his peripheral vision,

playing the game, pretending he didn't know she was interested.

What he saw surprised him. Usually, the first women to approach him would be the local floozies, the brazen females who were cruising for one-night stands and nothing more. Either that, or they'd be the desperate types attempting to drown their sorrows in booze and sex. He preferred his companions sober, and while he wasn't in any position to offer a long-term relationship, he usually wanted—and got—more than one night.

The woman beside him looked to be in her early thirties, and while her clingy knit blouse showed her ample bosom to its best advantage, she was otherwise dressed relatively demurely in a pair of loose-fitting khaki trousers. Definitely not floozy attire. And she didn't have that wild-eyed look of the desperate ones, nor had she yet drummed up the courage to speak to him.

The Underground never had live music, but the jukebox was always playing full blast, and there was a small area clear of tables that served as a tiny dance floor. There was a moment of near-silence as the music changed, then a twangy country ballad started up. Most of the bar's patrons groaned or rolled their eyes, and the crowd on the dance floor thinned. While the Underground was host to any number of tastes, country wasn't one of them.

With his acute hearing, Drake picked up the quick intake of breath that suggested the woman was about to speak to him, but when the song came on she closed her mouth so quickly her teeth clicked together. He fought a smile. A slow dance was, apparently, too much of a challenge to her courage. No doubt she was one of those women who believed deep down that men should make the first move.

Being more than a hundred years old himself, Drake found the old-fashioned attitude rather charming. He bent a little closer to her so he could speak without shouting.

"Would you like to dance?"

She almost jumped out of her shoes, then color rushed to

her face. She put a hand to her throat and laughed shakily. "Sorry," she said, blushing harder. "You startled me."

He smiled at her, exerting just a touch of glamour in hopes that it would soothe her obviously brittle nerves. There was something innocently appealing about her, something that made him hope she'd say yes.

"I'd love to dance," she said, her voice suddenly breathy.

Drake reeled his glamour back in. Calming her nerves was one thing. Clouding her judgment was another. He had little enough trouble finding women to warm his bed; he didn't need to seduce the reluctant.

But even without the glamour, she smiled shyly at him as he led her to the floor, their beers forgotten. "I'm Stacy," she said, holding out her hand for him to shake, then starting to jerk it back. Color flooded her cheeks again, and Drake had to fight the urge to laugh.

Obviously, she was new to the sport of picking up men in bars. He caught her hand and raised her knuckles to his lips, grinning at her as he planted a courtly kiss there.

"Pleased to meet you, Stacy," he said, not letting go of her hand. "My name's Drake."

"Hi," she said, grinning a bit herself. "You must think I'm the world's worst doofus."

He laughed, but didn't answer, figuring anything he said would make her feel worse. Instead, he put his hands around her waist and drew her to him, close enough for intimacy, but not so close as to be inappropriately forward with a complete stranger.

Tentatively, she put her arms around his neck and let him guide her as they swayed to the music. He grimaced at the syrupy lyrics.

"It really is a dreadful song," he said, then hoped it wasn't Stacy who'd put it on the jukebox in the first place.

She laughed, a little of the tension going out of her. "Yeah, it is. But at least it's got a good beat."

He drew her a little closer, until their bodies were almost touching. Her head barely came up to his chin, and she had to tilt back a bit to look up at him. Her eyes were an enchanting shade of hazel, almost green. The hint of uncertainty in them just made her more sexy. Her hair smelled of citrus shampoo, blended with a faint, floral perfume.

Yes, he decided as he smiled down at her. She had definite potential.

He stifled a groan when his cell phone vibrated against his hip. He wasn't exactly a social butterfly, being something of an outcast amongst the Guardians, so there was only one person who could be calling him. And it couldn't be good news.

The music was loud enough that Stacy couldn't hear the buzzing of the phone, but she got the hint when he let go of her and unclipped it from his belt. He tried glaring at it, but it kept vibrating.

He shook his head, giving Stacy an apologetic smile. "I'm really sorry, but I have to take this call."

She smiled gamely, despite her obvious disappointment. He offered her his elbow. She blinked at him in surprise, then took it as he flipped open the phone with his other hand.

"I'll call you back in a minute, when I get somewhere quieter," he practically shouted into the phone, then hung up.

The bartender had cleared both their beers. Drake insisted on buying her another one before he left.

"Maybe we'll meet again some day," he said.

"Maybe," she agreed, but she didn't believe it any more than he did.

He heard her sigh of regret after he turned his back and headed toward the door. Usually, he enjoyed the work he did for the Guardians, using his superior strength as a Killer to track down and destroy other Killers who preyed on the innocent. But that was before he'd learned some disturbing truths about Eli during his trip to Baltimore several months earlier. Ever since then, the job had become *work*.

Once he stepped out of the bar and into the relative quiet of the city streets, he speed-dialed Eli's number.

"Sorry to interrupt your evening's entertainment," Eli said, skipping the formal greeting.

Drake raised his eyebrows. Eli sounded odd, his voice a little tight, his tone a little sharper than usual. "What's up?" he asked, but he already had a suspicion.

"I think this is a conversation to be had in person. Can you come down to the house?"

Drake scrubbed his hair away from his face. It didn't take a genius to guess what caused that tightness in the Founder's voice. "It's Gabriel, isn't it? He's made good on his threat to come visit?"

"Just come to the house."

Drake took that to mean yes. He hung up and hailed a cab to drive him the fifteen blocks to Eli's house on the river.

Eli's house, perhaps more appropriately termed a mansion, was a stately Victorian that sat proudly on the banks of the Delaware. The house was surrounded by lovingly kept gardens and lawn, and bounded on all sides by a high fence. The fence, made of almost pure iron, was enough to deter any unwanted vampire visitors. And a powerful glamour like nothing Drake had ever felt before made the house all but invisible to mortals, except those special few he let in.

Drake felt the glamour close around him as he approached the gate, rendering the few mortals who were up and about at this hour oblivious to him as he rang the bell of the house they couldn't see. The gate buzzed and opened for him. He stepped through, careful not to touch the iron, which would leave a nasty burn.

The front door stood open, so Drake strode in and headed toward the meeting room, where he assumed Eli awaited him. The meeting room had no doubt been a ballroom when this house had first been built, but now made a convenient gathering place for all the Guardians.

No other Guardians were in there tonight. Eli stood by himself, his back to the doorway, staring into the fireplace—something he did often when there was actually a fire in the grate, but just now he was staring at an empty hearth.

Puzzled, Drake took another step into the room. That was when he noticed it. The faint scent of blood. His eyes scanned the room, quickly finding the source of the scent.

The woman lay on her back on Eli's fleur-de-lis rug, her hands crossed over her belly. Her throat had been practically torn out, and yet no blood seeped from the wound. Drake had a sinking feeling he knew why.

"I found her just inside my front gate," Eli said, still not turning around.

Drake frowned. "*Inside* the gate?"

Eli finally turned. His face was as impassive as usual, but there was something in his eyes that wasn't quite right. He was hurting. Badly. And trying very, very hard not to show it.

"He tossed her over the top of it and just left her there for me to find." The voice was flat, devoid of emotion, but that very flatness gave away more than he wanted.

"You're sure it's Gabriel?" Drake asked, though he knew the answer.

Eli nodded. "He let me sense him, for just the briefest moment, when he was far enough away to escape my glamour."

Drake regarded the Founder cautiously. "He *let* you sense him." He didn't quite phrase it like a question, but he asked the question with his eyes. Drake and the Guardians—and all other vampires he'd ever known—had to exert some effort to see with their psychic senses. Eli never seemed to need to. It was impossible to come within three blocks of his house without him knowing you were there.

"One of the quirks of his birth," Eli said. "He seems to be able to mask his psychic presence when he feels like it. Just like a master can mask his presence from his fledgling."

Drake ground his teeth to keep from saying anything he might regret. When Drake and Jules and Hannah had played their game of cat and mouse with Gabriel in Baltimore, Eli had never once thought to mention that Gabriel could mask his presence. But then, Eli protected secrets as if his life depended on it.

"That will make him rather harder to catch," Drake finally

managed to say, with a hint of dry humor that he hoped covered his annoyance.

Eli gave him a piercing look that said he hadn't managed to hide anything. "No doubt this is his way of firing a warning shot across the bow."

"No doubt." Drake regarded his mentor carefully. "And no doubt he knows you well enough to know just how to hurt you most."

Eli's expression wasn't quite a wince, but it was close. "Yes, he does. And unfortunately, it's not through doing anything to me."

Drake nodded. "He'll hurt you through us." He made a face. There was no "us." Drake wasn't a Guardian himself, was in fact just barely tolerated by the rest of them. "Through the Guardians."

"I'm afraid so."

"Which means you're going to have to tell everyone about him, no matter how much you'd rather sweep him under a rug."

Eli's eyes flashed with anger. "I haven't kept his existence a secret on a whim!" he snapped, which was an unusual display of temper for him.

Eli was under the impression that if the Guardians didn't think he was a saint, they wouldn't follow him anymore. He'd done everything in his power to keep Gabriel's existence and his own past a secret. Now, the secret was going to come out, one way or another.

"You know, Jules and Hannah and I all know about him, and we all still work for you. Maybe that ought to be a hint that you can have flaws just like the rest of us and we'll still respect you."

Eli's eyes locked with his, that sudden, penetrating gaze that always seemed to see below the surface. "And do you still respect me as much now as you did before you knew?"

Drake lowered his gaze, unable to face that knowing look.

"I'm not going to tell them much," Eli continued. "I'll

tell them that Gabriel is my son, and that he has a vendetta. But most of the details I'll keep to myself."

Now it was Drake's turn to get angry. "For God's sake, Eli! If he thinks it'll hurt you, Gabriel will find a way to make sure everyone knows every last sordid little detail, with some extra embellishment just for effect. If you've been honest with them, they won't believe any fabrications Gabriel tells them. But if you've lied to them, they won't know *what* to believe."

"I won't lie to them." Eli had the grace to look slightly abashed. "I just won't tell them everything."

It was futile to argue, though Drake was convinced the Founder was making a big mistake. "I presume you're going to give Jules and Hannah the party line too. Wouldn't want us all contradicting each other." He heard the hint of bitterness in his voice, but he was too angry to hide it.

He looked at the dead woman on the floor. She'd been pretty, and though her suit was rumpled from the rough treatment, it looked expensive. Would her people be looking for her? Would Gabriel try to lead the police to Eli's Guardians? And how many more dead bodies would Eli find on his doorstep in the near future?

"How do you plan to stop him, Eli? You're the only other person I've met whose power is as scary as his." He risked a glance at the Founder's face. "Can you overpower him?"

Eli nodded. "Despite his considerable talents, I did it easily two hundred years ago."

Two hundred years ago. When Eli had tried to force himself to kill his own son and discovered that he couldn't do it.

"However," Eli continued, "I doubt he plans to deliver himself into my hands for a fair fight."

"And you don't plan to leave the house to go after him."

Eli shook his head. "I can't do that."

Drake made a low growling noise. "Can't, or won't?" Eli refused to tell anyone why he wouldn't pass beyond the gates of his house, why the most powerful vampire he or any of the other Guardians had ever seen or even heard of, wouldn't help them fight the Killers.

As usual, Eli didn't answer the question.

"He could kill us all, if he wants to," Drake said softly. Eli didn't react overtly, but again Drake thought he saw a tightening around the Founder's eyes. "If you won't help us—"

Eli stopped the words in his throat with one icy glance. "The Guardians have destroyed Killers far more powerful than themselves before. They can do it again."

Yes, with Drake's help, they'd managed to destroy Killers who had one or two centuries' worth of experience and power. But Drake knew in his gut that Gabriel was an adversary too strong for any of them. Only Eli could prevail in a fight against his son. And there was no way Gabriel would get close enough for Eli to fight him.

Any way he looked at it, they were thoroughly screwed.

3

GABRIEL REGARDED HIS ONE and only fledgling closely, trying to absorb what she'd told him. He'd expected his bond with her to be different from the bond other vampires had with their fledglings. But he hadn't expected anything like *this*.

"You actually *felt* me feed," he murmured in disbelief.

She frowned and shrugged. "Yeah. I guess. I didn't know *what* I'd felt at first, but when I started thinking about it, these . . . impressions came to me."

"And you'd never felt anything like it before?"

She shook her head.

Which suggested the effect had something to do with his proximity. It wasn't as if he hadn't killed before during the months she'd been a vampire. At his age, he fed only a couple of times a month, though he suspected he could go a full month between feedings and be only mildly uncomfortable. Not that he'd ever been tempted to test this theory.

Jez stared at her hands, clasped in her lap. "I didn't like it, Gabriel," she said softly. She swallowed hard, and he thought he detected a hint of tears in her voice. "I didn't just feel you kill her. I felt your reaction." She shivered and hugged herself. They were sitting on her living room couch, and she leaned away from him, probably not even noticing that she did so.

His fists clenched in his lap, and his voice when he spoke was a low growl. "I'm sure it would have pleased you if I'd been overcome with remorse, filled with abject misery and despair." For all her tough talk, she was just like Eli's god-damn Guardians, judging and condemning him for a life he did not choose.

She turned her head slightly to look at him. "That's not what I meant."

He snarled. "The hell it isn't." He leaned into her, capturing her eyes with his glamour, forcing her to look at him, to face what he was, what she was bound to for the rest of her immortal life. "I'm a Killer, Jezebel. I kill mortals to feed, and I *like* it." His fangs had descended, and he pulled his lips away from them so she couldn't help but see.

"When I made you," he continued, "I gave you the choice not to kill." Had he been the average master vampire, he would have starved her until she was forced to kill to satisfy the hunger. And once she started killing, the addiction would make it impossible for her to stop. Instead, he had fed her on lamb's blood and thereby held the addiction at bay.

"It was a choice I never had," he continued. "But I haven't survived five hundred years by cursing my own existence, by wallowing in guilt and bemoaning my cruel fate. So fuck your delicate sensibilities, my dear. Deal with it!"

He released her from his glamour, and she jerked away. Fury coursed through his veins, looking for an outlet. He wanted to hurt someone, wanted it with an almost desperate passion. Jez was a vampire, could withstand immense amounts of damage without being permanently injured. He glared at her, and she met his gaze, not nearly as scared of him as she should be. It wasn't quite open defiance, but it wasn't the proper deferential attitude of a young fledgling, either.

Gabriel raised his fist, an almost instinctual reaction to the impulse to discipline his subordinate. But though the look in Jezebel's eyes dared him to do it, he felt no true temptation to strike her.

He leapt from the sofa, battling to rein in the anger. It was *Eli* who'd made him this freak of nature, not Jezebel. He focused his mind on the moment he'd left the dead woman on Eli's doorstep, remembered the triumph that had surged through his veins at the moment. *That* was his true battle— to punish Eli for the hell he'd put him through. If Jezebel feared and loathed him like everyone else, who the hell cared? He kept his back turned to her, breathing deeply, tamping down the rage as he promised to feed it well in the following weeks and months.

JEZ'S HEART SEEMED TO have taken up permanent residence in her throat. She stared at Gabriel's back, wondering if she dared speak to him. She'd thought she'd felt his rage before, when he'd bitten that woman. Now she knew that she'd only tapped its surface. She knew it because she'd *felt* it, not because she'd seen it on his face or heard it in his voice. Just as she could feel it draining away now.

"Gabriel?" she said tentatively.

He didn't turn toward her. "What?"

"Umm . . . I think things are even weirder than we thought."

That intrigued him enough to get him to turn around. His eyes still shone with that unwholesome anger, and he stroked his scarred cheek with the fingers of his right hand. She suspected he didn't even know he was doing it.

"When you got pissed at me just now," she said, looking up at him and hoping this wouldn't set him off too, "I felt that in here." She patted her chest. "I mean that literally."

"You *felt* it?"

She nodded. "Yeah." She shuddered. "It was like . . ." It was like nothing she'd ever felt before, and words stuck in her throat. How could she describe the indescribable?

Inspiration struck. "Did you ever see that movie, *Alien*?"

His brows drew together in puzzlement, but he nodded cautiously.

"It was like there was something like that alien inside me, struggling like hell to get out. But I had to keep it in, or just like the guy in the movie, I'd be dead." She shook her head. "I guess that's a pretty shitty explanation, but it was the strangest thing I've ever felt."

Gabriel's face lost some of its freshly fed color. He spoke after a moment of stunned silence. "Actually, I thought it an apt description." He returned to the couch and sat beside her. His eyes had a faraway look to them.

Her mouth was dry, and she found herself idly stroking her breastbone, as if still fearing a monster would burst through her skin. If that was how Gabriel felt when he got angry, no wonder he had such a penchant for cruelty. She thought she'd have done *anything* to get that horrible feeling out of her, even if that anything meant hurting someone.

"How did you manage not to hit me when you felt so much rage?" she asked in a bare whisper.

He blinked, coming back from whatever distance he'd retreated to. His expression lightened until there was a hint of a smile on his lips. "I've lived with it for five hundred years. If I hadn't gained some control over it, I'd have died or gone mad by now." He laughed, but there wasn't much humor in it. "Actually, I suppose many people would say I *have* gone mad."

She could see how some people might think that, but she knew Gabriel wasn't crazy. Frightening, angry, sometimes just barely in control of himself—but not crazy.

Not realizing she meant to do it, she reached out to him. As badly as he scared her at times, this little tantrum of his had shown her glimpses of things she'd never have guessed at before. She'd felt the pain that drove his rage. And that pain tasted familiar in her mind. She laid her hand lightly on his shoulder, wishing there was something she could do to ease him.

But whatever shields he'd dropped to allow her to see behind his façade were back in place. He stared blankly at her hand until she sighed and let go.

He pursed his lips and narrowed his eyes. "So, it would seem our bond allows you to share some of my . . . emotions." He said it like "emotion" was a dirty word.

"Something like that," she agreed. "Though I don't feel anything from you right now. Maybe the emotions have to be really strong for me to feel them."

He made a face that was half smile, half grimace. "And which did you like better? The ecstasy of the kill, or the alien chewing through the belly?"

She didn't dignify that with an answer, but she did venture to address the issue that had set him off in the first place. "I want you to know, I don't judge you. I'm the *last* person on earth who'd judge someone for the circumstances of his birth." Having been born to a junkie mother who had no idea which of the many men she'd slept with had fathered her, Jez knew what it was like to be scorned for something she had no control over. Her mother had been her scarlet letter, the cause of more sneers and insults than she could count. "But just because I don't judge you for enjoying the kill doesn't mean *I* have to like it. Do you understand?"

For a moment, it looked like her words would spark his anger again. But when he answered, both the words and the voice were mild. "Yes, I understand. And I'm sorry that our bond is causing you to experience things you'd rather not. I know so little about what I can do . . ."

Jez yearned to ask him *why* he knew so little. He couldn't be the only vampire in the world who was born that way. And at five hundred years old, she'd have thought he'd have learned more about his own abilities. But one thing she'd learned over the brief course of their acquaintance—Gabriel was about as eager to share information as Eli. She doubted Gabriel would appreciate the comparison.

Gabriel stood abruptly. "I need some time to think." He shook off some thought that seemed to bother him. "My

guess is that Eli will have to tell his Guardians something
about me, whether he wants to or not. Make sure you find
out what he has planned for me. I'll come to you tomorrow
night and you'll tell me what you've learned."

She opened her mouth to remind him that Eli wouldn't
necessarily share his plans with her, but apparently Gabriel
was tired of talking. He disappeared.

Jez shivered. She knew he hadn't really *disappeared*.
What he'd done was use his glamour to make her mind take
a brief vacation while he walked out the door. That didn't
make the effect any less unsettling.

But then, considering how unsettling it was to feel
Gabriel's emotions, she supposed she'd take the disappearing act any day!

CAMILLE AWOKE TO A sense of peace, the first she'd
known in . . . well, a long time. Perhaps ever since Eli had
cast her and Gabriel out of Philadelphia. Or perhaps even
longer ago, when Eli's hubris and Gabriel's lack of restraint
had seen them hounded from their home in a desperate
flight to the New World.

She sat up and stretched, and though hunger gnawed at
her senses, her head felt clear, her soul centered. Paris hardly
bore even a passing resemblance to the home she'd fled four
hundred years ago, but even so the place *felt* like home.
Like a piece of herself had slipped back into place, a piece
she hadn't known was missing.

She luxuriated in a long, scented bath, then dressed in
her favorite Chanel suit and swept her hair into an elegant
chignon at the back of her head. Shoes with toes as pointed
as her fangs completed the outfit, and she admired herself
briefly before the gilt mirror that adorned the dresser in her
room.

Satisfied that she looked as beautiful and as regal as she
could manage, she closed her eyes and reached out with her
senses.

It was no surprise to feel the presence of vampires below

her. If the power structure now was anything like it had been before she'd left, the *Seigneur*'s sentries would have sensed her invasion almost the moment she set foot in their city. They would give her perhaps a day or two before approaching her, as a courtesy to one of her advanced age. But she would not take a single step unobserved, and if she didn't formally present herself, her watchers would make themselves forcefully known.

She examined their auras carefully. None of the four who awaited her downstairs came close to her in age, she was sure. But they weren't fledglings, either. At a guess, they had two to three centuries on them apiece. Old enough that the four of them could overpower her despite her advanced age and power. But that didn't matter. She hadn't come here to fight, and there was no point in delaying her introduction to the *Seigneur*.

Taking a deep breath for courage, she left her room and waited what felt like an eternity for the elevator to arrive. The ride to the ground floor took even longer. But finally the doors opened, and she stepped into the elegant lobby.

Camille suspected she'd have felt the pressure of those four sets of eyes even if she *hadn't* detected the vampires awaiting her. They must have sensed her coming down the elevator, for they were all staring at her with unabashed curiosity.

They appeared to be a matched set, two men and two women. Their clothes were chic moderne, and all four were meticulously groomed. Camille was glad she'd chosen her own outfit with such care.

The petite dark-haired woman appeared to be their spokesperson, for she stepped forward to meet Camille. She smiled, but didn't offer to shake hands.

"You're trespassing," the little woman said, still smiling. Her French was fluent, but there was a touch of accent to it. German, perhaps. She used not a hint of glamour, but no one could have looked at that sweetly innocent, smiling face and guessed she'd just issued what amounted to a threat.

Camille inclined her head in acknowledgment. "I would have tried to make contact before I arrived, but I didn't know how," she responded in English. She'd have had no trouble speaking her native tongue, but she suspected her French would be . . . embarrassingly archaic.

The woman shifted easily to English. "Ah, so you are an American."

Camille couldn't help wrinkling her nose. "I was born here. In Paris. But I have lived in America for . . . quite some time."

Finally, the woman extended her hand. "I am Brigitte Arnault. I speak for the *Maître de Paris*."

Camille shook hands, stifling the urge to sigh. Only a few words exchanged, and already she saw that the vampires of the Old World still followed the almost feudal structure of yesteryear. In the U.S., there was no such thing as a "vampire society." Each vampire family operated independently, a nation unto its own. In Europe, the birthplace of their kind, there was structure, and protocol, and diplomacy. Which meant Camille would have to work her way through the underlings before reaching the *Seigneur*.

"I am Camille Crom—" she started, then stopped herself. She'd been carrying Eli's name for so long she'd almost believed it her own. Silly, really, as she was sure Cromwell wasn't Eli's real surname anyway. In fact, she suspected Eli was born before surnames even came into use. "Camille Hébert. I would like to beg an audience with the *Seigneur*."

Brigitte blinked a couple of times at what might have been an impatient-sounding statement. Still, that sweet smile stayed plastered on her face. Her three companions stayed well back, but eyed Camille with a combination of curiosity and distrust.

"It is up to the *Maître* to decide whether you shall speak to the *Seigneur*," she said. "Or have you been away for so long that you have forgotten protocol?"

Camille swallowed her first two responses. She could crush little Brigitte in a fight, but not Brigitte *and* her three friends. Besides, if she wanted to make a place for herself in the Old World structure, she had to play the bureaucratic games that were soon to follow.

"Your pardon, Mlle. Arnault. Americans tend to be more . . . forthright than perhaps you are accustomed to. I'm afraid I have absorbed some of their less attractive qualities. I will, of course, be delighted to meet the *Maître de Paris.*"

Brigitte's lips twitched into something more like a grin than a smile. "Of course you would. How could you refuse, when he's sent you such a welcoming committee?"

"Indeed."

The "welcoming committee" fanned out around her. It looked almost casual, as if they were joining her for a friendly talk, but only an idiot wouldn't see how they'd cut off her escape routes. As if she'd come all this way just to run away!

So she had to go through the *Maître* before she could petition the *Seigneur* for a place in his entourage. It was a price she was more than willing to pay. She gestured toward the front doors of the hotel. "Shall we?" she asked.

Brigitte flashed her that saucy grin again, then linked arms with her like they were best friends. *"Bien sûr!"* she said, and led Camille out into the welcoming Paris night.

As Gabriel had predicted, Eli called a meeting of the Guardians for the next night. Usually, the only time all the Guardians gathered together was on Wednesday nights, their regular weekly gathering. After the first few weeks of feeling like an interloper, Jez had started feeling comfortable during these meetings, getting to know the other Guardians, and even to like some of them.

Now she felt *worse* than an interloper. She was a mole, a spy. And she hated it.

She sat with head bowed, hands clasped in her lap as Eli told his Guardians about Gabriel. Well, not that he actually *told* them much of anything. He admitted Gabriel was his son, that he was born a vampire, and that he had a vendetta. But there was a lot he left out.

Even so, a sense of shock hovered over the collected Guardians. Jez raised her head and looked from face to face. Drake, Jules, and Hannah, who had all met Gabriel a few months ago on an ill-fated revenge quest in Baltimore, were unsurprised. Everyone else looked disillusioned, at best.

She swallowed hard and dropped her gaze as the Guardians started to bicker. The bickering was common enough—vampires as a general rule grated on each others' nerves unless there was a master/fledgling bond between them. Most gatherings of vampires—"families," as they were euphemistically called—consisted of a master and his or her group of fledglings. But Eli had no such bond with any of his Guardians, and it was only the force of his personality that kept them working together as a group.

Some worked together better than others. As usual when things started to get tense in the room, Jules and his nemesis, Gray James, started sniping at each other. Jez turned toward their angry voices, smiling even though the situation wasn't funny. God, the two of them were predictable!

Hannah, Jules's girlfriend and fledgling, had both hands on Jules's arm and was pulling hard, trying to get him away from Gray. Carolyn, Gray's mortal fiancée, was trying the same maneuver with him. Neither woman was having much success as Jules and Gray snarled at each other, flashing fangs.

"Enough!" Eli said, his voice cutting through all the arguments and grumbling. "Gray, Jules—sit down. Now."

Neither one of them was happy to back down, but they let their women pull them away from each other and shove them into chairs.

"I understand that many of you find all this very . . . disquieting," Eli said, his voice soft and yet full of power. "But fighting with each other is only going to play into Gabriel's hands."

"So what are we going to do about him, Eli?" Drake asked.

"He's a five-hundred-year old Killer, and we don't even know the full extent of his power."

Eli didn't answer, but one of the other Guardians, an especially aggressive hunter named Fletcher, stood up.

"What do you mean, 'What are we going to do about him?'" Fletcher asked. "We'll do the same thing we do when any other Killer decides to make himself at home in Philadelphia." He sneered a bit, giving Drake a disdainful look. "Except you, of course." He turned his glare to Eli. "We kill him."

If Jez hadn't been watching Eli's face closely, she wouldn't have noticed the slight tightening around his eyes that was almost a wince. But she *was* watching, and she *did* notice. No matter what Gabriel thought—and no matter what *Eli* thought—he wasn't eager to see his son dead.

"It isn't that easy, Fletcher," Drake said, his voice surprisingly calm when Fletcher was obviously trying to get a rise out of him. "I've met Gabriel. I've even fought him, or at least tried to." Drake shook his head. "I couldn't land a single punch. He was too fast, or his glamour was too strong, or a combination of the two. If *I* can't take him . . ."

"I wasn't offering to go up against him one-on-one in a fist fight," Fletcher retorted. "We're always outpowered by the Killers." He grinned, but it wasn't a nice expression. "Hell, I bet it would take at least four or five of us Guardians to take *you* down."

Jez rolled her eyes. Although Drake was an integral part of the Guardian organization right now, he was a Killer himself, and most of the other Guardians took that badly. Drake only killed "bad" people, hunting the really bad neighborhoods of the city where he fed on drug lords and murderous gang members. But he would always be an outsider, would always get those subtle—or sometimes not so subtle—little digs.

Drake had as hot a temper as any vampire, but though Fletcher pissed him off enough to draw a snarl, he for the most part didn't rise to the bait.

"Well, it would take more than four or five of you to kill Gabriel, even with my help. You don't understand what you're dealing with here."

Fletcher threw up his hands in exasperation. "What do you want us to do? Go hide under the furniture and pray he goes away? He's in *our* city. Killing *our* people. The people we've sworn to protect."

"No one's arguing that we don't need to kill him," Eli said, and he'd hidden any pain he might be feeling. "I should have killed him long ago, and I regret that I let sentimentality get in the way. The only issue up for debate is *how*. Drake is right—I'm not sure that all of you put together would be enough to stop him."

Fletcher gaped. "You've got to be kidding me!"

Eli shook his head. "There are only so many of you who could get to him at one time. Say, three or four. So imagine attacking him, three or four of you actually reaching him while the rest have to wait behind. He uses that immense glamour of his on the three or four who've reached him and tears out their throats while they're too stunned to resist. Then the next handful wade in. . . ."

"Sounds like a job for a gun to me," Hannah said, startling everybody.

Every eye in the room turned to her, and she shrugged. "If you can't take him in hand-to-hand combat, then you've got to shoot him."

Eli shook his head. "Letting someone with a gun get anywhere near him would be a disaster. He'd use that person to shoot everyone but himself."

Carolyn, who'd been a police detective and then a private investigator before she'd become the Guardians' mortal helper, spoke up. "So you have to make sure the person with the gun isn't close to him. You need a sniper."

Eli raised an eyebrow at her. "How far away can a sniper be and still have a reasonable chance to hit his target?"

"Depends on the sniper. And the equipment." She frowned. "But probably not far enough away for someone of Gabriel's age not to sense the sniper's presence. Obviously, if the sniper's a vampire, Gabriel would be far too suspicious to step into the trap. But if the sniper were mortal . . ."

Gray shot to his feet. "Don't even think about it, Carolyn!" he barked.

She blinked up at him with innocent blue eyes. "Think of what?"

Gray turned to Eli. "You are *not* sending Carolyn after this guy! I don't want her—"

Carolyn stood up and punched him in the arm. He turned to her indignantly. "If you're going to argue about it, argue with *me*," she said. "But ask yourself whether Gabriel is going to be suspicious if he senses a mortal presence fifty yards or so away from whatever trap we set up. If he's like most vampires, he'll dismiss me as no possible threat—if he even *deigns* to notice me."

"I don't remember you being a sniper when you were with the police!"

Gray was towering over her, his face flushed with anger, but though Carolyn was both petite and mortal, she stood her ground and didn't look the least bit intimidated. "I would need some practice time," she admitted. "It's been a while since I've fired a rifle, but it's not like I haven't done it before. And they're easier than handguns."

The argument raged on, but Jez tuned much of it out. She knew Carolyn was going to win, because Carolyn's argument sounded like it made so much sense.

Jez's chest ached. This sucked. Because she'd *promised* Gabriel that she'd tell him what the Guardians had planned. After everything he'd done for her, she couldn't go back on that promise, couldn't just let him be killed.

And if he killed Carolyn because of it?

Then she'd be questioning her decision—and her integrity—for the rest of her life.

DRAKE KNEW HE WAS being followed. And, unfortunately, he had a pretty good guess as to why. The meeting at

Eli's had left many Guardians unsatisfied. What better way to work off their displeasure than to take it out on the outsider?

He shook his head and sighed softly, reaching out with his senses and feeling three vampire auras behind him. The damn fools! If they were going to jump him, they needed more than three of them.

He spun around and glared at the advancing vampires. Fletcher led the way. No surprise there. The pup had a fiery Irish temper that he'd learned to keep contained in Eli's presence. Outside of Eli's influence, though . . .

At the middling age of forty, Fletcher was nevertheless one of the Guardians' best hunters, cunning and single-minded. At Eli's orders, he'd grudgingly accepted Drake's help from time to time, but he'd always made it clear that he thought Drake would look good with a stake through his heart.

The other two Guardians were younger and not as powerful, but their grim-faced hostility said they had no fear of taking on an older, stronger, more experienced Killer.

The three Guardians came to a stop about five feet away, Fletcher standing a little ahead with the other two hovering just behind his shoulders. The good news was, no one seemed to have drawn a weapon, which meant they probably didn't intend to kill him.

Drake glared at Fletcher, who was too smart to meet his eyes, though it must have offended his male ego not to be able to.

"You said yourself it would take four or five of you to take me," Drake said, readying himself for action as he probed with his senses to make sure no one else was sneaking up on him while he was distracted. "I only count three."

Fletcher grinned viciously. "You take what you can get."

Drake suspected if the pup wanted to spend a little more time planning, he could have gathered quite a posse. Resentment shot through him. They were happy enough to take advantage of his skills when they needed him. But it seemed nothing he did would ever make the Guardians accept him. No matter what Eli commanded.

Drake's fangs lowered. Adrenaline pumped through his system, bloodlust energizing him, narrowing his focus. And he suddenly realized why Fletcher dared jump him with only two helpers—the pup knew Drake would have to be careful not to kill anyone, which would significantly hamper his ability to fight. Damn it!

"This is childish," he said, knowing full well that wouldn't matter much to Fletcher and his buddies. "We're on the same side."

Fletcher rolled his neck from side to side, his spine making tiny popping noises as he loosened up. "So fucking what?" He charged forward, lowering his head like a battering ram.

Drake had a split second to decide on strategy as Fletcher's flunkies fanned out to come at him from the sides. He used his glamour to freeze both of them in their tracks, then braced himself for the impact as Fletcher's head slammed into his ribs.

Bracing did no good. Fletcher was strong and solidly built, and the two of them tumbled to the pavement together. Fletcher also fought dirty, so when they went down he made sure his knee landed on Drake's groin.

Even a century-old Killer was vulnerable to a blow like that, and the pain snapped Drake's concentration, freeing Fletcher's accomplices from his glamour. His head snapped sharply to the side from a brutal kick. Fletcher dug his knee in harder, but snarled at his buddy.

"Don't kick him in the head, idiot! You could break his neck."

Oh, good, Drake thought dryly as his vision swam and he fought for air. Fletcher was being *so* considerate, making sure Drake wasn't accidentally killed.

Drake couldn't suck in enough air to manage a well-balanced punch, but he didn't need much leverage to bite, so he sank his fangs into Fletcher's shoulder.

Fletcher screamed and reflexively tried to pull away. Drake's fangs tore through his flesh, leaving a huge, jagged wound. The pain and the blood stunned Fletcher enough that Drake was able to pitch him off and leap to his feet.

Fletcher's two buddies closed ranks, standing between Drake and Fletcher like guard dogs. Drake rolled his eyes, licking the Guardian's blood from his lips. The taste was sweet and coppery, but subtly different from the taste of mortal blood. Nowhere near as tantalizing.

"Relax, children," Drake said, baring his bloody fangs at them. "If I'd wanted to kill him, I'd have bitten something other than his shoulder." This was all so terribly civilized, no one trying to kill anyone. How long would that be the case, if Gabriel continued to hunt the city and raise tensions?

His wound was closing already, and Fletcher was regaining his composure. He pushed up to his hands and knees, still guarded by his friends.

"Good thing I'm not the enemy," Drake continued, giving Fletcher a droll look. "Never put your throat within reach of a Killer's fangs, puppy." Drake couldn't have killed him with a bite to the throat, but he could have hurt him badly enough to soften him for the killing blow. "Now, have we had enough for tonight, or do I have to teach you all some more lessons?"

Not surprisingly, they charged him again, all three of them together. But now he had a better clue as to how they fought, and he managed to keep his more vulnerable spots protected. A little touch of glamour confused the two youngsters, and they ended up hitting each other. Drake stepped aside to avoid Fletcher's charge, then used the puppy's own momentum to slam him into a brick wall, knocking the breath out of him. While Fletcher struggled for air, Drake got a hold of his arm and wrenched it up behind his back.

"Tell your flunkies to call it quits," Drake snarled in his ear.

"Fuck you," Fletcher panted.

Apparently, he wasn't going to give up until he'd been thoroughly thrashed. At this point, Drake was happy to oblige. He grinned as Fletcher's buddies finally snapped out of the glamour enough to realize they were pummeling each other.

"This is going to hurt like hell, puppy," Drake warned, then shoved upward on Fletcher's arm until he heard the sickening pop of his shoulder dislocating.

Fletcher howled, and Drake backed up to let him fall to the pavement. He turned to the others and smiled pleasantly, sure the expression in his eyes was anything but pleasant. "Unlike most wounds," he said casually, "this one won't heal by itself. You're going to have to pop his shoulder back into its socket first, then he'll be just fine." He grinned. "Of course, he won't like that very much, so I suggest you stay out of range of fists and feet and fangs."

The two of them stood there, cuts and bruises healing on their faces, as they looked back and forth indecisively between Drake and Fletcher.

Drake stared at them coldly. "Unless you'd like to find out first hand how lovely it feels to have a dislocated shoulder, I suggest you quit while you're behind."

They looked at each other, then at Drake, and then nodded simultaneously, holding their hands out from their sides in surrender. Both of their faces were pale with fear, all their toughness faded in the face of their leader's pain. At his feet, Fletcher moaned pitifully, his breathing labored.

Drake pressed his lips together. Fletcher might be in enough pain and be frustrated enough to be a danger to the others if they tried to pop his shoulder back into place.

Pissed though he might be, Drake didn't want anyone dying because of this foolishness. He lowered himself to one knee and stilled Fletcher's struggles with his glamour. He didn't make any attempt to kill the pain, though, figuring Fletcher was getting exactly what he deserved for trying to jump someone older and more powerful than himself. Matter-of-factly, he manipulated Fletcher's shoulder back into position, ignoring the howls of protest.

It would take a couple of minutes for the muscles and

tendons he'd torn along the way to knit themselves back together. With a final snarl that encompassed all three of his
would-be attackers, Drake turned his back on them and hurried away before Fletcher could recover enough to pick another fight.

4

JEZ WASN'T SURPRISED TO see Gabriel making himself at home in her apartment, even though her tentative probe before she'd entered had told her the place was empty.

He'd gone for his most aggressive look tonight, using some kind of product to make his short blond hair stick up in messy-looking spikes. His black leather jacket—way too hot for this temperate spring evening—was adorned with silver studs and chains. And his feet—which he'd rudely propped on her coffee table—were shod in boots that looked like they must have weighed five pounds each with all the metal on them.

She sighed quietly and closed the door behind her. After squirming through the entire meeting tonight, she could have used some time to herself to come to terms with what she had to do. Apparently, that wasn't one of her options.

With her back straight and proud, and her chin lifted, she faced her maker.

"I want you to promise me that you're not going to kill anyone," she said.

That startled him enough to get his boots off her coffee

table. One corner of his mouth quirked up. "Perhaps I have become hard of hearing in my old age," he said. "I thought I just heard you making what sounded suspiciously like a demand. But no, surely you're not that foolish."

She moved carefully, keeping a wary eye on him as she took a seat on the sofa beside him, just out of reach. Her heart fluttered in her chest as she met those cold, gray-green eyes, but whatever he was feeling right now, it wasn't strong enough to bleed into her.

"I know I made you a promise—" she started, but Gabriel cut her off.

"Yes, you did. And I expect you to live up to it. And do as you're told."

His voice, and the look on his face, chilled her to the bone, but she wouldn't, *couldn't* back down. Not this time. "You saved my life," she said. Her voice quavered a bit, so she lowered it. "In so many more ways than you know. I'm so thankful—"

"Cut the crap and get to the point," he snapped.

She narrowed her eyes at him. "This *is* the point. Sorry if being forced to listen to me is an inconvenience. If you wanted a slavishly loyal pet who wouldn't talk back to you, you should have gotten a dog."

He bared his teeth at her, but he hadn't lowered his fangs, so the threat wasn't as scary as it might have been. Then he shook his head and laughed softly. "You and Hannah must get along great. You have the smartest mouths of any women I've ever met."

She grimaced. "Actually, Hannah and I can barely tolerate each other," she admitted. "Eli decided she should teach me something about martial arts since, as he puts it, I fight like a girl. Hannah isn't exactly the most patient teacher, and for some reason she doesn't trust me. It's all very 'innocent,' but our sparring sessions all seem to end with me aching from head to toe."

He laughed again. "Yes, that's Hannah all right. Quite a little spitfire."

Jez was surprised at the zing of jealousy that shot through her. There was a hint of softness around his eyes that suggested he actually *liked* Hannah. Usually, he gave her the distinct impression that he didn't like *anyone*. She knew he and Hannah had met in Baltimore, and she knew he'd admired the woman's spunk. Too bad he didn't seem to feel the same way about Jez.

She didn't mean to say anything, but she just couldn't help herself. "So, Hannah can trade insults with you and you get all nostalgic about it, but if I even hint that I might not want to obey your every order, you get pissy."

He arched a single brow. "You're my fledgling. She's not."

"And 'fledgling' is the same as 'slave'?"

"My patience is nearing its end. What do Eli and his Guardians have planned for me?"

She almost snorted. His patience was nonexistent. Even knowing that, she held firm. "Promise me you won't kill anyone, and I'll tell you." A spark in the center of her chest told her she'd tweaked the well of anger in him, though his expression didn't change much.

"I don't make promises I can't keep."

She swallowed hard. There were so many worse things he could do to her than kill her. She didn't believe he'd do any of them, but if she was wrong . . . Even so, she had to stand firm, or she'd never be able to look herself in the mirror again. "Then I can't tell you what you want to know."

His eyes seemed almost to glow as he leaned into her space. She put her hand to her breastbone, feeling his anger seething in her center, creeping through her limbs.

"Think long and hard about defying me, my dear," he said, and his voice would have scared the devil himself.

The painful burn of his anger continued to spread and intensify. There was so much of it, boundless, bottomless, looking for an outlet. And here she was defying him, practically *daring* him to hurt her. Terror merged with the anger, forming a writhing, twisting struggle in her chest. Gabriel's eyes drew together in what she'd have described as puzzlement if she could think of any reason why he'd be puzzled. She could hardly breathe through the sensations in her chest, but she forced words out anyway. She had to reach through his anger and her fear, had to try to explain *why* she was defying him. He might not care. But then again, he might.

"All my life," she panted, "people have always thought the worst of me." Tears sprang to her eyes, and she wasn't sure if it was an emotional response to what she was saying, or a physical response to the pain. "I've been treated like the dog shit you scrape off your shoes, and nothing I could do would ever make them see me for who I really am." Visions of her grandmother's stony-faced disapproval flashed through her mind. The pain was unbearable, and her voice when she spoke was hoarse and broken. "Now, for the first time ever, I've got people who think I'm a good person." A sob escaped her. "If I betray them and you kill them, I'll have proved everyone else was right."

The pain pushed everything aside, made Gabriel's anger into a distant, unreal threat, her fear nothing but a nuisance. It was an old pain, one she'd been shoving into the back of her mental closet from the moment she'd awakened to find herself born anew. She drew her knees up to her chest, buried her head against them and drowned under the hurt of it.

And once again, she was a ten-year-old girl, standing at her mother's grave. Her mother, the junkie slut who'd accidentally killed herself with a heroin overdose. Her mother, who'd gotten lazy with little Jezebel's insulin injections and started using dirty needles because she was just too damn wasted to care.

Behind her stood her grandmother, her mother's mother, who would grudgingly take in her only granddaughter for however many years she'd manage to survive before the HIV grew to full-blown AIDS and killed her. Even as Jez's mother was being laid to rest, she could hear her grandmother talking worriedly with her like-minded friends. It was God's will that her mother had died, and God's will that had given

Jezebel HIV. It meant she was marked by the devil, a bad seed, doomed to follow in her mother's footsteps.

Afterward, she'd seen the minister take her grandmother aside. She'd snuck up close enough to eavesdrop, heard the minister counsel her grandmother to show "the child" a more Christian attitude. Her grandmother had been deeply offended by the suggestion that it was un-Christian of her to condemn a ten-year-old she barely knew as a lost soul. She'd demonstrated just how offended she was by switching churches.

Jezebel dragged herself back to the present by sheer force of will. All of that was behind her now. Not only was she no longer dying, she was practically immortal. And she would never lay eyes on her grandmother or any of the proselytizing, holier-than-thou bitches who formed her circle of friends, clucking worriedly about the state of Jez's soul while wisely nodding to each other and muttering that her mother's choice of name had been prophetic. Actually, Jezebel knew for a fact she'd been so named specifically to spite her grandmother.

She suffered a moment of disorientation as she stuffed the last of those memories back in her mental closet. Her head was pressed against the thick leather of Gabriel's jacket, one of the studs digging uncomfortably into her cheek. His arms were around her, but it was like he had no idea how to give a hug, and he felt stiff and awkward. He patted her back in what she assumed was supposed to be a comforting gesture. Apparently, he didn't have much practice at those either.

For a moment, she remained where she was, despite his awkward hold and the discomfort of the studded jacket. Though her nose was stuffy from crying, she smelled the warm leather-and-man scent of him, and it eased something inside her, helping her calm the inner demons his rage and her fear had inadvertently summoned. It felt good to be held, even by someone who sucked at it. Her grandmother had barely touched her, as if afraid the taint—or, more practically, the HIV—would rub off. Hell, she wouldn't even give Jez her insulin injections. Luckily, by the time she was ten years old, Jez had gotten very good at jabbing herself with needles because her mom wasn't dependable enough.

If only she'd taken over the job completely once she'd learned how. . . . *She* never would have used a dirty needle. *She* knew better.

Eventually, the awkwardness became too much, and Jez pushed away, surreptitiously wiping her eyes even though it was no secret she'd been bawling like a baby. Gabriel spoke before she had a chance to pull the last vestiges of her self together.

"I will offer you a compromise," he said, and his voice was strangely subdued. "I won't promise not to kill them, and I won't promise not to hurt or scare them, but I *will* promise that I won't kill unless it's absolutely necessary in self-defense. Which, considering my advantages, is unlikely to be the case. Will that ease your conscience?"

Jez swallowed the last of her tears and raised her head to look at him. In reality, she couldn't possibly hold him to any promise he might make. But his reluctance to make a promise in the first place suggested he might actually keep one he did make. The guilt would weigh heavily on her even if he didn't kill anyone, but she'd made him a promise, and she would keep it.

"All right," she said. "There's a mortal woman named Carolyn who's engaged to one of the Guardians. She used to be a police officer, and she helps the Guardians by doing things in the daytime and lending her expertise. They've decided to set a trap for you, though they haven't quite figured out how they're going to bait it yet. They'll have her planted with a rifle somewhere, and she's supposed to kill you as soon as you come into sight."

Gabriel's features hardened, the anger stirring once more. "You've got to love my dear old dad. He doesn't have the guts to kill me himself, but he doesn't mind sending someone else to do his dirty work for him."

"Yes, he does," she said softly, not sure Gabriel was willing or able to hear what she had to say. "I saw his face when he gave the order. He doesn't want to do it. If you weren't forcing his hand . . ."

He acted like he hadn't even heard her. "This ought to be . . . entertaining," he mused. "I'll have to see if I can help Daddy come up with a tempting trap. I will so enjoy turning the tables on him."

"Gabriel—"

"I promised not to kill anyone unless necessary. That's the best you can hope for from me."

He did another of those disconcerting disappearing acts of his, and Jez slumped down on the couch, praying that he would keep his word.

GABRIEL SAT ON THE front stoop of Jezebel's apartment building for a while, gathering himself. He was shaken enough that he actually dropped his glamour, but none of the mortals passing by paid him any attention.

What the fuck had he gotten himself into? He'd made Jezebel with only one purpose in mind—to use her as a weapon against Eli. Never had he imagined she might become a weapon against himself!

He'd barely begun to absorb the idea that she could feel his feedings and his anger. But what had just happened upstairs was even more unsettling.

It had started out as merely an uncomfortable ache in the center of his chest. Puzzling, but not enough to distract him from his anger. Then, when her voice had broken and her memories came flooding in, it felt like a booted foot had kicked him in the sternum. Worse, he'd seen her in his mind's eye, a hollow-eyed little girl standing beside an open grave. Blond hair pulled back into a severe pigtail that looked painfully tight. Body almost stick-thin, with an unhealthy pallor to her skin and hollow cheeks.

And he'd heard the whispers and muttering from behind,

from the family that was supposed to love and cherish her. She'd held her chin high, and not a single tear had escaped, but the pain of that moment . . .

He swallowed hard. He'd absorbed many a mortal memory during a kill. But as he limited his kills to the morally repugnant, and as he always forced the confession to bring the ugliness to the surface, all he'd ever felt was greed, and lust, and self-pity, and madness. Never had he felt the kind of . . . desolation . . . he'd sensed in little Jezebel's core.

He tried to reel himself back in, shove those aching memories away. He had enough painful memories himself—he didn't need someone else's!

But there was no denying the realization that had struck him when for a brief moment in time he'd stood in Jezebel's shoes. He was *not* the only person ever to be reviled by the only family they had simply because of an accident of birth. Not that he'd ever truly thought he was, but he'd always *felt* that way. Always felt like a foreigner, an alien, always "other."

And now by a quirk of dumb luck or fate, his life was bound up with someone who, despite a very different life, had felt very much the same.

Gabriel ground his teeth and shook his head. What the hell did it matter if her sob story resembled his? Through him, she'd been reborn to a new life, a life where she could shove it all behind her and start fresh. That option wasn't open to him. No, his only option was to punish the man who'd made him what he was today. For though his outright hatred of his father had started on the day Eli sliced his face with a sword, the fury had been building ever since he'd been old enough to realize his own father thought him an abomination before God.

Sucking in a deep breath of cool night air, tinged with the ever-present stinks of city life, Gabriel stiffened his spine and his resolve. What had happened tonight meant nothing. Jezebel's pain was her own concern, and if he had to tread delicately around her to avoid another dose of it, well, as he'd said, he'd had five centuries to learn self-control.

His business for tonight was not concluded, not by a long shot. Now he knew how Eli planned to kill him. But he had not the patience to wait until the sainted Founder built his trap.

A slow smile spread over his face. Eli wasn't the only one who knew how to set a trap.

Dismissing everything but his single-minded purpose, he rose from the steps and headed out into the night.

GABRIEL SLID THROUGH THE shadows, following Hannah at a discreet distance.

Locating her had been easy, since Jezebel knew her address. Getting her away from Jules, who apparently lived with her, had proven a little more challenging. He supposed he could have approached her even with Jules at her side, but he preferred to talk to her alone rather than dealing with Jules's hot temper and protective instincts.

Now, he'd gotten lucky, and she'd left her lover at home as she walked the city streets. He didn't know where she was going, but she walked with purpose. Was someone waiting for her? And would that someone become impatient if she didn't show up on time?

He decided he'd let her have her rendezvous, and then approach her on her way home. But she hadn't gone more than two blocks from her home before her purposeful strides altered. She paused to look over her shoulder.

Gabriel wrapped himself in a cloak of glamour, and her eyes slid right by him without noticing him. A furrow appeared between her brows. If he didn't know better, he would swear she could sense him, but even if he hadn't been masking his psychic signature, she was a very young fledgling, as young as Jezebel, and there was no way she could sense him at this distance.

She resumed walking, but her stride had lost some of its

confidence, and her shoulders were tight and twitchy. He followed for another block and a half, still keeping his distance, until she turned down a narrow alley that ran behind a row of shops. He paused and eyed the mouth of the alley suspiciously. What on earth could she be doing in *there*?

Gabriel peeked around the corner, still hiding behind his glamour, and saw Hannah standing in the middle of the alley, her arms akimbo, a look of studied concentration on her face. No question about it, something had tweaked her suspicions. He wondered what.

Finally, she shook her head. "Gabe, if you want to talk to me, just come talk to me. This stalker shit is getting on my nerves."

It was all he could do to suppress a gasp of surprise. Not only had she known she was being followed, she'd known *who* was following her! And yet, clearly she couldn't see him. Her eyes darted back and forth across the mouth of the alley without focusing on him. The woman had uncanny instincts.

Hannah leaned her back against the brick wall of one of the shops, feigning a casual pose. But her eyes were too wary, her posture was too stiff. Gabriel smiled faintly. She was leaning against the wall so he couldn't sneak up behind her.

But considering the strength of his glamour, he had no difficulty sneaking up in front of her. When he let up on the glamour, he was standing about two feet from her.

She must have been startled, but she hid it well, folding her arms across her chest and giving him a bland smile. "Hiya," she said. "Long time no see."

He returned her smile, though he doubted the expression reached his eyes. "Did you miss me?"

She sighed heavily. "What do you want, Gabe?" She looked him straight in the eye, challenging him, unafraid of his glamour.

For you to stop calling me "Gabe," he thought. But he was quite certain saying so would have the exact opposite of the desired effect.

"I presume you are aware of the calling card I left for my dear father," he said instead.

Hannah shuddered, though she visibly tried to suppress it, and her eyes slid away from his. "Yeah," she said softly. There was a hint of hoarseness to her voice. Apparently she hadn't thought much of his gift. "Very thoughtful of you."

He braced his hands against the brick wall on either side of her head, taking a step closer so that he crowded into her space. She tried to shrink away from him, but the wall at her back kept her right where he wanted her.

With palpable reluctance, she raised her eyes back to his. He heard the sudden speeding of her heart, practically *felt* her desire to put some distance between them.

He transfixed her with his gaze, not with any glamour, but merely with the intensity of his hatred. "I intend to enjoy my time here to its fullest extent," he said. "As I'm sure you know, I released Jules from his promise to tell me everything he knows about the Guardians."

He had extracted that promise from Jules in exchange for his help in tracking down and destroying Jules's maker. He'd known from the moment Jules made the promise that he didn't intend to keep it, and he'd looked forward to dragging every last drop of information from the Guardian's throat when the time came. But despite being an arrogant, annoying prick, Jules was not of the distasteful caliber of Gabriel's preferred prey. Besides, Gabriel had found Jez, and realized he had an even better way to gain the intelligence he needed to bring his father to his knees.

"Thanks," Hannah said, forcing the word out through clenched teeth. "That was very . . . decent of you."

He grinned down at her. "I thought so myself. But now I have a favor to ask you."

She eyed him warily. "Um, I don't want to piss you off or anything, but we're kind of on opposite sides here. I don't think I'm the best person to ask a favor of."

Still smiling, he lowered his fangs, leaning a little bit closer into her. "Perhaps 'ask' wasn't the right word."

He could smell the fear on her, and he saw her swallow hard, but she had more bravado than anyone he'd ever met before in his long life. Despite her fear, she forced a smile, flashing her own set of fangs.

"You know," she said with false perkiness, "I've got some of those now myself. Cool, huh?"

He closed his eyes and shook his head, but couldn't suppress a chuckle. She was just so adorable! Though he sincerely doubted she would appreciate the term.

He forced the amusement away, wiping every trace of emotion from his face. He could see that it worked by the way her eyes widened.

"I would like you to keep me informed of whatever plans Eli has for me," he said.

Hannah raised her chin and shook her head. "Huh-uh. Not going to happen, Gabe."

"Oh, I think it is," he argued, reaching out to her with his glamour, forcing her eyes to lock with his. "Here's the deal. You tell me anything they have planned for me. If you don't, I'll have to ask Jules. And him, I won't ask nicely, if you get my drift."

The blood drained from her face. If he'd actually intended to carry out his threat, he might have felt a hint of remorse. But of course, he didn't need Jules or Hannah to provide him the information. All he was doing was feeding them information they could use to try to "trap" him.

Because he knew that however frightened Hannah might be for herself or even for Jules, she would never betray the Guardians.

She drew in a deep breath, sweat beading her brow. Her voice when she spoke shook slightly. "I'm not going to betray my friends to you. I just can't do that."

He had to give her an excuse to pretend to give in, a reason for her to hope he might believe her.

He flashed her another one of his cold smiles. "Tell you what—I'll sweeten the deal for you, take out some of the sting. Tell me what I want to know, and I will promise not to kill any of your Guardians while I'm here. As I believe I've made quite clear, my quarrel is with Eli himself, not the Guardians."

Of course, he'd also told them before he wouldn't hesitate to kill anyone who got between him and his revenge.

Hannah pretended to think it over, puckering her brow as she cast suspicious glances up at his face. She was a terrible actress, and even if he hadn't known her well enough to guess she wouldn't give in, he would have read her expression easily.

"You're *not* planning to kill anyone?" she asked. "So, what, you're telling me you now like puppy dogs and long walks on the beach?"

Once again, she surprised a laugh out of him. Her little quips had made him laugh more often than he could remember laughing in the last century. He sucked in a quick breath and forced the amusement away. Laughing didn't do much for his hard-ass image!

"I find betrayal . . . distasteful," he said. Certainly true, although it had nothing to do with his current promise. "And betrayal unto death inexcusable. I would not ask that of you." He put a slight emphasis on the last word, suggesting he'd be perfectly happy to ask it of someone else. Like Jules.

She shook her head. "So now you're being considerate of my feelings?" she asked incredulously. "Have you had a personality transplant recently?"

This time, he didn't even try to suppress his grin. "All right. I'll cut the bullshit. The truth is, you're not a weakling, and I'm not a moron. There is no threat I could make that would cause you to betray your people if you thought the betrayal would cost lives." Actually, there was no threat he could issue that would make her betray them at all, but he thought this made a fairly decent cover story. He let the grin fade. "And so I offer you a trade you can live with. You help keep me alive by warning me about any plans that might lead to my death. And I refrain from killing anyone.

Or dragging the information out of your beloved maker, who caused me a great deal of inconvenience when he insisted on invading my city."

Hannah bit her lip, her face a mask of worry. She might talk tough, but he suspected she wouldn't much like the idea of baiting the trap to get him killed.

"I'll be generous," he said. "I'll give you forty-eight hours to think it over. Meet me here when those forty-eight hours are up. Alone, naturally. And if you're not here, expect me to pay a call on Jules sometime in the near future. Are we clear?"

She nodded, looking miserable. "Crystal."

He let his arms drop back to his sides but didn't give her any more space. She looked reluctant to brush by him, but she didn't have much choice if she wanted to get out of here.

He heard the hammering of her pulse as she slipped away and headed out of the alley at a pace just short of a run.

5

"CAMILLE HÉBERT," THE *MAÎTRE de Paris* mused, his back turned to the room. He stood before a window that faced the Place de la Concorde—within view of her hotel.

Not having been offered a seat, Camille stood straight and proud as recognition prickled at the back of her mind. She knew that voice, but without a face to put with it, she couldn't place it.

A chandelier with dimly glowing bulbs provided the only light in the room and left the *Maître* cloaked in shadow where he stood. Louis XV antiques decorated the elegant and sophisticated drawing room, and the walls rivaled the Louvre in the density of masterpieces.

Two of the vampires who had escorted Camille to this meeting stood flanking the door, hands clasped behind their backs, eyes fixed forward. The other two—Brigitte and her male companion—had excused themselves as soon as they'd presented her.

"When last we met," the *Maître* continued, "you went by the name Cromwell, did you not?"

Unease shivered over her skin. It was a given that there

would be many vampires in Europe who'd either met her or heard of her. In fact, she expected the *Seigneur* to be one of them. The youngest *Seigneur* she'd ever heard of had been five hundred and fifty years old, so whoever held the post now most certainly had been around when Camille was the consort of the *Maître de Paris*. But she hadn't been prepared to meet an old acquaintance just yet. If only she could place that voice, figure out whether he was friend or foe . . . Not that she would call any other vampire "friend," but it would have been nice to know if this one actively meant her harm.

"That may well be," she said, her voice showing none of her unease. "Have we met, then? I feel I recognize your voice, but perhaps this old woman's memory is a little faulty."

The *Maître* chuckled. "Oh, we've met, *Madame*. We've met indeed." Slowly, he turned around, letting the light play over his face, revealing first an awkwardly large ear, then a severe, angular cheekbone, an aquiline nose, and a pair of piercing, chilling blue eyes.

Camille's eyes widened in shock, and it took all her considerable willpower not to take a step backward, for she had indeed met the *Maître de Paris*. And he was the absolute last person she wanted to face.

Bartolomeo di Cesare laughed, throwing his head back and his arms to the side. "God is good!" he crowed, then reined in his laughter and pierced her with his eyes.

"You recognize me, then, *Madame*?"

Oh, yes. She recognized him. How could she not? It was because of him that she and Eli and Gabriel had been forced to flee for their lives.

Well, technically she supposed it was because of Gabriel, and what Gabriel had done to him.

It seemed likely she was going to die before ever meeting the *Seigneur*. She didn't imagine Bartolomeo would be inclined to forgiveness. But she would not abandon hope, not while any hint of it survived.

"Yes, *Maître*," she said, her voice soft and, she hoped,

conciliatory. "I recognize you. And for whatever it's worth, I did my best to convince Eli to hand him over to you. But Eli was my maker, and I could not defy him."

It had been the most bitter argument they'd ever had. At least, until the day he'd changed his stripes and forced her to leave Philadelphia. They'd known from the moment that Camille became pregnant that Gabriel's very existence would endanger them both. The *Seigneurs* had laid down a very clear law—no child born vampire was allowed to live. Camille had spent her entire pregnancy in reluctant hiding. And then, when Gabriel was born, Eli insisted on keeping him hidden, keeping him safe until he was an adult and no one could guess what he was.

And what did dear little Gabriel do once he came of age? He tangled with Bartolomeo di Cesare and committed the unpardonable sin of not finishing the job. He'd been "playing" with Bartolomeo when Bartolomeo's maker had interrupted. Gabriel had been forced to flee into the daylight. At less than one hundred years old, he should have died. And because he didn't, he revealed that he'd been born vampire, and the *Seigneur* ordered his death. To save the boy's life, Eli had uprooted them all and dragged them to the New World. Taken them from their home, made them suffer months of misery aboard a ship full of sailors they had to keep alive if they didn't wish to be lost at sea.

It was a nightmare she tried never to remember, and ever since, she'd cursed herself for going along. Just because Gabriel and Eli turned tail and ran didn't mean *she* had to. But by that time, she'd been with Eli for four hundred years, and she hadn't been able to bear the thought of being left behind.

Bartolomeo regarded her, arching his brows, the corners of his mouth turned downward. "So, you would have given me your own son?" he inquired.

She met his gaze. "He risked all our lives, when he . . . did what he did." She wrinkled her nose at the memory and tried not to let her eyes drift downward despite a voyeur's temptation. Had it grown back? Vampires could regenerate lost body parts, but Gabriel claimed that after cauterizing the wound with a hot iron, regeneration was impossible. Eli, typically, had neither confirmed nor denied Gabriel's assertion.

Bartolomeo gestured at a stiff, high-backed chair. "Please, have a seat. Make yourself comfortable."

She sat primly on the edge of the chair, back and neck held straight. The *Maître* gestured at his minions, and they left the room. She was now alone with the *Maître,* and though he was not young, he was not old enough to over-power her. Her eyes narrowed. What was he up to?

He crossed his legs and steepled his fingers in front of his face. "You wish to return to the land of your birth. Is that why you're here?"

She nodded slowly. "There is nothing to keep me in America anymore. And I would rather die in an attempt to win my way home than to continue to live in exile."

She winced as soon as she said it, for Bartolomeo him-self had lived almost his entire life in exile, his maker hav-ing uprooted him from his home in Venice and dragged him to France.

Bartolomeo smiled. "I gather you have not come to love your adopted home as I have mine," he commented, and she relaxed at his easy tone.

"No, I have not."

"You know, of course, that I cannot give you leave to stay. Only the *Seigneur* can do that."

"I understand."

"And unless I make an introduction, the *Seigneur* will not see you."

She hesitated. Protocol required the *Maître* to make a for-mal introduction. But perhaps she had already met the *Seigneur,* and the introduction wasn't necessary.

"Is Allain D'Anjou still the *Seigneur* of this region?"

Bartolomeo made a regretful face. "I am afraid not, *Madame*. He was killed in an air raid during World War II."

He smiled, but it was a strangely sad expression. "All our power, all our strength, and we are as helpless in the face of war as any mortal."

An exaggeration, of course, but she understood his point.

He lost the sad expression, his eyes filling with cunning. "So, I can choose to introduce you to the current *Seigneur*. Or, perhaps you can stand in for your menfolk as I indulge my thirst for revenge." His eyes glowed with an unwholesome light. "I would enjoy it immensely, seeing that legendary pride of yours wither and crumble."

She forced her face to give away nothing, though she suspected he could smell her fear. She was more powerful than he, and he'd sent his minions away. And yet, she felt sure he wouldn't have done so if he hadn't taken some sort of precautions to ensure his own safety.

He licked his lips slowly. "But perhaps you can offer me a sweeter revenge. Perhaps your dear son is still among the living?"

She dipped her chin in the slightest of nods, still keeping a wary eye on him.

His breath hissed in, his whole body stiffening as he leaned forward in his chair. "Take me to him. Take me to him and help me punish him for what he did to me. Do that and I will grant your introduction to the *Seigneur*. Don't do it, and I shall be . . . most displeased with you."

Camille's jaw dropped open. "But, *Maître,* he's in America!"

Bartolomeo gave her a bored look. "I had gathered that."

She sat back in her chair, stunned. No vampire more than a century or two old would willingly leave his home. Oh, they might make very brief visits to places nearby. But no one she'd ever known would go so far away unless forced, as she and Eli were forced. Gabriel alone of all the vampires she'd known seemed to have no special attachment to his home territory. But for someone as old as Bartolomeo, who'd risen in rank to *Maître,* to be willing to cross the ocean . . .

The *Maître* laughed, easily reading her expression. "Yes,

I hate him that much. I would travel to the ends of the earth to see him suffer." He leaned forward in his chair once more. "He took from me my most prized possession. And my pride. And I would dearly love to return the favor." He grimaced. "Unless your maternal instincts would keep me from my prize."

Now it was Camille's turn to laugh. "Maternal instincts?" she scoffed. "I have none." Her jaw tightened as she remembered the dreadful night when Gabriel had slaughtered each and every one of her fledglings before her eyes. She'd seen how much he'd enjoyed it—not just hurting her fledglings, but hurting *her*. His own mother! Who'd given up *everything* for him!

"I will gladly give him to you, *Maître*. And I would gladly watch him suffer." She frowned. "But even you and I together would not be able to take him. He's grown exceedingly powerful. More powerful than I could ever have imagined."

Bartolomeo sniffed disdainfully. "There is a reason born vampires are killed at birth, *Madame*. But I know ways to take down even the most powerful of vampires. Help me find Gabriel, and I will show you how."

Camille rose from her chair to offer the *Maître* a respectful curtsy even as her mind flitted worriedly from one thought to another. She probed at what had once been her conscience and felt no twinge at the idea of turning Gabriel over to the *Maître*. No twinge—maybe even some pleasure—at the thought of the *Maître* punishing the boy for his many transgressions. Gabriel had betrayed her, and anyone who'd ever betrayed her had suffered the agony of her wrath. Except Eli, of course. Only the worst kind of fool would mount an attack against a vampire of Eli's age and power. But then, Bartolomeo claimed he knew ways to take down even the most powerful of vampires.

"I will gladly help you hunt Gabriel," she said. "And I would even be happy to witness his punishment. But I would ask one favor of you."

The *Maître* gave her a narrow-eyed glare. "I am already

doing you the courtesy of letting you live. Do not try my patience."

One corner of her mouth tipped up. "I don't think you will find this favor distasteful." She was sure he had more than enough hate to go around. "I want you to help me hunt Eli. Much though Gabriel has angered me, it is Eli who is the root of all my troubles. He made me. He impregnated me. He dragged me from my home. And then he abandoned me. I would see him pay for all that he's done to me. And since it is he who has denied you your revenge all these centuries, I would think the idea might appeal."

Bartolomeo rose to his feet, smiling, a glow of genuine pleasure in his eyes. "To quote one of your quaint American movies, I believe this is the start of a beautiful friendship."

Camille curtsied once more, hiding her smile at his mangling of the famous line. Friendship was of course out of the question. But partnership . . . Yes, a partnership could very well be the perfect tool for both of them.

GABRIEL STOOD AT THE window of the penthouse apartment he'd rented and watched the sun slowly lower over the horizon. The smoggy city air seemed to catch fire in the red light of sunset. He leaned his forehead against the glass, fascinated. He'd never watched a sunset from this high up before, never seen the fire sink into the streets, pulling darkness in its wake.

He drew in a deep breath, surprised to find himself taking pleasure in something so . . . simple. Perhaps it was the lack of sleep. While young vampires were practically comatose during the daylight hours, older ones could walk even in the brightest light of day. One quirk of his birth was that Gabriel had been able to walk in the daylight ever since he hit puberty.

After his meeting with Hannah last night, he'd been too keyed up to sleep, and had spent the afternoon gazing at the TV while inane movies and talk shows provided background noise.

His first trap was now set. Hannah would tell Eli every-
thing and would then set herself up as "bait" for the trap.
Then, when he came to extract information from her, the
Guardians' mortal helper would shoot him in the head.

Or so she thought.

He smiled, imagining Eli's horror when he realized his
folly, what danger he'd put this poor mortal woman in. Yes,
this would make the perfect petty torment until Gabriel
found a way to plunge the knife deeper.

A sudden twinge of pain in his chest made him frown. He
touched his breastbone lightly, and the pain pulsed just beyond the reach of his fingers.

What the hell . . . ?

And then the twinge became agony, and with a wordless
cry he dropped to his knees and curled himself around the
pain. His breath seared his throat as he drew it in.

The pain vanished as quickly as it had come, but when he
raised his head, he found he was no longer in his apartment.
He blinked and rubbed his eyes, finding himself on his knees
on a garish floral rug in a meticulously neat living room.

Rubbing his eyes didn't make the room go away, and he
soon realized he wasn't alone. A young girl sat on a hard
wooden chair that looked like it had been dragged from a
classroom. He guessed her age as about fourteen, a girl on
the cusp of womanhood, with the first hint of breasts filling
out the Plain-Jane sweater she wore. Her hair was shorn
cancer-patient short, and dyed a hideous carrot orange that
made her skin look sallow.

A wound on the side of her nose bled steadily, the blood
running down the side of her face until it dripped off her
chin and spotted her faded blue jeans. She barely moved as
he stared at her, her eyes fixed on the floor, not a tear escap-
ing though the wound must have hurt.

Footsteps approached from the hallway, and the girl's
shoulders hunched. A muscle in her jaw ticked as she gritted her teeth.

Strangely, Gabriel found himself unable to move, unable

to turn around and see the figure that approached from behind. He reached out with his senses and felt nothing. Then, he realized he *smelled* nothing. He closed his eyes and drew in a deep breath through his nose. Still nothing. He should have scented the blood in the air if nothing else.

A washcloth sailed over his head and landed wetly on the girl's lap.

"Clean yourself off," a harsh voice demanded.

He recognized that voice, though it took him a moment to place it. He'd heard it only once before, when he'd been inadvertently dragged into Jezebel's memory.

Her grandmother.

He opened his eyes once more, and this time recognized young Jezebel, neither the child she'd been in the last vision, nor the adult he'd made his fledgling, but trapped somewhere in between. She held the washcloth to her bleeding nose, but her eyes remained fixed on the carpet.

"Jezebel Anne Johanson, you are a *disgrace!*" the grandmother pronounced. "Did you think for a moment about the risk you put everyone through? Did you warn anyone at that horrible place about your . . . condition?"

Gabriel could hear the sneer in the harpy's voice, though he still couldn't turn to see her.

Jez winced, and the pain that stirred behind her eyes was unmistakable. But her words showed none of it, betrayed only adolescent insolence.

"They wore gloves, Gram. No one's stupid enough to do a piercing without wearing gloves these days."

Ah. Now he understood the source of the blood. It seemed whatever piercing young Jezebel had gotten had been ripped from her nose. Rage stirred in Gabriel's center. She was a *child!* Who would do such a thing to a child? If the grandmother didn't like the pierced nose, she could have ordered Jez to remove the ornament.

"It was unthinkably selfish!" the harpy shrilled. "What if the gloves tore? You could have spread your filth to an innocent bystander all because you wanted to lash out at me."

Jez's eyes flashed with rebellion, and she reached over and pulled up her sleeve, displaying a bandage on her upper arm. "Don't you want to know what else I did while I was at the tattoo parlor, Gram?" She ripped off the bandage, and Gabriel saw the hideously ugly pentagram tattoo he'd removed from her skin while she'd slept during her transition from mortal to vampire.

The grandmother screeched, and Jez rose to her feet, sneering. But despite the angry, hateful expression, Gabriel had no trouble seeing the boundless hurt that lay behind it.

"And you know what?" Jez continued, holding her chin up high, a gesture he'd come to know well. "I fucked the owner to pay for it all."

A hand flew out of nowhere and smacked into Jezebel's cheek, so hard she fell sideways and crashed against the coffee table. The blood flow from her nose redoubled, and she touched her fingers to it. But instead of crying, or quivering, or in any way trying to protect herself, she held up her bloodstained hand and laughed.

"Wanna hit me again? Just make sure you don't hit too hard. You might break your own skin and then my *filth* will contaminate you."

"Say one more word, Jezebel, and I will toss you out on the street with not a penny to your name. I will not tolerate this insolence in my house. I have taken you in against all my better judgment. I have put up with you year after year, like I put up with your mother before you. But enough is enough. One more incident like this, and—"

"What do you think the child welfare folks would think of that?" Jez retorted, once again trying to stanch the blood flow with the washcloth.

"Take a look at yourself in the mirror. You dress like a whore. You've done . . . terrible things to your hair. You've admitted you traded sex for some hapless man's services. Who would disbelieve me if I said you just ran away from home?"

Gabriel wanted to kill the witch. He couldn't see her, he

couldn't smell her, had never met her. But he wanted her to die. Because he plainly saw the truth that Jez's grandmother chose not to see.

The tattoo on Jez's arm was strictly amateur work. It was entirely possible Jez might have done it to herself. And Gabriel knew for a fact she hadn't traded sex for *anything*. She'd been a virgin when the fledgling Killers had attacked her. He'd thought it odd when he'd read that from her memory when he transformed her, but now he understood. Despite her grandmother's condemnation, Jez would never endanger another person knowingly, would not take the risk of infecting someone else.

The scene around him began to bleed and waver, another scene taking its place. Jez was older now, her frame gaunt with sickness. She looked with desolate eyes over Gabriel's shoulder, and he knew who stood there just beyond his range of sight.

And suddenly, he couldn't bear to see anymore. He didn't know how this connection had happened, didn't know why he was reliving her memories with her, but it had to stop.

Acting on pure instinct, he imagined heavy steel doors slamming shut all around him, imagined dragging himself back into his body. And to his surprise, it worked.

He knelt on his apartment floor, his forehead against the carpet, his chest still aching horribly. His breath came in desperate gasps, and he felt a scream, a scream that was not his, rising from somewhere deep in his belly. He raised his eyes to look out the window, where the sun had yet to sink below the horizon.

A nightmare.

Jez would not have awakened from her daytime sleep yet. If he was sharing her memories, these intense sensations and emotions, she must be having a nightmare.

He forced himself to his feet and staggered to the phone. She might not be able to wake yet, but he had to try. The pain made it hard to breathe, hard to remember the numbers, but he managed to punch them in on the third try.

The phone rang, and rang, and rang.

And then suddenly, the pain stopped and he could breathe again. He drew in deep gasps, wiping the sweat from his brow, thanking God that it was over.

"Hello?" Jez's voice said. She sounded as breathless as he felt, and he imagined her heart still hammered from the nightmare. A nightmare she had actually lived.

"Hello?" she said again, more impatiently.

Trying to quiet his heavy breathing, Gabriel set the phone gently back in its cradle.

6

JEZ SAT AT HER kitchen table, groggy and shaken, feeling
as if she hadn't slept in a week. She'd been a vampire for
four months, and she'd let herself believe that it was actually possible to leave the past behind. Then Gabriel had
come to town and shattered it all by making her act like the
scum-sucking bottom feeder her Gram always told her she
was. And suddenly, she was having fucking nightmares!

She groaned and rubbed her eyes. Who knew vampires
could have nightmares? She thought the daytime sleep was
more like a coma. She'd never even had *dreams* before.

"Thanks a fucking lot, Gabriel," she muttered under her
breath.

She felt sick enough already without having to face the
ordeal of feeding, but Eli had pounded into her the necessity of feeding as soon as the slightest hint of hunger stirred.
If she didn't feed the hunger, there was a risk it would escalate faster than she expected and she could attack the first
mortal she laid eyes on. So she opened her fridge and
pulled out one of the stoppered green bottles that held pre-
served lamb's blood, and she pulled out the quart of milk

she'd bought last week. It ought to still be good. Not that she thought the meal could be any more revolting even if the milk turned sour. She poured a tall glass of half milk, half blood, then pinched her nose shut and chugged.

Her stomach seriously considered rebelling, but she clapped a hand over her mouth and forced herself to take slow, steady breaths. Sometimes, she wondered if it was really necessary to add the nauseating milk. It was certainly true that the milk made feeding a very unpleasant chore, but would she really feel any urgent need to kill mortals if she enjoyed her food?

She didn't want to find out. So she added the milk as Eli decreed, and tried not to hate him for it.

Geez, she was in a shitty mood this morning. She laughed at herself even as her stomach kept trying to toss her meal back up. When had she started to think of eight o'clock at night as "morning?"

Eli had called another meeting tonight, so she had less than an hour to pull herself together, get dressed, and get to his house down by the Delaware River. Usually, that would have been no sweat. Tonight, she felt like she was moving through molasses.

The dreams had been so goddamn vivid! And unlike the dreams she'd had as a mortal, they didn't seem to be fading away into unreality like they should. Maybe because they'd been too real. Memories relived, rather than dreams.

And she still remembered every cruel word her grandmother had said. Remembered how she'd instantly *assumed* Jez had carelessly risked spreading her illness to others. Had assumed Jez just went to some random tattoo parlor and bled all over people for the fun of it.

If Gram had bothered to ask, Jez would have told her she'd gone to her friend Harry's apartment. Harry was nineteen years old—way too old for her, and not that into girls, though she'd had a hint of a childish crush on him—and had HIV just like her. They'd met at the doctor's office, but of course Gram would never be caught dead acknowledging anyone who might share Jez's affliction, because as far as she was concerned, AIDS was God's punishment to the sinners of this world. And following that logic, Jez must be a sinner herself, or she wouldn't have HIV.

It had been Harry who'd pierced her nose, and he'd only done it because she said she'd do it herself if he didn't help her. Having worked at a tattoo parlor before he'd become infected, he'd been the perfect one to ask. He'd even been sensitive enough to warn her how Gram would react, but at the time, she'd said she didn't care.

Jez blinked away tears, leaning on the dresser in her bedroom, hating how memories could hurt so much even when she reminded herself that she'd never have to face Gram again. She dragged in a deep breath, then let it out slowly, trying to let the tension flow out of her. If she were like Gabriel, she'd head on back to Baltimore and pay her Gram a visit. She tried to imagine sinking her fangs into that self-righteous old biddy's throat, but the idea held no appeal. Vengeance just wasn't her thing.

Brooding and self-pity made her late to Eli's meeting, but she could always count on Jules and Hannah being later, so she wasn't the last to arrive. Eli gave her a funny look, like he could tell in an instant something was wrong, but thankfully he didn't press her.

There followed one of the most torturous hours Jez had spent since she'd been transformed, as Hannah recounted her meeting with Gabriel, and the Guardians planned their "trap." Jez hoped like hell her face wasn't giving away too much of her inner turmoil. Luckily, as one of the youngest Guardians, and having—as far as anyone knew—nothing to do with the case, she felt shrouded in a cloak of invisibility.

Carolyn had spent the day refreshing her rifle skills. She was confident that at close range, she'd have an excellent chance to get off a head shot. Everyone was in agreement she'd only get one shot. If she missed, Gabriel's glamour would make a second shot impossible.

For once, Gray and Jules were in agreement, begging Eli

not to let Hannah and Carolyn put themselves in so much danger. But only an idiot would bet against those two women in a battle of wills!

Hannah would stay home the next couple of nights, while Jules left on "errands." They were gambling that Gabriel would make contact before the scheduled rendezvous. Which, of course, he would.

Carolyn would arrange to be camped out on the roof of the house across the street from Hannah's apartment. Hannah would leave her living room windows and drapes open, and when Gabriel paid her a visit, Carolyn should have a clear shot from less than thirty yards away. She didn't need to be an expert marksman to make that shot. And Gabriel would have no reason to be suspicious if he sensed a mortal presence when surrounded by mortal residences.

If it weren't for Jez, the plan might actually have had a chance of working. The guilt squatted heavily on her shoulders, and she must have looked really miserable.

"Are you all right, Jezebel?" Eli asked, startling her out of her funk.

For half a second, she feared he saw right through her, knew she was a spy and a filthy liar. But then logic returned and she tried to answer calmly.

"I'm fine."

"You don't look fine," Hannah said, with her usual tact. She regarded Jez with unfriendly eyes. "What's wrong with you?"

It was on the tip of her tongue to deny anything was wrong, but who did she think she'd fool? So reluctantly, she told a bit of the truth. "I had nightmares," she said quietly. "I didn't know it was possible for a vampire to have nightmares."

"Oh yeah?" Hannah asked, and she still sounded suspicious. "What about?"

"I don't think this is a subject for a public forum," Eli chided gently. "This is a business meeting, if you'll recall."

Hannah shrugged. "Whatever."

The meeting resumed, but Jez could feel the occasional touch of Hannah's glance, full of curiosity and suspicion. Afterward, Eli made her stay behind and asked her if there was anything she wanted to talk about with him. Wishing desperately that she could, she smiled and shook her head, then got out of there as fast as she could manage.

HER NERVES WERE SHOT by the time she got home, so once again Jez rooted through her purse for her cigarettes. She grimaced when she took her first drag. She could swear they smelled and tasted worse each time. And she'd never liked them all that much in the first place. She'd started smoking because it pissed Gram off, and because she thought she'd be dead long before lung cancer became a concern.

She made it halfway through the cig before she discarded it in disgust, tossing the rest of the pack at the same time. Her body burned with excess energy, and she almost called Hannah to ask for a sparring session tonight. It would feel good to fight, even though she'd probably get her ass kicked again. But Hannah would start asking questions about what was wrong, and Jez didn't feel up to answering.

Searching for something that might soothe her, she settled for drawing a hot bath. She tossed in a handful of aromatherapy bath salts that were supposed to be peace-inducing, turned off the bathroom lights, and lit a single candle, making the bathroom as restful as she could. If only she could sip from a glass of wine as she soaked, it would be perfect.

For the first ten minutes or so, she felt like she might jump out of the water any moment. Then, the heat started to get to her, and finally, her muscles relaxed one by one. She let her eyes drift closed and leaned back into the water on a soft sigh.

She didn't know how long she'd been lying there, soaking in the warmth, breathing in the pleasant, though slightly medicinal, scent of the bath salts, before some sixth sense told her she wasn't alone.

She'd been expecting Gabriel to show up, of course. And she'd expected him not to bother knocking. She *hadn't* expected him to barge in on her in the bathroom. And yet, she *knew* he was here.

She kept her eyes closed, reaching out with her senses, but they as usual insisted there was no one here.

Wishing she could believe her vamp-dar, knowing her intuition was more reliable, she reluctantly lifted her eyelids just enough to let her peek out from beneath her lashes.

He stood in the bathroom doorway, staring at her with absolute attention. She'd turned the lights off in the hall, so the only illumination came from that one dim candle, which turned his handsome face into a collage of shadows and sharp angles. He'd dumped his leather jacket, instead wearing a plain black T-shirt and ratty, faded jeans, but he still looked dangerous. His eyes were night-dark, no hint of their usual gray-green color.

At first, she assumed his eyes looked so dark because it was dark in the room. Then, through her closed lashes, she watched his eyes travel up and down her body, a slow, luxurious tour that she felt like a physical caress. And she knew it wasn't darkness that caused his eyes to dilate.

Her nipples hardened, and a pulse of desire tugged at her center. Never before had a man looked at her like that. But then, ever since she'd come down with full-blown AIDS, she'd been perpetually skinny and sickly, not a curve on her.

She opened her eyes fully, but Gabriel was too intent on his inspection to notice. One corner of her mouth tipped upward. She supposed she should be annoyed at the invasion of her privacy, or at least embarrassed to be seen in the nude. Instead, she felt something almost like awe at the idea of being looked at like a desirable woman. What a novelty!

"Like what you see?" she asked, and he jumped.

She wasn't positive, but she thought his cheeks flushed just a tad pink at being caught staring. She expected him to cover for it with one of his nasty sneers or snide comments, but he didn't. Instead, he just smiled, though the desire in his eyes made the smile into something just short of a leer.

"I like very much," he said, and this time it was her own cheeks that went pink. Then, he had to ruin it. "The last time I saw you naked, you were bruised from head to toe and hadn't enough fat on you to keep a mouse alive."

"Gee, thanks," she said, sitting up and turning slightly away to hide her breasts. She still bore faint scars on both her breasts, on her throat, and on the insides of her thighs from the feeding frenzy that had almost killed her. That *would* have killed her, if Gabriel hadn't transformed her.

Gabriel didn't take the hint, coming instead to sit on the edge of the tub. "Get out," she snapped. "Let me put some clothes on."

He arched one eyebrow. "Now why would I want you to do that when I've just pointed out how lovely you look without them."

She crossed her arms over her breasts and glared at him, but he reached out and brushed her arms away, using his glamour when she tried to resist. Her heart fluttered strangely in her throat. Moments before, she'd enjoyed seeing the desire on his face when he looked at her. But that had been when he was clear across the room.

He reached out a finger and brushed lightly against one of the scars on the top of her breast. The touch made her shiver, and it had nothing to do with cold.

"Don't!" she gasped, and to her surprise he let his hand fall away. She risked a peek upward, and saw a look on his face she couldn't interpret. "Is something wrong?" she asked.

He blinked, and the strange look faded. He smiled, and it was almost charming. "I'm in a candlelit bathroom with a beautiful naked woman in the tub. How could anything be wrong?"

She narrowed her eyes at him. "My, aren't we mellow this evening." She'd never seen him even remotely like this before. What had gotten into him?

"I don't think mellow is the word you're looking for, my dear," he said, and his smile broadened until she saw that his fangs had descended. "Horny might be more like it."

That made her gulp, and, unfortunately, glance down at his crotch. One glance was all it took to confirm that "horny" was a good choice of words.

The water felt suddenly cold around her, and her shiver made her teeth chatter. She drew her knees upward and wrapped her arms around them, hiding as much of herself from him as possible, even while some small corner of her mind reminded her that if he'd walked in and not been turned on by seeing her naked, it would probably have hurt her feelings.

He stood up and grabbed the towel she'd left neatly folded on the back of the toilet. She thought he'd just hand it to her and go, but he unfurled it and held it by opposite corners, and she realized he meant for her to stand up and let him wrap it around her. The thought made fear and lust battle within her belly. But if he wanted to, he could just use his glamour to drag her to her feet, so she gathered her courage and stood.

He wrapped the towel around her, but made no move to grab her as she'd half-expected. She stepped out of the tub, and he moved back to give her room. His eyes were still almost black, and out of the corner of her eye she saw that his erection still strained against his zipper. She shook her head in confusion.

"Are you coming on to me, or aren't you?" she asked. "I always imagined it would be easy to tell, but I guess I was wrong." Most of the men she'd hung out with had been fellow HIV or AIDS victims, and most of them were gay. The few who were bi didn't seem to find her very tempting, so her experience with sexual overtures was disgustingly scant.

Gabriel met her eyes, his tongue playing with one of his fangs. "I'm trying to resist the temptation to pick you up and fuck you against the wall."

The growling ferocity of his voice made her take a step

backward. But the bathtub was behind her, and she kind of forgot about that. With a surprised cry, she lost her balance. The towel fell away, and she would no doubt have smashed her head against the tile wall behind the tub if Gabriel hadn't closed the distance between them, grabbed her by the shoulders, and stood her upright. She clutched his forearms, her legs unsteady, her heart pounding.

Fire coursed through her veins, and something throbbed between her legs. She closed her eyes and swallowed hard. Was this Gabriel's lust she was feeling? Or her own? She honestly couldn't tell, and that was scary as hell.

Gabriel's body pressed against hers, the torn denim of his jeans rough against her naked legs, the soft cotton of his T-shirt a sensuous caress against her hardened nipples. His mouth brushed against the side of her head, and she heard him breathe deep the scent of her. She couldn't help reciprocating, inhaling the scent of leather that clung to him even without the jacket.

If this was *his* lust she was feeling, she was damn lucky he hadn't already pinned her to the wall. And she couldn't help wondering what sex would be like if she could feel her lover's desire as strongly as her own.

Hell, she wondered what sex felt like, period! Having been gang-raped, she hardly qualified as a virgin, but whatever Gabriel had done to her memory made it all seem so distant she might as well have been. Common sense told her Gabriel wasn't the right man to satisfy her curiosity. Yeah, he was good-looking, and she found him sexy as hell, but he was also a basket case, so full of anger he wouldn't know a good thing if it bit him in the ass.

"Gabriel?" she whispered, not at all sure what she wanted to say.

His sigh was a breath of warmth along her cheek. Then, he let go of her and stepped back, his eyes averted.

"Come meet me in the living room when you're dressed," he said, and his voice sounded almost angry. He strode away before she had a chance to ask him what was wrong.

* * *

GABRIEL SAT ON JEZEBEL'S living room couch and willed his throbbing erection to go down.

He'd been entirely unprepared for his reaction to seeing her in that bathtub. When he'd transformed her, when he'd treated her wounds, he'd come to know every inch of her body, and had never once had a sexual thought about her. She'd been nothing but a tool to him then, a weapon to use to hurt Eli. He had to admit to himself that he'd barely even thought of her as a *person,* much less a woman.

Was it sharing her dreams that made him look at her so differently? Or was she blossoming now that she was out from under the influence of her poisonous family life? Or had he just gone too long without a good fuck?

If he hadn't feared she'd pick up on the strange vibes of it, he'd have ducked into the powder room and jerked off just to ease the strain. As it was, he merely gritted his teeth and tried not to imagine sliding his cock deep into her hot, tight sheath.

He rolled his eyes at himself. Jez was hardly an appropriate outlet for his ferocity in bed. She was practically a virgin. And even now that she was a vampire, there wasn't the faintest taint of corruption in her scent. She was a good person, and if he bedded her, he would cause her nothing but pain. Even if she genuinely thought she wanted him in her bed. Even if her apparent desire had nothing to do with his own lust bleeding over into her. No one in their right mind wanted *him* in their bed, not unless they were being well paid.

When he'd served as his mother's right-hand man, he could order any of her fledglings he wanted to his bed. None dared refuse him, no matter how much they might dread what he would do to them. Submitting to him—and to Camille—had been part of the price they'd paid in letting her bite and transform them. A price, he reminded himself, they'd paid willingly. Camille made them serve her as mortals for at least two years before she transformed them.

They saw what would be expected of them as fledglings, and they hadn't flinched. If the reality turned out to be a little harder on them than they'd expected, that was *their* problem. Besides, he'd never done anything to them that they hadn't done to someone else.

Now, he had no outlet. All Camille's fledglings were dead, and Eli's Guardians were too decent for his special brand of torment. At least, the ones he'd met so far were. Even Drake, the Killer, had no stink of corruption to him.

He supposed he could slake his lust on mortal prostitutes, but though he'd availed himself of such services many times in the past, he rarely found the experience worth the time or money. Mortal women were so fragile, he had to be careful not to break them, and where was the fun in that?

He was lost enough in the turmoil of his thoughts that he didn't hear Jezebel come in. He felt the couch dip with her weight, and his eyes popped open. He hadn't even realized he'd closed them. He was in a bad way!

She looked . . . vulnerable. She'd put on a pair of loose-fitting knit pants and a pretty, ice-blue camisole top that revealed plenty of peaches-and-cream skin. But the bruised expression in her eyes helped him shove thoughts of sex aside. He realized his abrupt retreat from the bathroom must have hurt her feelings, and though he was hardly in the habit of giving comfort, he found he couldn't resist.

"You're very beautiful, and very desirable, Jezebel," he said. "But as you've no doubt noticed, I am not a nice man." He allowed himself a small, bitter smile. "I have just enough decency to try to protect you from myself. Which means in the future, you should keep your clothes on in my presence."

The hurt in her eyes disappeared instantly. "Asshole!" she said, apparently not afraid of him anymore. Or maybe just too angry to care. "You walked into the bathroom while I was in the tub. It's not like I ripped off my clothing and begged you to fuck me!"

He bit the inside of his cheek to keep from laughing at

the fierceness of her response. Of course, she was dead right. "Forgive me. I'm trying to apologize. I'm not very good at it. I've had very little practice, you see."

Her anger faded as quickly as it had come, and she laughed softly. "Your technique could definitely use some work."

He shrugged. "I don't expect to make a habit of it. I'm an old dog, and this is one new trick I don't feel inclined to learn. Now, enough nonsense. Tell me what happened at Eli's meeting tonight."

The starch went out of her shoulders, the fire dying in her eyes. Gabriel's out-of-practice conscience twinged to see her misery. But he reminded himself that she'd agreed to his price, that he'd potentially saved her sanity by blunting the memory of that hideous attack. She might not like what she had to do in return, but he would hold her to that commitment.

"Tormenting them isn't going to change what happened between you and Eli," she murmured, not looking at him. "All you're doing is—"

"Don't provoke me, Jezebel!" he snarled, and he didn't even try to rein in his anger, let her feel it roiling inside him. She shrank away from him. "Tell me about the meeting and keep your morality lecture to yourself."

Even as she shrank from him, she gave him a knowing look. "It wasn't *morality* I was going to lecture about, but never mind."

He listened with only half an ear as she told him what the Guardians had planned.

7

CAMILLE GOT TO SPEND a grand total of two nights in her homeland. On the third, she found herself in the *Maître*'s limo, pulling up to the tarmac in front of a sleek white jet with its engines whining. Bartolomeo's chosen entourage—four of his youngest fledglings, as well as a handful of mortal males—milled around outside the jet. One of the mortals dashed up to open Bartolomeo's door as soon as the limo came to a full stop. The *Maître* stepped out onto the tarmac, then turned to offer Camille a hand out.

She sniffed daintily. There was something vaguely absurd about Bartolomeo playing the gentleman. Nevertheless, she accepted his hand after a slight hesitation. Let him have his pretensions of gentility!

He seemed not to have appreciated her hesitation. "You seem to lack some degree of enthusiasm for this hunt, *Madame*," he said as he escorted her toward the stairway that led up to the plane's door.

She shook her head. "It's not that. Believe me, *Maître,* I have no qualms about hunting Gabriel." Save fear for her own life, but she wasn't about to admit that. "I just . . ." She

smiled sadly. "Only three nights ago, I set foot in my homeland for the first time in four centuries. It's a hard thing to
leave again so soon."

Bartolomeo's brow darkened. "If you ever want to set
foot in your homeland again, I suggest you keep your complaints to a minimum."

She forced the sadness out of her smile and bowed her
head to acknowledge the rebuke, even as she dreamed of
ripping his throat out for treating her like this. She was his
elder and his better, and she deserved to be treated as such.
Why, once she was introduced to the *Seigneur,* she would
surely be elevated to the rank of *Maîtresse.* She smothered a
smile. Perhaps even the *Maîtresse de Paris.* Yes, she would
enjoy deposing her unwanted ally.

Camille had just set foot on the first step when another
car pulled onto the tarmac beside the limo. She turned to
look and saw Brigitte Arnault step out from behind the
wheel of an exotic-looking red sports car. Something Italian
and handmade, no doubt. Brigitte's companion, a tall, handsome male she had never bothered to introduce, stepped out
from the passenger seat.

Bartolomeo's shoulders stiffened, and he took up what
looked like a defensive position. Camille stepped back onto
the tarmac, curious. Why should Bartolomeo be tense because his underlings had arrived?

Brigitte wore a skintight black catsuit with a keyhole
opening that displayed what cleavage she had. She'd com-
pensated for her diminutive stature with a pair of high-
heeled black pumps that probably cost as much as most
economy cars. Her boy toy—or whatever he was—stood at
her elbow, dressed in a fine Italian suit, the shirt unbuttoned
halfway to his navel.

Smiling at Bartolomeo, Brigitte raised a set of car keys
and pressed a button. The car's minuscule trunk popped
open. Bartolomeo's driver, who'd already loaded their luggage into the plane, looked at Bartolomeo for direction.

"Brigitte. Henri. What a pleasant surprise." He tried a friendly smile, but the expression didn't reach his eyes. In fact, if Camille were pressed, she'd say he looked afraid of the pair. But why would that be?

Brigitte's smile could only be described as impish. "I'm glad you think so, *Maître*. Would you be so kind as to have your driver load our luggage?"

The white lights of the plane leached most of the color out of everyone's skin anyway, but Camille thought Bartolomeo paled. This made no sense, and Camille looked back and forth between them, trying to puzzle out what was happening.

"Are you sure this is . . . wise?" Bartolomeo asked, but he sounded desperate.

Brigitte laughed. "Probably not. But I'm coming anyway."

Yes, Bartolomeo was definitely pale. Frightened. Camille reached out with her senses, examining Brigitte's aura once more. But still, she guessed the woman's age at less than three hundred, with Henri even younger. They should be no threat to Bartolomeo at all.

"Mlle. Arnault," he said, and he sounded like he was begging, "please reconsider. Your mother—"

She snarled. "I have made up my mind, *Maître*. Henri and I are coming to America with you."

Sweat beaded Bartolomeo's upper lip. He stopped trying to hold onto his composure and openly pleaded now. "Don't ask this of me."

Brigitte smiled, her eyes twinkling with glee. "Oh, but I'm not *asking* anything of you. Have your men put our bags on your plane. If you don't, I'll have to tell Mother something beautifully inventive about your hospitality."

His face bleak and scared, Bartolomeo motioned his driver toward Brigitte's car. She nodded briskly, then practically skipped up the stairs into the plane, Henri trailing silently behind her like a malevolent shadow. Camille turned to Bartolomeo and raised her eyebrows.

He pulled a handkerchief from his pocket and mopped his sweaty brow. "Her mother is . . ." His voice trailed off, but Camille picked up the thread, making an educated guess.

"Her mother is the *Seigneur,*" she guessed. Obviously, the *Maître* was afraid of Brigitte's mother, which meant she had to be more powerful than he. But that also meant she had to be considerably more than three hundred years old. If the *Seigneur* was more than three hundred, and Brigitte was less than three hundred, then . . . "Brigitte is a born vampire."

Bartolomeo's eyes closed for a moment. He was still sweating profusely, and his face hadn't regained its color. "Oh, no, *Madame,*" he said. "It is far worse than that. Mlle. Arnault is indeed a born vampire, but her mother is not the *Seigneur.*" He swallowed hard, his Adam's apple bobbing. "Her mother is *La Vieille de la Nord.*"

Camille's mouth dropped open. *Les Vieux,* the Old Ones, were creatures of legend. Vampires of such enormous age and power that even the *Seigneurs* bowed to them. No one she knew had ever seen any of the Old Ones, and some people claimed they were a myth, a kind of vampire bogeyman, used by the *Seigneurs* to frighten those who weren't sensible enough to be frightened by the *Seigneurs* themselves.

Bartolomeo stared up at the plane. "If *La Vieille* discovers we've taken her to America, we will both die more horribly than you can possibly imagine."

Camille felt like screaming in frustration. She didn't need this extra complication! But she understood Bartolomeo's predicament. If Brigitte were to tell her mother some tall tale about Bartolomeo's behavior, he was as dead as if he took her to America. Which would be fine with Camille, if only she hadn't gotten caught in the crossfire.

Brigitte popped her head out the door and called down the stairs toward them. "Well? Are you coming or aren't you? I'm anxious to see the famous New World with my own two eyes."

Sighing, Camille climbed the stairs and heard Bartolomeo

start up behind her. Perhaps having a born vampire in their midst would prove to be an advantage in their battle against Eli and Gabriel. The *Maître* seemed smugly confident that they could handle Gabriel, but he hadn't explained just how he planned to do it.

Gabriel had a good two centuries on Brigitte, but with Camille and Bartolomeo's combined support, they might actually stand a chance against him.

Telling herself not to think too far into the future, she stepped through the doorway and into the plane.

GABRIEL HID IN THE shadows a block away from Hannah's apartment, and surveyed the situation. In his otherworldly vision, he saw Hannah's aura as she paced relentlessly. She must be nervous. For as far as his senses could stretch, he caught no hint of another vampire's psychic footprint. Perhaps even if he *hadn't* known about the plan in advance, her very vulnerability would have made him suspicious.

He couldn't see the mortal woman who was concealed on the roof of the building across the street, but he could feel her. Unlike Hannah, the mortal seemed steady and sure, hardly moving. He lowered his fangs and smiled.

"Let the games begin," he murmured to himself, then slipped around the corner.

He'd been watching Hannah's apartment all day, keeping just far enough away that Jules wouldn't be able to sense him when he woke. He'd scoped out the neighboring houses, making sure he was intimately familiar with the area. And because of his vigilance, he'd seen the mortal woman, Carolyn, when she arrived in the late afternoon to take up her position.

He wasn't sure exactly how she'd managed it, but she'd somehow gotten up to the roof from the inside of the building. Gabriel decided to take the more obvious route—climbing the fire escape.

He climbed effortlessly most of the way. The last few feet

from the top of the fire escape to the lip of the roof were something of a challenge, but he used his telekinesis to give himself the boost he needed. He landed silently on the black tar roof, which sprouted antennae and chimneys like a forest of butt-ugly weeds.

Carolyn lay on her stomach beside one of those chimneys on the opposite side of the roof. She squinted into the sights of a high-tech rifle that was propped on what looked like a two-legged tripod. Then she lowered her head away from the rifle and stretched her neck. He could hear her spine crackle and pop even though he was still a good fifteen yards away. He moved a little closer.

Her concentration was fixed on the rifle and her view of Hannah's window. There was no reason it would occur to her to look behind her. He inched even closer. This little demonstration would be of no use if Hannah didn't know he was here, so he waited patiently for her to sense him. As a fledgling, her range wouldn't be very good, and it would take a lot of energy for her to keep reaching out. But he knew she'd do it, knew she'd want an early warning of his approach to her apartment. He just had to get close enough for her to be able to feel him.

He was only about five feet behind Carolyn when he felt Hannah stop pacing. Once again he smiled. This was it. He *had* to be close enough now. He stepped a little to the side so that the chimney wasn't blocking his view of her window.

A low buzzing sound emanated from a pocket in Carolyn's pants. Her cell phone. She cursed softly and reached for it.

Hannah appeared in her window, face white as ashes, phone to her face. Her eyes strained out into the darkness and found him. He gave her a jaunty wave. Carolyn put the phone to her ear.

"What is it?" she hissed.

"I think Hannah's calling to warn you that I'm standing right behind you," Gabriel said, and watched her entire body go tense. He didn't see any sign of another gun on her, and he didn't think she could swing that rifle around and get a shot off at him, but he stilled her with his glamour anyway as he reached down and plucked the phone from her fingers.

He made a clucking sound with his tongue as he watched Hannah watch him. "A little too obvious, my dear," he said into the phone. "You seem to forget, I'm not a moron."

He heard her swallow hard. He could even swear he heard the pounding of her heart, though even *his* senses weren't that strong. Spitfire though she was, she didn't seem to be able to find anything to say at the moment.

"You'd better lock dear Jules in my father's basement," he warned. "Otherwise, I'll have to make good on my threats."

"Gabe—"

"You just stand right where you are and watch. There's nothing you can do to stop me now." He hung up the phone on Hannah's wail.

She stood frozen in the window, shouting to him across the space that separated them. He tuned her out and focused on his would-be assassin.

She lay as he'd left her, futilely struggling against his glamour. He reached down and grabbed her under the arms, hauling her to her feet. Her pulse throbbed under his hands, sweat dewing her face as her breath came in short little gasps. He inhaled her scent, but as he expected, no taint clung to her.

He waited for the thrill of power that usually flushed his veins when he drank in someone's terror, but it didn't come. Then again, despite what his father thought, Gabriel didn't make a habit of preying on the innocent, so perhaps it was no surprise that he took no pleasure in Carolyn's fear.

Across the street, Hannah was crying, something he knew she didn't do easily. An uncomfortable sensation stirred in his gut. Perhaps he should have set *Jules* up for this little drama instead of Hannah. He doubted Jules's distress would have felt so disconcerting.

Carolyn trembled in his grip. He could only imagine

what she thought he was going to do to her, given his fear-
some reputation. And though he'd had every intention of
scaring her half to death, something unpleasantly reminis-
cent of guilt troubled him.

Pushing his second thoughts aside, Gabriel moved to the
very edge of the roof, dragging Carolyn with him. It was
late enough for traffic to be sparse, which was part of his
plan. He didn't need any civilian witnesses. A single taxi
cab cruised down the street, and there was no pedestrian
traffic. No one to see what he was about to do, except Carolyn and Hannah.

His conscience nagged at him, and he whispered in Carolyn's ear. "Have courage. I'll catch you before you hit."

Then, he shoved her off the edge of the roof.

Both Carolyn and Hannah screamed, their voices merg-
ing into one as Carolyn fell. Gabriel leaned over to watch,
gathering his power to stop her fall before she splattered on
the pavement.

A loud crack sounded from across the street, and at almost the same moment, something slammed into his shoulder, knocking him backward. It took every ounce of his
concentration to reach out with his power even as he landed
on his ass and pain blossomed and grew. Blood spurted
from the wound, and the pain redoubled. The best he could
do was to slow Carolyn's fall, not stop it completely.

He heard a thump and a cry of pain, and once again he
heard Hannah scream. He clapped his hand to his wounded
shoulder, gritting his teeth against the pain.

He stood up and staggered to the edge of the roof, keeping a low profile this time in case Hannah was lining up for
another shot. But she no longer stood in her window.

Carolyn lay on her side on the pavement below, but even
as he watched she pushed herself up to a sitting position.
She would be all right. His relief at the realization surprised
him.

Hannah charged out the front door of her apartment building and crossed the street without a glance in either direction.

If a car had been coming, she'd have been road kill. She fell to her knees by Carolyn's side, and the sound of her sob made something tighten in his belly.

The bleeding in Gabriel's shoulder had slowed, though the pain was a relentless throb as his body worked to expel the foreign object. He slipped away from the edge of the roof, making his getaway before Hannah had a chance to recover her composure and come looking for him. He wasn't sure how well his glamour would work when the pain was so distracting.

He *deserved* to hurt. He'd told Hannah he wasn't a moron, and then he'd gone and acted like one, so focused on his plan for Carolyn that he hadn't looked up and realized Hannah had drawn her gun. In Baltimore, Hannah had held a gun directly to his head and hadn't been able to shoot. But he wasn't at all surprised she found the will to shoot when she thought he'd just murdered her best friend.

Worst of all, he felt no spark of triumph from winning this little game. He'd expected to enjoy sticking a knife into Eli. He *hadn't* expected to feel remorse for making Hannah cry!

The bullet popped out of his flesh, rolling down the inside of his shirt until it got trapped at the waistband of his pants. The pain receded. He untucked his shirt and plucked out the bullet, wrapping his fist around it.

This was a just punishment for his arrogance. He would be more careful next time. No matter how great his powers, if he grew careless enough to let someone shoot him, and that shot should penetrate his heart or head, he was as dead as any mortal man.

And if he was going to end up dead when all was said and done, it would be because Eli killed him with his own two hands.

JEZ THOUGHT SHE MIGHT very well be going crazy.

Tonight was the night Gabriel would spring his trap, and though she felt fairly confident he wouldn't kill anyone, she

couldn't be sure. The not knowing was driving her nuts! She
wanted it over, one way or another, but hour after hour ticked
by and still no word. And although Gabriel could break into
her apartment at any time of the night or day, could contact
her whenever he damn well pleased, he'd given her no way
to get in touch with him.

Man, she wished she could still drink alcohol. A couple
of beers would have been real welcome just about now.

To distract herself from thinking, she stuck a Kanye West
CD in the stereo. She'd have loved to turn it up to ear-
splitting volume, but though she'd used her music to torture
her Gram whenever possible, she didn't want to wake her
neighbors.

Somehow, at moderate volume, it just didn't have the
same effect. Nonetheless, she danced to the heavy beat, trying to let herself drown in it, putting her whole body into it
until she was drenched in sweat. She'd always been a good
dancer, when she wasn't too sick to dredge up the energy,
and her friends at one of her favorite dance clubs had
dubbed her Funky White Girl. It felt good to channel all the
excess energy into motion, and for a little while, she actually managed to forget her worries.

Then, when she was in the middle of a particularly ener-
getic leap, pain exploded in her shoulder.

She fell to the floor in a heap, grabbing her shoulder,
searching for the wound her mind insisted was there. Except there was nothing. She closed her eyes against the relentless throbbing, the bass of her stereo making the floor
vibrate beneath her.

And she felt him, stanching the flow of blood from his
shoulder, then gritting his teeth in pain as he made his way
clumsily down a fire escape, using only his left hand, his
right arm cradled to his chest. When he reached the ground,
he ran, each step jarring the wound on his shoulder.

"Gabriel!" she gasped. But of course he couldn't hear her.

Her long history of illness and doctor's visits had made
her no stranger to pain. Jez coached herself to ride the tide

of Gabriel's pain, a calm, dispassionate voice in her mind
telling her to breathe in deeply and breathe out slowly.

It would have been easier if she weren't feeling . . . other
things as well. Remorse. Confusion. And, of course, the
ever-present anger. Anger that hadn't been relieved by anything he'd done tonight.

Jez shivered as she lay on the floor and concentrated on
breathing. The CD played on, and she wished she had the
strength to get up and shut it off. But the pain sapped her
will, and only half her mind seemed to be in the apartment
with her. The other half stalked the streets with a very dis-
satisfied, angry Killer.

Eventually, the pain let up, but the flood of emotions
didn't. This was supposed to be his *revenge*. It was supposed
to feel good, supposed to ease some of the pressure that had
been building up inside of him for centuries. Instead, he felt
fucking *guilty*! Jez felt his snarl in her own throat.

He'd made his way to a more populous street, mortals
crowding around him even though it was past two in the
morning. She couldn't actually *see* through his eyes, but she
could feel his distaste for the press of humanity around him.
She felt his control balancing on a razor's edge, the anger so
fierce it demanded he find an outlet.

Then he brushed by someone, and she felt something . . .
strange. Almost like a sense of recognition, though that
wasn't the right word for it. The rage crystallized inside him,
no longer a formless, roiling mass but now a guided missile.
And he began to follow whoever it was who'd touched him.

Jez opened her eyes and stared at the ceiling, willing herself to see nothing, to feel nothing, to put some walls up to
separate her from her maker. Because she knew what she'd
just felt in him. Knew he'd chosen a victim, chosen a mortal
to kill just for the pleasure of venting his rage. He didn't
need to feed, wouldn't need to for another couple of weeks,
but that wasn't going to stop him. And she didn't want to be
riding along with him when he did it.

It worked, amazingly. Suddenly, she was alone in her

own head. There was no longer any pain in her shoulder. The CD had finished, leaving the apartment shrouded in the city's equivalent of silence.

Jez blinked and was surprised to feel the dampness of her eyes. Gabriel was about to kill someone in an effort to fix whatever was broken inside him, or at least to make the pain of that break go away for a little while. And it wasn't going to work.

A tear leaked from the corner of her eye, running down the side of her face and dripping into her ear. She squinched her eyes shut in an effort to stem the flow.

Looking at Gabriel was like looking in a mirror. So much anger, and it all arose from an abiding hurt. One that no act of desperation or defiance would heal. In fact, ten to one he'd feel *worse* after the kill instead of better.

She scrubbed her eyes, obliterating the tears. Tonight was just another sign that he was way too fucked up for her to get involved with. When *she'd* wanted to stick it to her Gram, she'd gotten pierced and tattooed. When *Gabriel* struck out, he killed people. Jez had given up her wild ways and found she didn't miss them. Gabriel, however, couldn't give up the kill even if he wanted to.

He was just another self-absorbed, self-destructive addict. Like her mom. If he wanted to wallow in his anger, then that was *his* problem, not hers.

But none of these logical arguments stopped her from wishing she could reach out to him and make him see how badly he was hurting himself in his attempt to hurt Eli.

8

CAMILLE STARED OUT THE window at nothing as the jet soared through the darkness of the night. Bartolomeo had fallen asleep almost as soon as the plane had lifted off, and now his snores rivaled the plane's engines for sheer volume. Disgusting creature!

She saw movement out of the corner of her eye. Reluctantly, she dragged her attention away from the window to look at Brigitte, who had slid into the seat across from her. Brigitte smiled, then toed off her expensive shoes and stretched.

"I was wondering if you'd be so good as to satisfy my curiosity," Brigitte said. "Obviously, the *Maître* hates your son with an impressive passion. Everyone knows *something* happened between them before your family fled to America." She stuck her lower lip out in a pout. "But no one seems to know exactly what it was, and the *Maître* isn't talking."

Camille glanced sidelong at Bartolomeo, who was far too deeply asleep to hear their conversation. Yes, she could well imagine why he'd want to keep the details a secret, though she was rather stunned he'd managed to do so.

"I'd be happy to tell you about it," Camille said. "If you'll tell me why you're coming to America with us."

Brigitte laughed. "Well, *that's* no great secret. Obviously, you know the rules where born vampires are concerned."

Apparently, she expected a response, for she looked at Camille pointedly. Camille nodded. "The last I knew, the *Seigneurs* had decreed that no born vampire should be allowed to live."

She laughed again. "Oh, no. It is not the *Seigneurs* who made that rule. It is *Les Vieux*. The *Seigneurs* are merely the enforcers of the rule. But because my mother is *La Vieille de la Nord*, I am the exception." The twinkle of mirth left her eyes. "At least, I have been so far. As long as her pet *Seigneurs* are strong enough to control me, I have her protection. But I'm getting old enough to be dangerous. My mother's maternal affections are as changeable as yours. When I become old enough to pose a real threat, she'll have me killed." She made the statement with no inflection in her voice, as if it hardly mattered to her. The intensity in her eyes belied her seeming nonchalance. "I've been thinking about leaving for decades now, but I couldn't figure out where to go. Now that I know I have a potential kindred spirit in America, it seems the obvious choice."

Camille narrowed her eyes at the girl. "But you know why we're going there." Was Brigitte going to interfere with the plan to kill this supposed "kindred spirit" of hers?

"Yes, I know. And if he's weak enough for you two to kill him, then he's of no interest to me." The offhand contempt in her voice pricked Camille's temper, but she managed to keep her mouth shut. "I only plan to observe," Brigitte continued. "I'll neither help you nor hinder you."

"And where does Henri fit into this equation?" Camille asked, looking past Brigitte to where Henri sat just out of hearing distance. He was staring at the two of them with great intensity, but Camille couldn't read his expression.

Brigitte waved her hand dismissively. "He's my fledgling.

He'll do as he's told." She smirked. "Perhaps he and Gabriel shall become fast friends."

Camille highly doubted that.

"Now," Brigitte continued, "I've answered your questions and it's your turn. What did your son do to the *Maître*?"

The corners of Camille's mouth tightened to think about how Gabriel had shattered her life with his lack of restraint.

"Eli, my maker and husband, was the *Maître de Paris*. Bartolomeo's maker came to visit, bringing Bartolomeo as part of his entourage. He and Gabriel took an instant dislike to one another. Gabriel kept trying to pick a fight, but Eli wouldn't allow it." Eli had always kept Gabriel on a tight leash. It had been for Gabriel's own good, but the boy had always been too hot-headed to see that. She shook her head. "My son had little self-restraint. He knew it would be a death sentence to reveal he was born vampire, and he was less than a hundred years old. He had to pretend to be weaker than he was, and he didn't much like it."

"I can sympathize," Brigitte said with a slight smile. "But go on. What happened?"

"Gabriel slipped Eli's leash. As a visitor in our territory, Bartolomeo was naturally forbidden to hunt. But Gabriel had heard of the disappearance of a couple of local peasant children, and for some reason he believed Bartolomeo was responsible. He followed Bartolomeo to the house where he was staying and caught him in the act of raping a little girl."

Brigitte's nose wrinkled, and she cast a look of disgust on the *Maître*. "No wonder he doesn't want anyone to know what happened." She gave Camille a pointed look. "And he will never introduce you to the *Seigneur*, not with the threat that you might reveal his history."

Camille blinked in surprise. "Why should the *Seigneur* care that the *Maître* raped a little girl four hundred years ago?"

"Because when the *Seigneur* was mortal, he had a young daughter who was raped. He will turn a blind eye to whatever his people do to adults—as long as they do not draw attention to themselves—but to harm a child in his territory is a death sentence." She looked at the still-snoring *Maître*. "Now I understand why he seemed so agitated when you arrived." She turned back to Camille. "But you haven't finished the story. Your son caught the *Maître* indulging his perversion. What then?"

Camille gritted her teeth. "Gabriel indulged his own perversion. When he'd discovered Bartolomeo was poaching, he should have reported the breach to Eli. Eli would have demanded his death, and Bartolomeo's maker would have had to hand him over or fight Eli. Although Eli was no more than a *Maître*, everyone knew he was old and powerful enough to be a *Seigneur* if he wanted. No one with an ounce of common sense would have fought him, especially not over such a blatant breach of protocol.

"But if Gabriel had reported the poaching to Eli, Bartolomeo would have died a quick death, and that would not have satisfied my dear son's lust for cruelty. So instead of following protocol, Gabriel attacked Bartolomeo. They were approximately the same age, but Gabriel overpowered him easily, not bothering to hide his superior strength because, as he later explained, he did not expect Bartolomeo to live to tell anyone.

"My son then proceeded to remove his, er, equipment."

Brigitte's eyes widened, and she gasped. Camille couldn't read beyond the surprise in her face. Was she shocked? Horrified? Gleeful?

"The girl Bartolomeo had been tormenting had been severely burned with a hot iron. Gabriel then took that hot iron to *him*. He says he cauterized the wound."

Another gasp, and Brigitte looked more closely at the sleeping *Maître*. "If that's the truth, then one might suppose he has artificially stuffed his pants."

Camille had thought the same herself, but she felt no desire to take a closer look. "Unfortunately for all of us, Bartolomeo's maker interrupted Gabriel's fun before Bartolomeo was dead. Gabriel was forced to flee into the sunlight, and that was the end of the charade."

Brigitte nodded sagely, then cocked her head. "What happened to the little girl?"

Camille gave her a disdainful look. "She died, obviously. She'd seen far too much to be allowed to live."

"Naturally. But did your son kill her?"

"Yes." At least, he said he did. Eli had accepted it as the truth. In his typically sanctimonious manner, he'd acknowledged that the girl's death was necessary while still managing to convey his disapproval of Gabriel's action. Gabriel had pronounced the death of a peasant child no great loss, which had infuriated Eli, just as he'd no doubt intended. It had turned into a stunning row.

The whole incident made Camille wonder how a man as wise as Eli could be so blind to the evidence before his face. How could he believe Gabriel indifferent when he'd gone to such brutal lengths to punish Bartolomeo? But then, Eli had never been able to see straight where Gabriel was concerned. He'd once confessed to her that he considered fathering Gabriel to be his "greatest sin." And yet he hadn't hesitated to uproot them all when Gabriel's life was threatened.

Brigitte nodded thoughtfully. "Thank you. The story was most enlightening. I very much look forward to meeting your son."

And with that, she retreated into her own thoughts, ignoring Camille so thoroughly that she might as well not have been there.

Camille shook her head. She still didn't understand what Brigitte was after. And now she knew for sure that Bartolomeo had no intention of letting her return to her home after she'd helped him kill Gabriel.

Somehow, she was going to have to use the two of them against each other. Otherwise, she'd never get out of this alive.

9

JEZ LAY ON HER back on her bed, staring at the ceiling. The physical pain was gone, but she still felt like she was being crushed by the weight of Gabriel's pain.

Despite her attempt to cut off contact between them, she'd felt him kill. And it had been nothing like the previous kill she'd experienced with him. No pleasure in it whatsoever, just a desperate attempt to vent his rage and his confusion.

But there was something else she'd noticed, another thread of emotion snaking through the anger and pain. Disgust. Some of it no doubt directed at himself, but more of it directed at his mortal victim. It was something she didn't understand. He seemed to like mortals just fine. Why had *this* one spurred such a reaction in him? Because it *had* been something about this particular mortal, she was sure of it. He'd chosen his victim for a reason, had reacted to him in some odd way different from his reaction to everyone else.

She sighed and rubbed her breastbone, where a formless ache troubled her. He was still out there, roaming the streets,

seething, hurting. So desperately alone. How could she feel
that desolation in him and not want to help?

"You're not alone, Gabriel," she whispered into the air. "I
know what you're feeling. And I understand it."

She closed her eyes and imagined calling out to him, following whatever psychic thread connected them, wondering
if she could reach him. Probably, it was the height of stupidity to do so. If she did reach him, if he did come to her,
she might be putting herself in danger. She understood that
his anger overlaid a heavy base of pain, but she also knew
he was perfectly capable of lashing out at anyone or anything around him.

And yet still she called to him, urging him to come to her,
to talk to her, to share a moment of connection with another
person.

She had no idea whether her call was working or not until she heard the front door of her apartment open. She sat
up in bed and drew her knees to her chest. This could turn
out to be a bad, bad idea. But too late now. He was here.

Moments later, he appeared in her bedroom doorway. His
eyes were cold and distant, his posture wary.

"You heard me calling to you," she said quietly.

Gabriel blinked, and a furrow of confusion appeared on
his brow. "What?"

Was it possible he'd just turned up here by coincidence?
True, he'd come to her every night since that first kill, but
still . . . What she'd felt in him had suggested he planned to
stay away tonight, to spend his time restlessly brooding.

Jez licked her lips, worried about how he might take this.
"I felt a lot of the things that happened tonight. And I tried
to use our connection to call to you."

He curled his lip in a snarl, but she saw and felt his defenses going up, knew the angry face was a cover for fear.
"And what happened tonight, my dear? Please, enlighten me."

She met his eyes steadily. "You got shot, for one. And
you didn't enjoy springing the trap you'd set."

The snarl grew more pronounced. "Anything else?" He took a step into the room, his posture radiating menace.

Jez's heart skipped a beat, but she forced herself to continue, still holding his gaze. "You killed someone. A mortal you passed on the street and decided to follow."

He laughed, a sound as brittle as breaking glass. "Indeed. I couldn't let my dear father think I'd gone soft, now, could I?"

"That's not why you killed him."

Between one blink and the next, he'd crossed the distance between them. Suddenly, he was on the bed in front of her, hands gripping her shoulders, fingers digging in brutally as he glared at her from within inches of her nose.

"Don't *presume* to tell me why I killed!"

The ferocity, the almost-madness, of his gaze should have frightened her into silence. But it didn't. Even though he was hurting her with his brutal grip, she didn't really feel afraid of him. She met his angry eyes steadily, not saying anything.

He was used to *everyone* being terrified of him. Even Hannah, who'd boldly traded quips with him, had feared him. No doubt, Jez was being foolish not to. But instinct told her she was in no danger, and she listened to her instincts.

Gabriel lowered his fangs, baring them at her. "I killed a boy tonight, just for the pleasure of killing. I wasn't hungry. I didn't feed. I just killed him." His fingers dug in even harder. "I killed him because I felt like it. Because I'm a Killer, and that's what Killers do."

"Bullshit."

His eyes widened in almost comical shock. "What?" He was so surprised, he forgot to keep up his crushing grip on her shoulders.

"Something about him set you off," she said. "I don't know what it was, but it was something. It wasn't a random kill. And you didn't enjoy yourself."

He shoved her away from him with a sound of inarticulate rage. But considering his strength, the shove hadn't been very hard at all. And he didn't get up off the bed. Instead, he stared at the floor between his feet, his whole body radiating tension. And confusion.

Jez rubbed the sore spots on her arms. If she were mortal, she'd be sporting bruises for days. As it was, they'd be gone in a minute or two.

"I used to tell my Gram all kinds of crap about the terrible, depraved things I did. When I was fourteen, I told her I was dating a nineteen-year-old bisexual black guy. He was really just my friend, but since my mother was a total slut, Gram assumed I was too. I knew she wouldn't believe the relationship was innocent, so I told her I was fucking him. And do you know why I did that?"

He wasn't looking at her, but she saw the tightness at the corners of his eyes. "Ask me if I care."

You care, she thought, but didn't say. "Because I thought it would hurt a hell of a lot less if I claimed I was fucking him and my Gram believed it than if I claimed I wasn't and she *didn't* believe it."

The tightness of his eyes became a full-fledged wince. Recognition, perhaps?

She moved closer to him, putting her hand tentatively on his back. She took it as a good sign that he didn't immediately push her away.

"You killed that boy for a reason," she said with utter conviction. "You're not some mindless killing machine." *And you don't have to pretend to be to protect yourself from me.* But she didn't think he could take that much truth, so she kept the thought to herself.

He turned toward her, his eyes still guarded. "How can you believe that, after everything I've said and done?"

She smiled, her hand sliding over the taut muscles of his upper back. "I don't know. I just do." She moved closer still, until her side pressed up against his arm. To her surprise, he slid that arm around her waist and drew her against him.

He didn't say anything, just held her there as his muscles relaxed under her hand. With a soft sigh, she laid her cheek against his shoulder, breathing in the scent of him. The coppery smell of his blood blended with his leather-and-man scent, and she wished she could offer him a fresh shirt. Then, she wished she could just get him out of his current shirt, to hell with the fresh one.

The thought surprised her. But she'd been held so rarely in her life, and it felt so good. She wished she could get even closer to him, feel his skin against her cheek. He turned toward her, putting his other arm around her and hugging her close. She wrapped her arms around his waist and rubbed her cheek against his chest, hearing the thump of his heart as it picked up speed.

Snuggling against him, she supposed that he'd been held as rarely in his life as she had in hers. When his fingers began to play up and down her spine, she let out a little sigh of pleasure.

"That feels good," she murmured, just in case he didn't get the hint.

"Yes it does," he whispered back, and there was a hint of a smile in his voice.

Tentatively, she placed one hand against his sternum. When he didn't push her away, she stroked over the planes of his chest, wondering at the feel of him under her hand. His chin brushed over the top of her head. She turned her face into him and planted a soft kiss on his collar bone. His heart stuttered under her hand, its beat coming harder and faster. She raised her head a little until her lips found the bare skin of his throat.

His quick intake of breath and the tightening of his arms around her emboldened her. Her tongue flicked out to taste his throat, and her whole body thrilled to it. Her fangs descended as an ember glowed in her core.

Gabriel tipped her chin up, and before she realized what he was going to do, his lips were on hers. She gasped and wrapped her arms around his neck, clinging tightly to him as she opened her mouth and welcomed him in.

He was as tentative as she, at first, the touch of his lips

feather-light against hers. But then he deepened the kiss, a little growl of hunger rumbling in his chest.

It was like nothing she'd ever felt before. None of the boys in school would have dreamed of kissing her. Hell, they were afraid to get within five feet of her, as if the contagion could leap over vast distances. At sixteen, desperate to know what it felt like to kiss a boy, she'd persuaded one of her friends from the clinic to kiss her. He'd even given her a little tongue action, but there had been no pleasure in it for either of them. He'd just been providing a demonstration, and she'd just wanted to satisfy curiosity. There was no chemistry, no attraction, and she'd been left wondering what the fuss was about.

Her only other sexual encounter had been with her friend Harry. Again, it had been persuasion on her part that had moved him to try anything. Because they were both infected, they felt safe with each other. But although Harry was bisexual, he really liked guys better, and he couldn't muster enough enthusiasm. Had she been any more enthusiastic herself, that might have hurt her feelings. As it was, she'd simply thanked him for trying and tried to reconcile herself to the idea that she would die a virgin.

Gabriel's kiss was everything those others hadn't been. His lips made her heart speed, made her breath come short, made her feel all warm inside. When he brushed his tongue over hers, she moaned softly and practically climbed onto his lap, wanting more. He buried his hand in her hair, holding her head at just the angle he wanted, and plunged his tongue deep into her mouth.

She couldn't believe how good it felt, how good he tasted, how much more of him she wanted. She shifted her position until she really was sitting on his lap, her legs straddling his hips. Under her bottom, she felt his growing enthusiasm, and fire surged through her veins.

His hands slid downward until they were cupping her bottom. Her cotton knit pants were gratifyingly lightweight, letting her feel that touch all the way to her center. She sucked at his tongue and swallowed his groan of pleasure.

Gabriel's hands tightened convulsively on her butt, fingers digging in hard enough to hurt as he pressed her against his erection. The pain of that grip should have killed the mood. Instead, the evidence of his desire made her want him even more, and she gasped at the shock of it.

And suddenly he let go. She tried a murmur of protest as he broke the kiss, but he ignored it. He wrapped his arms around her again, letting her stay poised over the tempting heat of him, but she felt the tide of his desire stutter to a stop. She closed her eyes and fought against tears of disappointment.

"Don't cry," he begged, and he sounded horrified. He pressed her head to his chest and cradled her against him. "Please don't cry, Jezebel. I'm sorry. I didn't mean to hurt you."

And in the midst of her tears, she began to laugh. He slid her off his lap, putting enough distance between them so he could look at her.

Tears still streaked her cheeks, and she kept hiccuping, but the laughter bubbled through it all. Gabriel looked at her like she was crazy, and she couldn't blame him. She tried to talk, but burst into giggles again.

Her reaction was taking on an edge of hysteria. She closed her eyes and took a deep breath, trying to calm herself. When she thought she could talk without laughing or crying, she opened her eyes and met Gabriel's confused gaze.

"You think I was crying because you hurt me?" she asked. The laughter bubbled up again, and she ruthlessly tamped it down. "I was crying because you stopped, idiot."

He blinked and looked even more confused. "Jez, I *know* I hurt you. I didn't mean to, but—"

She shrugged. "Yeah, it hurt a little. I really didn't give a crap at the moment."

He stared at her like he didn't believe her.

She sighed. The heat of the moment had definitely passed, and letting herself get romantically involved with her maker was a really stupid idea anyway. But she couldn't let him believe he'd hurt her.

"I had diabetes ever since I was too young to remember," she said. "Then I had HIV and AIDS. I don't know how many times I've been stuck with needles, but it's a really high number. I had my ears pierced multiple times. I had my eyebrow pierced. I had my nose pierced. Twice, because the first time my Gram pulled the nose ring out. I got a homemade tattoo on my arm. And you think it's going to make me cry if you hold me a little too tight?"

He looked as uncertain as she could ever remember seeing him. She grinned at him.

"You know, for someone who was just a few minutes ago telling me what a hard-ass he was, you've turned into quite a wuss."

He snarled at her, but there was no venom in it. Not when his eyes sparkled with amusement. He patted her thigh lightly, then stood up.

"I'd better be going."

She swallowed a protest. She'd accomplished what she'd set out to do, and her chest no longer ached with his complicated welter of emotions. She'd brought him—and through him, herself—a little bit of peace. It was more than she'd had any reason to hope she could do. Now, she had to give him time to absorb it all.

"Will you come see me tomorrow night?" she asked.

The expression on his face wasn't quite a smile, but it was close. "I think that's a safe assumption." He visibly forced the smile from his face. "I'll want to hear about how Eli liked my present."

His eyes met hers, daring her to show him some sign of condemnation. She wasn't going to give it to him.

In fact, she now knew exactly how she was going to spend the hours between sunset and whatever time Gabriel graced her with his presence. She was going to get on the

Internet, and she was going to look up everything she could find out about the two victims Gabriel had left for his father. And every instinct in her body told her she would find something very interesting indeed.

10

DRAKE STOOD BEFORE THE gates of Eli's mansion and wondered what the hell was going on. He knew that the trap had backfired, that Gabriel had been ready for it. But since no one had been seriously hurt, he couldn't imagine what had caused Eli to sound so distressed when he'd called.

His conviction that something was dreadfully wrong was confirmed when he took a good look at the house as he hesitated by the front gate. At first glance, it looked as it always had, stately and somewhat imposing. But then he'd seen the shards of glass that littered the lawn. Eyes widening, he stared at the house more closely and saw that all the windows in the meeting hall were broken, the jagged edges resembling menacing fangs.

Drake wasn't at all sure he wanted to know what had happened. Of course, he couldn't just ignore Eli's summons. But right this moment, the idea of ringing that bell had little appeal.

As he paced indecisively, Drake caught a glimpse of movement out of the corner of his eye. He peered into the shadows of the tree-lined path that led to the front door, but saw nothing. Then he reached out with his psychic senses and felt the vampire presence lurking there.

"Eli?" he asked, his voice tentative.

"Who else?" Eli responded, stepping out from behind a tree. The gate swung soundlessly open in an invitation to enter.

The night was overcast, and very little light from the streets reached inside Eli's property. The darkness hid his eyes, hid his expression. Not that his face usually gave away much, but he seemed to have become considerably less inscrutable since Gabriel had come to town.

At least there was no chill in the air.

"What happened?" Drake asked, indicating the shattered windows with a sweep of his hand.

"Gabriel left me another present. Come inside."

Eli didn't wait for an answer, leading the way into the house and into a library on the first floor. It was another massive room, furnished in floor-to-ceiling bookcases, all crammed full of books. A well-used, incongruous-looking computer desk sat in a back corner like a naughty child, but the rest of the room looked like it was still trapped in the nineteenth century.

Eli sat in a well-loved wing chair by the fireplace, and Drake took a seat opposite him.

"Tell me what happened to the meeting hall, Eli," Drake said.

"As I told you, my son presented me with another body. Here's the note he left with it."

Drake took the sheet of paper from Eli's hand and read it.

I promised Hannah not to kill any Guardians. As you know, Father, I am a man of my word. But the mortals in your city are fair game, and it is they who shall suffer for your every misstep. If you want to kill me, you're going to have to do it yourself. But first, you have to catch me. Enjoy the hunt.

"The victim was just a boy," Eli said softly. "He couldn't have been more than nineteen. And Gabriel didn't need to feed again so soon. He ripped that boy's throat out just to get at me." The temperature in the room started to dip.

"And how does that explain the windows?"

Eli looked mildly embarrassed. "I'm afraid I lost my temper."

Drake supposed it was lucky no one was around when *that* happened. "We can't afford to have you go to pieces on us," he said.

Something flashed in Eli's eyes. Annoyance, perhaps, though when he spoke his voice was mild enough. "I am aware of that. I've gotten it out of my system."

Drake highly doubted that. "It's just going to get worse. You know that."

Eli nodded briskly.

"And you know that the Guardians aren't strong enough to fight him."

Eli gave him one of those annoying, penetrating stares of his. "Your point being?"

Survival instinct urged Drake to keep his mouth shut. He ignored it. "My point being, the only one who can stop him is you."

Not surprisingly, Eli shook his head. "I can't hunt him."

"Why not?"

"I just can't."

Drake grunted in exasperation. "How are you going to explain this to the Guardians? Gabriel's out there killing people at his whim, and you won't lift a finger against him. Everyone's going to wonder—"

"They've wondered before!"

"But this is different, and you know it. You've told us Gabriel is too powerful for us to defeat. The natural question then becomes, why won't you hunt him yourself?"

Eli visibly struggled with himself. Then, he heaved a heavy sigh. "You won't understand this," he warned.

A strange thrill of excitement vibrated through Drake's nerves. He'd known Eli for more than a century, and the mystery of his self-imposed imprisonment had roused his curiosity from the very first. He'd long ago resigned himself to the idea that Eli would never explain.

Of course, if it took having Gabriel on the warpath in Philadelphia to get that explanation, Drake would have been happy to do without.

"Before I became a vampire, I was a man of God," Eli said quietly. "The church was my life, was my everything. I made a sacred vow that I would never set foot outside the gates of my home again. When I became a vampire, I broke every vow I'd ever made. This one, I will not break."

He stopped speaking, and for a moment Drake thought that was all the explanation he was going to get. Then, he recognized that distinctive, speculative look on Eli's face. The look that said he was measuring someone up, making an important decision.

Drake tensed as a sense of foreboding descended on him. "Why are you looking at me like that?"

Eli didn't answer immediately, just continued to stare and consider. When he finally spoke, he didn't exactly clear things up.

"I can't explain my vow without telling you something I feel it would be better for you not to know."

Drake sat up straighter, the foreboding growing stronger. "You have my undivided attention."

Another long silence. Then, "You've accused me of being a Killer," Eli said.

It was an assumption Drake had always made, amazed that the Guardians had never suspected as much themselves. Eli was vastly more powerful than any other vampire Drake had ever met, vastly more powerful even than the oldest Killers he'd ever encountered. That he could be that powerful and *not* be a Killer was unthinkable. And, as Drake had learned a few months ago, Eli had once been the Master of Philadelphia, ruling as head of his own vampire family, Killers all.

"I didn't accuse you of anything, Eli. I merely made an

observation. If you're not a Killer, then why on earth did you make Camille? And how could you have been the Master of Philadelphia?"

"Because back then, I *was* a Killer."

Silence hung heavily in the room as Drake absorbed that. Then he spoke again, carefully, making sure he'd heard correctly. "You were then, but you're not now. Is that what you're telling me?"

Eli nodded.

"Then the addiction is curable." The idea sat in Drake's stomach like a lead weight. Since he'd first met Eli, since he'd first known that not all vampires had to kill, Drake had believed his addiction to the kill was incurable, that it had been too late for him after those first few kills of his, made in ignorance. It was that knowledge that had allowed him to function, and to accept himself as a Killer, for more than a century.

Knowing he had no choice but to kill if he wanted to survive, Drake had assuaged his conscience by killing only the scum of the earth. Given his choice of victims, he'd probably saved as many lives as he'd taken. But it was one thing to kill because he had no choice, and quite another to kill because he didn't know he had an alternative.

Anger rose up from deep inside him, but Eli slapped it aside before it had time to surface.

"No, Drake," Eli said very quietly. "It's not curable. Not for you. I was already more than a thousand years old when I tried it, and I almost died. My 'cure' would kill you."

The anger still milled about, ready to take hold should Eli slip up. Drake licked his lips, hoping to get some moisture back into his mouth, and was startled to discover that his fangs had descended without him noticing. "But you found a way to cure the addiction. And you kept that knowledge from me."

Eli met his eyes steadily. "Yes, I did. You are one of the few vampires I've ever known who is completely at peace with himself. That's rare even in the Guardians, much less in Killers who have not completely discarded their consciences. I did not want to disturb your peace of mind."

Drake clenched his fists and his jaws, the Killer within him stirring. "What the hell gives you the right to make that decision for me?" he growled, and right that moment, he thought he might actually *hate* Eli for that deception.

"What difference would it have made if I'd told you? You're far too young to—"

"I've had enough of your goddamn secrets! I don't care anymore why you keep them." Drake's pulse raced, his muscles taut with the need to take action, and yet he forced himself to stay seated, using every ounce of his self-control. "You can skip the excuses. Just tell me why you won't leave the house. You owe me that, at least."

A shadow of pain crossed Eli's face before he quickly erased it. He clasped his hands in his lap and stared at them. "I'm sorry for any distress I've caused you. I did what I thought was right, but I can understand how you'd see it differently."

Drake shook his head. Eli had been like a father to him ever since Drake had come to Philadelphia. A far better father than Drake's own. But these last months had revealed some highly unpalatable truths, and he was no longer sure he'd be able to forgive the Founder for the secrets and the deceptions.

He gave Eli his coldest stare. "Tell me why you won't leave the house. Tell me why you're throwing me and all the Guardians to the wolves."

Eli winced and looked away. "I'm not throwing you to the wolves," he protested. "We will figure out some way to deal with Gabriel. It's just that it will take some time—as it always does when we hunt a Killer."

Drake crossed his arms over his chest and said nothing.

"All right," Eli said. "I'll tell you why I don't leave the house, although you won't understand." He rose from his chair and turned his back on Drake, moving to one of the windows and looking out. The overcast must have cleared, for a shaft of moonlight illuminated his profile.

"As I said, when I was a mortal, I was a man of God. When I became a vampire, I was sure my immortal soul was damned for all eternity, that there was nothing I could do to return to a state of grace. I thought about committing suicide, but I wasn't eager to begin my eternity in Hell, so I did what was necessary to survive.

"At first, I was a virtual slave to my maker, just as Camille's fledglings were her slaves. But after a few centuries, he died, and I was finally free of him. I was his oldest fledgling, and I easily destroyed my 'brothers.' I planned to spend the rest of my existence as a hermit. But even though vampires are not naturally social creatures, we aren't made to live in complete solitude either.

"Eventually, I couldn't stand being alone anymore. So I transformed some people as companions. Thus I became a master, creating other Killers like myself while living in a constant state of guilt.

"It was during that time that I met and transformed Camille. She wasn't always as she is now." He allowed himself a wry smile. "Not that she was angelic by any means. I had enough conscience that I refused to transform anyone I didn't believe was bound for Hell anyway. Camille was a courtesan who'd made extra money by betraying an important man or two to their deaths.

"You don't need to know all the details. Suffice it to say that I was as resigned as I could be to eternal damnation. Then, about two hundred years ago, I met a young seminary student named Patrick McNabb. I usually kept my distance from mortals, except when it came time to feed, but for whatever reason, Pat drew me to him. We discussed matters philosophical and theological. He was the first person I'd felt was actually a friend ever since I'd been transformed.

"We were still friends after he was ordained. I'd told him I was a lapsed Catholic, and he'd been gently urging me to return to the arms of the church ever since we'd first met.

I think he sensed the longing in me. Of course, I couldn't tell him why it was impossible for me to rejoin the church.

"But he kept after me, assuring me there was no sin God couldn't forgive. I assured him there was. Then he told me the story of Tannhäuser." Eli risked a glance at Drake. "Are you familiar with the story?"

Drake shook his head. He'd heard the name before, but knew nothing of the story.

"The legend is that Tannhäuser was a terrible sinner who went to the Pope to ask for absolution. The Pope was horrified by the magnitude of Tannhäuser's sins, and said that his staff would sprout leaves before God could forgive a sinner such as he. Dejected, Tannhäuser left and returned to his life of sin. And three days later, the Pope's staff sprouted leaves."

Eli smiled faintly in remembrance. "It's just a legend, of course, but the story moved me, and I let Pat talk me into giving him my confession. I told him everything, never expecting that he'd believe me.

"But he *did* believe me. Sometimes I think he was a bit clairvoyant, that he'd known all along that I wasn't a normal human being.

"He convinced me that redemption was possible, even for such an ancient sinner as myself. I vowed that I would never again kill a mortal. I bought myself a new house." He gestured to encompass his house. "And I told my family and fledglings that I needed some time to myself. Then I locked myself in the basement with no food and prepared to die. It was suicide, which of course was a terrible sin in and of itself, but I deemed it the lesser sin than continuing to kill others so that I might live.

"I don't know how long I was down there before Father Pat found me. It must have been at least a couple of months. I went mad with hunger along the way, destroying everything in the room. I was comatose when he found me, very nearly dead. He force-fed me lamb's blood in an effort to revive me. And it worked.

"Believe me, I'd tried many, many times before to subsist on animal blood. Because my vampire strengths grew as I aged, and my vampire weaknesses dwindled, I hoped that someday I wouldn't need to kill anymore. Apparently, I needed to take myself to the edge of death first." His smile turned wistful. "Or perhaps it was simply the grace of God.

"When I returned to full strength, I knew I'd been given a second chance.

"At first, I tried to convert my fledglings. My two oldest, next to Camille, volunteered to try the experiment. They both died. I tried to force-feed them for days, but they rejected the lamb's blood. My other fledglings were unwilling to risk their lives for a chance to cure the addiction. It was then that I realized I had to kill them all. I had created them, unleashed them on the world. It was my duty to right that wrong.

"So I destroyed my fledglings, and I tried to force myself to kill Gabriel." His voice tightened. "But of course, I couldn't. I let him and Camille leave the city, and I'm paying for that folly now.

"I founded the Guardians then. At first it was just me, but then I experimented with a newly made vampire who hadn't killed yet and discovered he could live on animal blood. He became my first Guardian.

"I went back to church, attending services as often as possible. I went to confession, though I could only confess to Father Pat. Those were some of the happiest years of my life. My relief at being saved was indescribable."

Eli's face clouded, old misery haunting his eyes. "I had three decades of the closest thing to peace I've ever felt. Then, Father Pat fell ill. I think it was some form of cancer. He was in constant pain, and yet he lingered, and lingered, and lingered.

"I visited him as often as I could, and when I was with him, I used my glamour to erase the pain from his mind. But I couldn't be with him twenty-four hours a day, and so he suffered terribly.

"One day, I just couldn't stand to see him suffer anymore. I went through the ritual of confession with him, and I confessed that I was going to kill him."

A lump formed unexpectedly in Drake's throat. No matter how furious he was, the pain in Eli's voice was almost unbearable to hear.

"If I hadn't seen that spark of hope in his eyes, I wouldn't have done it. But for one unguarded moment, he showed me how desperate he was to end the suffering.

"Oh, he begged me not to do it. Not because of any fear of death, but because he was still trying to save me. He couldn't absolve me of a sin I hadn't yet committed, because absolution requires repentance. If I was still planning the sin, then I obviously did not repent. He'd saved my immortal soul, and he begged me not to throw it away on his account.

"I vowed to him that even if there was no chance of redemption for me, I would do penance all the rest of my days. And then I killed him."

Eli's eyes shone with what might have been the glimmer of tears. "I will never repent what I did. He deserved to be released from his suffering. After all that he did for me, I couldn't stand by and do nothing."

He breathed in slowly and deeply, then let his breath out just as slowly. One blink dispelled the glimmer in his eyes, and when he spoke again, his voice was deceptively even. He turned away from the window, meeting Drake's eyes for the first time since he'd started talking.

"My final vow to Father Pat was that I would make of this house my prison, never to set foot outside its gates again. My soul is already damned. But I will not break that final vow. No matter what my son does to torment me."

Drake looked at the Founder's face and knew he faced an implacable will. Eli would not break his vow, no matter what happened around him, no matter what Drake said or how convincingly he argued.

There was no mistaking the soul-deep pain that ate away

at the Founder. Drake even felt some pity for his mentor's moral dilemma. But more than anything, he felt anger, for whatever Eli claimed, he was indeed throwing his Guardians to the wolves.

And there wasn't a damn thing Drake could do or say to change his mind.

11

DESPITE HIS PROMISE OF the previous night, Gabriel found himself reluctant to stop by Jez's apartment. He felt unsettled by her, and by the strangeness of the bond between them.

He'd *suspected* it would be different even before he'd bitten her. And when he tasted the first drop of her blood, he'd *known* it would be different. But he'd thought he would merely have more power over her. How could he possibly have known she'd develop this unnerving empathy? And how could he possibly have known that she'd have power over him as well?

Because although he wasn't yet ready to admit it to her, he had indeed felt her call last night. He hadn't known what it was, at first. Just a nagging feeling, like some kind of intuition. When he'd started walking toward her apartment, the nagging had eased. When he'd tried veering away, it had strengthened. Until he arrived on her doorstep and it went away.

Yes, she was definitely more than he'd bargained for.

The reluctance pounded at him as he mounted the stairs, but his feet kept moving. He wasn't one to break a promise.

Usually, he just let himself in. His telekinetic powers were delicate enough to allow him to coax the locks open. Tonight, however, he knocked. The door swung open moments later, and he felt something almost like shock at how good it felt to see his fledgling.

Jez stood in the doorway, her hip cocked, a sardonic grin on her face. A bra-top camisole in royal blue left her shoulders and the tops of her breasts bare to his view. A multicolor peasant skirt that didn't quite clash with the top skimmed her knees, and her feet were bare save for a toe ring topped with a glittering blue stone on her big toe.

His pulse sped, and his body hardened. He stood there like a fool, staring, not knowing what to make of his own reaction.

True, it was hardly unusual for a man to become aroused when faced with a beautiful woman. But it was unusual for *him*. He enjoyed sex a great deal, and was painfully aware that he hadn't had any in too long. But before Jezebel, the intention to have sex had come first, and the arousal had come later. He'd never been one to let his cock make decisions.

Jezebel was different. Jezebel made him hard when he had no intention of bedding her.

"Well?" she said drolly. "Are you going to stand there in the doorway ogling or are you going to come in?"

He gave her a repressive look, hoping to hide his embarrassment. "I was not ogling," he answered with as much dignity as he could muster.

She laughed and stepped away from the doorway, gesturing for him to come in. "Right. And that's a banana in the front of your pants."

He stepped into her apartment, closing the door behind him. The heat in his cheeks suggested he might actually be blushing. He couldn't remember ever feeling such a thing before.

Had she worn that oh-so-sexy top because she knew he'd be stopping by?

Gabriel wanted to slap himself silly. He was acting like a besotted teenager! Jezebel was a tool in his revenge against Eli. Nothing more. Perhaps it was time he reminded her of that fact.

"I did some research this evening," she said, before he had a chance to chastise her. "I called Eli and got the names of the two victims you left on his doorstep."

Gabriel stumbled to a halt as Jez took a seat on the sofa, picking up two sheets of paper on the end table beside it. She pulled her feet up onto the sofa, and the skirt slid up to reveal a hint of thigh.

"Margaret McCall," she said, reading off the first piece of paper. "In 2004, she was questioned in the bludgeoning death of her six-year-old daughter. She was eventually released due to lack of evidence, and her husband was convicted of the murder. To this day, he claims she did it and framed him."

She shuffled that sheet to the back, and her finger skimmed down the next page. Gabriel wanted to tear the paper from her hand, stop her from reading any more, but he seemed not to be in full control of his body.

"George Parks," she read. "Eighteen years old, twice questioned and released in regards to the rape and murder of girls who attended the middle school near his home. Again, not enough evidence to hold him, although when I dug at it a little bit more, I found a couple of assault charges against him when he was still a minor. No convictions, but I'd say there's a pattern of behavior here."

She put the papers aside and stared up at him, blinking innocently. "This is just a coincidence, right? Of all the people in Philadelphia, you just happened to pick two people who might have gotten away with murder." Again, the innocent blink.

For once in his life, Gabriel was utterly speechless. Despite all the evidence of his ferocity, despite having felt his ecstasy at the kill, she didn't believe he was a soulless Killer.

She'd said something to that effect last night, but he'd dismissed it as a case of wishful thinking on her part. Apparently, she'd been convinced enough to spend her evening chasing down the facts.

He stared at the tips of his boots, not sure the floor beneath his feet was stable and solid. Jezebel waited patiently for him to speak. He had to say something. He could deny her allegations, but that would merely make him seem stupid.

He swallowed, clenching his fists so hard his knuckles cracked. "Parks had two more victims the police didn't know about. Transients no one missed."

"Why don't you come sit down," Jezebel said gently, patting the sofa beside her. "And take a deep breath or two. You're making my chest ache."

He winced slightly to realize his emotions were bleeding into her. Then, she rubbed between her breasts, and his eyes fastened on her fingers in fascination.

He managed a shaky laugh as he lowered himself onto the couch. "Are you making any more sense of all this . . ." He searched for a word to describe what he was feeling, but came up blank. He settled for a vague hand movement. ". . . than I am?"

She smiled at him. "I think it's called confusion. You're not used to having anyone call your bluff."

He sat up straighter. "It's not a bluff," he growled.

Jez made a face. "Yeah, yeah, I know. You heap bad Killer." She made a claw with one hand and scratched the air. "Grr. Grr." He opened his mouth for an outraged reply, but didn't get it out in time. "But there's more to you than that."

She gazed at him earnestly, sliding closer to him on the couch. He felt an insane urge to run away, even as he couldn't help noticing the enticing view down the front of her top.

"You have a heart, Gabriel," she said. "You just don't have much practice using it."

He laughed bitterly. "I wouldn't go that far, my sweet. Having a conscience and having a heart are not the same thing."

She shrugged. "If you say so." She reached out and took his hand, moving still closer to him on the couch, till her thigh brushed up against his.

He breathed in deeply the clean scent of her, perfumed with herbal shampoo and spiced with womanly musk. And all the inner turmoil in the world couldn't stop his body from responding to her. She licked her lips and raised his hand to the smooth, warm skin just above the neckline of her top. He could see the outline of her pebbled nipples through the thin, stretchy fabric.

Suddenly, his pants felt about two sizes too small, and he squirmed. "Are you trying to seduce me?" he asked, a trifle breathlessly.

She smiled and licked her lips again, a hint of nervousness in her eyes. "Yeah. Is it working?"

He took a deep breath to calm himself, but that was a mistake, for he couldn't help noticing the increasing muskiness of her scent. He closed his eyes, fighting for self-control.

"It's a bad idea," he warned.

"But it's working?"

Her voice was so hopeful he had to open his eyes and face her. He gently moved his hand away from her chest and cupped her cheek.

"You are a very beautiful, very desirable woman," he told her.

She grimaced. "I sense a 'but' coming."

A sudden twinge in his chest let him know he was hurting her. As if he couldn't have read that in her eyes.

What could he say to explain this to her? He wasn't about to use the old chestnut, "It's not you, it's me." Accurate though it might be.

"You are in many ways still a virgin," he tried, and her eyes narrowed.

"Yeah, you know, you have to go through that being-a-virgin thing before you become *not* a virgin. It's not some incurable disease."

He shook his head and tried again. "Your only experience with sex so far has been a dreadful, brutal, painful attack."

"So what you're telling me is because I was raped I should never have sex again in my life?"

Now she was being deliberately obtuse. "I am not a gentle man," he said, putting a hint of a growl in his voice to emphasize his point. "The games I enjoy in the bedroom are not the thing for genteel women."

She snorted. "Since when have I been a 'genteel' woman? Gabriel, you're reaching."

"Damn it! No, I'm not. I'm trying to tell you I might very well hurt you. And that's something I don't want to do."

Her brow puckered as she thought that one over, but she didn't look as alarmed as she should have.

"Don't you get it?" he asked. "I'm a sadist." As everyone had been telling him since he was about twenty years old, though, of course, they hadn't had a word for what he was back then. "I *like* hurting people. And I like hurting people in bed."

One corner of her mouth lifted. "I got it, all right? I gather I'm supposed to be shocked and horrified. You're forgetting my oh-so-genteel upbringing. If there was an alternative lifestyle I could attach myself to, I attached myself to it. The more it horrified my Gram, the more I was into it. I couldn't *participate*, not with my illness, but believe me, I've been thoroughly exposed." She gave him an impish grin. "Some of my best friends are sadists, and you're not shocking me."

Maybe not, but she was shocking the hell out of him. She must have sensed it, or seen it on his face.

She raised her eyebrows. "You do know that lifestyle exists, right? That there are people out there who like pain during sex?"

He squirmed uncomfortably and cleared his throat. "Uh. Yeah. I know." But in a severe case of the pot calling the kettle black, he'd always thought of them as "deviants." He looked into Jezebel's ingenuous face. "Are you saying you're one of them?"

"How should I know?" Another mischievous grin lit her face. "I could be a lesbian for all I know. After all, you've given me the only real kiss I ever had."

He couldn't help answering her grin. And despite all his warnings to himself, he reached down with his index finger and brushed lightly over her nipple, feeling it bead under his touch.

"I don't think you're a lesbian," he said, his cock hardening yet again.

Boldly, she reached out and put her hand behind his neck, drawing him to her. He could have resisted. But he didn't.

"No, I guess not," she murmured as their lips brushed.

His conscience screamed at him to stop before things went too far. Despite Jezebel's tough words, seeing something and doing it weren't the same. She was an innocent, and he was . . . Well, he wasn't an innocent, anyway.

Despite the screaming of his conscience, he slipped his arms around her and pulled her closer, until her breasts were pressed up against him and she had to bend her head backward to let him kiss her. He speared his fingers through her silky hair and thrust his tongue into her mouth.

They moaned in unison, and he deepened the kiss, his tongue playing with the delicate fangs that had descended. The taste of her went to his head, made him dizzy.

He'd never felt anything like this before.

Not the desire. Desire he'd felt before. But this was different. For one thing, he didn't want the kiss to end. Usually, he'd allowed only the most perfunctory of kisses, and had never much enjoyed them.

Jezebel climbed onto his lap, straddling him as she knelt on the couch. The position pushed her skirt up, revealing more of her thighs, which he stroked with one hand while the other held her head in place. She put both hands on his chest, her fingers caressing him through his T-shirt, finding his nipples. His cock lurched at the sensation, and she gasped.

His hand slid up her thigh, under her skirt, and the way she pressed herself harder against him proved that she liked it just fine.

Underneath her skirt, he found a tiny pair of silk panties, soft and cool to his touch. But cool wasn't what he wanted. He slipped his hand inside to cup her hot little bottom. She shivered at his touch, but there was no mistaking her reaction for anything but pleasure.

The phone rang.

Jez pulled away from the kiss with a mewl of displeasure, glaring at the offending machine.

"You'd better answer it," he said, reluctantly removing his hand from her panties.

"Yeah," she murmured, but she didn't move from her place on his lap. Her eyes were dark and dazed, her lips swollen from kissing, her fangs still descended.

Much as he enjoyed having her right where she was, he knew she had to answer that phone. "Come now, my sweet," he said, picking her up and moving her to the side, where the phone was in reach. "You wouldn't want anyone worrying about you."

With a long-suffering sigh, she answered the phone, while Gabriel tried to calm the desire that still pounded through his veins. Then, his keen vampire hearing picked up the voice on the other end of the phone, and all hints of arousal vanished.

"Would you be so kind as to come visit with me tonight?" Eli asked.

Jezebel gave Gabriel a doubtful, worried look. She knew he could hear that voice. His lips pulled back from his teeth in a snarl.

"Does it have to be tonight?" she asked.

"You have something more important to do?"

Gabriel snarled again at his father's condescension. Of course, no one could have anything important to do if it didn't revolve around him and his fucking Guardians!

Before he even knew what he was going to do, Gabriel had snatched the phone from her hand. Her eyes went wide and her jaw dropped.

"Yes, Father. She has something better to do," he said.

Dead silence on the other end of the line. Jezebel crossed her arms over her chest and looked worried. He covered the mouthpiece on the phone and whispered very softly.

"Don't worry. I'm not going to blow your cover."

The reproachful look she gave him told him that wasn't what she was worried about. He moved his hand away from the mouthpiece.

"Well, Father? Have you nothing to say? It's been, what, two hundred years? Give or take."

Eli sighed heavily. "What can I say that you'd want to hear? I'm not going to hurl threats at you over the phone. I don't expect to be able to talk you out of your vendetta. What does that leave?"

Fire burned in Gabriel's chest and belly. Jezebel winced and hunched over. He'd have liked to spare her the pain of his turbulence, but it was well beyond his control.

"Won't you beg me for the life of this pretty little Guardian? She's been quite the fount of information, but I've no more use for her. Perhaps I should leave another calling card at your doorstep. I'm sure you've enjoyed my others."

"If I thought begging you for her life would save her, I'd do it," Eli said, and there was not a hint of emotion in his voice, while Gabriel was awash in it.

"You cold-blooded, cold-hearted bastard. You don't give a goddamn about anyone, do you?"

"I care. I just—"

But Gabriel couldn't listen to that impassive, unexcitable voice for a moment longer.

"Fuck you, old man!" he raged, then threw the phone across the room so hard it left a gaping hole in the drywall.

Jezebel reached out toward him, but he couldn't stand any more of her sweet compassion, either. He seized her with his glamour, and her eyes went blank.

He didn't release her until he was so far away he couldn't hold her anymore.

12

THE *MAÎTRE* HAD RENTED a suite of rooms in the Rittenhouse Hotel, one of the finest hotels in the city, with a breathtaking view of Rittenhouse Square. The *Maître*, Camille, and Brigitte each had their own private rooms, with the entourage occupying a pair of much more modest rooms one floor down.

Camille had barely had time to settle in before Bartolomeo demanded entrance. With a soft sigh, she let him in. For a long moment, she considered the possibility of killing him where he stood. She was older and more powerful than he, and his guard dogs were downstairs. Then she could return home to Paris and try again.

If it hadn't been for Brigitte, she might very well have done it. After she'd finished him off, she could take out his companions, and when she returned to France she could claim Gabriel killed them all.

But Brigitte was an unknown quantity. Camille had had no idea just how powerful a born vampire could be, hadn't realized how much of his strength Gabriel concealed from her until it had been too late. Although Brigitte was considerably younger, Camille couldn't be sure how powerful she was. And if Brigitte lived, she would no doubt tell *La Vieille* about Camille's treachery, and *La Vieille* would order her death.

So for now, Bartolomeo would live, and Camille would cooperate to the best of her abilities. And if he could help her get her due from Eli, she might even feel a slight stirring of remorse when she killed him.

She smiled. Probably not.

"Is there something funny, *Madame*?" Bartolomeo asked, giving her a hard stare.

She schooled her features. "Not at all. To what do I owe the pleasure of your company, *Maître*?"

He made himself at home in her room, striding to the window and throwing open the curtains. The lights of the city glimmered and twinkled before them. Camille came to stand beside him, looking out into yet another city that had once been hers and that she had lost because of Eli.

"Where will we find your son?" the *Maître* asked.

Camille lifted one shoulder in a delicate shrug. "He didn't leave me an address where I could reach him. I don't know where he is." She glanced sidelong at Bartolomeo. "And when we find him. What then?"

Bartolomeo crossed his hands behind his back, raising up slightly on the balls of his feet. His eyes shone with unmistakable hate. "Then, we play. For as long as we like, in as many ways as we like."

Camille wrinkled her nose. While she wouldn't mind seeing Gabriel suffer, "playing" with him herself would seem somehow . . . incestuous. "You can have my son. Do with him what you wish. *I* want Eli."

He turned those glittering eyes toward her. "First, you give me Gabriel. Then, I will aid you in your own endeavor."

Unfortunately, she had to take what she was given. She lowered her head in a hint of a nod. "Understood. But I'm still not clear on how you plan to take Gabriel when the two of us together are not strong enough to overpower him."

"We don't have to overpower him. We'll use this."

Caught completely unprepared, Camille didn't even get fully turned around before the *Maître* jabbed something into her upper arm. Something stung, hot and sharp. She gasped and tried to muster her power for a fight. Nothing happened, and her knees started to wobble.

The *Maître* had his hands behind his back once more and was smiling at her. "You'll find your glamour useless, I'm afraid," he said.

Her wobbling knees collapsed, and Camille dropped to the floor, catching her fall with her hands. The floor seemed to buck and pitch beneath her. Her upper arm where he'd jabbed her burned fiercely, the heat spreading slowly from a pinpoint source, crawling down her arm and over her shoulder. And it intensified.

"I've given you a fairly low dose," Bartolomeo continued. "I'll give your dear son more."

The pain continued to creep over her, climbing up her neck and sliding down her torso, until it was all she could do not to scream. She bit her tongue to keep herself silent.

Bartolomeo knelt before her, sliding a hypodermic needle out from the inside pocket of his jacket. When he reached for her, there was nothing she could do to stop him. He pulled the cap off the needle with his teeth, then turned her over onto her stomach and hauled her skirt up. She tried to issue a protest, but found even her mouth didn't want to work, and all that came out was a garbled mumble.

A sharp sting on her hip, and then he pulled her skirt back down.

"Antidote," he said. "It will take a minute or two to work, but you'll be good as new soon enough." He tucked the used syringe back into his jacket, then rose to his feet once more and dusted off his knees. He took a seat on a chair near the window and just watched her, a malicious little smile on his face.

Sweat beaded her brow as she gritted her teeth harder and fought to contain the pain. She glared at the *Maître,* hoping

Gabriel had used a dull knife and gone slowly when he'd removed his cock and balls. But as the pain dwindled, then died, she had to admit this demonstration had been most effective. No matter how great his power, Gabriel would be helpless under the influence of this insidious drug.

She just hoped that once Eli and Gabriel were dead, there'd be another dose or two left for Bartolomeo, just to show him what he was missing.

JEZ DIDN'T EVEN BOTHER trying the phone that Gabriel had flung against the wall. It was clearly dead. She hadn't the faintest idea what to do now, except that she had to call Eli back and let him know she was okay.

She retrieved the phone from her bedroom and dialed, wondering what on earth Gabriel expected her to tell the Founder about his little visit with her.

"Jezebel?" Eli answered on the first ring. If Gabriel thought his father didn't care about anyone, he'd never heard that particular tone of voice before.

"Yes, and I'm fine. My phone and my wall will never be the same, but he didn't hurt me."

Perhaps Gabriel expected her to tell Eli some bullshit story about how he'd tortured her. If he did, he should have stuck around and told her so.

"I want you to call a cab immediately and come straight to my house," Eli said.

Ugh. She'd really have loved a little time to pull herself together, but she didn't think Eli had meant that as a request. "All right," she agreed. "You said you wanted to talk to me anyway, right?"

"Yes, but that can wait until you get here in person. Please hurry. Gabriel might come back."

She really hated this shit. "I'll be out of here in five minutes."

"I'll be waiting for you."

Great.

She hung up the phone and took a deep breath. It wasn't

Eli's fault he'd interrupted her attempted seduction, and it wasn't his fault Gabriel had gone ape shit. But right now, the last thing she wanted to do was tap dance around the truth, trying not to blow her cover while her head was spinning with more thoughts than any one person should be allowed to have.

Of course, if she didn't go, Eli would send someone to bring her to him, so she had no choice.

Reluctantly, she called a cab, then tried to think of what story she should tell Eli about what had happened tonight. She'd learned to be a fairly good liar over the years, as she made up ever more outrageous tales to shock her Gram with. Of course, it might not have been her skill as a liar that made Gram believe her. Perhaps she was just an especially receptive audience.

Eli, on the other hand . . .

Just before she left the apartment, her eyes lit on the printouts she'd made of the stories of Gabriel's victims. He would absolutely hate it if she showed those to his father. He'd chosen those victims for maximum hurt value, making his father believe he'd killed innocent, upstanding citizens. But he hadn't specifically forbidden her from showing them to Eli, which meant she wasn't directly disobeying his orders.

One corner of her mouth lifted in a grim smile as she folded up the papers and stuck them into her purse. Why did she somehow think he wouldn't see it that way?

But Eli deserved to know his son wasn't quite the monster he pretended to be. And although she knew her own Gram would never have believed that she wasn't completely corrupted by her mother's influence, she thought Eli might be open-minded enough to see the truth and to accept it.

Jez paused with her hand on the doorknob, suddenly recognizing the direction her thoughts were spiraling in.

She was doing it again. Casting herself as the knight in shining armor, the superhero who would save the day. Time and time again as she was growing up, she'd tried to save her mother from herself. She'd begged her to give up the drugs. She'd cried, she'd pleaded, she'd made endless promises to be the best little girl ever if only her mother would stop making herself so sick.

And you know what? It hadn't done a damn bit of good. Once or twice, her mom had seemed to hear her, had checked herself into a rehab and made vows that from now on everything would be different. And every fucking time, she'd gone back to business as usual. Teaching young Jezebel one very important lesson—you can't save someone who doesn't want to be saved.

It wasn't her job to save Gabriel from himself. It wasn't her job to reconcile father and son. Certainly it wasn't worth facing Gabriel's wrath to do something that probably would have no effect on his relationship with Eli anyway.

Face it, Jez. The two of them are just too fucked up to save.

Trying to ignore the little voice in her head that told her she was being a coward, she pulled the articles out of her bag and left them on the table beside the door.

WHEN CAMILLE HAD FULLY recovered from the drug that Bartolomeo had injected her with, she excused herself to the bathroom to fix her hair and makeup. He smirked at her, knowing she was stalling, giving herself a few minutes to recover her composure as well. But if she didn't get out of his sight, she was going to forget all the reasons she shouldn't kill him, and that would be . . . unfortunate.

In the bathroom, she slipped off her suit jacket and examined her arm, where an angry red patch of skin surrounded the injection site. She touched it gently, and found the skin tender and hot to the touch.

When she emerged from the bathroom, she'd regained enough control over herself that she didn't fear she'd kill the *Maître* at the first ill-considered word.

She took a seat on the room's second chair, sitting stiffly upright, her back not touching the back of the chair. Bartolomeo lounged in his own chair, legs stretched out in front of him, crossed at the ankles. His face looked oh-so-smug, and she had to fight fiercely against an urge to wipe the smugness from his expression.

She knew just how she could do it, too. The position he sat in drew his pants tightly against his groin. *Something* caused a slight bulge there, but she was quite sure it wasn't any male equipment. Too bad taunting him about it as she'd like wasn't an option.

"Now you know what we will do when we find Gabriel," Bartolomeo said, and Camille forced herself to focus. "But first we have to find him. Do you have any suggestions?"

In truth, she hadn't given the matter a great deal of thought. She was much more concerned about how she was going to deliver that nasty injection to Eli. His unwillingness to leave his house would prove quite the impediment.

But if she didn't give Gabriel to Bartolomeo, that would become a moot point. One problem at a time.

Happily, an idea came to her with gratifying speed. "Gabriel created a fledgling a few months ago. He sent her ahead to Eli. He never explained exactly what he planned to do with her, but I'm sure he's using her as a spy. If we find her, we can use her against him." She made a face. "My son is anything but stupid, but he is capable of being strangely sentimental. If we had his fledgling, he might take foolish risks in order to get her back."

"And how would we acquire this fledgling?"

Camille smiled. "Why, we keep a watch on Eli's house, of course. She's sure to come and go from there on a regular basis." Her smile faded. "Although Eli would sense it if a vampire were lurking near enough his house to see her leave."

Bartolomeo shrugged. "So we send a mortal to keep watch instead. He can follow her until she's out of Eli's range, and one of my fledglings can take her from there."

"It might work," she conceded. "But the mortal would experience some difficulties around Eli's house. The glamour that surrounds it is impressive. Even knowing the house is there, I doubt a mortal could see it, unless Eli wanted him to."

"But my mortal doesn't need to see the house. He just needs to see the fledgling. If you can give him a fair description, I'm sure he'll manage admirably."

Camille nodded her agreement. She hadn't seen Jezebel in three months, but she had a clear enough image in her head that she felt sure she'd be able to describe the little wench.

Soon, she told herself. Soon she would have her revenge on the man who'd shattered her life. And after that, she could return to her true home and start anew. And when she did, she might even consider that Gabriel had done her a favor when he'd betrayed her and shown his true nature, because if he hadn't, she might never have seen her homeland again.

JEZ SAT CROSS-LEGGED ON the super-comfy leather couch in Eli's library, tucking her skirt in carefully around the edges so as not to flash him. It was something of a nervous gesture, and she forced herself to stop fussing.

When she looked up, Eli was staring at her with that intense, knowing look of his, and it was all she could do not to squirm. She suspected she looked guilty as all hell.

"You're sure you're all right?" Eli asked gently, and his concern made the guilt spike.

She let out a deep breath. "Yeah, I'm fine. Just a little shaken up."

"What did Gabriel want from you?"

Apparently there was to be no small talk, and no beating about the bush. She'd been thinking furiously about how she'd answer that question all through the cab ride here. Unfortunately, it was far too short a ride, and she was stuck mostly winging it.

"I'm not entirely sure," she said, looking down at her hands, which were clasped in her lap. "You called before he got around to doing much other than stomp around and look scary."

"I'm surprised he let you answer the phone."

She was pretty sure she heard a hint of suspicion in his voice, but maybe that was her own guilty conscience talking. "Wouldn't it have been suspicious if he hadn't? He made sure I understood that there would be dire consequences if I wasn't careful about what I said." She shrugged. "Maybe he just guessed it was you and wanted a chance to tell you what he thought of you."

"Hmm. And afterward, he just . . . left?"

She nodded. "He threw the phone at the wall. Then the next thing I knew, he was gone. Smoke and mirrors stuff, you know?"

Eli took his time considering what she'd said, watching her carefully.

"Why did you want to know the names of Gabriel's latest victims?" he asked, out of the blue.

"Morbid curiosity."

But of course, he wasn't buying that. He leaned back in his chair, crossing his hands over his belly. "I got to wondering after you'd asked, so I got on the Internet to see what I could find out about them."

Jez's eyes widened. She probably looked pretty silly.

Eli smiled. "Yes, I know how to use a computer. One does not reach my advanced age without becoming adept at adapting to the times."

That made sense. "And what did you find?" she asked, but of course she already knew what he'd found.

The piercing look again. "Same thing you found, I'd expect."

She didn't bother with a denial. He looked far too sure. So much for all her angst about whether she should share her findings or not. She met Eli's eyes, trying to gauge what he'd made of the stories. Unfortunately, his eyes gave nothing away.

When she didn't speak, Eli continued.

"What I'd really like to know is what made you think of looking."

Obviously, she couldn't tell him the whole truth. But there was part of the truth she *could* tell. She looked down at her hands once again. "I didn't have a good home life," she said. "I was raised by my grandmother, and she didn't like anything about me. I used to do all kinds of things just to piss her off. And a lot of times, I told her I did things I didn't do. My teenaged version of psychological torture.

"Gabriel didn't kill Carolyn when he had the chance. Instead, he went out and found someone else. I wondered why, and it got me to wondering if he and I had something in common. So I looked the victims up and found they both may have gotten away with murder."

"Is that the whole story?" Eli asked, in a voice that clearly indicated he didn't think it was.

"It's as much of the story as I'm willing to give you."

"Jezebel, if you have some kind of connection to Gabriel, then you have to help us stop him before he kills again."

She raised her chin. "Even if I had a connection to him, I wouldn't be eager to help you kill him. Considering how angry he is with you, I think he's shown a hell of a lot of restraint."

"But he's been here less than a week, and already he's killed two people."

"Two people who, it seems, deserved to die."

The Founder's eyes hardened. "That is not Gabriel's decision to make."

Jez's temper stirred. "Let me see if I've got this straight. It's all right for *you* to decide who gets to live or die, but it's not all right for *him*?"

The temperature in the room dropped, a sure sign of Eli's anger. "It isn't like that."

"Yes it is!" The air temperature continued to plummet, but though she figured persisting was probably dangerously stupid, she wasn't going to back down now.

"Why is it okay for your Guardians to kill Killers?" she

demanded. Eli opened his mouth to answer, but she interrupted before he had the chance. "Because they're bad guys
who murder innocent victims, so it's okay for you and the
Guardians to do the whole judge, jury, and executioner
thing, right?"

"That's not the same thing!" he said indignantly.

"All right, then why haven't you killed Drake?" She saw
her barb hit home. "He's a Killer, Eli. If being a Killer is an
automatic death sentence, then why is Drake still alive?"

Eli visibly struggled for an answer, and Jez rammed the
point home. "You haven't killed him because the people he
chooses to kill are scumbags. If that's okay for him, why
isn't it okay for Gabriel?"

"I made my bargain with Drake because the Guardians
need his power. And, yes, because he doesn't kill the innocent. But—"

"Don't you think Gabriel's power would be an asset to
the Guardians?"

Eli laughed. He sounded genuinely amused, but the expression on his face was brittle. "Somehow, I don't think
joining the Guardians is quite what my son has in mind."

"Maybe if you invited him, if you gave him some scrap—"

But Eli shook his head. "No, Jezebel. I'm not inviting
Gabriel to join the Guardians. Even if I could actually contact him to ask. Even if I thought there was a chance he
might accept. He was born vampire, and he's . . . unstable."
A hint of sadness crossed his face. "Maybe it isn't his fault.
Maybe it's just the circumstances of his birth. I've heard ru-
mors that born vampires tend to be mentally unbalanced,
but I've never known one other than my son."

"He's not crazy."

"If you don't know him, then how can you say that?"

"Because if he were crazy, he would have just killed Carolyn. And me, for that matter. He's shown mercy, and that's
not the sign of a crazy man."

"Enough," Eli said, making a slashing gesture with his
hand. He'd put on his impassive face, but the expression

was far from perfect. "This subject is not open to debate. Now, since Gabriel knows where you live, and since despite your assertions he may very well be crazy, I suggest you stay in my guest room for the time being."

The way he said it told Jez he expected her to argue. He was definitely on suspicion overload right about now, and she had no desire to make it worse. She tried to make herself look and sound relieved. Even though staying at Eli's would mean there'd be no more seduction attempts in her near future.

"Thanks, Eli," she said. "I'm sure I'll feel much safer here. I think you're wrong about him, but I'd hate to find out you're right the hard way. Let me just dash home to pack an overnight bag. I should be back in an hour."

She didn't think her act did much to convince him, but it was the best she could do.

13

GABRIEL SAT ON THE river bank, staring out at nothing. It was peaceful out here this time of night. Very few cars, very little foot traffic. No need to use his glamour to keep the annoying mortals away. The lights of New Jersey shone across the river, reflecting on the water.

Yes, it was the perfect spot to find serenity. But Gabriel didn't think he was going to find that rare commodity any time soon.

Had he scared Jezebel with his explosion? He hoped not. That was the last thing he wanted, though it was just as well Eli's call had interrupted before he'd let himself do something unutterably rash.

There were so many reasons he should stay away from Jez he wasn't even sure he could count them all. Most of them had very little to do with her inexperience in the bedroom.

He'd seen enough through her dreams and memories to know that she'd had a tough life. Getting entangled with someone like him was not at all what she needed.

Much as he hated to admit it, she needed someone like

Eli, like the Guardians, to make her feel accepted for the first time in her life. But because of Gabriel, neither Eli nor his people would ever fully accept her. Not if they knew the truth.

He was sinking into self-pity, and he knew it. Perhaps another kill would turn his mind away from all this guilt-ridden emotional drama that always disgusted him when he saw it in others.

He tried to imagine hunting the streets once more, searching for that distinctive, tainted scent, tearing the throat out of a mortal who would otherwise never be punished for his crime. The prospect held no appeal.

If only he could talk to Jez before it got too close to dawn! If nothing else, he owed her an apology. He grimaced. And a new phone. But of course, she had run straight to Eli's, and though Gabriel knew she was there, it wasn't like he was going to go knock on the door.

No doubt Eli would insist she stay with him now that Gabriel had threatened her. Cutting off his only access to his fledgling. The nights were long enough *now*. What would they be like if he didn't at least have a visit with her to look forward to?

Thinking of Jez, he closed his eyes and breathed in deep, reminding himself for the thousandth time that she was supposed to be nothing but a tool.

Suddenly, his head felt . . . weird.

He frowned, his heart picking up speed for no reason he could understand. Soon, his brow was bathed in sweat, though he was doing nothing but sitting still.

The clamoring kept up until he finally realized what he was feeling. Fear.

He sprang to his feet, eyes popping open, scanning the area for any potential threat. But he saw nothing, nor did he feel anything with his vampire senses.

Gabriel, help me!

The voice was nothing but the faintest whisper in the back of his mind. He took a hesitant step forward even as he dedicated most of his concentration to following the elusive link that connected him to his fledgling.

He found the link, like a thin psychic tether that reached out from his chest toward the heart of the city. And he felt the link stretching, thinner and thinner.

He started to run, not thinking, just following the feeling, trying to strengthen the link. Still, it kept thinning. He had to get to her fast.

A lone car drove rather forlornly down Front Street. Gabriel leapt out in front of it.

The driver slammed on the brakes and leaned on the horn, but then Gabriel's glamour seized him and he put the car in park and stepped out, eyes glazed.

Gabriel gave the man a shove onto the sidewalk where he wouldn't get run over, then hopped into the car and floored it, barely remembering to close the door after himself.

The thread that connected him to Jez was so thin he could barely feel it anymore. Tires shrieked as he turned the car around, trying to keep enough of himself grounded in the physical world to avoid crashing while still searching with his otherworldly senses.

There! He felt the thread, growing stronger again. He screeched around a turn, sighing in relief as the connection solidified.

Once he was sure he was going in the right direction, he slowed down a little. He didn't have enough concentration to drive, follow the trail, and use his glamour to keep the cops from noticing his creative interpretations of traffic law all at the same time.

"I'm coming, Jezebel," he said under his breath, trying his hardest to send that thought through the psychic pipeline. He thought he might have felt a twinge of response from her, but he couldn't be sure.

The thread grew firmer, more solid, and it no longer took so much effort to hold onto it. He swerved around a gaping pothole, then blew through a red light. And then, he was close enough to "feel" her, to feel the pale, unfinished aura of a new vampire.

And to feel that she was not alone, that she was in the presence of another vampire. A fairly young one—Gabriel guessed the age at around sixty—but easily old enough to overpower a fledgling Guardian.

Jezebel's fear pounded through him, making his heart race and his palms clammy. What the hell was going on? Surely she wouldn't be afraid of any of Eli's Guardians. And there shouldn't be any other vampires in this city. But there was no questioning her fear. He could practically taste it, a bitter flavor on the back of his tongue.

He ran another red light, and then he could see them, two small, indistinct figures three blocks away. He let go of the psychic thread that connected him to Jezebel and concentrated on wrapping himself in his own peculiar brand of glamour, the glamour that made other vampires unable to sense him at all.

As he drew closer, safe in his cocoon of psychic dead space, he tried to figure out exactly what was going on.

The vampire who was causing Jezebel such distress was a young blond male, dressed in fancy tailored pants and an impeccably pressed dress shirt. He had his fingers wrapped around Jezebel's upper arm, but he didn't seem to be physically forcing her to walk with him. There was no sign of resistance at all, and Gabriel realized she was under the influence of the vampire's glamour.

Gabriel pulled his "borrowed" car into an illegal parking space and got out, leaving the keys on the seat. Jez and the hostile vampire were only a half block away, and he followed them at a brisk pace, eating up the distance between them.

A breeze blew down the street, carrying the smells of the city, and the scent of his prey. He tensed as he rolled that scent around his mind.

Tainted. Very, very tainted. This vamp smelled as bad as

Camille's fledglings. And he had Jezebel, was forcing her to come with him for some unknown reason.

Gabriel's fangs descended, and his hands clenched into fists. The beast within him stretched and flexed its muscles, ready to play, and he made no attempt to contain it.

The strange vampire, unaware of his impending death, continued to guide Jezebel down the street, his long strides forcing the shorter woman to practically run to keep up. Gabriel was close enough now to smell her fear, and a monstrous rage rose up from inside him.

There were too many people on the street for Gabriel to kill the vampire here. But there was a subway entrance not too far ahead where no doubt they could find some privacy.

He reached out with his glamour and seized the vampire, who made a feeble, useless attempt to resist. His hand fell limply to his side, and Jezebel jerked away.

She turned slowly, and her eyes widened as Gabriel closed the short distance between them. Her attacker stood slack-jawed beside her, but terror shone in his eyes.

"Gabriel!" Jez cried, running to him and flinging her arms around him.

At any other time, he would have found the effusive greeting gratifying. But right now, the rage was too raw within him, the beast screaming for her attacker's blood.

"Let go, Jezebel," he said. He hated the coldness in his own voice, hated the twinge in his chest that told him he'd hurt her. But he couldn't even look at her, his gaze instead focused on the enemy.

Jezebel obeyed and took a step back from him. "You heard me calling for you," she said.

He nodded, but didn't answer. Instead, he started walking toward the subway entrance he'd noticed, dragging her attacker with him, forcing him to walk to his death on his own power. Jezebel fell into step beside him, though she kept a wary distance between them.

"Wait for me here," he ordered.

"Gabriel—"

He didn't look at her. "This *thing* touched you. Wanted to hurt you." He bared his fangs, and Jezebel's attacker practically pissed his pants.

"Gabriel—" she tried again.

"You don't want to see what I'm going to do to him."

She laid a hand on his arm. His gaze snapped to hers, and she saw something in his eyes that made her let go and take a hasty step back. That pricked his conscience, but the bloodlust ran too keenly through his veins for him to protect her delicate sensibilities.

"Wait for me here," he said again, and this time she nodded faintly, her face pale and her eyes wide.

Gabriel steered his soon-to-be victim down into the subway tunnel as the beast within him crowed in delighted anticipation.

IT WAS A BEAUTIFULLY warm spring night, but Jez shivered and hugged herself as she stood rooted to the sidewalk, waiting for Gabriel to emerge from the subway.

She knew it would be only Gabriel who emerged. And she couldn't say she felt bad to think the vampire who'd grabbed her was going to die. It was the how of it that made her insides want to curl up in a ball and hide.

She'd seen, and *felt,* the madness within her maker for the few moments before she'd mustered her mental forces and somehow managed to block him out. She didn't want to know how he felt as he killed the guy, and she certainly didn't want to know what he did to him before he died.

Tears pricked at her eyes, and she blinked rapidly to keep them from falling. The vamp who'd grabbed her deserved everything Gabriel was going to do to him. She didn't know who he was, but he'd made it very clear what he was planning to do to her when he got her to their unknown destination. And he'd also made it clear he wouldn't be the only one doing it.

No, he had not been alone, and Jezebel hoped Gabriel had enough sanity and self-control to ask some questions before he . . .

She swallowed hard, her ears straining for any sounds that might leak out of the tunnel. But whatever Gabriel was doing, he was being quiet about it.

Her knees felt weak and wobbly, so she went to sit on the front stoop of a charming little bookstore, locked up tight for the night. She wrapped her arms around her legs and hoped her feeble glamour was strong enough to shield her from the mortals who prowled the city streets at night. This wasn't a particularly bad neighborhood, but there weren't many streets in this city that felt safe for a lone woman at this time of night. The last thing she wanted right now was a fight.

She didn't know how long she'd been sitting there hugging her knees before Gabriel finally emerged from the tunnel. She looked up and met his eyes, seeing that familiar dead expression, the one she hadn't seen for a while now. Her heart thumped unhappily, and her throat constricted.

Without a word, he came to sit on the step beside her. She drew in a deep breath, noticing against her will that there was no scent of blood on him. Of course, he didn't have to make someone bleed to make him hurt a whole hell of a lot.

She blinked away tears and fought to stop more from coming.

"Are you all right?" Gabriel asked softly. "Did he hurt you?"

She shook her head, sniffling. To her surprise, he put his arm around her and drew her close to him, giving her comfort. She'd thought he'd moved beyond her reach, emotionally.

Feeling like a helpless victim, and hating it with all her might, she snuggled closer to him. Tears leaked from her eyes one by one, though she tried to stop them.

Gabriel wrapped his other arm around her and held her tight, his chin resting on the top of her head. She laid her hand against his chest and breathed deeply the scent of him, more glad than she could possibly express that he didn't reek of blood.

"Thank you for coming for me," she said, her voice a bare whisper as still she fought the tears.

His arms tightened around her. His lips pressed softly against the top of her head. But he didn't say anything.

Even though she knew the answer to the question, she couldn't help asking, "Is he dead?"

"But of course," Gabriel said.

She swallowed hard, trying to quell the tears without spectacular success. "Did you find out who he was? Why he was trying to kidnap me?"

"Yes." Even in that one word, she could hear the grimness in his voice.

It was the last thing she wanted to do at the moment, but she pushed away from him. He still had that flat, dead look in his eyes, but she could feel the turmoil that churned beneath the impassive surface. Whatever he'd learned, he didn't like it one bit.

He dropped his gaze, staring at the pavement. "I'm sorry, Jez. You were being used to trap *me*."

She gasped. "What?" For an endlessly horrifying moment, she thought he meant the Guardians had been behind the attack. But he quickly clarified.

"Nothing to do with Eli. Well, not really." He grimaced. "Apparently, leaving my mother alone in Baltimore was not my wisest decision ever. It seems she made a field trip to Paris, where we lived before we came to America. And she's brought back someone who wants me dead even more than my father does."

That wasn't hard at all, seeing as Eli didn't *really* want Gabriel dead. He just thought that's what he *should* want.

A strange, tinny version of Darth Vader's theme suddenly emanated from Gabriel's pocket. He curled his lip in distaste as he pulled a cell phone out. She knew without having to ask that it wasn't his.

He flipped the phone open and grunted a greeting vague enough that the caller didn't realize it wasn't who he was expecting.

"Well?" a man's voice asked, sounding terribly impatient. "How close are you? I expected you to have brought our prize home by now."

Gabriel's eyes seemed almost to glow in the dark with hatred. "Bartolomeo di Cesare," he said. "How good of you to come to town so I can finish what I started all those long years ago."

Jez heard the caller's harsh intake of breath.

"I'm afraid your fledgling's met with an unfortunate accident," Gabriel continued, chuckling harshly. "And if you, or my mother, or any of your flunkies lays a hand on my fledgling again, I'll see how many of your other parts I can cut off without killing you. So unless you'd like to live eternally as a paraplegic with no ears, nose, or eyes, I'd suggest you get the fuck out of Philadelphia and thank the gods above that I don't follow you and hunt you down."

Before di Cesare could muster an answer, Gabriel snapped the phone closed.

And once again, Jezebel felt that simmering hatred rise inside him. And she knew that he'd meant every word he'd said.

GABRIEL TRIED TO CALM himself, the beast once again writhing and twisting in his chest and belly. He knew from the tight squinch of Jezebel's eyes that she felt it too.

Who would have thought his mother had the guts to fly to Europe to look for help against him? Certainly he had never considered the possibility himself. No, he'd been sure she was a broken woman, her mind shattered by the knowledge of just exactly how helpless she was against him.

But for her to have joined forces with di Cesare! Cruel though she might be, he hadn't thought her so twisted as to ally herself with a rapist and murderer of children.

Not that di Cesare had been capable, of raping anyone since Gabriel had divested him of his weapons centuries ago.

"Who is he?" Jez asked, nodding at the phone he still clutched in his hand.

He ground his teeth. "A very evil man."

She sniffed. "I picked up on that. Give me the specifics."

He suffered a flash of resentment that she would issue what sounded suspiciously like an order, but he didn't think there was any reason to keep di Cesare's story to himself.

The version he gave her was highly abbreviated, but he left out none of the important details. He watched her face, looking for any sign of horror or censure. After all, he could have simply killed the animal when he caught him. But death had seemed too good for him, though Gabriel had intended to leave him dead in the end.

Jez's face gave no indication that she was horrified or disgusted by him. But then, having been victim to a terrible rape herself, perhaps she did not have an abundance of sympathy for men who committed it.

She leaned her head against his shoulder, a silent show of solidarity that made his heart squeeze in the strangest way. He closed his eyes and breathed deep of her clean scent, reveling in it. He couldn't ever remember having this much contact with anyone who was genuinely good before.

He'd hurt the vampire who'd attempted to kidnap her no more than was necessary to extract the information he required. In the past, he would have made that death last an hour, at least. He would have enjoyed every drop of terror he could wring from his victim, drunk in every sound of pain that escaped him.

This kill had been different. Oh, he didn't feel the least hint of remorse for it, or for the pain he'd caused during his brief interrogation. But there had been no great joy in it, either, no feeling of blessed release.

Jezebel's phone rang, and she cursed. She pushed away

from him, fumbling through her purse for the phone. The way she suddenly avoided his eyes and looked anxious told him who she thought the call was from.

"Eli again, eh?" he asked, feeling no surge of fury at the mention of his father's name.

She bit her lip and nodded. "He's 'suggested' I stay with him for safety, and I should have been there by now."

She found the phone but hesitated to answer.

He smiled reassuringly at her. "Don't worry. Your cell phone is safe from my wrath."

Jez didn't look convinced, but she answered the phone anyway.

"Sorry, Eli," she said in lieu of a greeting. "I got delayed a bit."

"But you're all right?"

"Yes, I'm fine. I should have called."

Gabriel heard the relief in his father's voice, and realized Eli did care about her after all. It was for Gabriel that he'd reserved that peculiar, uninflected tone that gave away nothing.

In the few moments that he listened in on the phone call, he realized a few other things as well. For one, he had no desire to let Jezebel move into his father's house for protection. If she were living there, then Gabriel wouldn't be able to see her, and that was unacceptable.

For another, much though he hated to admit it, Eli should be warned that an animal like di Cesare was in the city. Freed from the control of the *Seigneur* and *Les Vieux*, di Cesare might very well decide to indulge his unnatural appetites while he was here. The Guardians should be warned. And who knew, perhaps they would be able to hunt him down and destroy him.

The conversation was winding to a close when Gabriel reached out his hand and gestured for Jez to give him the phone. He saw her fingers tighten around the phone as her eyes went wide.

"Is something wrong?" Eli asked at the sudden silence.

Gabriel repeated the gesture, and Jez reluctantly handed

the phone over. He took a deep, steadying breath before he spoke.

"I wish to call a truce, Father," he said, the words sour on his tongue.

Jezebel gasped and gaped at him. He wanted to give her another reassuring smile, but he couldn't muster one, not with the effort his words were costing him.

"So," Eli said, his voice back to that infuriating flatness he seemed to reserve just for Gabriel. "You're the delay that came up."

"No, not exactly. It seems I'm not the only one who's come to Philadelphia with revenge in mind. I've discovered that my mother has come for me, bringing an old friend."

Eli was silent.

"She's brought Bartolomeo di Cesare."

Eli's sigh was soft, but audible, though still he didn't speak. Gabriel swallowed his own reluctance and forced himself to continue. The time for subtlety was past. When the truce was over, there would be straight-out war.

"Jezebel is mine," he said. She gasped yet again.

"Yours," Eli said softly. "As in . . . ?"

"As in I made her. Yes. I'm sure Jules and company told you about the dying mortal woman we pulled from Ian's hiding place."

"Ah. I see."

Gabriel heard a combination of disapproval and anger in his father's voice. If it had been directed at him, he'd have ignored it. "It's not her fault I sent her to you under false pretenses." A sidelong glance showed him the tears that snaked down Jezebel's cheeks. She lowered her head, letting her hair shield her face from view.

His heart squeezed again, and he put his arm around her. She snuggled easily against him. His throat tightened at her trust.

"I'm sure you understand, Father, that as my fledgling she did not dare defy me."

"No. Of course not."

The disapproval was still in his voice, but Gabriel didn't think he could do anything to make it go away. "For the moment," he said, "I'm going to keep her with me. It seems that my mother and her new pet thought to get to me through Jezebel."

"She would be safest at my house," Eli commented.

Physically, maybe. But Gabriel wasn't about to subject her to Eli's subtle, poisonous brand of emotional punishment. "You would treat her like a traitor. I won't have that. She stays with me."

"Gabriel—"

The anger rose within him, urging him to lash out, but he did his best to keep it leashed. "She's staying with me and that's final. And I will call a truce with you until di Cesare is dead. I would not loose him on the unwary citizens of your fair city and then distract you from the hunt."

"How very thoughtful of you."

A soft whimper told him his grip on Jezebel had grown too tight, and he hastily released her. He couldn't trust his temper. His heart thudded against his breastbone, and he wanted to reach through the phone line and grab Eli by his sanctimonious throat.

"Listen, you old—"

"Also thoughtful of you to rid my 'fair city' as you call it of Margaret McCall and George Parks."

Gabriel's voice died in his throat.

"I thought it odd that Jezebel would ask for your victims' names, so I looked them up," Eli continued.

Gabriel swore under his breath.

"I'm thankful to learn that you have not taken the innocent in your desire to hurt me." Eli sounded like he was choosing his words with great care. "However, I want to make it clear to you that my position hasn't changed."

Gabriel growled deep in his throat. "Glad to hear that, Eli. Because mine hasn't either. Over the centuries, I've become quite proficient at finding ways to hurt people. If my kills no longer cause you distress, I'll find something that does." He swallowed back some of the bile. "But not while di Cesare still hunts the city. I would even offer to rid you of his odious presence, if your Guardians should locate him and discover him beyond their abilities. I can't imagine they've ever had to deal with a vampire of his age before."

As far as he knew, he and Camille and Eli were the oldest vampires in the New World, or at least were before di Cesare had arrived. For Eli's Guardians, an "old" vampire would be one of, say, two hundred years.

"A generous offer," Eli said dryly, his tone indicating that he had no intention of taking Gabriel up on it.

"Fine!" he snapped. "If you think your little band of toy soldiers can handle a Killer of his caliber, have at it! If you change your mind, you can contact me through Jezebel.

"Oh, and one more thing. In addition to di Cesare, my mother has apparently brought another 'friend' from home. And this little chippie is the daughter of *La Vieille de la Nord*."

Gabriel smiled in satisfaction to hear his father's gasp of surprised dismay. Then he turned off Jezebel's phone and snapped it shut.

14

DRAKE GLIDED THROUGH THE darkness of the ghetto, shrouding himself in glamour, turning all mortal eyes away from him. Sometimes he used himself as bait when he went hunting. An unknown white man parading boldly through this neighborhood at this time of night was certain to attract all the wrong kinds of attention. But that was a dangerous game, one that tempted fate. Aside from punks with guns, there was always the threat of witnesses. The world at large didn't believe vampires existed, and it was best that way.

The temptation to attract a crowd tonight was stronger than he would have liked to admit. Although he was somewhat more even-tempered than most of Eli's young, impetuous Guardians, an excess of energy made him restless and irritable. He'd love a good fight, not his usual clean, merciful kill.

Across the street, a likely candidate for dinner caught his eye, and he began to follow discreetly.

The punk looked to be in his late twenties, and dressed in full gangbanger regalia, complete with chunky gold jewelry and trousers so baggy the crotch practically dragged on the pavement. But it wasn't the clothing that caught Drake's eye. It was the swagger, the attitude. The cruel, deadly expression, and the way others on the street subtly tensed when he approached, then relaxed when he was past. Once in his distant past, he'd have caused a similar reaction when he walked the streets of his home.

A patrol car cruised by, mostly ignored by the predators who mingled in the streets. Both officers in the car were black. The hostility that vibrated through the air here suggested that police officers would be only marginally safer than civilians.

The details were different, but in atmosphere and mood, this place was an aching reminder of his misspent youth. Misery. Poverty. Violence. Prejudice. All present day in and day out, crushing the human spirit.

When he was in his darkest moods, as he was tonight, he wondered if his bite wasn't the ultimate mercy for most of his victims.

His target turned a corner, and Drake hastened to catch up. He reached out with his senses, discovering that the next street over was empty of pedestrian traffic. A good spot for an ambush.

But he pulled up short before he rounded the corner himself, because at the last moment, he sensed something else entirely.

Swearing under his breath, he turned to look behind him, where he'd sensed a vampire following him. Not surprisingly, it was Fletcher again.

Fletcher's glamour wasn't as strong as Drake's, and every once in a while, a mortal would glance in his direction and begin to notice him. Fletcher turned the attention away in time, but he must be exhausting himself doing it.

For the puppy's own good, Drake ducked around the corner to the deserted street rather than confronting him in front of a crowd. Drake's intended victim was pounding on a door halfway down the block. Someone opened the door, and he shoved his way in just as Fletcher came into view again.

Drake sighed and shook his head. He was so tired of all these games of one-upmanship. And he was tired of being the responsible one, the one who was always looking out for everyone's best interests. Right now, the idea of snapping Fletcher's neck was more tempting than he'd like to admit.

He lowered his fangs and snarled at Fletcher. "If you couldn't take me with two buddies, you can't take me single-handed."

Fletcher held up his hands in surrender, but the look in his eyes said he didn't mean it. "I'm not here to start a fight," he said.

Drake narrowed his eyes. Like hell he wasn't! He hadn't opened his mouth wide enough to show the fangs, but the hint of a lisp said they were down.

Damn it, he'd had enough of all this! He'd had enough of the Guardians, and he was beginning to think he'd had enough of Eli too.

Of course, if it weren't for Eli, there'd be no place in the world for him. If he tried to move to another city, he'd step on the toes of the city's master, and end up dead. If he moved to some place quiet in the country, he'd never find enough prey of the sort his conscience could stomach killing.

He was trapped, and that didn't help his temper any.

"One false move, puppy, and that dislocated shoulder is going to seem like a bee sting."

Fletcher's face went red with anger, but he answered in a deceptively mild voice. "I said I didn't come to fight, and I meant it."

Drake grunted in disgust. "So what did you come for?"

The Guardian's smile was singularly unpleasant and revealed the fangs Drake knew were there. "Nothing. Nothing whatsover. Please, just go on about your business as if I weren't here."

So, that was his game. "You think you can disrupt my feeding by following me around." Drake laughed. "If you think I'll refrain from killing just because you're watching me, you're sorely deluded."

"Far be it from me to interfere," Fletcher responded. "As I said, please, go about your business."

What was the damn fool's game?

The gangbanger Drake had been following emerged from the house. Drake thought he heard the echo of a feminine sob before the door banged closed, but he couldn't be sure. He glanced at Fletcher indecisively.

"Don't mind me," the Guardian said, eyes glittering.

Drake still had no idea what the puppy was up to. But the reality was, he needed to feed, whether Fletcher was watching or not.

Ignoring the Guardian as best he could, Drake set off down the street after his meal.

GABRIEL WAS BROODY AND silent throughout the walk to his apartment. Jez bit her lip to keep from pestering him with questions.

Was his last conversation with Eli a good sign? Did it mean the chasm between them was narrowing? Or was it just that Gabriel hated this di Cesare person even more than he hated his father? She longed to know, but she didn't dare ask.

Besides, as shaken as she was by tonight's events, she couldn't help thinking that perhaps she'd been given a second chance at her evening's attempted seduction. Smiling faintly, she slipped her hand into Gabriel's. His face barely acknowledged her touch, but his fingers closed around hers.

His apartment turned out to be a penthouse with a fantastic view of the city. At any other time in her life, Jez would have stood at the windows to drink in that view. Tonight, she had other plans, and with dawn only a few hours away, she had to get those plans into action.

"There's a guest room—" Gabriel began, but Jez cut him off by throwing her arms around his neck and pressing her mouth to his.

For a moment, he resisted, putting his hands on her upper arms and trying to push her away. Not trying terribly hard, though, or he would have succeeded. She'd have been discouraged, if she weren't pressed up against him from chest to hip, if she couldn't feel how his body responded to her.

She licked along the seam of his closed lips, and he made a sound, half growl and half groan. He grabbed a handful of her hair and pulled her head away from his. His eyes bored into hers, and he bared his fangs.

She should have been frightened by the rough handling and by the implied threat. Maybe a part of her was. Her heartbeat seemed strangely erratic, and butterfly wings flapped in her belly. But at the same time, heat gathered at the core of her, spreading outward, engulfing her.

"Be careful what you ask for, my sweet," Gabriel growled, his grip tightening on her hair. "You just might get it." He clapped his other hand to her ass and ground himself against her.

Her breath came in short, frantic gasps, the desire an almost unbearable ache. But the fear was there too, making her limbs tremble.

With a start, she realized it wasn't her own limbs trembling. It was Gabriel's. It was *his* fear that pounded through her veins.

She sucked in a deep breath of air and met his eyes. "I trust you, Gabriel," she said. "You won't hurt me."

He closed his eyes, as if her words hurt. "Then you're a fool, Jezebel."

But when their emotions bled over into each other, pretenses became difficult. She knew how much he wanted what she offered. And she wasn't about to let him pull away.

She raised up on her tiptoes and once again touched her lips to his, ignoring the pull of his hand in her hair. He kept up his resistance for about half a second. Then, his hand flattened against the back of her head, holding her steady as his tongue stabbed between her lips.

She gloried in the pleasure of it, stroking his tongue with hers, marveling at how good he tasted. Her knees trembled, and if it hadn't been for the way he held her so tightly against him, she thought she might have fallen.

His hand squeezed her bottom, then slid down the back of her thigh. His fingers tangled in her skirt and started inching the fabric upward. When he found the hem, he slipped his hand underneath.

She moaned at the touch of his hand on the bare skin of her thigh. But that wasn't where she wanted his hand. She tried an experimental grind of her hips, pressing the hardness of his erection into the softness of her belly.

"Jez!" he gasped against her lips.

But if she let him talk, he'd talk himself out of this. She bit down gently on his lower lip, careful not to catch him with her fangs.

With another of those sexy groans, he seized her lips once more, and his hand moved up to her bottom. He caressed her lightly over her panties. Then, with a quick, ruthless jerk, he tore the flimsy lace away from her, and his hand cupped her.

His fingers dipped between her legs, stroking her most tender flesh, the touch both urgent and gentle. She'd never felt anything so wonderful in her life, and she wanted more!

Even as his fingers teased and tortured her, she felt him pulling away again, so that when he broke the kiss she wasn't surprised.

"Don't you dare stop now!" she growled, glaring up at him. But it was hard to glare too fiercely when his fingers kept finding ever sweeter places to torment.

"If I don't stop now," he said breathlessly, "I'm going to fuck you till you can't walk. Is that what you want, Jezebel?"

The fierceness in his eyes should have been terrifying. Instead, it inspired her to spread her legs a little wider to give him more access. His chest heaved with his heavy breaths, and his skin where he touched her seemed to burn with an inner fire.

When instead of taking advantage of the access she'd

granted him, he pulled his hand away, she almost howled in frustration. But there was something about the glow in his eyes that stopped her voice in her throat. She watched, wide-eyed, as he raised his fingers to his mouth and tasted the moisture that glistened on them.

"Is this what you want?" he repeated in a molten murmur, sucking his fingers clean one by one.

Arousal stole her ability to speak, and she could only nod. Her heart felt like it might explode out of her chest at any moment.

Gabriel surprised her once again when he suddenly bent and hauled her off her feet, slinging her over his shoulder. Somehow, her skirt ended up bunched around her hips, her bottom bare. One arm clamped down on her knees, pressing them against his chest. He clapped his other hand against her butt and continued his sensual torment as he carried her, presumably toward the bedroom.

Jez took advantage of her position by grabbing a double handful of his shirt and tugging it loose from his pants. She grunted in frustration to realize she was too short to reach his butt.

They passed through a doorway into a darkened room. Gabriel closed the door behind him with his foot, then slid her off his shoulder to her feet, steadying her shaky balance by lightly holding onto her hips.

When she was no longer in danger of falling over from the head rush, he took a step back from her. Though the room was dark, the curtains were open and city lights illuminated his face enough for her to see the hungry glow of his eyes. He folded his arms across his chest and looked down his nose at her.

"Strip."

She swallowed hard, nerves suddenly buzzing. But that was ridiculous. He'd seen her naked before! More than once, in fact. So there was no reason to be bashful. And yet something about the way he was looking at her made this into something entirely different.

"Don't make me repeat myself," he said, his voice a soft but dangerous croon. There was a glitter of challenge in his eyes, and she realized that once again he was trying to scare her off. He was just being more subtle about it this time.

She heaved an exasperated sigh. "How many times do I have to prove to you that I really want to do this?" she asked as she reached behind herself to unclasp her bra.

He pulled his lips away from his teeth, tonguing first one fang, then the other. "As many times as I tell you to."

Well, he definitely had his Master of the Known Universe hat on tonight! If he thought he was genuinely scaring her, then he had to be blocking out her reactions. Jez felt certain that once again, it was *Gabriel* who was scared, not trusting himself. Perhaps as he said, it was foolish of her to trust him, but she did. Despite his snarls and his threats, she was sure he wouldn't hurt her.

Now, all she had to do was prove it to *him* so he could get the Rock of Gibralter off his shoulder.

A slow smile spread over her lips, sensual and yet full of mischief. She knew it unnerved him, because some of the swagger left him.

"You want me to strip?" she asked sweetly. Then she crossed her arms over her chest, mimicking his stance. "Make me."

His eyes widened in shock. "Jezebel . . ." he warned.

A sense of power surged through her, a deep-seated understanding of just how desperately he wanted her. It went to her head like alcohol, and she laughed.

"Yes?" she goaded. "What are you going to do to me if I don't do what you tell me?"

His Adam's apple bobbed as he swallowed hard. Even in the dim light of the darkened room, she could see the sheen of sweat on his brow. Smiling at him, she cupped her hands under her breasts, pressing them together to give her even more cleavage. A glance at his groin showed him just how much he liked the view.

"Don't tempt me!" he snapped, but there wasn't much of his trademark ferocity in his voice.

She did a little bump and grind with her hips, laughing at the hiss of his sharply intaken breath. She reached down and pulled her skirt up to mid-thigh.

"Come and get me," she taunted.

And that was the end of his restraint.

He was on her before she realized he was coming, grabbing the straps of her top and yanking downward until her breasts popped free. A startled gasp escaped her. Then he wrapped one arm around her, hauling her toward him, while his other hand cupped her breast and his mouth descended on the nipple.

She moaned in ecstasy as his lips fastened around her hardened nipple and his tongue flicked across it. She let her head sag backward, let her eyes fall closed so she could concentrate on the overwhelming sensations he sparked in her center. His teeth scraped gently over her and she arched her back.

He moved to her other breast, sucking and licking and nibbling until she thought she'd go crazy with it. One hand slid between her legs, the touch almost, but not quite, rough enough to hurt. She widened her stance, and his finger slid into her sheath. Air whooshed out of her lungs, but before she'd had a chance to absorb the strange new sensation, he stopped.

She was trying to muster enough brain cells to form a protest when he suddenly propelled her onto the bed. Her butt hit the edge of the bed and he pushed her shoulders down. She tried to wriggle backward until she was all the way on the bed, but he grabbed her legs, spreading them and then pulling her back to the edge of the mattress.

A flick of his hand had her skirt up around her waist. He pinned her to the bed with his eyes as his hands went to his belt and ripped it open.

Her skin felt like it was on fire, and her heart slammed frantically in her chest. Some tiny remnant of prudishness urged her to close her legs, protect herself from his ravening gaze. But though she trembled slightly, she stayed right where he had put her, gasping for breath as his zipper rasped down and he freed himself.

Her breath caught in her throat at the sight of his rampant arousal. His erection looked huge and threatening, a weapon that would split her in two. Goose bumps prickled over her skin and the trembling got worse, some of her bravado fading. She didn't have a hymen for him to rip through, but logic told her there was no way he could shove that monster into her without it hurting, not when she was so inexperienced. She closed her eyes, bracing herself.

Then, he was on her. He buried himself to the hilt in one thrust, and she cried out in anticipation of pain.

Only, there was none.

She opened her eyes to find him leaning over her, forearms resting beside her head. His eyes locked with hers, and he gave another hard thrust. Again she tensed, but again it didn't hurt.

Gabriel's lips whispered over hers. "I'm too hungry to be gentle," he murmured, slamming into her again. "But glamour has its advantages."

A little moan escaped her throat, and she wrapped her legs around his pistoning hips. This cruel, brutal, "sadistic" Killer was using his glamour to make sure he didn't hurt her. The realization quelled the last of her fear, and she relaxed into him, feeling the delicious sensation of him moving inside her, drinking in the dark desire in his eyes, the musky scents, the sweat that trickled down the side of his face.

His hand slid between her legs as he rode her hard.

She'd thought it felt good *before*. Now, his fingers played with her hardened nub as he stroked her deep inside. The pleasure mounted rapidly. She wanted to rein it in, slow it down, make it last. But the fire burned too brightly, and all too soon the pleasure spiked and she arched her back as a cry rose from her throat.

Gabriel lasted only a few more strokes before his own release shuddered through him. Breathing raggedly, sweat bathing his face, he lowered his forehead to hers.

Jez wrapped her arms around his neck, holding him close as her heart continued to hammer as if it wanted out of her chest. She wanted to say something, but words couldn't express what she was feeling right now. So she settled for holding him tight and hoped the psychic bond they shared allowed him to feel just how good it had been for her.

15

THE HEAVY DRAPES BLOCKED out the sunlight, leaving the room bathed in darkness. Gabriel reached over to the nightstand and turned on the light, squinting in the sudden brightness. He sat up and looked beside him, where Jezebel lay naked on her side, deeply in the grip of the daytime sleep.

He couldn't help the fond little smile that tugged at his mouth, even as the more sensible part of him warned he was on the roadway to disaster.

He lay back down, propping his head on his hand and regarding her sleeping form. Her shoulder-length blond hair was thoroughly tousled, her cheeks still rosy from their last tumble. He reached out and brushed away a lock of hair that had caught in the corner of her mouth. A sleepy sigh escaped her, and he smiled again.

Gabriel swallowed hard around a sudden tightening in his throat. A couple of hours rolling around in bed with Jezebel had shifted his entire perception of reality. He felt confused, unbalanced, uncertain. Like the world he'd known had taken a giant step to the side and everything was just a little off.

He rolled over onto his back and stared at the ceiling, fighting off something that was almost panic.

He couldn't even begin to count the number of women—and men, for that matter—he'd bedded during the near five hundred years he'd walked this earth. None of that had prepared him for Jezebel.

He'd been rough with her that first time, but not out of any desire to hurt her. It had been only the urgency of his need, and a touch of glamour had made certain his lack of finesse caused her no pain.

Before last night, he'd have said he couldn't get off without causing at least some pain. When he'd hired mortal prostitutes, he'd always paid whatever premium they demanded for the privilege of slaking his unnatural tastes. Even then, he'd always experienced some measure of guilt afterward.

He hadn't felt guilty when he'd taken heavily tainted vampires to his bed, no matter how badly he'd hurt them in the process. But he'd always felt somehow unclean afterward. Not guilt for hurting his bed mate, but perhaps some guilt over the fact that he'd enjoyed it.

Last night, the thought of hurting Jez for his pleasure had never even entered his mind.

He rubbed both hands over his face, wishing that would clear the muddle of his mind. Not so long ago, his life had seemed orderly and clear, filled with single-minded, short-sighted purpose—to hurt Eli in any way he could find. He'd never let himself look past his quest for revenge, knowing that in all likelihood, he'd be dead when all was said and done. Eventually, it would come down to a fight, and he had no hope of defeating Eli.

Now, one little slip of a girl had him thinking about the future, had him wondering if he shouldn't cut his trip short of that final confrontation. And even had him wondering just what his quest to hurt his father would accomplish.

Grunting in disgust, Gabriel rolled over on his side again

and turned off the light, practically snapping the switch off in his irritation.

So he'd had a good time in bed with his little fledgling. So what? Two hours of pleasure couldn't undo five hundred years of cruelty and pain. He was what he was, and he'd learned to accept himself that way long ago. When Jez awoke for the night, he would remind her that she'd taken a monster to her bed. No doubt he'd hurt her feelings, and no doubt he'd hurt himself in the process, but it wasn't fair to either of them to let illusion cloud their vision.

Grinding his teeth, unhappy with his decision but nonetheless resolved, he closed his eyes and willed himself to sleep.

DRAKE KNEW HE WAS most likely going to regret this, but he wasn't willing to let Fletcher win their little mind game. The puppy still trailed behind him, watching but not interfering. Drake could simply kick his ass again and hope he got the message, but he had a feeling violence would only escalate the problem.

With a gentle touch of glamour, he steered his victim toward a subway entrance, wrinkling his nose as he breathed in the stink of the place. Urine and vomit were the prevailing scents, with lingering traces of sweaty human bodies.

It was late enough at night that the subways weren't running anymore, but in this neighborhood everything, even the grates and fences that guarded the subway entrance after hours, was decrepit and broken. Drake had no trouble gaining entrance to the silent, darkened tunnels.

"God, it stinks down here!" Fletcher complained, pinching his nose and making a horrible face.

"Then go home," Drake called over his shoulder.

No such luck. Fletcher's footsteps echoed through the tunnels behind him.

Drake guided his victim to a graffiti-covered wooden bench. The gangbanger sat as commanded, his vacant eyes staring out into the darkness. Even over the reek of the

subway tunnels, Drake could smell his victim's atrocious
body odor, blended with the scent of cum and something
sweet and smoky. Hash or pot, most likely. Even more
faintly under that, there was blood.

Not a whole lot of it, but enough for a vampire's sensitive
nose to pick up. The scent of blood came from the skinned
and bruised knuckles of his right hand, and from a set of
scratches that trailed down one arm. The blood and cum
scents hadn't been on him before he'd entered that house.

Drake tilted the man's head until it was at just the right
angle. Then, with an extra pulse of glamour to make certain
his victim's mind was too fogged to feel any pain or even
fear, he sank his fangs into his throat.

Fletcher moved closer to watch, lips pulled away from
his fangs in a grimace of distaste. But something glittered in
his eyes, something that wasn't distaste.

Guardian or not, Fletcher was a vampire, and the smell of
fresh human blood had to excite his senses. Drake would
have liked to close his eyes and revel in the sensory overload of the kill, but he didn't dare, not with Fletcher so
close.

Like a dog guarding a bone, he growled at the Guardian,
warning him away as his victim's heart stumbled in its pace.
He drank until he could drink no more. The mortal's heart
had stopped beating within a minute of when Drake first
sank his fangs. He wasn't quite empty of blood, but it was
close.

When Drake raised his head once more, the gangbanger's
lifeless body tumbled to the floor of the platform. Drake
licked the last remnants of blood from his lips, still eyeing
Fletcher. The Guardian was staring at the body with a look
of mingled awe and horror. His fangs were still out, and
Drake was sure it wasn't from any desire to fight.

"There, but for the grace of God . . ." Drake murmured
softly.

Fletcher's head snapped up, and a fire seemed to burn

behind his eyes. "Fuck you!" he shouted, his voice echoing eerily against the stone and tile.

Drake rolled his eyes. If the idiot wanted to pretend he'd never felt the lure of the kill, that was his problem, his delusion.

"Are you satisfied now?" he asked, hoping that Fletcher wasn't planning to follow him anymore.

Without a word, Fletcher knelt by the body, turning it over onto its stomach. Patting down the pockets, he eventually found a wallet and, inside, a driver's license. He stuck the wallet back into the dead man's pocket, and tucked the license into his own. Then he stood up and dusted off his hands.

"*Now*, I'm satisfied," he said.

Fletcher left the platform, climbing back up into the relative cleanliness of the night air, leaving Drake confused and more than a little concerned. Whatever Fletcher was up to, Drake didn't understand it. And whatever it was, it couldn't possibly be good.

GABRIEL HADN'T THOUGHT HE'D succeed in sleeping, but he must have, for when he next opened his eyes, his senses told him the sun had set.

Jez had snuggled up behind him, spooning him, her body a wall of warmth at his back, her breath tickling the hairs at the back of his neck. He smiled in spite of himself, wondering if she was awake yet. Then her fingers started making light, teasing circles on his chest, and he had his answer.

His smile broadened, then froze. He raised his hand to hers and flattened it against his chest, shoving aside the last remnants of sleep. He heard Jez breathe in as if about to speak, but then she must have felt it too, the subtle wrongness in the room.

He opened his eyes, searching the shadows at the far end of the room. The psychic footprint said vampire, about three hundred years old. But there was something decidedly strange about it, something he couldn't interpret.

Something he should be paying no attention to! There was an intruder in his apartment, and now that he was fully awake, he sensed another, just outside the door.

The intruder switched on a lamp, and Gabriel squinted through the sudden onslaught of light. A three-hundred-year-old vamp would be helpless against his glamour, so he reached out even before his eyes cleared enough to see his quarry.

And his glamour seemed to bounce off some kind of invisible psychic wall. He blinked, and the colorful spots stopped dancing before his eyes.

In the corner of his bedroom sat a petite, dark-haired vampire with an almost cherubic face. She was smiling at him, and she made no hostile move, but that didn't ease the flood of adrenaline that surged through his veins.

"You must be Gabriel," she said, still smiling sweetly. Her English was perfect, though colored with a hint of a Germanic accent.

Gabriel sat up slowly, mentally urging Jez to stay down and stay behind him. For once, she obeyed.

"And you must be Brigitte," he said. The daughter of *La Vieille de la Nord*. Another born vampire, like himself. The only other one he'd ever heard of, let alone met. That would explain her unusual psychic footprint, though not why she seemed to turn his glamour so easily. He was still two centuries her senior. His power ought to be greater.

"Ah, I see Bartolomeo's man spilled all his secrets."

Gabriel snarled at that hated name. Brigitte laughed.

"Don't worry," she said. "He's no friend of mine. Just a convenient tool."

"What do you want?" Gabriel asked, even as he reached out with his glamour again, trying to find a way around her shields.

Brigitte waved her hand in a dismissive gesture. "You may be older than me, but my fledgling is far older than yours, and I know how to draw power from him. If I stayed here long enough, you might be able to penetrate the shield, but I don't plan to stay that long."

Gabriel sensed the other vampire, the one in his living room, moving closer to his bedroom door.

"What do you want?" he repeated.

She shrugged, a delicate little motion. "I wanted to meet you," she said. Then she grinned. "Actually, I had other plans, but I see your bed is already occupied at the moment."

The bedroom door opened, and the other vampire—Brigitte's fledgling, Gabriel assumed—stepped in. Brigitte rose from her chair, moving over to stand by her fledgling, who was staring at the bed with wide, lust-filled eyes.

Gabriel snarled and used his body to block Jez from view. Under the covers, her hand reached for his.

I don't like him, her voice whispered in his mind, and he tasted her fear in the air.

I don't either, he responded. He spared only a moment to be startled at how clearly they'd just communicated with each other, then focused his attention. The smell of corruption wafted from Brigitte's fledgling in sickening waves, though he caught no similar scent from her. Strange. She couldn't possibly have a fledgling that tainted and not be tainted herself.

Brigitte touched her tongue to her upper lip. "Of course, I'm sure Henri would be happy to entertain that sweet little morsel of yours if you like what you see." She cupped her breasts suggestively, but even if Gabriel had had the slightest interest in her, she was too flat-chested to make the gesture terribly alluring.

"If either of you lays a hand on her, you will both die in more pain than you can possibly imagine."

Brigitte giggled. "Big threat from someone whose glamour can't even get a foothold." She sobered suddenly. Perhaps the giggling had been just an act. "But honestly, I'm not here to fight." An impish grin. "Maybe some other time."

The grin disappeared as fast as the giggles. "I just wanted to meet the man who made a woman out of Bartolomeo di Cesare.

"I'm not your enemy," Brigitte continued. "At least, not at the moment." She grinned again. "I'm not your friend, either. I'm neutral, like Switzerland. But, should you wish to be, er, 'friends,' I could teach you much about what it means to be a born vampire. I could teach you how to use your little fledgling to your best advantage." Her smile turned into a sinister leer. "Or maybe I could persuade you to trade her in for a more suitable model. You should choose a fledgling to complement your abilities instead of picking a pretty little bed toy."

"Get out!" he demanded, but she ignored him.

"You're wasting your talents. You could be so much more, with the right tutor. And if you turned out to be an apt pupil, then I could even help you kill your old man."

Jezebel's fingers tightened in his. But, much though he'd love to see Eli dead, he wasn't about to make this devil's bargain.

Brigitte shrugged, perhaps seeing the refusal in his expression even though he didn't speak. "I'll give you some time to think it over," she said. "Assuming your mother and Bartolomeo don't succeed in capturing you, I'll call on you again some night." She flashed him another of those sweet smiles, an expression that now looked absolutely wrong on her face. "It's been a pleasure."

Before he had a chance for a scathing response, she and her tainted fledgling were gone.

16

GABRIEL WASN'T USED TO feeling unsure of himself. He was not enjoying the experience.

He desperately wanted some time to himself, some time to let his chaotic thoughts settle. But he didn't dare leave Jez alone. While he doubted Bartolomeo or his mother could locate her here in his apartment, Brigitte obviously could. He didn't know what the little bitch was up to, but she'd made it clear she saw Jez as a rival. And he hadn't liked the way the fledgling, Henri, had looked at her. Not one bit.

"Gabriel." Jez's voice had a sharp edge to it, one he'd never heard before. He stopped in mid-pace, blinking and turning to her.

"Yes?"

Her hand rubbed over her breastbone. A gesture he was becoming familiar with, so her words didn't surprise him even if her harsh tone did. "You're giving me heartburn. Can you just, I don't know, chill out or something?"

He swallowed a snappish answer and let out a frustrated sigh. "Sorry." He shook his head, wondering how he'd managed to get himself in such a muddle. "This trip is not working out like I'd planned," he muttered.

She let out a nervous little laugh. "Really?"

He tossed her a sour look. "I don't know why you're finding this so terribly funny. You're in far more danger than I am."

She came to stand right in front of him, so close she was almost touching, her head tilted back so she could meet his eyes. "I'm not worried," she told him. "I have you." She dropped her gaze almost immediately, and color warmed her cheeks.

Her words sent a shiver down his spine. No one had ever depended on him before. Now was not a good time to change that. He should never have slept with her, no matter how good it had been, should never have given her that false hope.

He hardened his heart and said what had to be said. "Don't forget what I am, Jezebel." He almost winced at the coldness of his own voice, but it was for her own good.

She blinked and looked up at him once more, raising her eyebrows. "And what is that?"

There was a hint of challenge in her gaze, one that raised his hackles immediately. "I'm a Killer. A monster."

She rolled her eyes. "You know, we've had this conversation before."

"And we'll keep having it until it sinks in!" He wanted to shake her, to rattle her teeth until her common sense snapped back into place.

With a grunt of disgust, she moved away from him, plopping down heavily onto a love seat that faced the breathtaking view out his living room window. Her lovely face reflected back at him in the glass, but she didn't meet his gaze, instead staring out at the city.

"I wasn't finished talking to you," he snapped. Jez didn't even acknowledge that he'd spoken. Something like anger welled up inside him, only it wasn't that familiar, roiling, uncontrollable mass. Maybe "annoyance" was a better descriptor.

If one of his mother's fledglings had treated him like this, Gabriel would have him screaming for mercy by now. He needed to remind her who was boss. But how could he punish a fledgling he wasn't willing to hurt?

He reached out across the psychic line that connected them, slipping inside the barriers of her mind, sensing her disgruntled irritation with him and her complete lack of fear.

"I can feel you in my head, you know," she said without turning around.

No, he didn't know that, but he wasn't about to admit it. "Can you feel this?" he asked as he reached out with his power and lifted her off the couch and into the air.

Jez gave a startled little squeak and tried to grab onto the couch. He jerked her quickly up and out of reach, then turned her upside down. Her skirt slid down her legs and she reached up to hold it down.

He hadn't released the psychic connection between them, and he casually, almost accidentally, tasted her reaction. As he should have known by now, there was still no fear. A little flare of anger, then the warmth of embarrassment as she tried to keep her skirt covering everything that needed covering.

He smiled at her smugly as her face turned red from being upside down. She made a little snarling noise that failed to intimidate him, and for a few seconds, he thought he might actually have made his point.

When the anger left her face and she smiled back at him, he knew he was in trouble. She let her skirt fall, displaying a tiny pair of red satin panties. His mouth went dry.

Jez tucked the hem of the skirt into its waistband so it wasn't covering her face. She licked her lips ostentatiously, then reached up and lightly rubbed her fingers over the triangle of red satin.

"Can *you* feel *this*?" she asked, her smile as smug as his had been.

Something skittered over the line that connected them, a

tickle of pleasure that went straight to his groin. His breath left him in a gasp.

Was he really feeling her touching herself? Or was he just reacting to the visual? Which was becoming more stimulating by the moment as her fingers rubbed a little harder and her thighs parted.

Hoping to regain his equilibrium—and his control of the situation—he spun her in the air until she was upright. With the hem of her skirt tucked in the waistband, his view remained unobstructed. He had the vague idea that he'd been meaning to punish her, to show her her place. He briefly considered bending her over his knee, but enticing though the mental image was, it would involve hurting her, and that he wouldn't do.

"You know," she said, "if that would excite you, I'd be willing to give it a try."

He was so startled he almost dropped her. She fell a good six inches, yelping in alarm and putting out both hands to try to catch herself. He regained just enough control to lower her gently to the floor.

"You saw what I was thinking?" he asked, and there was no hiding the shock in his voice. Damn, just how closely connected were they?

"Yeah," she said, cautiously. "I had a real clear image in my mind." She grinned. "Naughty, naughty."

Gabriel pinched the bridge of his nose. His cock still pulsed with desire, but he was too intrigued by this revelation to let it go. He'd seen snippets of her memories before, but only when she was in great distress.

"I can *feel* things from you," he said. "But I can't *see* things."

"Maybe you aren't looking hard enough," she suggested. "I'm going to imagine doing something wicked to you. See if you can guess what."

Jezebel closed her eyes, her cheeks flushed rosy with desire, her smile positively lascivious. He clenched his fists, stifling the urge to cross the distance between them and touch her anywhere, everywhere. His cock throbbed in time to his pulse, but he forced himself to concentrate on the connection. He closed his eyes, narrowing his concentration further, straining his metaphysical eyes.

And then, he saw it. A vision as clear as if it were really happening. Jezebel on her knees in front of him, taking every inch of his cock between those sweet, sensuous lips of hers. A groan escaped him, and he wasn't sure if it was real or imagined.

It was like watching in a mirror, but even more real. Jez's head bobbed as she mimicked a thrusting motion. He reached across the distance between them, his mind affecting her fantasy Gabriel. His hands stilled the movement of her head. Her eyes widened, and he sensed her surprise to find herself no longer completely in control.

He smiled down at her, flashing fangs. Then, holding her head still to receive him, he began to thrust. She surrendered to him, letting him ram his cock all the way in. Perhaps she was too inexperienced to know she couldn't take that much. Or perhaps she knew, but in her fantasy it didn't matter.

His arousal reached painful proportions as he watched himself fucking her mouth, but as clear as the vision seemed, there was no physical sensation to go with it. He knew if he didn't touch her soon, he was going to go mad with desire.

Gabriel pried his eyes open, reluctant to let go of the fantasy despite the urgency of his need.

Jez's eyes were darkened coins as she regarded him, her scent spiced with arousal. Then a furrow appeared between her brows and she cocked her head to one side.

"I'm not sure how I'd manage that trick with these things in my mouth," she said, indicating her fangs.

He grinned at her, moving closer and cupping his hands around her flushed cheeks. "I'd be willing to take that risk."

Her laugh was as warm and soft as velvet. "Yeah, I'll bet." She turned her head, her lips seeking the palm of his hand and brushing a soft kiss across it. Then she looked up at him, and there was the devil in her eyes. "But I don't get to indulge my fantasy unless you get to indulge yours."

Infuriating woman! His hands dropped away from her face, and he shook his head. How she'd managed to claim giving him a blow job as *her* fantasy, he wasn't sure. "Forget it," he growled.

She put her hands on her hips and looked as exasperated as he felt. "For God's sake, Gabriel! How can you be five hundred years old and be such a prude?"

He took a step back from her, affronted. But it was hard to stay indignant when her skirt was still raised up high enough to display those incredibly sexy panties.

"I am *not* a prude!" He'd never met anyone, male or female, who could unbalance him as easily as Jez could. Her expression of polite skepticism tweaked his male ego. He crossed his arms over his chest, knowing he looked defensive, but unable to resist.

"I'm *not*!" he repeated. Not the most convincing of arguments, but he honestly didn't know what to say to her.

"Then why are you freaking out so much over this? You've said you're a sadist, and I'm offering you the chance to indulge your fantasies."

"I don't want to hurt you!" he said stubbornly. And that was the truth. Thinking about causing her pain was making his erection go down in a hurry. He wanted to make her scream, all right—but he wanted it to be pure pleasure.

One corner of her mouth tipped up. "Then I guess you're not really a sadist, are you?"

The words struck him like a slap in the face.

Could it be that his assumption of his depravity had been faulty, or at least exaggerated, for all these years? But no, that couldn't be. He remembered what it had felt like to take his mother's fledglings to bed, remembered how he'd reveled in their fear, in their pain. He closed his eyes to try to block the images out. He didn't want to remember, didn't want to think about it, not when Jez might be able to see through their psychic link.

His eyes popped open when Jez took both his hands. He hadn't sensed her closing the distance between them.

"Let me in, Gabriel," she said. "Let me share whatever it is you're thinking that's got you looking so miserable. Maybe I'll be able to understand it better than you."

He recoiled, slamming closed his mental doors and reinforcing them as strongly as he could. There was no way in hell he wanted Jezebel seeing the things he'd done! She had some naive idea in her mind that he wasn't as bad as he claimed. If she saw him for what he really was, she'd never let him touch her again.

And, he realized suddenly, that was what he had to do. Hadn't he been telling himself all along that she was better off without having any inappropriate romantic attachments? What better way to set her straight than to let her see the beast that resided within him.

He set his jaw and stared into her eyes. "All right, Jezebel. I'll let you in. But don't say I didn't warn you."

She nodded solemnly. "I won't. Now, come sit down."

Still holding his hands, she pulled him toward the couch. He noticed with a hint of chagrin that she'd untucked her skirt, but he supposed they'd gone past the point of seduction. He doubted he'd be seeing those sexy red panties again. He tried not to let the thought depress him.

Laying his head against the back of the couch, he closed his eyes and let out a deep breath.

At first, he was so reluctant to let Jez see inside him that his shields remained resolutely up despite his effort to drop them. It wasn't like this was something he'd done before, wasn't like he'd even known it was possible before a few days ago. He wasn't even sure he knew *how* to do it.

"Relax," Jezebel said in his ear. "Don't think about letting me in. Just let your mind go."

Skeptical, he nonetheless tried to do as she suggested.

She didn't think he was a sadist? Well, he'd show her! And he wasn't as benevolent as those people with "alternative lifestyles" she'd encountered in her rebel years. *Those* people had enjoyed it only with others who shared their tastes, who were consensual partners. Not at all like his own exploits.

He focused his mind on one of the most reprehensible of his reluctant playmates—Ian Squires.

Gabriel had despised Squires from the moment he'd first met him. He'd felt the same way about all of his mother's fledglings, but Squires had been the worst. His stink offended Gabriel's nostrils every time they were in the same room together.

Squires joined his mother's entourage as a mortal, patiently waiting for the gift of her bite. And when she finally granted it to him, he ran away, delusions of grandeur making him imagine himself a master vampire with a harem of groveling fledglings.

He'd run to Philadelphia, where he'd paid a visit to his old friend, Jules Gerard. The slimy bastard had used his glamour to make the rigidly straight Jules think he was succumbing to a seduction when Ian raped him. He then transformed Jules as his first fledgling.

Luckily for Jules, the Guardians had caught wind of Ian, and he was forced to flee Philadelphia for his life. He'd come crawling back to Camille, who allowed Gabriel to punish him for running away.

Gabriel had forced Ian to share every intimate detail of his time in Philadelphia, where he'd indulged a taste for cruelty that he'd barely kept under the surface as a mortal. Once he became vampire, he shrugged off all the constraints of humanity and reveled in his power.

Ian had been a sadist in the most unimaginably ugly sense of the word, preying upon the weak and the innocent. He fed when he wasn't hungry, just for the sheer euphoria of the kill. And even a forceful taste of his own medicine hadn't tempered his cruelty, for the Killer was incapable of even the most basic empathy.

Gabriel had used his glamour to force Ian to beg for every blow that fell upon him, and to thank him afterward.

And his glamour had dragged sounds of feigned pleasure from Ian's throat with every indignity Gabriel had forced on him.

The feel of Ian's soul cringing in horror had made lust surge through Gabriel's veins, had made—

"That's not lust," Jez said, interrupting his forced march down memory lane.

Gabriel shook his head to clear it. His brain felt all cobwebby. He'd almost forgotten Jez was here. And that she was marching down that memory lane with him.

He shut down the mental gates, cutting off contact so abruptly it made his head hurt. How could he have let her see that? She was the one person in the world who *didn't* think he was a monster, and he was destroying everything there was between them.

"Did you hear me?" she asked. She didn't sound as disgusted as she should have.

Gabriel buried his head in his hands, unable to look at her. He'd never felt ashamed of what he'd done before. Now, the weight of guilt crushed him down into the couch. He was as disgusting, as tainted, as Ian himself! All these years, he'd told himself it was all right to indulge himself with his less-than-innocent victims. Now, he wondered how he could possibly have deluded himself that much.

Jez put a hand on his shoulder and gave him a small shake. "Snap out of it, already."

He raised his head and forced himself to meet her eyes, trying to damp down his feelings, trying to make sure they didn't bleed over into her. There was no reason she should share this swamp of remorse he was wading through.

He lifted one corner of his lip in one of his trademark sneers. "Now what do you think of me, my sweet?" he asked in a vicious undertone. "Do you still think I'm not a sadist? Do you still think I'm not a *monster*?"

He expected her to flinch away from him, but she didn't. "I think," she said carefully, "that you're a very, very angry man. I think that no matter what you say, *you* blame yourself for the circumstances of your birth, not Eli. And I think you punish yourself for it by trying to make yourself into the monster you think you are."

"But if you were a monster, it wouldn't be just creeps like Ian you'd be picking on."

Gabriel snorted. "Tell yourself that, if it makes you feel better."

"I recognized Ian in your vision, you know," she said.

He blinked at her, not quite getting it.

"He was the guy who picked me up when I was hitchhiking. The one who raped me, then watched while his fledglings took turns doing the same during their feeding frenzy. You've cut off my emotions about that, but not the memory itself. I know from first-hand experience just how evil he was. Let me just say that as bad as what you did to him was, it couldn't have happened to a nicer guy."

That, he couldn't argue. "That's not the point, Jez. The point is, I *enjoyed* what I did to him."

She frowned at him, her pretty face all squinched up with thought. "I don't know that 'enjoyed' is the right term. It felt like justice to you." She reached for his hand, fingers urging his fist to unclench. "It had nothing to do with sex or pleasure."

His jaw dropped, and he looked at her in disbelief. "Did you feel *anything* of what I felt?"

"Of course."

"Then how can you say that?"

She gave him a look of undisguised challenge. "Did you enjoy making love to me last night?"

The change of subject practically made him dizzy. "What?"

Her lips twitched in a hint of a smile, quickly suppressed. "I think the question is self-explanatory. So, did you enjoy it?"

He watched her face, feeling something very much like suspicion. "Yes, of course I did," he said slowly.

"And did anything you felt last night bear any resemblance to what you felt with Ian?"

"That's not the same thing!"

"My point exactly."

He opened his mouth to argue with her, but apparently she'd had enough of arguing. Before a word escaped him, she'd climbed onto his lap, wrapped her arms around his neck, and planted a breath-stealing kiss on his lips. He couldn't help surrendering to that kiss, couldn't stop his arms from wrapping around her and holding her close. Languorous warmth spread out from his center, and his hands moved restlessly along her back, finding their way under her top until he touched her soft, smooth skin.

"*This* is sex," she murmured against his lips. "*This* is desire." She drew the tip of her tongue over his lower lip. "*That* was something else entirely."

Her kiss traveled from his lips to the edge of his jaw. His eyes closed, heavy with pleasure, each brush of her mouth triggering aftershocks that he felt all through his body.

"Is this how it felt when you were with Ian?" she whispered hotly as she traced the line of his jaw upward.

A soft groan escaped him as he shoved the memory of Ian out of his mind. He didn't want to think about that, didn't want that taint to color this moment.

"Shut up, Jezebel," he murmured, then turned his head into her kiss, his mouth seeking out her lips once more.

She melted into him, her tongue tangling with his, her hands kneading his shoulders like little kitten paws. Holding her securely in place, he turned them, then laid her back on the couch, her head comfortably nestled against the armrest. With a gentle nudge of his knee, he parted her legs and settled himself between them.

The contented, purring sounds she made as he kissed her electrified him. Primal instincts urged him to bury himself in her as fast as possible, claim her as his own, but he fought against them. Last night, his need had been too urgent to contain. The need was no less urgent tonight, but he felt more in control—more human, for lack of a better word.

He pulled away from her, drawing a cry of protest. The

protest died in her throat when his fingers found her breast and began circling softly. She bit her lip and stared up at him with lust-fogged eyes as her pulse jumped in her throat. He smiled as he watched the color that flushed her cheeks, as he saw her nipple tighten and bead beneath the fabric of her top. His fingers played all around it, circling close but never quite touching. She squirmed beneath him, the movement grinding his almost painful erection into the softness between her legs. They both drew in quick, sharp breaths.

"Be still!" he said sharply, trying for an expression of stern command. Her impish grin told him he fell short of the mark, but she lay still anyway. For the time being. The corners of his mouth turned upward against his will. "Now, where was I?" he mused.

"I think you were right about here," Jez murmured, reaching up to cup her own breast, skating her fingers over the perky nipple.

Gabriel grabbed her wrist with a feigned snarl. "None of that!" he said, pinning her wrist above her head. Her other hand was trapped between their bodies and the back of the couch. He settled his weight more comfortably above her, then resumed his sensual torture.

He gave her nipple just the tiniest stroke with one finger, a touch that made her back arch and drew a moan from her throat. Then he shifted his weight so he could pull her blouse up and over her breasts, revealing a red satin bra that matched the panties. The satin barely covered her nipples, and he traced his fingers along the edge, loving the softness of her skin and its creamy color.

She kept up her squirming, trying to move so that his fingers stroked where she wanted them. The feel of her moving under him made his cock throb, and he was afraid the stimulation would become too much and overpower his self-control. A touch of glamour stilled her struggles, and she gasped.

He met her startled eyes. "If you don't hold still, this will be over far too fast," he said. He felt the shiver that rippled through her body, saw the hint of doubt in her eyes. He stroked her cheek with the back of his hand. "I'll let go if this is frightening you."

She swallowed and licked her lips, then let out a shuddering breath. "I'm okay," she said.

He brushed a kiss over her moistened lips, his tongue dipping in for the briefest taste. "If that changes, tell me."

She made a vague sound of agreement, and he returned his attention to her breasts, teasing along the edges of her bra with fingers and tongue. She couldn't squirm anymore, but his glamour didn't stop the sexy little moans and gasps that told him just how much she liked what he was doing. And just how much it frustrated her.

When he judged she couldn't stand the torture any longer, he popped the catch on her bra. Her perfect breasts spilled out, and he took a long moment just to admire them, smiling at Jez's muffled oath.

She forgot her complaints when he took one dusky peak into his mouth. Her taste shot an arrow of desire to his groin, and once again he fought for control. Much though he wanted the mind-blowing pleasure of release, the touching and the tasting, the sounds of pleasure he drew from Jez's throat, were too delicious to come to an end so soon.

He tasted first one breast, then the other, using lips and tongue and, very gently, teeth until the nipples were hard and sharp as pebbles. Then he raised his head to look at her flushed face, pondering how to torment her next.

"Are you feeling this?" she asked breathlessly.

He knew immediately what she meant. Even the idea of opening up the psychic link between them, of experiencing what she was feeling right this moment, took him perilously close to blastoff. He gritted his teeth and fought it off.

"Some other time," he said, his voice strangely strangled.

Her little smirk told him she enjoyed that feeling of feminine power. He narrowed his eyes at her, once again envisioning taking her over his knee. The vision crystallized, the details clear. Her skirt flung up over her hips. Those insanely sexy red panties down around her ankles. Her bare, breathtaking ass just waiting for the slap of his hand.

Her cheeks burned with color, and Gabriel laughed, having confirmed his suspicion that she had left the psychic connection wide open. He visualized putting up a wall around his mind, cutting the connection.

Jezebel pouted. "Now why'd you do that?"

His grin no doubt held a touch of evil. "Because I don't want you coming until I'm good and ready, and I'm planning to very much enjoy what I'm going to do next."

Her eyes widened a bit at that.

Sitting up, he positioned her more comfortably on the couch, releasing the glamour so she could move. When she was settled, he slid her skirt up to her hips, revealing her panties once again. His cock twitched eagerly. *Not yet,* he told it.

As stunning as she looked in those panties, it was time for them to go. Her skin shivered under his touch as he drew them slowly down her legs. The musk of her arousal filled his senses, and he wasn't sure how much longer he could last.

He tapped with one finger on the inside of her thigh, and she spread her legs in response to the silent command. He began again the maddening tease, not sure which one of them he tormented most as his fingers explored the soft, sensitive skin of her thighs, her hips, her lower belly.

"Please, Gabriel," she gasped, her hands clenched into fists beside her.

He grinned at her. "Please what?" he asked, but at just that moment his fingers brushed against the curls between her legs, and her voice was lost in a gasp.

The look on her face, the little breathy moans, the scent of her, combined in a heady blend of erotic energy that seized him by the balls. He'd never felt anything like this before, never ached so desperately for release while still denying himself. Never known how unbearably arousing it could be to bring his partner pleasure, how her pleasure could be as intoxicating as his own.

He spread her legs wider, and she held her breath as he kissed the inside of her thigh, just above her knee. Moving a little higher up her thigh, he pressed another kiss to the tender skin there, then followed the kiss with a quick flick of his tongue. Jez's breath hitched, and he smiled.

The smile faded momentarily when he found the mass of scar tissue where her attackers had torn her open to get at the femoral artery. Would a kiss there trigger an unpleasant association despite the shroud he had drawn over the memory? There was only one way to find out.

A pleasured sigh eased his concerns, and he traced the scars with the tip of his tongue. He was so close to her tantalizing warmth! But he feared if he tasted her now, he might lose the last of his control. He didn't want to be distracted by his own pleasure when she came, wanted to drink up every quiver, every spasm, every cry.

"Please," she moaned again.

His glamour wasn't pinning her anymore, but her muscles trembled with the strain of keeping herself still. And despite his desire to take everything glacier-slow, he couldn't resist her for another second.

He was woefully inexperienced at giving women pleasure, having in the past concentrated on his own selfish needs. But Jez's responses were so transparent, there was no doubting that she enjoyed what he was doing. When he finally allowed himself the luxury of tasting the glistening flesh between her legs, she almost jumped off the couch, her back arching wildly, an incoherent cry bubbling from her lips.

Draping one arm over her hips to hold her down, he used his other hand to part her, then took a long, tantalizing tour with his tongue, noting her reactions, seeking out the spots she liked best.

"Oh," Jez moaned, "there!"

He allowed himself one quick, smug smile, then set to work, flicking her sensitized flesh with the tip of his tongue, then trying a tentative suckle. Her hips bucked under his arm, and he settled into a rhythm, eyes closed, all his other senses tuned into the rhythm of her body. He knew she was close, knew her release when it came would be explosive. He slid his finger inside her just in time to feel her sheath spasm, her cry almost a scream, the firm grip of his arm the only thing keeping her on the couch.

He didn't let up stroking her until he'd milked the last possible shudder out of her and her breath came in frantic wheezes and gasps. He raised his head, making a pillow of his hands right above her sex and laying his chin on them as he regarded her face. He was pretty sure the smug smile was back, but he didn't much care. His cock was still rigid, still ached with need, but for the moment he preferred to revel in the satisfaction of having so thoroughly pleased his beautiful little fledgling.

Jez opened her eyes on a contented sigh. She met his gaze and laughed suddenly.

He raised his eyebrows. "What?"

Still giggling, she shook her head at him. "You look like the cat who ate the canary." The look on her face said she heard the double entendre just half a second too late.

"Meow," he said, then licked his lips slowly and sensuously.

She shivered, and her eyes darkened with desire once more. "I'm one happy canary."

He raised his head from his hands and began climbing up her body. "Should I make a remark about how happy the pussy is, or would that spoil the mood?"

She laughed and grabbed him by both ears, dragging him up to her a little faster. With her urging him on, he finally let go of the reins of his desire. And when he slid inside her, the sense of connection was so much more than just the joining of two bodies.

Something deep inside him cracked, a small, hairline

fracture that wasn't quite a break. A chip in his defenses that could one day be his downfall. And even as the pleasure and the joy of his union with Jezebel sang through his body, he knew that he would have to work swiftly to mend that crack before all was lost.

17

CAMILLE KNEW A TEST of her resolve when she saw one. But resolved as she was, even *she* found her current errand distasteful. Not that she'd ever been particularly fond of children, or that she had any deep maternal instincts. It was just that some remnant of the human being she'd once been insisted she was about to cross the final line, make the final transition from human to monster.

She smiled faintly as she approached the playground, which teemed with screaming brats under the only sometimes-watchful eyes of their parents and guardians. It was time—past time, really—that she lay the last of her humanity aside, embraced her true nature and blossomed.

She'd dressed in her casual best for this little adventure, wearing hip-hugging designer jeans and a crisp button-down blouse. She looked eminently respectable. No one gave her a second glance as she sat on a bench and watched the children playing. No one so much as guessed that a wolf sat in their midst, looking for the perfect sheep.

Gabriel, with his strange squeamishness around mortals, would probably be moved to stupidity no matter which child she selected. However, she was determined to pick the one that would push his buttons the hardest.

A girl, naturally. And a pretty one at that. Young enough to tug at heartstrings, but not so young she wouldn't understand exactly what was going to happen to her.

A little boy, probably no more than four years old, tripped over his own awkward feet and sprawled on the asphalt. An older girl, very likely his sister, ran to him and gathered him up in her arms, making cooing noises even as she rolled her eyes and shared a long-suffering look with her giggling friends.

Camille studied the girl with the eyes of a connoisseur. She guessed the age at somewhere around eleven or twelve. The cusp of womanhood, but not there yet. No sign of budding breasts, no telltale curves. Long, straight dark hair was tangled messily in a scrunchie, and her clothing was cheaply nondescript. But her face was sweetly heart-shaped, her eyes large and expressive.

Yes, she would be perfect. Trussed up like the proverbial Christmas goose, eyes red and swollen from crying, lips trembling as Bartolomeo held her in his lap and smiled for the camera, she would call to Gabriel's all-too-human sense of pity, and he would realize just what the cost of avoiding his fate would be. The pitiful fool would walk straight into their trap, no doubt thinking himself more than a match for his adversaries.

And when Bartolomeo finally had his hands on his longed-for target, Camille knew exactly how she could use both of them to catch Eli as well.

The last of her qualms buried, Camille rose from the bench and started down the street. Her glamour called out to the child she had chosen. The girl broke away from her friends, an expression of mild confusion on her face, and followed haltingly in Camille's footsteps.

DRAKE STOOD IN A corner, far away from the rest of the Guardians. Eli had called an emergency meeting, and Drake had been sorely tempted to play hooky. He didn't imagine the Founder could have much to say that he'd want to hear. And yet, he'd come anyway, out of long habit, or curiosity, or sense of duty.

Amazingly, the meeting hall looked as it always had, all the windows repaired, no sign of the overpowering rage that had stormed through it only a few nights past. The news, however, was grim in the extreme.

As if Gabriel himself weren't enough of a threat, Camille and at least two other Killers had come to town as well. And they were down one Guardian, because Jezebel turned out to be Gabriel's fledgling and spy.

Eli handed out assignments, trying to treat this massive invasion like he would any other hunt. His explosion of the other day must have had a calming effect on him in the long run, for he seemed much more sure of himself tonight, much less distracted and emotional. Drake approved of his aura of calm confidence, even as he wondered how long it would take everyone to realize it was a smoke screen.

The meeting was nearly over, and Drake was anxious to get the hell out, when suddenly Fletcher rose to his feet, drawing everyone's attention. Drake had been leaning one shoulder against the wall, but something about the glitter in the Guardian's eye made him stand up straight. He knew without a doubt that he didn't want to hear whatever the puppy had to say.

Fletcher reached into his pocket and pulled out an envelope, dumping the contents onto his chair and then picking through them and holding up a wallet-sized photograph.

"There's been a vampire kill in our city that I thought everyone should know about," he said, passing the photograph to the Guardian nearest him, then picking up another from the pile and handing it to the Guardian on the other side of him.

"His name was Antwaan Evans," Fletcher said, his eyes homing in on Drake. "He's served time on drug charges and for assault and battery, but his record has been clean the last couple of years." He leaned down and picked up yet another picture, this one a little larger, of an attractive young black woman, holding a pudgy infant. "This is his widow, Tawnya, and his son, Antwaan Junior." Another picture, this of a white-haired woman, scrubbing at her eyes with an embroidered handkerchief.

The room had fallen eerily silent as the Guardians passed the pictures around.

"This is his mother, LaShanda. She had three boys. Antwaan was the youngest. Her first boy was killed by a stray bullet in a drive-by shooting when he was only nine. Her second died in a car accident, hit by a drunk driver, when he was twenty-two. Antwaan was twenty-nine when a Killer sucked every drop of blood from his body, and then left him on the subway tracks for a train to mangle beyond recognition."

Drake's heart beat somewhere up around his throat as every eye in the room fixed on him. He held his head high and gritted his teeth. He was *not* going to get drawn into this, was *not* going to defend himself.

Fletcher met his eyes again, daring him to say something. Drake refused to give him the satisfaction.

"He was a human being, Drake," Fletcher continued. "He wasn't a saint, he probably wasn't what you'd call a nice guy, but he was human. He had people who cared for him, who relied on him. And you killed him without a second thought. So don't give yourself airs, don't pretend you're one of the good guys. You're a Killer just like the rest of them, and you don't belong anywhere near the Guardians."

"That's enough, Fletcher," Eli said quietly.

Drake bit down on a surge of anger. Couldn't Eli have spoken up earlier?

Fletcher held up his hands. "I've said my piece." He gathered up the contents of the envelope, sticking the pictures back in it, then headed for the door, passing by Drake on the way. He dropped the envelope at Drake's feet without looking at him.

Everyone else watched him, eyes boring into him. A few

faces showed sympathy and understanding. Most of them, though, held unbridled hostility and condemnation. He glanced at Eli, wondering if the Founder was going to defend him, but Eli was staring at the floor, his eyes troubled.

Leaving Drake out to dry.

Drake had a sudden flash of understanding for how Gabriel must have felt when Eli had tried to kill him. Being left out in the cold by someone you'd counted on sucked. He clenched his fists and promised himself he'd deal with the pain of it all later. For now, he just had to get out of this room alive, which could prove a challenge if Eli had removed his protection.

"I do what I have to do to live," he said quietly, hoping his words would spur Eli into action. But Eli still had that lost look on his face, almost like he hadn't heard anything. "When I was turned, my maker failed to mention that the kill was optional. I've never had the choices you all have had." He frowned, those words resonating strangely in his head. Then he remembered where he'd heard them before— Gabriel, sneering at him and Jules for their sanctimonious attitudes. Gabriel, who like himself, had never had the choice not to kill. No choice other than death, that is.

He looked at Eli again, and realized the Founder was making the same comparison. *That's* why he looked so troubled, so haunted. That's why he didn't speak in Drake's defense. He was thinking of Gabriel, once again.

"You know," Gray said, interrupting the oppressive silence that had fallen, "nothing's changed."

All eyes—except, naturally, Eli's—turned toward Gray. Drake was glad to have the attention move elsewhere, but he wasn't sure Gray was doing himself any favors by speaking up. He, too, hovered around the fringes of Guardian society, for he'd killed a mortal when he was turned. With some vampires, one kill was enough to make the blood addiction take hold, but Gray had dodged that bullet. Still, even that single kill made him suspect in many of the Guardians' eyes.

"We've always known that Drake is a Killer," Gray continued. "That's why he's been such a help to us."

"I hate to say it," Jules said, making a face, "but I agree with Gray." A few of the Guardians chuckled at this once-in-a-lifetime occurrence. "We've been thankful enough for his help in the past. Seems rather hypocritical to sit here and sneer at him now just because Fletch has shown us a bunch of pictures."

Eli finally came back from whatever mental distance he'd disappeared to. "I've killed far more people than Drake could ever dream of," he said, and once again a stunned silence descended on the room. "Let he who is without sin cast the first stone."

No one spoke, and no one seemed to know where to look.

"Go home, everybody," Eli said. "You have jobs to do. Killing Drake isn't one of them."

There were a few grumbles and murmurs, and lots of speculative looks. Drake was sure many of the Guardians were dying to ask Eli what he'd meant when he'd claimed to have more kills than Drake. No one was **brave** enough to ask, though.

When Drake made to follow the crowd out, Eli beckoned him to stay behind. He hesitated for a long moment in the doorway. Then, he shook his head.

"No, Eli. I'm going home. I've had enough for one night."

"I'm sorry," Eli started, but Drake didn't want to hear it, not now.

Turning his back on his mentor, he hurried out of the house and hoped the rest of the Guardians weren't waiting out there to kill him.

JEZ SLID QUIETLY OUT of Gabriel's bed. He mumbled sleepily, reaching over toward the warm spot she'd just vacated and pulling her pillow up against him, but didn't wake up.

She'd never actually seen him sleep before. He was usually

far too wired, too full of conflict and painful energies. For him to be sleeping when it wasn't even daytime must mean she'd really tired him out!

The thought brought a smile to her lips as she donned her shirt and panties and crept out into the living room.

She turned on the TV, muting the sound and then flipping absently through the channels. Naturally, there was nothing on at this late hour, but she didn't much care. She found an unfamiliar black-and-white movie and left the TV tuned to that station, the sound off.

It was a good thing she was a vampire, or she'd probably be too sore to move right about now. Gabriel was capable of being gentle when he wanted to be, but he obviously preferred it passionately rough. Making love, to him, was almost an act of desperation. She didn't like the idea that his passion was motivated by despair, but she certainly liked the passion itself!

She drew her knees up to her chest, stretching her shirt over the top of her legs.

She liked the passion *too* much. She was sailing dangerous waters, losing her heart in bits and pieces. It felt wonderful. Addictive. But just like the cigarettes she'd been addicted to as a mortal, Gabriel could turn out to be a fatal addiction.

He wasn't the heartless, soulless monster he made himself out to be. Yes, he had a streak of cruelty to him—a *wide* streak—but it was much more controlled than he liked to admit. Unfortunately, the fact that he wasn't a monster didn't mean he wasn't severely fucked up.

The two of them were so much alike it wasn't funny. They'd both reacted to their family's scorn by pretending to be something other than what they were. The difference was, Jez had escaped from her Gram's poisonous influence when she was eighteen, and in the six years since, had come to understand how badly she'd been hurting herself in her effort to hurt her Gram.

Gabriel had never escaped. He'd been beating himself up

with Eli's opinion of him for five hundred years now. How could she possibly expect a wound like that to heal? And how could they possibly have anything like a relationship when he was so full of anger and self-loathing? They might be able to stumble along for a while, but anything between them was doomed to fail.

A tear trickled down her cheek, and she wiped it angrily away. She hadn't even known she was crying.

Why did she always find herself surrounded by fucked up people? Why couldn't she find someone nice and sane and well-adjusted to spend time with?

She swallowed her tears and took a deep, shuddering breath. She knew the answer to her own question. No matter how much she told herself that she'd grown up, and *wised* up, she still had this ridiculous hero complex. She still wanted to save the world. Some childish, wistful part of her soul still thought that if somehow she could save someone else she cared about, it would make up for not having been able to save her mother.

Before she could sink deeper into her funk, her cell phone rang. She leapt from the couch and dove for her purse, hoping to silence the damn thing before it woke Gabriel. Aside from the fact that he probably needed the sleep, she didn't want to face him right now, when her soul felt so raw.

It took three rings before she dug the phone out from the bottom of her purse, but at least the bedroom door was closed. She moved to the other end of the room from the door and flipped the phone open.

"Hello?" she said, *sotto voce*.

"Hi, Jez. It's Drake."

She frowned. He wasn't exactly someone she'd have expected to call her.

Had Eli told everyone that she was Gabriel's?

"May I speak to Gabriel?" Drake asked, answering her question.

"Um, he's asleep right now. I'd rather not wake him."

Drake paused. "It's two-thirty in the morning. What's he doing sleeping at this hour?"

Jez felt the color rising to her face, then shook her head at herself for being embarrassed. Her Gram had treated her like the Whore of Babylon when she was still a virgin, but that didn't mean having slept with Gabriel made her a slut.

Geez, she kept telling herself she'd escaped the poisonous influence, but obviously that was wishful thinking. She forced a smile she didn't feel, and hoped it translated into her voice.

"Let's just say I tired him out."

"Oh," was Drake's brief, unembarrassed reply. "Do you think there's any chance you could talk him into calling me when he wakes up?"

She raised her eyebrows at that. "Why? So you can lead him into some kind of trap so Carolyn can take a shot at him?"

There was a long hesitation before Drake spoke again. "It's been pointed out to me that I'm not really in a position to throw stones. Eli told us what you'd learned about Gabriel's victims. He's declared hunting Camille and di Cesare the more urgent mission at this moment. But you and I both know the Guardians aren't equal to this challenge, and Gabriel probably is."

Anger surged through her veins. "Oh, so yesterday it was 'off with his head,' and today, he could be useful so you'll generously allow him to live?" Maybe Eli and the Guardians really *were* as hypocritical as Gabriel thought. "Go to Hell, Drake. And right this moment, I wouldn't even mind if you took Eli with you!"

She snapped the phone closed and turned off the ringer. Then she jumped like a cartoon cat at the sound of clapping hands.

She whirled around to see Gabriel standing stark naked in the bedroom doorway. He was grinning at her, his gorgeous gray-green eyes twinkling with amusement.

He looked good enough to eat. He'd taken a shower

between lovemaking sessions and hadn't bothered to put any product in his hair. It lay soft and silky against his skull, so much more attractive than his usual porcupine look. And his body! Lean and nicely toned, with the powerful legs of an athlete, his harsher angles smoothed by a dusting of very light blond hair. His cock jerked to life at her visual inspection, though he made no sexual overture.

"My little hellcat," he said with a fond smile, though it didn't take long for the smile to harden around the edges. "Have you changed your mind about Saint Eli?"

Her heart lurched in her chest. She was pissed at Eli right now for not seeing that on the scale of good and evil, Gabriel was no worse than Drake. Well, she mentally amended, perhaps a little worse, with that cruel streak of his, but not so much worse that he deserved to die while Drake deserved to live. But despite all that, she still respected Eli, respected his mission, and respected his judgment about everyone except Gabriel.

She shrugged as casually as possible and turned her back as she plopped the phone down on the coffee table.

"He's being a hypocrite," she said, "happy to avail himself of your services when convenient."

"But that was Drake on the phone, not Eli."

"Yeah. So?"

Apparently not at all worried about what people in neighboring buildings might see through the open curtains, he trotted into the living room, still naked. "So, Eli would never in a million years ask for my help. He may be a hypocrite, but he's also a stubborn ass. He's already turned down my offer, and he's not going to change his mind. I suspect our friend Drake has something else in mind."

She bit her lip. Possibly true. But it was also possible that it was a trick. "So, are you going to call him back?"

Gabriel's eyes scanned up and down her body, and no amount of anxiety about Drake's motivations could stop the pulse of desire that throbbed between her legs the moment he looked at her.

The corners of his mouth tipped upward, as did other portions of his anatomy. "I might," he conceded, moving toward her at a predatory stalk. "But it isn't my first priority at the moment."

She giggled and put a chair between herself and him. "What, *again*?" she asked incredulously. "I've had battery-operated toys that have less stamina than you!"

She reached across their psychic connection and politely knocked on the doors of his mind. He invited her in with no hesitation, and she saw just how much he liked the image of her with her battery-operated toys. Then his mind filled with other images, creative uses that she'd never have thought of herself, and heat flooded her from head to toe.

"Tomorrow, we're going vibrator-shopping," she informed him, looking forward to enjoying the wicked possibilities.

"Anything you say, my sweet," he agreed amiably. Then his power wrapped around her, lifted her off her feet, and sailed her straight into his waiting arms.

18

Bartolomeo's mortal servants had been busy during the daylight hours, renting a fixer-upper of a warehouse on the banks of the Delaware. The place was a mess, with cracked windows, rusted fixtures, and crumbling mortar. Pigeons had made themselves at home in the rafters, leaving their telltale calling cards splattered everywhere.

But the warehouse was a standalone building, and none of the nearby buildings were exactly bustling centers of activity. Also, there were several convenient observation posts available, so that someone could watch the building on all sides if necessary. A watcher could even see the river side of the building, thanks to a helpful pier that jutted out into the water about a block away.

The perfect setting for a trap. Now, it was time to bait it.

Camille sat in the back seat of the car while Bartolomeo's entourage surveyed the surroundings to make sure no prying mortal eyes would see them. Camille could have saved them the trouble—a psychic probe had shown the area completely deserted except for themselves—but Bartolomeo seemed to think the inspection necessary. Perhaps simply because it appealed to his sense of self-importance.

Between them sat the child that Camille had lured away from the playground last night. Her hands were bound behind her, and a gag cut tightly into the corners of her mouth. The *Maître* had his arm around her, as if trying to comfort her, but Camille knew he was merely soaking in the luxury of her fear. While he lacked the equipment to indulge in his own particular brand of perversion, he had enjoyed the experience vicariously through one of his fledglings.

Disgusting creatures, both of them, but she would tolerate them a little longer. Just long enough to get Eli where she wanted him.

When his entourage declared the coast clear, Bartolomeo, Camille, and the child made their way into the stinking, stiflingly hot warehouse. The sun had gone down two hours ago, but with no climate control, the building had absorbed the heat and held it trapped. Sweat dewed Camille's face moments after she'd stepped inside.

The inside of the warehouse was empty, save for the few items Bartolomeo had ordered his servants to acquire. In the center of the floor sat a four-poster bed, each post fitted with adjustable restraints. Bartolomeo dragged the struggling girl to the bed. He could have stilled her struggles with glamour, but chose brute force instead. The little whimpering sounds that escaped the girl's throat made the minions' eyes glow with pleasure, and made Camille vaguely sick to her stomach.

If she had her way, they would take a few pictures to send to Gabriel, then they would put the child out of her misery. But somehow, she didn't think she would be getting her way.

When the child was secured, Bartolomeo lay down on the bed beside her, propping his head on his hand and draping one of his legs over her midsection. Tears drenched her cheeks, and her eyes showed white all around.

Camille swallowed her revulsion and flipped open her

camera phone. The lighting was terrible, even with the spot-light the minions focused on the bed. Bartolomeo grabbed the girl's chin and turned her head to face the camera. Camille snapped the picture and was pleased to discover it came out just fine, despite the poor lighting.

Then, Bartolomeo summoned his pedophile fledgling to the bed, just to prove this was more than an empty threat. The fledgling positioned himself on top of the girl, then leaned his face closed to hers and licked her cheek. Camille snapped another picture, this one more heart-rending than the last with the child's face squinched up in disgust. She nodded in satisfaction.

"Yes, I'm quite sure these pictures will bring my son running to the rescue," she said.

Bartolomeo rolled off the bed. His fledgling remained behind.

Camille took the *Maître*'s offered elbow and let him lead her from the building. "How long do you plan to keep Gabriel alive once we have him?" she asked.

Bartolomeo laughed, an evil sound if ever there was one. "Until he's broken or I'm tired of playing, whichever comes first."

She touched her tongue to her upper lip, debating briefly whether this was the time to discuss the idea this trap for Gabriel had spawned in her head. But Bartolomeo was in an uncommonly jolly mood at the moment, so she decided to proceed.

"I have a proposition for you," she said.

Playing the gentleman, he opened the car door for her. She slid in, and he followed. His driver closed the door, then rounded the front of the car to take his own seat.

"What might that be?" the *Maître* asked.

"In his own way, Eli is as sentimental as Gabriel. Actu-ally, more so. I'm sure Gabriel's presence in his city has caused him no end of annoyance, and I'm sure he's doing his best to hunt him down and kill him."

"Your point being?"

"I'm getting there. Eli had the chance to kill Gabriel once before and found he couldn't do it. I suspect he'd find the will to finish things now. But I also suspect it would twist a knife in his gut to see Gabriel suffer."

Bartolomeo made an impatient sound. "I thought you said you were getting to the point."

I'd get there faster if you'd stop interrupting, she thought. "I believe the same trap we're setting for Gabriel might work for Eli. We could torture Gabriel for years, and he could survive anything we did to him. Heal any injury we caused him." She smiled her most unpleasant smile. "Regrow anything we cut off."

Bartolomeo's eyes glowed at that thought.

"Eli might be able to stand by and see Gabriel killed. But were we to show him evidence of just what we were doing to his precious boy, I suspect he'd throw all his scruples to the side and come charging to the rescue."

"Hmm," Bartolomeo mused. "Is he really that much of a fool?"

She thought about it a moment. Remembered all the trouble Eli had gone through over the centuries to protect Gabriel, even though they had never exactly seen eye to eye. And she knew in her heart that Eli could never stand to see his son suffer, not if he thought he could do something about it.

"Yes, *Maître.* He is. And he's so sure of his own power that even if he knows he's walking into a trap, he will firmly believe that he can escape it."

Bartolomeo nodded. "The idea has possibilities."

Camille wasn't sure that was a "yes," but for the moment she would bide her time. They had to catch Gabriel first. Then, she could concentrate on her real target.

WHEN DRAKE CALLED JEZ'S phone for the third time in two hours, Gabriel finally decided to talk to him. He could see from the look in her eyes when she handed him the phone that Jez had long ago gotten over her fit of pique

about the request for aid and was now hoping Gabriel would
ride in on his white horse to save the day.

It showed how clouded her judgment was.

"So," he said into the phone, watching Jez out of the corner of his eye, "you've gotten tired of being Eli's little yes-
man."

Drake hid whatever annoyance he might have felt fairly
well. "I'm looking to make a practical alliance to get some
dangerous Killers out of our city. Eli can't see straight where
you're concerned. I can."

Gabriel laughed. "So you're calling me to appeal to my
better nature? Delusions about me seem to be contagious."
He caught Jezebel's sharp glance, but didn't acknowledge
it. The last time he'd made love to her, he'd felt the cracks in
his defenses spreading and widening. Amazing how much
damage one little slip of a girl could do in just a few hours.
At first, he'd convinced himself he could hold out at least a
few days, could enjoy her in his bed and by his side just a
little longer before his defenses crumbled completely.

Now, he knew he didn't have the luxury of time. He had
to stop the bleeding, and fast, before he gave her the power
to destroy him completely. And there was no better way to
shore up the walls of his defenses than to remind her just
what kind of a man he was.

"You called a truce because this Killer, this Bartolomeo
di Cesare, is such a monster even *you* can't stomach him,"
Drake continued. "If that's the case, then I hardly think an
appeal to your so-called better nature is necessary. You and
I both want the same thing—to see him dead. We can help
each other."

Gabriel snorted. "Even if I were inclined to help the
Guardians, why should I team up with you? I can kick your
ass without breaking a sweat, and my mother and Bartolomeo would find you similarly inconsequential. You have
nothing I need."

"I have knowledge of the city. Knowledge from *this* century. And I have decades of experience as a hunter."

Again, Gabriel laughed. "I was hunting centuries before you were born. Try a new angle."

"You've hunted mortals. Any mortal would do. You weren't hunting for a *specific* mortal, nor have you hunted for a *specific* vampire. It's a different skill."

"Be that as it may. I didn't come here as a philanthropist. If Eli doesn't want my help against di Cesare, then he can take him on himself. I'll stay true to my word and stay out of your way. But I will not hunt him, and if you find him, he's all yours."

"Gabriel—" Jez interrupted, but he silenced her with a glare.

"I was under the impression that you wanted to see this man dead," Drake said.

Gabriel shrugged, though of course Drake couldn't see it. "I divested him of the equipment he would need to commit the worst of his atrocities. Perhaps living without his cock and balls is punishment enough."

Jez looked at him with obvious reproach, but she wisely didn't try to interrupt again.

Drake made a growling sound on the other end of the line. "You wouldn't have offered Eli your help in the first place if you didn't—"

"If Eli wants my help, he can fucking ask me himself!" Gabriel's fangs descended, and he didn't even try to control his temper. "I offered my help, and he laughed in my face. Well, to hell with him! Let *him* deal with the consequences of having di Cesare and friends making themselves at home in his city."

"I'm not Eli," Drake said, trying to sound reasonable. It didn't take a genius to hear the anger that shaded his reasonable tone.

"That's the point, you fool. If Eli asks for my help, I'll help. But if he's just going to sit around behind his fence with his head up his ass, then it's his problem."

"Look, I know you have every right to be angry with him, but—"

Gabriel hung up before Drake could finish the sentence. He thrust the phone back toward Jez. "If he calls again, I'm not talking to him."

She took the phone from him, looking at him with a wary expression he hadn't seen in days. "Don't you think—"

"No!" he snarled, baring his teeth at her. He felt a faint vibration over the psychic line that connected them and snarled again. "And get the fuck out of my head!"

She jerked backward, her eyes filling with hurt and shock. His first instinct was to apologize and gather her up into his arms. He fought that instinct, slamming shut his mental doors, making sure she'd see no sign of remorse. When he took a step toward her, she took a corresponding step back. And right that moment, no matter how unreasonable it might be, he hated her for it.

This is exactly what you want, he told himself. He wanted to get her head out of the clouds, wanted her to see who he really was, not who she wanted him to be. Naturally, if she saw that, she would draw away. Only the worst kind of fool would harbor tender feelings toward him as he really was.

He reached out with his glamour and forced her eyes to meet his as he stood toe to toe with her.

"There are to be no illusions between us, my sweet," he said, his tone rough and harsh as sandpaper. "I am not the white knight, come to save the day. I am here to torment and, if possible, kill my father."

A tear dribbled down her cheek, and he fought the urge to kiss it away. It wasn't only himself he was protecting by shoving this brutal spoonful of reality down her throat. He was hurting her now, but he'd hurt her far worse if he let her continue looking at him through rose-colored glasses.

He curled his lip up in a nasty sneer. "We've had some good times together. And I will admit to feeling a certain fondness for you. But don't you dare to question me again. I might not particularly enjoy hurting you, but don't fool yourself into thinking I won't do it if you disobey me."

He let up on the glamour, and Jezebel hurried to put some

distance between them, her eyes glistening with tears as she averted her gaze. The sight of her hurt was like a knife in his gut. If he didn't get out of here, his resolve was going to crumble and he'd end up giving her yet another set of mixed signals.

"I'm going for a walk," he announced.

He pushed past her without a backward glance and slammed the door when he left.

FOR ABOUT FIFTEEN MINUTES after Gabriel had left, Jez sat on the couch with her face buried in her hands, fighting sobs.

She understood him too well not to see what he was doing, not to see that he was willfully erecting walls between them because their connection tonight had scared the shit out of him. But she saw more than that. She saw the well of bitterness and anger inside him. For a few hours, he'd let that anger slip away, had allowed himself to feel what she felt sure was genuine joy. But the anger was still there, five hundred years' worth, and it was a foe too great for her to battle.

Still sniffling and wiping her eyes, she got up off the couch and hurried to the bedroom to pack up the few belongings she'd brought with her. It would be dawn in an hour or so, but she suspected she'd be able to get to Eli's with time to spare. Assuming he was still willing to shelter her after her deceit.

She made a quick phone call on her way out and was relieved beyond measure when Eli assured her she was still welcome.

All the way to Eli's, she kept hoping that Gabriel would leap out of the shadows, beg her to stay with him and promise not to explode like that again.

It was just as well he didn't. Any promise of change he might make would be short-lived, at best. It would be just like the times her mother had promised to stop drinking. She'd really meant it at the time she said it, had every intention of turning her life around and becoming a good mother. Those good intentions had amounted to nothing.

People didn't change—one of life's hard lessons that she had to learn to live with. But oh, how she wished the fairy tale were true and the kind-hearted soul could tame the savage beast.

19

GABRIEL WAITED UNTIL AFTER the sun came up to return to his apartment. He wasn't positive he could stand firm in the face of Jezebel's hurt and disillusionment, so like a coward he'd stayed away until he was sure she'd be asleep.

He wasn't in the least bit tired, but he felt inexorably drawn to her, so within five minutes of returning home, he headed toward the bedroom. He'd taken two full steps into the room before his mind registered its emptiness.

He came to a halt, his heart lurching in his chest. His first thought was that Brigitte had returned to take out what she saw as her "competition," and the horror of that idea was like a thousand lead weights collapsing on his shoulders. How could he have been so self-centered, to have left Jezebel alone and undefended when he knew Brigitte could get into his apartment?

Even when he saw the sheet of paper sitting on the bedspread, he thought it must be some sort of ransom note. It wasn't until he'd forced his heavy feet to move and picked up the note that he realized what had really happened.

Jezebel had left him.

The desolation that slammed into him at that thought was like nothing he'd ever felt before. His knees wobbled beneath him, and he sat heavily on the edge of the bed, Jezebel's short note clutched in his fingers.

You asked for this, you fool, he reminded himself as the pain threatened to crush him. No, he hadn't thought things through enough to consider that his earlier outburst might make her leave him, but he had wanted to put distance between them. His plan had succeeded, had worked better than he could possibly have hoped. He should be rejoicing that he'd gotten out in time, before she had the power to destroy him.

The ache in his heart suggested that maybe he hadn't gotten out in time after all. A lump formed in his throat, but he swallowed it down. No matter how much this hurt, it was for the best. Jezebel would be safer and happier without him. And if this feeling that overwhelmed him was anything like that elusive, unfamiliar emotion of love, then he should be selflessly looking out for her best interests instead of his own.

His fingers curled in on themselves, crushing the note. Selflessness had never been one of his virtues. Even knowing she was better off without him, he had to fight the urge to go after her. It helped when he considered the likelihood that she'd fled to Eli's house, rather than back to her own apartment.

"What's done is done," he said aloud, trying to convince himself.

His cell phone rang. Hope surged in his chest, hope that it was Jezebel calling to say she'd made a terrible mistake and wanted to come back. Hope that died even before he'd pulled the phone from his pocket, because, of course, she wouldn't be awake at this hour.

He flipped open the phone, and a lump of fear formed in his gut when he saw the caller ID. It was his mother. Had she somehow gotten her claws on Jezebel? If she had, he would kill her without a second thought.

Steeling himself, trying to get his tempestuous emotions under control, he answered the phone.

"Why, hello, Mother dear," he said, his tone betraying none of his turmoil. "I hear tell you missed me so much you've come all the way to Philadelphia to be near me again."

"Yes, my son," she answered, her voice as oily as his. "And I'm so anxious to see you again that I've arranged a little party in your honor. Let me send you a picture of just what I have set up for you."

The hand that wasn't holding the phone was clenched into a white-knuckled fist, and he hoped his heart wasn't beating so loud that his mother could hear it over the phone. If she had hurt a single hair on Jezebel's head, he would see her—

He looked at the picture on his phone, and for half a second was flooded with relief that it wasn't Jez. Then, his mind made sense of the image he was seeing, and nausea roiled in his stomach. Another picture filled the small screen, this time showing the poor child covered by the body of an unfamiliar man who was licking her cheek.

"She's a pretty little thing, isn't she?" Camille's voice warbled over the phone.

He raised the phone back to his ear, too sick even to manage a comeback.

"Thanks to your handiwork," Camille continued, "Bartolomeo can't enjoy her as much as he would have once, but he seems to get a great deal of pleasure out of watching his fledgling—"

"I knew you were a sick bitch, and I knew you'd teamed up with di Cesare, but I never imagined you had sunk this low."

She laughed, sounding genuinely amused. "If the girl were a vampire, you'd have found the sight so exciting you'd be fondling yourself at the moment."

He flinched, hating that she'd managed to shoot a barb past his defenses. But no, she was wrong. If there was one thing Jezebel had done for him, it was to make him see that he wasn't the cold-blooded sadist he'd once thought he was.

"But of course," Camille continued, "the girl is not a vampire. She's merely a pretty mortal child. I believe Bartolomeo and his man will continue to find her entertaining for another day or so. After that, they'll want some variety. I'm sure we can find another lovely little girl for them to enjoy when they've used this one up."

Words stuck in Gabriel's throat. He couldn't think of a single thing to say, couldn't think of a curse vile enough to hurl at her.

How had he allowed himself to serve her for as long as he had? As soon as Eli had cast them out of Philadelphia, Camille had been free to indulge the taste for cruelty Eli had kept firmly in check. She'd tormented her victims, hurt and frightened them beyond what was necessary in order to feed. And she'd frequently allowed her fledglings to "play" with them before she actually fed.

And Gabriel had stood by and let it happen, out of some twisted, misplaced sense of loyalty. A fist clenched around his heart. No, not just out of loyalty. Out of the pathetic illusion that she was the one person who could love a monster like himself.

Which one of them was the most sick, and the most sickening?

"I take it you are unmoved by the poor child's plight?" Camille asked.

Hate crystallized in Gabriel's chest. "I made a terrible mistake when I allowed you to live. That isn't a mistake I'll make a second time."

Once more, she laughed at him. "Do you think you can manage it, my son? I'm not alone, you know."

He bared his teeth in a feral snarl, wishing she could see it, sure that even in her supreme confidence, that expression would shake something deep inside her. "Were you alone when I took your eight fledglings apart limb by limb in front of you?" he asked. He'd thought he'd broken her at the time. She had tried so hard to control him, to stop the slaughter, and her glamour had barely slowed him down.

"But they were merely fledglings. My allies at the moment are considerably more potent. Let's have it out, shall we, dear boy? A showdown of epic proportions. You all by your little lonesome, against me and Bartolomeo and our friends. It ought to be most entertaining, don't you think?"

Gabriel hesitated. No vampire of Camille's power or age would offer up anything like a fair fight. Camille and Bartolomeo had to know they were no match for him. But perhaps they were expecting Brigitte and her fledgling to fight on their side? Brigitte had claimed she would neither help nor hinder his mother's cause, but she could well have been lying. And she'd already proven herself a formidable foe.

But perhaps it didn't matter. He couldn't stand by and do nothing while Camille and di Cesare made a sickening feast of the city's children. He could hope that he was more than a match for anything they would throw his way, but if he wasn't . . .

He shrugged. Hating how pathetic it sounded even to himself, he had to admit that the world might be a better place without him in it.

"Very well," he said. "Let's have this showdown of ours. Where and when shall we get together to try to kill one another?"

"Tonight at midnight seems an appropriate appointment, don't you think? If you have a piece of paper handy, I'll give you the address."

Heart and mind both blessedly numb, Gabriel wrote down the address she gave him.

JEZ SUFFERED A MOMENT of disorientation when she first woke up. She wasn't in the familiar double bed in her apartment, nor was she in Gabriel's plush king-sized bed, with his body warm beside her. A hint of alarm tingled in her blood, warning her that something bad had happened, warning her that she didn't want to wake up and remember where she was or why.

She tried to burrow more deeply under the covers, tried to let sleep take her again, but the shot of adrenaline the worry caused made that impossible. Hard though she tried to hold the memory off, it came crashing down on her again.

She'd walked out on Gabriel.

Tears stung her eyes. She bit her lip hard and told herself she was *not* going to cry about this anymore. Yes, she was the one who'd physically done the leaving, but not until after he had slammed the metaphorical door in her face.

Groaning and rubbing her eyes, she sat up. She opened her mental shields, searching tentatively for her connection with her maker, but though she found the line that connected them, she couldn't travel along it, couldn't penetrate the shields he'd erected around himself. If she'd hoped to find him open and pleading for her to return to him, she was sorely disappointed.

A long hot shower cleared her head somewhat, though it didn't make her feel any less miserable. When she couldn't delay it any longer, she trudged down the stairs and into the library, looking for Eli. She'd arrived so close to dawn this morning that she hadn't had much of a chance to talk with him. Now, it was time to face the music, as well as time to let him know some of the secrets Gabriel had been hiding from him all these years.

He was reading a book when she entered the library, or at least he was pretending to. She knew he'd felt her coming long before she'd walked through the door. He slid a bookmark between the pages of the antique-looking hardback, then set it down on a side table and looked up at her, his expression carefully neutral.

Taking a deep breath, she sat in a comfortable chair across from him and tried to relax. The fact that he'd let her stay here last night was a good sign, a sign that he would forgive her for her betrayal. Still, despite all the reasons why she hadn't had a choice in the matter, she couldn't help the guilt that clung to her like sticky cobwebs.

"For what it's worth," she said, looking at the floor instead of at him, "I'm really sorry I lied to you."

Eli's only answer was a soft grunt that could have meant anything.

"He promised me that he wouldn't kill anyone," she continued.

"And you believed him?" His voice was as neutral as his face, giving away nothing of what he thought or felt.

Jez forced herself to meet his eyes, her chin stubbornly raised. "Yes, I believed him. If for no other reason than because he made me work so hard to drag a promise out of him." She suspected there was more to it than that, that her deepest instincts had spoken to her from the very beginning and told her he wasn't as he appeared. But that was something she doubted Eli would understand.

Eli sighed. "I'd like to promise the Guardians will welcome you back with open arms, but I doubt that's the case. Once upon a time, my word was law. Gabriel has weakened my authority."

Anger pulsed through her veins. "Don't put this all on his shoulders! You may not have lied outright, but you've certainly deceived everyone about a lot of things for a long time. Maybe if you'd been honest from the beginning—"

"If you're planning to take me to task for my mistakes, then perhaps you would prefer to sleep under your own roof from now on." Eli's eyes flashed and his jaw clenched.

Jez swallowed her own indignation. Most likely she would be compelled to leave the Guardians and take care of herself eventually, but with Brigitte out there potentially regarding her as a rival, and with Camille and di Cesare seeing her as bait, she really didn't want it to be now.

Another deep breath helped calm some of her anger, though she wasn't about to apologize for what she'd said. "There are some things I think you should know about

Gabriel," she said. "Things I'm sure he'd rather I didn't tell you, but maybe they'll make you understand him better."

Curiosity and irritation warred on Eli's face. Apparently, curiosity won. "Such as?"

She rubbed her hands nervously up and down her pants legs. "Such as, our bond is different from the usual bond between master and fledgling. We can communicate telepathically, and sometimes we feel each other's thoughts over the connection. I've been in his head for both of his kills."

The lines around Eli's eyes and mouth tightened. "You've already established that they were potentially killers themselves."

But she shook her head. "Not potentially. Gabriel didn't know either of them. He picked each of them out from a crowd. I don't completely understand it, but there's something about his power that lets him sense these people."

"I hardly—"

Jez ignored the interruption. "When he bites them, he shares their memories. They were both guilty, Eli. And it wasn't just that he suspected they were, he *knew*. That's how he's always picked his victims."

She could read the doubt on Eli's face. "If that were truly the case, he would have said so," Eli argued.

She shook her head, not at all sure he'd be able to understand. Her hands had curled into fists in her lap, and she forced them to relax. "You always disapproved of him, and it hurt him more than he could ever admit. So he let you think he was a heartless Killer because he couldn't have borne the pain if he'd told you he wasn't and you'd still disapproved of him."

Why she was bothering to tell Eli any of this, she wasn't sure. She'd already established in her own mind that the rift between father and son was irreparable. And she'd established that it wasn't her job to try to repair it. So why didn't she just keep her mouth shut?

Eli sat there and stared at her, his thoughts hidden behind

his impassive face and dispassionate eyes. Jez clenched her teeth and fought the urge to argue her case any further.

Finally, Eli looked away. "You're in love with him, aren't you?" he asked, sucking the air out of her lungs.

Was that what she felt for Gabriel? Love? Certainly the pain she felt at leaving him would suggest a depth of feeling she hadn't allowed herself to acknowledge before. But was that feeling truly love?

"Maybe," she admitted. "But he loves his anger more than he loves me." And for once in her life, she'd decided she deserved better.

Eli nodded sagely. "Very well, then. I'll give you shelter for as long as you need it. But I will restrict you to your room whenever the Guardians meet here. Tensions are running high and I'd prefer not to spark them."

Jez ground her teeth. "You don't actually think you're fooling me, do you? You want to lock me in my room so that I don't overhear your latest plan to kill Gabriel and warn him about it."

He didn't bother to deny it. "As long as he insists on remaining in Philadelphia to torment me, he is under a death sentence. When he gets frustrated and angry enough, there's a good chance he will start killing Guardians, and that I won't allow."

Jez bit her lip to keep from arguing, though she was sure deep down in her gut that Eli was wrong. No, she didn't think Gabriel was going to let go of his vendetta any time soon. But as tough as he talked, he wasn't going to start killing the good guys just to get back at his father.

When Eli dismissed her, she tried one more time to reach across the psychic connection to touch Gabriel's thoughts. But the doors of his mind were locked and barred against her.

20

GABRIEL DIDN'T HAVE DRAKE'S cell phone number, nor did he know exactly where the Killer lived, but thanks to Jezebel he knew the general vicinity. From there, it was a relatively simple matter to seek out the psychic footprint of the only century-old vampire in the neighborhood.

Drake lived in a quaint old brownstone in Society Hill. Gabriel climbed the three stairs to the front door, then rang the doorbell.

He felt Drake's cautious approach, and for a moment thought he might have to unlock the door and let himself in. But Drake had to know he couldn't keep Gabriel out, so he opened the door and leaned against the jamb.

"Well," he said, raising an eyebrow, "I wasn't expecting to see *you* on my doorstep after our conversation last night."

Gabriel shrugged. "In all honesty, I don't want to be here. But I'm potentially going to my death tonight.

"I've got a rendezvous with Camille and di Cesare," he continued, watching Drake's eyes widen in surprise. "We've decided to get together and try to kill each other like civilized people."

Drake snorted a laugh. "And you've decided to accept my offer of aid after all?"

Gabriel shook his head. "You'd be out of your league, old son." Drake would be more of a hindrance than a help, Gabriel was sure. "But I do have a favor to ask of you."

Again, Drake laughed. "You're a piece of work! Why on earth would you think I'd want to do you a favor?"

The tone caused Gabriel's fists to clench, but he managed to keep his own voice calm and level, even as his lip curled in distaste. "Because I think you're a basically decent fellow, and because you know what it's like to be on the outside looking in." Drake looked like he was about to say something, but Gabriel cut him off. "Jezebel has gone back to Eli's," he said. "I suspect Eli will forgive her because he knows she had no choice but to do as I ordered, but I doubt she'll get the same understanding from the rest of the Guardians."

Drake cocked his head, no longer looking wary or amused. "Just what are you asking me to do?"

"Just . . ." Gabriel's voice almost gave out on him, his throat tightening at the sense of loss. He cleared his throat. "Just keep an eye out for her, will you? I know Eli won't let anything happen to her while she's at his house, but once she returns home . . ." He shrugged, sure he'd made his point even if he hadn't been as articulate as he might have liked.

Drake nodded slowly. "All right. I'll look after her." He grinned. "At least, as much as she'll let me."

Gabriel returned the grin, though it felt strained. He had a feeling Jez wouldn't accept anywhere near as much help as she needed, but that would have to be her decision.

"Thank you," he said. He nodded briefly, then started down the stairs.

"Gabriel."

He stopped at the bottom of the stairs and turned to face Drake once again. "Yes?"

Drake straightened up, then descended a couple of steps, holding out his hand. "Good luck."

Strangely moved by the gesture, Gabriel shook the Killer's hand. "Thank you. Again."

CAMILLE FELT LIKE A sitting duck. Which, in many ways, she was. Bartolomeo and his fledglings were waiting for her call, on the other side of town, well out of reach of Gabriel's vampire senses. She was alone in the warehouse, except for the frightened little girl who was still tied to the bed.

If Gabriel charged in like an enraged bull, she'd be dead before she even knew he was here. But no, there was little chance of that. He was far too old to be incautious. And while he might hold her in some amount of contempt, he would not make the mistake of thinking her stupid. He would sense in her solitary presence a trap, and he would proceed accordingly.

In the darkness of the deserted industrial neighborhood, the tripwire that stretched across the bottom of the warehouse door was invisible, even to Camille, who knew it was there. All she had to do was lure Gabriel inside. She leaned into a tiny patch of moonlight, glancing at her watch. It was almost midnight. He would be here soon.

The child had fallen asleep, exhausted by her ordeal. Camille prodded her awake and removed the gag. A few childish whimpers ought to help ensure that Gabriel would enter the warehouse.

It took very little effort to induce the girl to comply.

DRAKE SAT IN THE library, with Eli and Jezebel. He'd debated whether to tell them of Gabriel's visit, but it had been a brief debate. If nothing else, Eli should know that Gabriel was planning to do battle with Camille and di Cesare tonight.

Jez had taken to pacing across the room, her eyes swimming with worry as she chewed her lower lip raw. Eli watched her pace and said nothing. The tension in the room was as thick and oppressive as the humid summer night.

"They wouldn't have agreed to fight him if they didn't think they had an ace in the hole," Jez muttered, voicing what they all knew to be true. She turned to Eli. "He *has* to know that. And yet he's going anyway."

There was an accusatory tone in her voice, and the hardness in Eli's eyes said he heard it.

"His feud with di Cesare predates his feud with me," Eli said, his voice milder than his expression.

Neither Jez's voice nor her expression could be called anything like mild as she threw up her hands in disgust. "He's right! No matter *what* he does, you're determined to see him in the worst possible light!"

"Jezebel—"

She put her fists on her hips and glared at him, too angry to be as circumspect as she should have been. Tears glimmered in her eyes, but didn't fall. "You should be helping him, Eli! He shouldn't be going out there to face them alone. And no matter what you tell yourself, he's not going out to fight them just because he hates them more than he hates you. He's doing your fucking job!"

Drake felt his jaw drop open, then quickly snapped it shut. No one talked to Eli like that. Not if they wanted to live.

Predictably, the room was growing cold.

Drake had promised Gabriel he'd look after Jez, but he hadn't expected to be trying to protect her from Eli. Or from herself, for that matter. Still, he could see that she'd completely lost the reins on her temper, and if he didn't intervene, she was going to dig the hole deeper. With a silent apology, he reached out with his glamour and stilled her.

It was harder than it should have been, considering she was such a young fledgling, and she wasn't a Killer. She glared furiously at Eli.

"Don't glare at *him*," Drake said. "*I'm* the one holding you."

Her eyes narrowed to slits as she turned her head toward

him. He had to suppress a shiver. She shouldn't have been able to turn her head, not with his glamour holding her.

Was it all a lie? Was Jez actually a Killer? But even if she were a Killer, she shouldn't have been able to resist him when he was so much older.

He hoped his face didn't reveal how unnerving he found that single small gesture.

"Having a temper tantrum isn't going to help anything," he told her. "Gabriel would be pissed as hell if you got yourself hurt or killed defending his honor to Eli."

Now it was Eli's turn to glare at Drake. "I had no intention of hurting or killing her, as I'm sure you know."

Drake met his stare steadily. "Once upon a time, I thought I knew you. But I didn't." The words felt like a lead weight on his soul. "You're willing to abandon everything you believe in just because you're pissed at Gabriel. You're not the man I once thought you were."

Eli blinked, like he didn't know what to do with that statement. His expression still gave little away, but there was a hint of a crack in his façade. The room had warmed up, so no matter how much he didn't like what Drake was saying, he was apparently not reacting with anger.

That increased the odds that Drake would live through saying his piece.

"Fletcher was right about me," he said. "The people I kill may be scum, but they are still people. I'm a murderer many times over, just like Gabriel. And just like you." Eli actually flinched at that. "And even your Guardians are murderers. How many have they killed since you founded the Guardians?"

"They've destroyed Killers!"

"Yes," Drake agreed promptly, "they've killed very bad people. Just like I have. And, apparently, just like Gabriel has. The only difference is that Gabriel and I kill mortals, while the Guardians kill vampires."

Eli shook his head violently, though the troubled expression on his face showed that Drake's words were having an effect. "You are not like Gabriel!" he argued. "Maybe you're right, and the mortals he has killed over the centuries have been reprehensible human beings all. But he also takes pleasure in torturing his victims."

"No, he doesn't!" Jezebel said.

Again, Drake had to suppress a shudder. He hadn't released her from his glamour. At least, not consciously. But she'd shaken him off completely. He didn't dare try to hold her again and find out he couldn't.

Drake and Eli both turned to stare at her.

"If he had just killed di Cesare instead of stopping to torture him, then we wouldn't be having this discussion right now," Eli argued.

Jez dismissed that with a wave. "I didn't say he hasn't hurt people. And I didn't say I approve of it. What I'm saying is he doesn't really enjoy it. He just thinks it's justice. An Old Testament, eye for an eye kind of justice, but that's what it is to him. It's not about getting his jollies."

"I'm sure his victims would be most comforted to know that."

The look in Jezebel's eyes suggested she was about to take her life in her hands again, so Drake jumped in.

"Arguing about this is pointless," he said. "Eli, you're not going to convince Jez that Gabriel's the anti-Christ. And Jez, you're not going to convince Eli that he's an avenging angel. There's nothing we can do to help or hurt him right this moment. So why don't we all just shut up so we don't hurt each other anymore."

To his surprise and relief, both Jez and Eli backed down. But how long would the peace last?

GABRIEL HAD THE CAB drop him off a good four blocks from the rendezvous point. He wanted to get the lay of the land before he approached. He quickly sensed the psychic footprint of a vampire in the direction of the address he'd been given. A quick examination showed a vampire of eight hundred years, which he assumed was his mother. He focused his senses on her, sweeping around her in ever-increasing circles. He found a mortal, very close to her.

And then nothing. Sparks of mortality flickered here and there in the nearby buildings, but the area directly around where Camille awaited him was devoid of life.

What was she up to? She couldn't possibly hope to defeat him alone. And yet, there was nowhere her cohorts could hide from his psychic survey.

Using his unique ability to mask his presence, he slowly made his way toward the rendezvous, all his senses, psychic and otherwise, on full alert. And still he felt nothing, no sign of life anywhere near where Camille awaited him.

Wishing he had some idea what her game was, knowing it had to be a trap of some sort, he walked into it anyway.

The address where Camille had told him to meet her was a decrepit-looking warehouse on the river front. He inspected the building for a good five or ten minutes, hiding in the shadows, hoping to spot the trap. But he saw nothing.

Most of the windows were boarded over, and those that weren't were broken and cracked. The building looked like it hadn't been used in at least a decade. But, he supposed that's why Camille and friends had chosen it. No prying mortal eyes to get in the way.

Facing the river was a loading dock, but the massive metal doors there were locked and barred. A smaller door off to the side stood open, an invitation.

If he could have found a different door, Gabriel would have used it for the surprise factor. He even considered entering through one of the windows, but the only ones he could get through would require him to levitate, smash out the remaining glass, and then jump through and land without hurting himself. By the time he did all that, the surprise factor would be gone.

Not sure what else to do, he reached out with his glamour and took hold of Camille. He felt her feeble attempt to fight him off, but he brushed her aside as easily as a mortal would swat a mosquito.

Camille, fighting and stumbling the whole way, moved to stand in the doorway, where the glow of a street light could illuminate her face. Her eyes were wide and frightened-looking, her pulse racing. His nostrils flared at the scent of fear in the air.

This made no sense. If she was so afraid, why was she waiting for him here alone? He took a couple of steps closer.

"What are you playing at, Mother?" he asked, cocking his head at her.

"I'm the bait," she said, her voice wobbling slightly. "I'm to call Bartolomeo and his men when you've arrived. They didn't want any chance that you would sense their numbers and decide not to come. I told them you weren't such a coward, but . . ." She shrugged.

Gabriel laughed derisively. "Is this like one of those horror movies? 'Gee, a horrible monster is hunting us and trying to kill us. Let's split up?' "

She visibly swallowed hard. "They figure I'm expendable," she said.

His fangs slid down. "Funny, I feel the same way about you." He let up on his glamour and took a step toward her.

Camille took a couple of hasty steps back, holding her hands up as if to ward him off. "Think about this a minute. If you kill me, I won't be able to call them. Bartolomeo will get away."

She kept retreating, her heart beating loudly enough that he could hear it. He cracked his knuckles, a feral grin on his face.

"I guess I'll just have to persuade you to make the call before I kill you," he answered.

He took two giant strides toward her, his glamour halting her retreat. She made a small whimpering sound in the back of her throat as he crossed the threshold into the darkened interior of the warehouse.

There was a soft popping noise, and then something sharp and stinging smacked his shoulder.

He took a giant step to the side, turning and searching for

his unseen adversary as he checked out the wound in his peripheral vision.

A nasty-looking little barb clung to his skin. A tranquilizer dart, he guessed. His brows drew together in puzzlement. Tranquilizers didn't work on vampires, so what the—

Camille was smiling at him, the fear gone from her eyes. He plucked the dart out, but the injection site hurt like the devil. He winced.

Camille moved closer to him. And that was when he realized his glamour wasn't holding her any longer.

Swaying on his feet, he tried to grab hold again. But the pain from the injection site was spreading, fire burning through his muscles. His legs buckled, and he fell to his knees.

Camille stepped closer, staying just out of reach. "It seems the European vampires have discovered a drug that can disable one of their own. A very convenient discovery, don't you think?"

He tried to answer back with a sarcastic, unworried quip, but his tongue felt thick in his throat and his brain stumbled on the words. The pain hammered at him, eating away at his strength until all he could do was lie still and clench his teeth while Camille gloated in victory.

21

JEZ HAD RETREATED TO the guest bedroom, needing to put some distance between herself and Eli. Father and son were more alike than either of them would like to admit, if in nothing else than their basic hard-headedness.

She wasn't entirely sure what to do with herself right now. There was a TV in the downstairs parlor, but this floor of the mansion had no such modern accouterments. And she hadn't had the foresight to grab a book while she was in the library.

She flopped onto the bed, rolling over onto her back and staring at the ceiling, trying not to think.

A sharp sting suddenly lanced through her shoulder, and she gasped. She slapped her hand over the sting, but could find no source for the pain. She sat up hastily and looked around the room, thinking surely there must be a bee or wasp flying around. But there wasn't, and the pain was spreading, a wave of stinging heat radiating out from the initial non-existent wound.

Heart thumping, she slipped off the bed and tried to stand up, but her knees buckled. What the hell was wrong with her?

Gabriel!

She stopped trying to stand, instead resting her back against the bed and closing her eyes. The pain kept getting worse, kept spreading. She forced deep, even breaths, shunting the pain aside as she reached across the psychic connection.

Gabriel? What's the matter? Where are you?

A vision flashed before her eyes. Camille, standing in a doorway, smiling in malicious triumph.

Jezebel.

Her whole body was shaking with the strain of holding the tenuous connection while fighting off the pain.

Where are you? she asked again.

Be safe, Jez, he responded.

And then he cut the psychic connection, like a door slamming shut between them.

"Gabriel!" she howled out loud. "Don't you dare shut me out!"

The pain was gone now, blocked out by Gabriel's barriers. She concentrated all her will on re-establishing the connection, but no matter how hard she pounded on that door, it remained firmly shut against her.

Damn, him! Damn him to Hell!

Tears streaked her cheeks. She wrapped her arms around her legs and let the sobs tear through her.

GABRIEL HAD NEVER FELT pain like this before, so all-encompassing, unrelenting. It pulsed through him with every beat of his heart, sapping his strength, bathing his body in sweat. He lay helpless on the warehouse floor as Camille called Bartolomeo and reported the success of their plan.

He kept trying to muster his glamour, but his mind refused to focus. It took all his mental resources just to keep Jez out of his head; the last thing he wanted was for her to come running to his rescue and get herself killed. And he certainly didn't want her sharing this pain!

It felt like hours that he lay there on the floor, incapable of movement, wondering how it could be possible he was still breathing when the pain was so overwhelming. Eventually, Bartolomeo di Cesare arrived. Gabriel heard him and Camille congratulating each other on a job well done, but then he tuned them out, closing his eyes.

A brutal kick to the injection site on his shoulder startled his eyes open. Di Cesare knelt beside him, eyes gleaming in malicious glee.

"Don't you want to hear what we have planned for you?" he asked.

"Fuck . . . you," Gabriel managed to gasp out.

Di Cesare laughed. "Is that the best you can do?" He laughed some more. "Maybe I can inspire you to be more creative."

Gabriel would have spat in his face, but his mouth was too dry. How he wished he'd killed the beast long ago. But when he'd seen what was left of the child di Cesare had kidnapped, a quick death had seemed far too good for him.

Perhaps if it hadn't been for his own sense of pity, he would have finished di Cesare off before his master came to the rescue. But the girl had been in such dreadful pain, her cries so piteous that Gabriel had to help her. He couldn't bring himself to kill her, even though his psychic senses were already refined enough to see from her aura that she wouldn't survive. But he'd spent a good half hour or so using his glamour to cloud her mind and kill the pain. At a hundred years old, he hadn't been powerful enough to keep di Cesare captive, ease the girl's pain, and carry out his punishment all at the same time.

Di Cesare slapped his face, lightly, just trying to bring his attention back.

"I'm very grateful to you for not killing me quickly when you had the chance," di Cesare said with a savage grin. "So grateful, in fact, that I'm going to do you the same favor. Let's see if you'll thank *me* for it some day." He gestured toward his henchmen. "Come hold him down," he said. "He won't have much fight in him, but I don't want him squirming around too much."

The henchmen did as ordered, one sitting on his legs, one holding his left arm down, one holding his right. Di Cesare drew a wicked-looking knife from a bag he'd laid on the floor beside him. He brandished the blade for a while, letting the light play along its edge.

"I had this specially made," he said, touching the blade with an almost loving caress. "It's steel, but with a very low iron content. It won't prevent you from regenerating." He sighed happily. "Just imagine how much fun we're going to have!"

Di Cesare put his hand over Gabriel's, tucking Gabriel's fingers into a fist. All except the index finger. He held the blade to the light again, making damn sure Gabriel knew what he was about to do.

Gabriel doubted the pain of losing the finger was going to be much worse than the pain that wracked him now. Even so, he shored up his mental defenses, making sure whatever he felt wouldn't leak over into Jez. Di Cesare set the blade against his finger, pressing down just hard enough to draw blood.

"Enjoying this so far?" he asked. His eyes gleamed with pleasure, and his cheeks were flushed with it. He pressed down a little harder, the blade slicing easily through skin and tissue until it hit bone.

Gabriel gritted his teeth, but though he felt the pain of that cut, it was nothing compared to whatever poison was coursing through his system. Di Cesare applied more and more pressure, the pain building steadily. Gabriel had to bite down on his tongue to keep from crying out.

As di Cesare must have intended, the anticipation made the pain that much worse. When would the pressure become too much? When would the knife slice through bone? Just how long was he going to make Gabriel wait?

Not much longer. Gabriel tasted blood in his mouth, having

bitten his tongue in his effort not to give di Cesare the satisfaction of crying out. But when bone gave way to steel, and
the knife clinked against the cement floor, a scream tore
from his throat despite his best efforts.

THEY GAVE GABRIEL ANOTHER shot of the "tranquilizer," just to be safe, and chained him to a pair of whipping
posts with cuffs and chains of iron, strong enough to burn
even Gabriel's age-toughened skin. The air stank of burning
flesh and hair.

Camille placed her son's severed finger in a cotton-lined
gift box, then closed the lid and handed the box to one of
Bartolomeo's mortals. Delivering it to Eli was something of
a challenge, as he would sense any vampire who came near
his house, and any mortal they sent wouldn't be able to see
the house in the first place. So she'd come up with the idea
of planting the box and having Eli send someone to pick it
up. The mortal was to drop the box in a trash can at Fifth
and Chestnut.

The mortal had just left the building when Brigitte arrived,
her faithful fledgling in tow. For the most part, Camille and
Bartolomeo had left her out of the planning, and she'd
seemed generally uninterested. Most of the time, they didn't
even know where Brigitte and Henri were. Camille would
have preferred it stayed that way.

Bartolomeo, predictably, started sweating.

Without a word, Brigitte came to stand in front of Gabriel,
looking him up and down with apparent admiration. She
touched a delicate finger to Gabriel's sweating chest, drawing a line down his sternum and along the line of hair that
disappeared into his pants. Gabriel tried to twist away, but of
course, he couldn't.

Brigitte giggled, then touched her tongue to that finger,
seemingly savoring the taste of his sweat. Camille wrinkled
her nose and wished the little bitch would just go away.
Brigitte circled the whipping posts, taking a slow survey.
When she'd completed the circle, she frowned.

"Here you've got him all nicely trussed up, stretched between the whipping posts, and yet he doesn't seem to have tasted the lash yet," she said.

Bartolomeo gestured to Gabriel's hand, where the finger was already starting to regrow. "I had other things in mind."

Brigitte nodded approvingly. "So I see." She blinked coquettishly. "But you do *have* a whip, don't you?"

Bartolomeo nodded toward the wooden chest that sat within easy reach of the posts. His mortals had been very busy indeed, combing the city and buying every instrument of torture they could find.

With the delighted squeal of a child at Christmas, Brigitte hurried to the box, flinging open the lid and rooting through the contents. Camille wished she understood what Brigitte was up to. After all, she'd suggested that she was coming to the U.S. to meet up with her fellow born vampire, her "kindred spirit." And yet, she seemed quite eager to join in Bartolomeo's fun.

When she found the whip, Brigitte touched her tongue to her upper lip, her cheeks slightly flushed. She rose and uncoiled the whip, letting it trail on the floor behind her as she walked up to Gabriel and smiled into his pain-filled eyes.

"You were rude to me and to Henri when we came to visit you," she said.

Camille couldn't restrain her start of surprise. Brigitte had visited Gabriel? When? And, more importantly, why? Bartolomeo gave every impression that he was about to ask these questions out loud, but Brigitte stopped him with no more than a casual glance.

"Shall I make you pay for it?" Brigitte asked, once again looking up at Gabriel, her fingers caressing the fall of the whip. He just glared at her, an expression that managed to chill Camille to the bone, even though it wasn't directed at her, even though the ferocity was overlaid with pain.

Brigitte reached up and patted his cheek. "But no," she said, tossing the whip aside. "I wouldn't want to put a damper on our friendship." She winked at him, then gave one of his nipples a quick, hard tweak. He hissed at her, but she just laughed. Beckoning Henri to follow, she headed back out into the night.

Camille kept a psychic eye on them until they disappeared into the distance. "Perhaps we should use the same trap with her that we used on my son," she suggested to Bartolomeo.

But he shook his head. "Much as the idea pleases me, I don't want to give *La Vieille* any cause to be unhappy with me."

Camille wondered if she could arrange Brigitte's death herself, and then blame Bartolomeo for it. It was worth thinking about. But for now, she had a phone call to make.

Smiling in anticipation, she dialed Eli's number.

FROM SOMEWHERE DOWNSTAIRS CAME the sound of a ringing phone. Jez ignored it, sitting on the reading chair in Eli's spare bedroom, her feet gathered up under her as she continued to sniffle.

Gabriel was still alive. That, she knew, because she could still feel the psychic line that connected them. But he'd been in such terrible pain when she'd last touched him, and she'd seen Camille gloating. Somehow, they'd found a way to disable him. And the fact that he wasn't dead yet meant . . . bad things.

She should tell Eli what she knew, but right this moment she wasn't sure she could bear to look at him. If he weren't being so blind and pig-headed where Gabriel was concerned, maybe—

The air turned arctic all of a sudden. Jezebel gasped, and she saw her own breath. Her teeth chattered, and she wrapped her arms around herself for warmth.

She knew what that cold meant, knew Eli was seriously pissed about something. And she guessed it had something to do with the phone call he'd just gotten. Common sense told her to stay as far away from him as possible. He was angry and dangerous, and she was angry and incautious. Not a good mix.

Despite her conviction that it was a dumb move, she found herself heading downstairs. It wasn't warming up any. In fact, it might still be getting colder. She should have grabbed a blanket off the bed on her way down!

Eli was in the library. The chill deepened with every step she took in that direction, but her feet kept moving.

When she crossed the threshold, she saw Eli sitting in the chair by the phone, his posture rigidly straight, his eyes closed. The air felt heavy, hard to breathe, and it was more than just the penetrating cold.

"Eli?" she asked, her voice smaller and weaker than she'd have liked.

He opened his eyes, and it took all her courage not to back out of the room and run for her life. When she met his gaze, it felt like an icepick had stabbed through her eye all the way to the back of her head. Gone was the kindly old man, and even the angry, conflicted father. In his place sat a predator, a Killer, of terrifying power.

"Where is he?" Eli asked, and even his voice didn't sound like his own, the words vibrating through her bones. There could be no doubt who he meant.

"I don't know," she said, her answer forced out through a tight throat.

Eli rose slowly from his chair, and this time, Jez did take a step back. His glamour seized her by the throat, and she couldn't even struggle against it as he came to stand only inches away.

"Where is he?" he repeated, still in that awful, sepulchral voice.

Jez trembled under the weight of his gaze, her voice nothing but a frightened whisper. "I swear, I don't know. Something hurt him and seemed to disable him. Camille was there. But he's blocking me out. I don't know where he is. I don't know what's happening." Tears filled her eyes again.

Eli pulled his lips away from his teeth, displaying his fangs. She'd never once seem him lower those fangs before. The sight made her knees knock.

"Please, Eli," she whispered. "I'm scared." She wasn't even sure whether she meant of him, or just for Gabriel. All she knew was that fear saturated her every pore.

He blinked, still flashing fang. "Camille claims to have left me a 'present,' as she called it, in a trash can at Fifth and Chestnut. I've asked Drake to retrieve it for me."

"What is it?" she asked. Her stomach lurched.

"She said it would be a surprise." Eli growled, a low, animalistic sound. Maybe it was her imagination, but she could swear his fangs grew longer as she watched.

Jez licked her lips, but there was no moisture anywhere in her mouth. "If you could stop being so terrifying for a moment, I can try again to reach him." Her chattering teeth made the words indistinct. The room still hadn't warmed, and between the fear and the cold, she was surprised she managed to talk at all.

Eli closed his eyes and sucked in a slow, deep breath. He let it out again just as slowly.

It took three more of those deep breaths for his fangs to start to recede. Perhaps a half dozen more before the room stopped feeling like a walk-in freezer.

He opened his eyes again, but meeting his gaze still made her head hurt, so she looked away.

"Sit," he told her, putting a hand on her arm and guiding her to the nearest chair. His voice no longer made her want to pee her pants, but it wasn't exactly warm and fuzzy either. "Try to reach him."

She did as he commanded, concentrating as hard as she could. Gabriel's barriers were still locked and barred against her, and, under her breath, she called him every foul name she could think of.

"Is he alive?" Eli asked. "Can you tell that at least?"

She nodded. "He's alive."

The air turned colder once more. Danger or no danger, her gaze snapped to Eli's.

"You're *angry* that he's alive?" she said indignantly, not

that she should be surprised. "How could—" Her voice died in her throat, killed by Eli's glamour.

"If he's still alive," Eli said, "it means they plan to kill him slowly. Do you have any idea what kind of damage a vampire can withstand without dying?" His voice choked off for a moment. He moved back to his chair, eyes now glazed over with grief. "I could barely stand the thought of killing him, even though I knew it was the right thing to do. But the thought of him suffering like that . . ."

Jez suppressed a miserable moan, not wanting to even think about what might be happening to him right now. "You love him, don't you?" she asked.

Eli nodded, not looking at her. "Of course I love him. He's my son."

"He's Camille's son, too," she ventured. "She doesn't seem to have the same feeling."

Eli didn't get to answer because the buzzer at the front gate sounded. Both of them tensed.

"Is it . . . ?" Jez asked, unable to finish the question.

"Yes, it's Drake," Eli responded, buzzing him in.

They stood side by side, waiting for Drake to display Camille's "gift." It seemed to take him an uncommonly long time to make it from the front gate to the front door, and then even longer to make it from there to the library. When he came into view, every line of his body radiated tension. In his hand, he held a gift box, about the size of a pack of cigarettes.

"Have you looked inside?" Eli asked.

Drake's chin dipped in the faintest of nods. His Adam's apple bobbed as he swallowed hard, looking back and forth between Eli and Jez.

"Show me!" Eli demanded.

Drake's gaze flicked toward Jez. She *so* didn't want to see. And yet, just like Eli, she had to. "Open it," she whispered through the dread.

With a grimace, Drake lifted the lid off the box. Inside was a finger, displayed on a bed of bloodied cotton.

A sob escaped Jez's throat, and her hand flew to her mouth. It wasn't like she hadn't known what to expect, but that didn't make the certain knowledge any easier. Drake hastily closed the box.

Once more, the temperature in the room dropped. Eli moved carefully, as if too jarring a movement might break him, as he walked to his chair and gingerly sat down. His control was hanging by a thread; anyone could see that.

"What are you going to do?" Drake asked softly.

"Camille has promised to call again to arrange a rendezvous. She says she and her friends would like to have it out with me, a war for the ownership of Philadelphia. But she won't tell me where to meet her until di Cesare has had sufficient time to entertain himself."

Jez's stomach threatened rebellion, but since she hadn't fed lately she doubted she would actually puke.

"What are you going to do?" Drake asked again.

Eli raised his head and smiled. His fangs had descended again, and the expression was more terrifying than anything Jez had ever seen before. "Why, I'm going to meet her, of course. And she, and every one of her accomplices, is going to die."

22

GABRIEL KEPT HIS EYES firmly closed, trying to wall himself off from everything around him. From the unrelenting pain. From the gloating of Bartolomeo and Camille. From the helpless cries of the little girl he'd come hoping to rescue. Bartolomeo's henchmen, both mortal and vampire, were as sickening as Bartolomeo himself.

Through it all, he felt over and over the pounding on his mental barriers that meant Jez was trying to reach him. Stubborn wench! She'd quit for a few minutes now and again, but every time he thought it was safe to relax his guard, she was there again.

Much though he worried about her, hard though it was to protect her from what was happening to him, he couldn't help feeling warmed by her loyalty. He wished he could spare her from the grief, and yet he was paradoxically glad that *someone* would mourn him.

Bartolomeo, Camille, and the rest of the vampires left the building well before dawn, but the mortal henchmen stood guard in shifts, regularly dosing him with that horrible drug. When the sun rose, Jez was finally forced by sleep to discontinue her siege. Gabriel breathed a sigh of relief. For the daylight hours, at least, he didn't have to worry that she would break through the barriers and experience his pain.

The day passed in a welter of agony. One of the mortals wanted to play with the whip and had a jolly old time ripping Gabriel's back to shreds. Gabriel didn't give him the satisfaction of crying out. The disgruntled mortal then turned his attentions to the child. This time, Gabriel did cry out in helpless rage.

He thought he might have passed out for a few hours somewhere in the middle of the afternoon. When he came back to himself, the child was gone. He had no doubt that she was dead. He swallowed another howl of rage. But at least she was now out of reach of her tormentors.

The mortals spent the rest of the afternoon rigging the warehouse with a complicated array of explosives.

Explosives?

Clearly, they weren't meant for *him*. Bartolomeo would want to kill him up close and personal, he felt sure of that. Perhaps this was their plan for dealing with Eli in the unlikely event Camille was right about him and he would actually leave the house on Gabriel's account. The idea seemed laughable.

Camille and Bartolomeo returned to the warehouse just before sunset. They inspected the mortals' handiwork and seemed to find it sufficient. Bartolomeo then ordered Gabriel taken down from the whipping posts. The finger he had lost last night had grown back, up to the first knuckle. Bartolomeo attacked his other index finger, cutting it off one knuckle at a time.

Gabriel felt Jez wake during the last cut. He felt her reach across the distance that separated them, once more demanding entry into his mind. He just barely managed to block her out.

When they stretched him out between the whipping posts again, his soul shrank in horror as he realized his defenses were weakening. Jez's assault on his mental barriers was a constant, nagging pressure. And he knew it was only a matter of time before she got through.

JEZ DIDN'T EVEN BOTHER to get out of bed. She lay on her back and stared at the ceiling in between bouts of psychic assaults on the fortress of Gabriel's mind. She wasn't sure, but she thought for a moment there, right when she first woke up, that she'd been close to reaching him. That little hint of hope was all it took to convince her that the effort was worthwhile.

Around ten o'clock, the phone rang. Shortly afterward, the air turned frigid again.

Jez clenched her fists and gritted her teeth against a burst of fury. She didn't need to go downstairs to know that Eli'd received another "gift." Not long afterward, she heard the front door buzzer and knew Drake had retrieved the "gift." Jez felt no desire to find out what part of Gabriel they'd cut off this time.

Around midnight, Eli came upstairs and bullied her into feeding. She wasn't sure her stomach could keep anything down, but when Eli argued that she needed her strength if she wanted to break down Gabriel's barriers, she had to concede the point. She chugged down the blood and milk concoction. When her stomach complained, she snarled at it to quit its bitching. Then she lay down again, closed her eyes, and renewed her efforts.

She didn't know how long she'd been at it when Gabriel's barriers started to crumble. A long time, she was sure.

She felt the pain, first. A steady throb all through her body. If she hadn't known it meant she was getting through to him, she would have struggled against that pain. Instead, she embraced it, pushing harder against the doors, even though the pain grew greater with every second.

Finally, the doors burst open.

Pain like living flame engulfed her, and she choked back a scream, holding the doors open with all her strength.

Damn it, Jezebel! Gabriel's voice shouted in her mind. *Stay out of my head!*

No, was her simple answer. *Tell me where you are.*

You can't help me.

I didn't ask if I could help you. Tell me where you are.

She felt his frustration, his fury. *I don't want you feeling this. Please, just leave me alone.*

She didn't much want to feel this either, but she forced herself to breathe as steadily and deeply as she could, focusing all her concentration on her connection with Gabriel, not on the pain. *I'm not leaving you alone, so quit asking.*

I'm not asking. I'm telling you, leave me alone.

Despite the pain, despite her fear for him, she laughed. A laugh that no doubt traveled through the psychic pipeline. *Or what?* she taunted.

Don't make me beg, Jez. Leave me what little pride I have left.

I'm not giving up on you.

I thought you already had.

As soon as he said it, she felt his rush of remorse, of self-loathing. A lump formed in her throat, and she wished she could be with him physically, could throw her arms around him and hold him close.

I didn't give up, she told him. *Not really. I just needed a rest.* She swallowed the lump in her throat. The pain had taken on a life of its own now, writhing through her body, burning and biting. Sweat soaked through her clothes, but she held on to the connection for all she was worth.

I love you, Gabriel. She felt his gasp of astonishment. She was almost as surprised as he was. She hadn't thought she'd allowed things to go that far, had clung to the illusion that she'd kept some small corner of her heart safe. Now, she knew that wasn't true.

Then why did you leave me? Gabriel asked, his voice small and frightened-sounding in her mind.

We'll talk about that later. In person. You need to tell me where you are.

Why? So you can come get yourself killed?

No, dumb-ass. So Eli can come get you out of there.

This time, it was Gabriel who laughed, and she could hear it just fine. *Yeah, like that's going to happen.*

It is. You should have seen him last night, when they sent . . . She swallowed hard, the night's meal making an attempt to crawl back up her throat. *I've never seen or felt anything like that. He loves you, Gabriel. He doesn't want to, he doesn't think he should, but he does.*

Yeah? Well, he has a funny way of showing it. The sarcasm was as thick as heavy cream.

He might have been able to reconcile himself to seeing you dead—though I doubt it—but he can't stand to see you suffer. He's already said he'll come for you as soon as Camille tells him where to meet her.

Gabriel was silent a long time, and if it weren't for the constant pain, she might have thought the connection had broken.

I understand now, Gabriel said, and she felt both pain and relief in those words. *He's coming to kill me.*

He's not— But Jez cut herself off before she finished her sentence.

Gabriel was right. That's exactly what Eli planned to do. Tears burned the back of her throat.

It's all right, Jez. Gabriel's voice was like a caress in her mind, full of softness. *I deserve it.*

You don't! she argued fiercely.

Never mind. Just tell Eli to be careful if he comes. They've rigged the building with explosives. They caught me with some kind of tranquilizer dart, but by the time Eli comes, I guess they'll be finished playing.

Tell me where you are, she demanded for the umpteenth time.

No, Jez. You are not to come anywhere near me. And I'd rather let them torture me for days than let you know where I am. I won't risk you, not for anything.

She cursed him, using every foul word she could think

of. When she felt Gabriel's amusement, she only got angrier.

Let me close the doors now, Jez, he begged. *I'm not going to tell you where I am, no matter what you say. And thinking of you feeling what I'm feeling just makes the pain worse. Please. Let me go.*

Right now, she wanted nothing more than to walk up to him and smack him. Unfortunately, that wasn't an option. Also unfortunately, she knew she wasn't going to talk him out of his position.

All right, she agreed reluctantly. *I'll back off. But only if you make me a promise.*

What promise? He sounded so suspicious she almost laughed again.

Promise that if I try to communicate with you again, you'll let me in.

Jezebel—

Promise me, damn it! Even a pig-headed asshole like you has to know there could come a time when I need to talk to you, and the last thing I want to do is spend a million hours fighting and clawing to get through. I won't try to reach you just to chat!

She thought she heard the echo of a sigh.

All right. I promise.

It wasn't much, but it was the most she could hope to get out of him. She wanted to tell him again that she loved him, but he might feel guilty that he couldn't say it back, so she didn't. Instead, she retreated from his mind, closing the door softly behind her.

When her eyes popped open and she was fully back in Eli's house, the pain now only a horrible memory, she rolled onto her stomach, buried her head in her pillow, and sobbed.

LATER, ELI ROUSED HER from her bout of misery, giving her a handkerchief and looking away while she dried her eyes. She shared the meager information that Gabriel had given her.

"Is he right, Eli?" she asked. "Are you going to kill him if you find him?"

His shoulders sagged and he sighed heavily. "Honestly, I don't know. I still feel that I ought to—though I don't expect you to agree." He offered her a hint of a smile, which quickly faded. "But the last time I tried, I wasn't able to force myself to do it, no matter my convictions. I'm not sure if anything has changed."

She resisted the urge to argue with him, to try to convince him that Gabriel didn't deserve to die.

"I'm tired of waiting," Eli continued. "My vamp-dar, as Hannah calls it, is quite strong. And if that drug has weakened him so greatly, Gabriel shouldn't be able to mask himself from me. I think it's time I take a walk through my city. Perhaps I'll get lucky and find him before Camille and friends are ready for the showdown."

Jez's eyes widened. "So you're really going to leave the house?"

Eli nodded, his jaw visibly working. "I've broken every vow I've ever made," he said bitterly. "What's one more?" His tone was so hard and sharp it made her head hurt.

Before she had any time to offer sympathy, he'd risen to his feet, his face determined. "I need to gather a few things. Meet me at the front gate in ten minutes."

"I get to go with you?" she asked, hardly daring to believe it.

"If by some miracle I do find him, I might need you to communicate with him."

She leapt eagerly from the bed, hope making her almost giddy. "I'll be ready the moment you are!"

The corners of his mouth almost twitched upward, but his expression was still far too grim to be called a smile. He left without another word.

Five minutes later, Jez was pacing in front of Eli's front gate, nervous energy pumping through her. She couldn't deny how eager she was to locate Gabriel. But she also couldn't deny how worried she was about what would happen if they did. Would Eli kill him? A better fate than the one di Cesare and Camille had planned for him, perhaps, but that wasn't much comfort. Somehow, she was going to have to protect him, though what a fledgling like her could do against an ancient vampire like Eli was anyone's guess.

Her misgivings rose to epic proportions when Eli strode down the path from his front door. Her jaw dropped, and she couldn't help staring.

He was dressed as he always was, in dark trousers with a crisply ironed dress shirt. Except for the sword belted at his side, that is. He stopped right in front of her, standing straight and proud, looking every bit the warrior, his right hand reaching across his body to grip the sword hilt.

Jez swallowed hard. Was that the sword that had scarred Gabriel's face? And just who was Eli planning to use it on?

She didn't dare ask either question.

Eli punched a button to set the iron gates swinging open. His knuckles where he gripped the sword turned white, and a bead of sweat rolled down the side of his face.

The gates stopped moving. Eli took a deep breath, then started forward. Still gripping the hilt of his sword, he looked like a soldier marching into battle, a battle that would lead to certain death. Jez felt almost sorry for him, sorry he had to break a vow that obviously meant so much to him.

She had just started to follow along behind him when Eli seemed to slam into a wall.

There was nothing there, just the gates hanging open, but Jez could both see and hear the impact as Eli bounced back, letting go of his sword and windmilling his arms to keep his balance. His face was almost white with shock.

Having no idea what was going on, Jez drew up beside him and gave him a questioning look.

"I don't know," he said in answer to that look. He took a couple of steps forward again, both his hands held out in front of him. When he reached the line where the gates would usually be, his hands stopped moving.

"Dear God," he whispered, shaking his head. He slapped the invisible wall with both hands, and Jez heard the impact. This wasn't his imagination.

She stepped up beside him, reaching out tentatively, expecting to feel some kind of invisible barrier, thinking it must be some kind of trick of their adversaries, a vampire magic that even Eli didn't know about. But her hand passed right through the barrier.

She and Eli stood side by side, both of them trying to cross the plane of the gates, but only Jez could do it. With a roar of rage and frustration, Eli tried to bull his way through, only to be knocked back once more, landing on his butt on the path.

The humid spring air now held a distinct chill. Jez put a little distance between herself and Eli, watching him warily as he pushed to his feet. He drew his sword, holding it with both hands and charging forward, slashing at the air. And the sword bounced off whatever invisible barrier was keeping him in.

Jezebel shivered in the sudden arctic cold and wondered if Gabriel's last hope of rescue had just faded.

23

ELI HAD TRIED FOR another ten minutes to get past whatever barrier seemed to be keeping him within the gates of his house, but it was pointless.

"This is God's way of telling me that this is one vow I cannot break," he muttered under his breath when he finally gave up. Frost had formed on the grass and bushes around him. He turned and strode back toward the house, frost coating the path behind him until the warmth of spring melted it away.

Jez stood by the gates and watched him go. Maybe she should go with him, try to ease his mind somehow, but her feet were rooted to the ground. Despair threatened to overwhelm her, but she shoved it back.

So, Eli couldn't leave the house after all. That left Jezebel as the only person in the world who cared enough to try to save Gabriel.

If only she had some clue how to do it!

She stepped through the gates onto the sidewalk outside, closing her eyes and groping for Gabriel's presence in her mind. She found it quickly, but resisted the urge to knock on his mental doors. Instead, she tried to figure out if that feeling of his presence was coming from any particular direction. After all, when Bartolomeo's goon had ambushed her outside Eli's, Gabriel had tracked her down via the connection, so maybe she could track *him* that way, too.

Try though she might, she couldn't put a direction to the feeling. But anything was better than sitting around Eli's house worrying, so she picked a direction at random and started walking.

She'd gone about three blocks before she decided to stop and try again, hoping the sensation would be either stronger or weaker, hoping for some clue. The moment she reached out with her senses, she found a pair of vampires, not fifty feet behind her. With a gasp, she whirled around.

Brigitte smiled and waved, looking delighted to see her, as if they were bosom buddies. Standing just a little behind her and to the side, Henri did not look similarly thrilled.

Jez considered the possibility of running for her life, but decided against it. For one thing, she figured Brigitte's glamour was enough to stop her in her tracks. For another, Brigitte and her fledgling were predators, and the last thing Jez wanted to do was tweak their instincts to give chase.

Trying to pretend she was brave, she held still and waited for them to approach. Brigitte gave her a long once-over. Behind her, Henri merely stared at Jez's chest and licked his lips.

"What do you want?" Jez asked. She was pleasantly surprised to find that her voice came out firm and bold, without a trace of a quaver. Score one for bravado.

Brigitte feigned surprise, reaching back and slapping Henri's shoulder. "Did you hear that, Henri? It speaks!"

Henri grunted. It might have been a laugh, but then again it might not.

Jez's fangs descended, an instinctual response she couldn't help. "I do indeed speak," she said, voice still steady. "Does *it*?" she asked, pointing at Henri with her chin.

Henri bared his impressive fangs. Brigitte laughed as if

that were hilarious. "Only when spoken to," she responded. "But then, talking isn't what I usually want my men doing with their mouths, if you know what I mean." The bitch winked, still doing the best-friends routine.

"What do you want?" Jez repeated.

"Gabriel."

Jez's mouth dropped open. "Huh?"

"Not very bright, is she?" Brigitte asked Henri over her shoulder.

"No, but she's got nice tits," the fledgling responded, proving that he did indeed speak when spoken to. Jez would have preferred he kept his mouth shut after all.

Brigitte turned back to her. "Gabriel is the only other born vampire in the world, as far as I know." She put her arm to her forehead and infused her voice with melodrama. "We are fated to be together!"

When Jez just stared at her, Brigitte heaved a sigh and let her arm fall to her side.

"All right," she said, taking a step forward and hooking her arm through Jez's elbow. "Let's take a walk, and I'll explain it to you in small words, so you'll understand."

Jez had no desire to go along, but resistance wouldn't do her any good. Gritting her teeth, she allowed Brigitte to steer her toward the riverfront, Henri following about three paces behind.

"I presume Gabriel has told you that in the Old World, born vampires are outlawed. Slaughtered at birth." She looked over at Jez, who nodded. "Do you know why?"

"He said it was something about them fearing your power."

Brigitte smiled. "Yes, something like that. Has he told you of *Les Vieux*?"

Jez thought about it for a moment, but couldn't remember him mentioning the term. "No."

"*Les Vieux* translates to something like the Old Ones. They are the oldest, most powerful vampires in the world. As you no doubt realize, vampires get more powerful as they age—such a lovely contrast to the human condition, don't you think? But even among the oldest of them, there are variations in power. Variations in potential. *Les Vieux* are the vampires whose potential was the greatest, who have achieved the pinnacle of power.

"My mother is one of them. Hence, the reason I am alive, while Gabriel would have been killed if anyone knew about him." She stopped walking, turning to face Jez. "Do you know what differentiates *Les Vieux* from other vampires of great age and power?"

Since Jez had never heard of them before today, obviously she didn't. She mustered just enough willpower to resist making a sarcastic comment to that effect. Instead, she shook her head silently.

"They take root," Brigitte said, as if that made perfect sense.

"Huh?" Jez asked.

Brigitte regarded her with piercing eyes. "They become bound to the land on which they live."

Jez suppressed a gasp, not sure she was understanding Brigitte's implications. Brigitte grinned at her.

"We think that's where the legend of vampires having to have the soil of their homelands in their coffins comes from. *Les Vieux* must have the soil of their homelands beneath them at all times."

"You mean . . ." But Jez didn't finish, because of course she knew exactly what Brigitte meant.

Brigitte laughed, no doubt at Jez's stunned expression. "Yes. It seems that sometime in the last couple of centuries, Eli has taken a leap in power without even knowing it."

Jez gaped at her. "How can you call that a leap in power? He's a prisoner in his own home!"

"Oh, I think if he plays around awhile, he'll find that taking root has certain advantages."

"What advantages?"

"The greatest advantage of all—he can create avatars."

Brigitte looked at her expectantly, making Jez want to swallow all her questions. But her curiosity was too strong.

If Brigitte wanted her to jump through hoops and ask questions, she'd just have to live with it.

"What's an avatar?" she asked, rolling her eyes at the little game.

"A *Doppelgänger*. An illusion. The most powerful glamour of all. That is the power of *Les Vieux*. They cannot leave their homes in body, but their avatars can walk the length and breadth of their territory, limited only by the Old One's power. And the best part? The avatars can't be killed. So the Old One stays safe and secure in a fortress of a home, shielded by powerful glamours, while still enjoying the freedom of traveling the land."

Questions continued leaping to Jez's mind, but she shouted them all down except for one. "Why are you telling me all this?"

Brigitte's smile turned mischievous. "Why, just a little girl talk, of course." She shared a look with Henri, who had come up behind Jez. Uncomfortably close.

"There's got to be some reason you're being so chatty all of a sudden."

"Well, yes. I suppose there is. I'm trying to explain why I want your master, but I'm afraid it's a long story." She glanced up at the sky. "You have at least a full hour before the sun rises. You can spare the time."

When she saw she had Jez's undivided attention, she continued. "Having just watched Eli's performance at his front gate, I can say with certainty that he has become an Old One. Whatever conceit he devised to explain his reluctance to leave his house was no doubt a construct of his subconscious.

"And that brings us to Gabriel, and why born vampires are outlawed in the Old World. You see, a born vampire from a strong bloodline can eventually become an Old One too. Only, these Old Ones aren't bound to the land. They are known as *Les Vieux Marchants*. We only know of one who ever attained this level of power in the last millennium. Just imagine what a creature of that power can do, free to roam anywhere he pleases! The last *Vieux Marchant* killed three of the Old Ones and took over their territories before the rest of them mustered an army powerful enough to defeat him. Naturally, the current Old Ones do not wish to see history repeat itself, and the easiest way is to ensure that no born vampires are allowed to live." She frowned. "At least, not past a certain age."

The frown disappeared as fast as it had come. "So, to make a long story short, I would like to live long enough to become *Vieille Marchante* myself, but I doubt I will be allowed to live even to Gabriel's age. What I need is an ally. One powerful enough to help me fight off the assassins who will no doubt come after me when my mother realizes I have gone. And there is no better ally for me than a five-hundred-year-old born vampire. Especially when his father has become an Old One and proven his bloodline strong.

"Who knows? Being older than I, he will make the transition to *Vieux Marchant* sooner, and perhaps together we can return to the Old World and show *Les Vieux* what true power is." Her eyes glowed with fervor. "And in these modern times when hardly anyone believes in vampires, it will be next to impossible for them to raise an army against us." She raised her hands over her head. "We can rule the world!" she hollered, then laughed maniacally.

Is this nutcase for real? Jez wondered for a moment. Then Brigitte abruptly stopped laughing, her eyes twinkling with genuine humor.

"Just kidding," she said, though Jez wasn't sure that was entirely true. "I mostly just want to stay alive, and Gabriel seems like my best hope."

Jez crossed her arms over her chest. "Then get him away from di Cesare and Camille. You could take them both all by yourself, couldn't you?"

"Possibly," she agreed. "At least, I could with Henri at my side, though it would be a real battle. Remember, I'm

not as old as Gabriel. But here's the thing—he didn't seem
too interested in having me in his bed when he already had
you there."

Oh shit, Jez thought, but she wasn't in any position to defend herself. All she could do was stand straight and proud
and look her death in the face.

Brigitte waved a hand at her carelessly. "Oh, don't get all
jumpy. I'm not going to kill you. I seriously doubt Gabriel
would forgive me for that and stand by my side as I need
him to."

Brigitte stepped in closer, and Jez couldn't help taking a
hasty step back—right into Henri, whose hands clamped
down on her shoulders and squeezed as hard as they could
without breaking bones. Jez couldn't help the wince that
tightened her features.

"No, I have to be a little more subtle than that," Brigitte
continued, reaching up to touch Jez's face, then stilling her
with glamour when she tried to pull away.

"I'm not going to get him out of that warehouse myself,"
she continued. "But I'm going to tell you how you can use
your bond with him to help set him free."

24

DESPITE HIS DISGRUNTLEMENT WITH the Founder, Drake answered Eli's summons, arriving at the mansion shortly before sunrise. At his age, Drake could stay awake another hour or two, as long as he kept out of direct sunlight. It took most of that time for Eli to explain to him what Jezebel had learned through the born vampire, Brigitte. And it took most of Drake's willpower not to express his outrage that Eli had been willing to leave the house to save Gabriel when he hadn't been willing to leave to stop him.

Swallowing the bile as best he could, Drake kept his voice steady. "And why did you call me here at dawn to tell me all this?" he asked.

Eli probably heard the anger under the steady tone, but he didn't react beyond a sharp look. "Because I need help determining just what this avatar can do."

Drake raised an eyebrow. "So you really can do it?"

The lines at the corners of Eli's mouth tightened. "I've managed to create a faint illusion once or twice. Nothing more than that so far. But I'm going to keep trying. I'm hoping to have something more solid by the time you awaken for the evening. Then you and I can test out the avatar's limits. If it's even remotely possible, I mean to put a stop to all this tonight." His face became even more grim. "Before Camille sends me another part of my son's body."

There wasn't time for much more discussion. The rising sun was already making Drake's mind and body sluggish with sleep. He retired to one of the guest bedrooms, collapsing onto the bed and trying not to think.

Luckily, his daytime sleep was dreamless, and when Drake awoke he felt rested and ready. The resentment was still there, an ever-present companion, but despite his mixed feelings he knew he had to help Eli deal with Gabriel and with the other Killers who'd invaded their city. Afterward, the two of them could have a long talk about Drake's future with the Guardians, but now was not the time.

He found Eli in the library, where he'd left him last night. The Founder was fast asleep in his chair, snoring softly. Drake had never seen him sleep before, never seen his face look so open and unguarded. For just a moment, Eli looked almost human, as vulnerable as the rest of them.

"I wonder if I've always snored," Eli said.

But the voice didn't come from the figure in the chair. The hairs on the back of Drake's neck stood on end, and he slowly turned toward the sound of that voice.

Eli stood behind him in the doorway, smiling faintly. Drake looked back and forth between the smiling Eli and the sleeping one. A chill crawled down his spine, and he suspected his face lost its color.

"What do your senses tell you?" Eli asked. "Do you sense one of us, or both of us?"

Drake closed his eyes and reached out with his senses, finding the psychic footprints of two vampires in the room with him. Reluctantly, he opened his eyes.

"Both," he said, and the smiling Eli smiled more broadly.

"Good. Hopefully, that means Camille and her friends will sense the avatar as a vampire and will therefore be convinced it's really me."

Drake looked back and forth between the two Elis again. "That is very unnerving," he commented. It was an understatement.

The smiling Eli disappeared, and the sleeping Eli opened his eyes. "Sorry," he said, not sounding terribly apologetic. He sat up straight in his chair, stretching. "I'm getting better at it, but I still can't seem to keep the avatar going for more than about five or ten minutes at a time."

Drake took a seat. "And how far from the house can your avatar go, or have you tried leaving the house yet?"

Eli nodded. "I've tried. I've managed to send it a couple of blocks from the house, and I've managed to wrap it in glamour so mortals can't see it." He frowned. "But obviously that's not far enough. Not yet." His frown deepened. "I seem to be getting better with practice, but I don't know how long it will take before I'm good enough to take on vampires of Camille and di Cesare's age. If indeed it's possible for me to have that kind of strength."

"And you don't know how long the two of them are going to keep Gabriel alive," Drake finished for him.

Eli nodded. "Precisely. I need to keep pushing. And I need you to spar with me. With my avatar. I need to know what my limits are."

Drake couldn't think of any excuse to refuse. "All right."

"Thank you," Eli said, sinking back into his chair and closing his eyes. A ghostly image of him formed in front of Drake's eyes, growing progressively more solid.

"Let's take a walk, shall we?" Eli's avatar said.

Once again suppressing a shudder, Drake nodded silently and followed the avatar out of the house.

JEZ LISTENED WITH ONLY half an ear as Eli described his plan of attack. He hadn't come right out and said it, but she could tell from every nuance of his body language and tone of voice that he wasn't expecting to get Gabriel out of that warehouse alive. It made her almost wish she hadn't told him everything Brigitte had told her.

Well, actually, she hadn't told him *all* of it. She'd told him what Brigitte knew of the Old Ones, and she'd told him where Brigitte said Gabriel was being held. She *hadn't* told him about Brigitte's plan to both free Gabriel and get rid of Jez all in one fell swoop.

"Have you heard anything I've said, Jezebel?" Eli asked, snapping her out of her reverie.

"Yeah. You're going to send that avatar thing to storm the building." She swallowed hard. "And you're going to try to use it to set off the explosives and kill everyone inside."

Eli stiffened. "That's *not* what I said."

"But it's what you meant."

Eli shared a quick but significant look with Drake. Jez understood that look perfectly well. There was a reason Drake was here at the moment, and it wasn't because Eli needed his help carrying out this brilliant plan.

"If I can get him out of there alive, I will," Eli promised.

Jez snorted. No doubt he meant what he said, but she knew he wasn't planning to try terribly hard. Why should he, when he'd made it perfectly clear that Gabriel was still under a death sentence?

"I mean it," Eli said earnestly. "I will try to get him out of there alive. Whether he stays alive after the smoke clears is up to him."

She swallowed a sharp retort. Arguing with him was only going to strengthen his conviction that he needed Drake to act as prison guard and keep her in this house while he went off to save the world.

Damn, she was turning bitter.

For two seemingly endless days and nights, Eli had practiced with his avatar, stretching his range until he knew he could make it all the way to the warehouse. Mock battles with Drake had shown him that his power waned the farther he got from his house. By the time he'd stretched to the warehouse, he wouldn't be much stronger than Jez herself.

Maybe if he'd been willing to wait a little longer, practice a little longer, he'd have a better shot of getting Gabriel out alive. But each night, Camille had called to let him know another body part was waiting for him at a new drop-off point, and tonight he'd decided he couldn't wait any longer.

Which was for the most part fine with Jez. She couldn't go help Gabriel all by herself. Brigitte had given her an explanation of just what it was she had to do to give Gabriel the strength to break free of the drug, but it was mystical, metaphysical shit that wasn't easy to explain in words. It was going to take a considerable amount of trial and error to figure out how to accomplish it. And while she was trying, Camille and her cronies would sense her presence. And that would be that.

She needed the diversion, needed Eli there to distract them while she figured out what to do. She just wished she had faith that he would buy her enough time.

"So, when are you going?" she asked.

Again, Eli and Drake shared a look.

"What?" she asked. "Why do you guys keep doing that?"

To her surprise, it was Drake who answered, not Eli. "Because you're being way too quiet and accommodating. What are you planning?"

Great. Now she'd gone and made them suspicious! She narrowed her eyes and glared at both of them. "Why should I bother arguing?" she asked, and it wasn't hard to get a convincing dose of bitterness into her voice. "It's not like you'd listen to me. You're going to do it your way no matter what I think, and if Gabriel gets killed . . ." She exaggerated a shrug. "Oh well!" Her voice had risen steadily, and she felt the hot flush of blood in her cheeks.

"I've told you, I'll get him out alive if I can," Eli said. "What more do you want from me?"

"I want you to *mean* it! I want you to do everything you can, not just make some half-assed effort." She let tears of frustration flood her eyes. Nothing like a bout of screaming hysterics to put a pair of men into a state of mental shutdown! If she was lucky, she'd knock them off balance enough to kill their suspicions.

"Calm down," Eli said in a soothing croon, a tone that had calmed many a temperamental Guardian.

Jez let it have the exact opposite effect on her. "No, I *won't* calm down! I won't be a good little girl and be quiet!" Her voice became shrill. She could hardly recognize it as her own. "If you get him killed, I will *never* forgive you."

Mentally crossing her fingers, she covered her face with her hands, letting the sobs bubble up from deep inside her, and ran for the door.

And Eli let her go.

She ran for the first few blocks, trying to put as much distance between herself and Eli as she could, getting out of range of his vampire senses. She had hoped that like most men, he'd be unwilling to intervene in a bout of feminine hysterics. It seemed that even thousand-plus-year-old vamps could be flummoxed by tears.

The tears weren't entirely fake, however, so she had to stop and pull herself together. She huddled in the shadows between the stoops of two houses, letting the tears run their course, giving in to terror now so that she could be calm later when she needed to be.

When she wiped away the last of the tears and got shakily to her feet, she found herself face to face with Drake. Her shoulders slumped. Apparently, she hadn't diverted suspicion after all.

She refused to look the Killer in the face, though she figured his glamour was probably strong enough to subdue her without eye contact.

"Please, Drake. Just leave me alone. You and Eli both."

"Whatever you're planning to do, you don't have to do it alone," he responded. "And don't pretend you don't have some kind of plan. You're not fooling me any more than you're fooling Eli. Who, by the way, is already on his way to the warehouse."

Alarm jittered through her nerves. She didn't have time to waste arguing. "Get out of my way."

Drake stepped aside and she frowned at him. "I'm following you wherever you're going," he explained. "Feel free to get started."

She briefly considered trying to talk him out of following her, but she doubted she'd have much luck, so she pushed past him and started walking briskly. He fell into step beside her. At least he hadn't tried to stop her yet.

"So, what's the plan?" he asked.

She cast a sidelong glance his direction. She'd refused to tell Eli her plan because he would go all protective and try to stop her. But maybe Drake would treat her like an adult, capable of making her own decisions and allowed to take her own risks.

She took a deep breath and let it out slowly. If Drake tried to stop her, he would win. So she just had to hope he wouldn't try to stop her.

"Brigitte says I can use my bond with Gabriel to draw the pain away from him so that he can function again. If he can break free while Eli is there, the two of them together stand a fighting chance."

For about half a block, Drake said nothing, the only sound the steady thump of his shoes against the pavement as he kept pace with her. At least they were still moving.

"Draw the pain away from him," Drake mused. "You mean draw it into yourself, don't you?"

She nodded. "When he's been hurt before, I've felt it. Apparently if I can manipulate our connection enough, I can make it so I feel it and he doesn't. Which should clear his head enough to let him break free."

"Uh-huh." Another block passed in silence.

"And why do you think Eli wouldn't let you do this?"

"Because it's dangerous." Brigitte had been quite clear on just how dangerous it was. A fledgling of Henri's age could manage the trick with minimal risk. But someone as young and inexperienced as Jez would almost certainly fry her brain in the process.

"How dangerous?"

"Dangerous enough that Eli would never let me do it."
And neither would Gabriel, if he had any idea what she was
up to. She would have to convince him to open the psychic
connection, then figure out how to siphon off his pain without him realizing it until it was too late.

Drake stopped her with a hand on her arm, and she almost screamed in frustration.

"Goddammit!" she said, trying to jerk out of his grip. No
luck. "This is *my* decision to make. Not Eli's, and certainly
not yours!"

"I'm not arguing," Drake responded, though he didn't release her arm. "If this is truly what you want to do, I won't
stand in your way. Even though I promised Gabriel to look
after you and I don't think this is quite what he meant."

She gaped at him. "When did this happen?"

He ignored her question. "I just want to make sure you've
thought it through. Do you think Gabriel would be happy to
live at the cost of your life?"

"No," she admitted. How to explain to Drake something
she wasn't even sure she understood herself? She mulled it
over for a moment, then answered. "But he deserves to have
someone who loves him unconditionally. Who loves him
enough to risk everything to save him."

Drake looked down at her gravely. "Maybe so. But if you
die in the process, he *won't* have you."

She raised her chin. "Then I'll just have to make sure I
don't die."

He didn't look happy. But he didn't drag her back to
Eli's, either. "All right. I won't stand in your way. And I'll
help you however I can."

Her smile was forced, but she gave herself an "A" for effort. "Great. You can keep the minions away from me while
I try to pull this off. Brigitte says the closer I am, the more
likely this'll work, so I have to get too close for comfort."

"And you believe this Brigitte is telling you the truth?"

He'd finally let go of her arm, so she started forward

once again. "Yes, I do," she said, remembering the satisfied glow in Brigitte's eyes when she'd told Jez about the likely consequences of success.

Jez was certain Gabriel wouldn't team up with the psychotic little bitch even if Brigitte wasn't directly responsible for her death. But she'd seen no reason to tell Brigitte that.

Hoping that Drake wouldn't change his mind, hoping that Eli wouldn't sense her and interfere, hoping that Gabriel would let her in, Jezebel made her way toward the warehouse.

25

GABRIEL HAD NO IDEA how many days and nights had passed since Bartolomeo's men had taken him. It seemed like an eternity.

The mortals had gotten bored with tormenting him during the daytime, but so far Bartolomeo showed no signs of getting bored himself. Gabriel had thought himself a master of cruelty. He'd been a soft touch in comparison to Bartolomeo.

Pain consumed his every waking moment. Sapped every ounce of his strength, reduced him from a quasi-human being to a mindless melange of skin, blood, and bones. The only good news was that Jez had not tried to contact him again. He still felt her there in his mind, still felt that connection between them, and it actually gave him comfort at times. But, thankfully, she had resisted the urge to share in his pain.

Even as that thought occurred to him, he realized he "heard" her knocking on his mental doors. How long had that been going on? Everything about him felt sluggish, his reflexes, both mental and physical, almost non-existent.

The pounding in his head grew more insistent. He didn't

want to let her in, but he had made her a promise. And even if he hadn't, he didn't think he had the strength to resist her for long.

What is it, Jezebel?

He felt her wave of relief before she spoke in his head.

You scared me, she said. *I thought you weren't going to answer.*

I promised I would. Now, what is it?

He could almost hear the deep breath she drew in. *I thought you should know that Eli is on his way.*

Gabriel was sure he'd heard wrong. Or perhaps the pain was making him delusional. *What?*

He's on his way to get you out of there.

Impossible! But even as he denied it, hope flared in him. Was it possible this pain would end soon? Even if Eli was coming to kill him, at this point Gabriel would thank him for it.

I wouldn't tell you that if it weren't true. Her psychic voice softened. *He loves you, Gabriel. The idea that they're hurting you has practically driven him mad. And he's not going to take it anymore.*

If that's the case, get out of my head. There's no reason for you to suffer. He tried a push on his mental doors, but he wasn't surprised when Jez resisted.

Hang on a minute! she protested. *I told you I wouldn't contact you just to chat. Eli might need some help. I need to stay in contact with you in case we need to send in the cavalry.* He didn't want anyone else in danger unless it was absolutely necessary.

Why did that feel like a lie? He couldn't imagine what reason Jez would have to lie to him at a time like this. He tried to probe into her mind, but the damn drug seemed to deaden that power as well as all his others. He supposed he was lucky he could even communicate with her.

Then he realized why her words didn't ring true.

Why would Eli need help? he asked. *He's far more powerful than Camille and di Cesare, and their little minions are practically useless against a vampire of any significant age.*

She hesitated a moment, then rushed to cover up the hesitation. *It's a long story. One I can tell you when you get out of there. Let's just say that Eli isn't at full strength and leave it at that for now.*

He was about to question her some more, but he heard a sudden buzz from the assembled minions. He opened his eyes and looked around the darkened warehouse.

Everyone was scurrying around frantically. Camille and di Cesare were arguing in low, urgent voices. Di Cesare insisting they needed to flee for their lives. Camille insisting it was too late and they needed to stand and fight.

I guess he's here, Gabriel said, feeling a sense of wonder under the oppressive blanket of pain.

Good, Jez replied. But even with his sluggish, deadened senses, he felt the alarm that tingled through her.

SHE HAD TO STAY calm, Jez reminded herself. Gabriel was getting suspicious, hearing nuances in her mental voice that she couldn't mask. She didn't dare let him feel her fear and turmoil, didn't dare risk that he would close the doors between them.

What's everyone doing in there? she asked. She needed to keep him "talking" as she worked her way around his mind, trying to figure out how to siphon the pain away. Brigitte had said it was a visualization technique. Jez had to visualize Gabriel's pain, and then draw it into her.

Only, of course, it wasn't as easy as that.

She only half-listened as Gabriel described the action in the warehouse. She kept trying to visualize his pain as a solid mass that she could reach out to and grab, but it wasn't working. Frustration made her frantic.

Jezebel! Gabriel's voice was sharp in her head. *What aren't you telling me? What's the matter?*

Nothing! Except the man I love is in danger and I'm relegated to sitting here on the sidelines.

That shut him up. She hadn't meant to say that, hadn't meant to remind him that she'd foolishly lost her heart. She felt the turmoil her words engendered, felt him struggle under the weight of the unspoken expectation that he'd admit to loving her too. But that was too much to ask of someone who couldn't even love himself.

She steadied her nerves and redoubled her efforts to visualize the pain. She had an image in her mind, an image of an amorphous black glob that surrounded Gabriel, clinging stubbornly to him. She reached out and tried to grab the blackness, but it turned to mist and her fingers passed right through it.

What's going on? Gabriel asked. *Eli's here, but he hasn't neutralized anyone yet. Not even the mortals.*

Oh shit, she thought. She didn't have much time. Eli might even now be trying to figure out how to use his telekinesis to set off the bombs.

She didn't have the time or the concentration to answer Gabriel's question, so she ignored him, grabbing ever more frantically at the black mist that surrounded him. But it still wasn't working.

Panic threatened to overwhelm her, but she shoved it aside. There had to be something wrong with her visualization technique. Either that, or Brigitte had been feeding her a load of shit.

Trying to ignore the time pressure and the increasing urgency of Gabriel's demands for an explanation, she backed off for a moment and thought.

When she reached into that cloud of blackness that surrounded Gabriel, her fingers passed straight through. She either had to change the way she was visualizing the pain, or she had to change the way she was trying to siphon it off.

The answer clicked suddenly in her head. *Siphon* it off!

In her mind's eye, she saw herself sticking a straw into that black cloud and inhaling. And suddenly, the pain she'd been feeling from the moment she'd made contact with him grew worse.

Jez? Gabriel's voice was weak and uncertain in her mind. *What's happening?*

I love you, she told him again. Then she inhaled another lungful of pain.

GABRIEL'S HEAD SPUN WITH confusion as the pain of the drug and of his healing wounds ebbed. Even the iron cuffs that held him chained to the whipping posts no longer seemed to burn as severely into his flesh.

Jez was doing this, somehow. He felt certain of that, though he didn't know how. And every instinct in his body told him she *shouldn't* be, that it was dangerous.

Jezebel! he howled, but she ignored him.

Suddenly, the pain was gone. Completely. He tried reaching for Jez across their connection, but though he felt that fragile bond, he couldn't seem to reach her.

Practicality won out over concern, and he blinked the sweat from his eyes and looked around.

Camille and di Cesare stood to one side, looking perplexed as their minions grappled with Eli. One mortal lay dead at Eli's feet, his head twisted at an unnatural angle. As Gabriel watched, Eli lost his footing and went down hard, three vampires landing on top of him. He should have been able to shove them off with ease. And yet, he didn't. One of the humans was readying a syringe.

Gabriel didn't wait any longer. His limbs still felt weak and sluggish, but his mind seemed to be all his. He used his telekinesis to unlock the cuffs. His legs trembled but held him as he eased away from the whipping posts.

Neither Camille nor di Cesare had noticed that he was free, their attention entirely focused on the struggle with Eli. Gabriel risked a glance in that direction and saw the mortal plunge the needle into Eli's shoulder. A slow smile spread on Gabriel's face as his strength continued to return. Just as well to have Eli out for the count. That meant Gabriel got to have all the fun.

Eli went still, and the three vamps who'd been holding

him down rose to their feet, looking terribly pleased with themselves. Gabriel would have liked to have taken his time with them, paid them back at least in part for the misery they'd caused him, and for the atrocities they'd committed on the mortal child. But even with whatever Jez was doing to help him, he wasn't at full strength, and he didn't know how long the reprieve would last. Best to finish things up quickly.

The oldest of the three vamps was only two hundred. None of the three of them could resist Gabriel's glamour. He froze two of them where they stood, then bade the third to snap their necks. Gabriel then sent him after the remaining mortal helpers as he turned his attention to Camille and di Cesare.

They'd noticed him finally. Lowering his fangs, he took a step toward them. Both of them backed up, eyes wide and unbelieving. Camille's face had drained of all color. Di Cesare snarled and tried to look fierce, but like most bullies he was a terrible coward and was practically pissing himself.

Gabriel smiled at Camille. "Don't go anywhere, Mother. I want a word with you."

Then, he leapt at di Cesare, who turned and tried to flee. Gabriel didn't even bother using glamour to stop him. Di Cesare hadn't gotten more than three steps before Gabriel slammed into him and knocked him to the floor. Di Cesare struggled wildly, limbs flailing, the stink of his fear heavy in the air as his glamour beat helplessly against Gabriel's mental shields. Gabriel grabbed his head.

"This is so much quicker than you deserve," he growled. Then, with a hard jerk of his hands, he broke the Killer's neck. Di Cesare went limp.

Behind him, Gabriel felt Camille trying to run away, but he seized her with his glamour, keeping her still until he was ready to face her. Brushing off his hands, he rose slowly and turned toward her.

All the malice, all the gloating pride, had faded from her countenance. Tears snaked down her cheeks, and she was actually trembling. Gabriel stalked toward her, ignoring the sounds of scuffling coming from the far end of the room. He'd have thought the battle there would be over by now, that the fledgling he'd compelled would now be coming to his senses and either charging at Gabriel or running for his life.

But he'd take care of that later.

Camille swallowed hard. "All I wanted was to go home to Paris," she said in a shaking voice.

Gabriel sneered. "Yes, I could see you were really heart-broken at the price you had to pay for admission."

"I didn't have a choice! He would have killed me if I hadn't promised to give you to him."

He laughed. Did she actually think there was a chance in the world he was going to buy her pathetic excuses? What di Cesare had done to him might not have been her idea, but she had never once uttered a word of protest.

She held up both her hands to ward him off. "Please, my son. Let us come to some kind of . . . agreement."

Gabriel spat, her groveling leaving a nasty taste in his mouth. "You have nothing I could possibly want," he said.

She turned and tried to run. Gabriel took two steps in pursuit, then blinked in confusion to see Eli appear seemingly out of nowhere. Camille saw him at the same moment, screaming shrilly.

And that was when Gabriel saw the sword in his father's hands. A sword he knew all too well himself. A sword he could have sworn Eli hadn't been carrying when he first arrived.

The sword sang through the air. Moments later, Camille crumpled to the warehouse floor. Her body landed in an undignified heap. And her head rolled to a stop about five feet away.

Gabriel stood frozen, staring at his mother's head, at the look of surprise and terror on her face. Then, swallowing hard, he raised his gaze to Eli and the bloody sword.

For one long moment, father and son met each other's

gaze. Gabriel braced himself for the assault of Eli's glamour. Eli had let him live once before and had come to regret it. He wouldn't make the same mistake twice, though Gabriel was damned if he'd go down without a fight. He clenched his fists, wishing he had a weapon to counter that sword.

Eli opened his mouth as if to say something. Then, he vanished, leaving Gabriel to stand gaping like a fool.

WHEN JEZEBEL HAD COLLAPSED, Drake had done his best to revive her, gently slapping her cheeks and shaking her. Nothing seemed to be working, though her pulse was strong and her breathing steady.

He didn't sense any vampires coming their way on the attack, but he also didn't see any point in leaving her lying here helpless as they waited for the outcome of the battle.

Hoping he was doing the right thing, he scooped her up in his arms and carried her back to Eli's.

When he arrived back at the mansion, he found Eli conscious, but exhausted. He explained what Jezebel had done—at least, he explained it as best he could. He expected Eli to give him hell for letting her risk her life, but the Founder merely instructed him to take her upstairs and tuck her into her bed.

"I didn't hear an explosion," Drake said before he turned to go. "Is Gabriel . . . ?"

Eli's eyes looked far away. "He's alive. The others are all dead."

Drake wanted to ask for more details, but he suspected they wouldn't be forthcoming.

GABRIEL HAD NEVER FELT so exhausted in all his long life. Apparently, it was adrenaline that had fueled him for the last few minutes, because now that the danger had passed, his knees wobbled beneath him.

Sure that he should be getting the hell out of here as fast as possible, he nonetheless took a seat on the floor before he fell down. The air reeked of blood. And of fear.

He stared at his hands. Most of his fingers were in some state of partial regrowth. Even the one he'd lost tonight had healed over. In a few days, his hands would be whole again. He closed his eyes, sucking in a deep breath despite the stink.

What the hell had happened in here? What had Jezebel done to give him back his power? And how could Eli just vanish like that? So many questions, so few answers.

He reached over the psychic line, trying to reach Jez, but though he still felt her presence in his head, he couldn't contact her. He had to find out if she was okay. No matter his exhaustion and injury.

He pushed himself up to his feet, heading toward the open warehouse door. When he stepped outside, he came to an abrupt halt.

Brigitte smiled at him, her eyes seeming to glow with pleasure in the moonlight. "Well!" she said. "You seem to be doing better than the last time I saw you."

He mustered a snarl, though he felt so depleted he feared he'd make easy prey.

"Oh, don't be so grumpy," she said. "If it weren't for me, you'd still be in there waiting to see what body part you'd lose next."

He stiffened. "What do you mean?"

"Who do you think taught your fledgling how to help you?"

Gabriel's hands closed into fists. "What did you do to her?"

She raised her eyebrows. "Do to her?" She shook her head. "Nothing whatsoever. I just gave her the information she needed to save your life."

"Don't fuck with me!" he snapped.

Brigitte wrinkled her pretty little nose. "Americans are so vulgar."

He took a menacing step her direction, at which point Henri stepped out from the shadows.

"You're in no condition to fight us," Brigitte pointed out.

"Your little fledgling has taken the pain away, but you will still be somewhat weakened until the drug has completely worked its way out of your system." She made a moue with her lips. "Besides, I don't want to fight with you. We should be friends, you and I. Perhaps the only two born vampires in the entire world. It's a natural alliance."

"I want nothing to do with you!" He still couldn't find the scent of corruption on her, but he decided that had to be another side effect of her being a born vampire. There could be no doubt in his mind that she was as tainted as her fledgling.

Brigitte shrugged. "Perhaps not now. You've been through a lot in these last few days. And I can certainly understand that I might not be your favorite person in the world if you associate me with that lot." She jerked her chin toward the warehouse. "But they were merely a means to an end, a way to get me to America and—"

"Tell me what you did to Jezebel!"

She rolled her eyes. "I've already answered that. I did *nothing* to her. All I did was instruct her on how to cure your pain."

Another quick psychic probe showed him Jez was still out of reach. Something was most definitely wrong. It wasn't like he was hitting her mental barriers. It felt . . . different.

"Then why can't I reach her?" he demanded.

"Ah," Brigitte said softly, making a pitying face. Her eyes filled with false sympathy. "I warned her to be careful," she said. "I warned her not to press too hard or too fast." She shook her head, again making one of those sad faces he didn't believe. "She knew it was dangerous, what she was trying. For a fledgling as young as she, especially. She had to tread with the utmost care to keep herself safe. It seems that she failed to follow my instructions."

"You lying little bitch!" Again, he took a step toward her.

Henri stepped up to her side, and the two of them stared at him intently. Suddenly, his legs refused to obey him and take another step.

"As I told you," Brigitte said, "you're in no condition to fight us just now. I am truly sorry that your fledgling's mind didn't survive the effort to save you. I warned her of the risks. It was her decision to proceed regardless.

"I know that you felt some attachment to her, and that she was your first fledgling. But you can make others, and I can help you train them so that—"

"She's not dead!" Gabriel snapped, testing the connection for the millionth time and finding it still there.

Brigitte shrugged. "She might as well be."

Gabriel's eyes blazed and he redoubled his efforts to break through the glamour. But he was still weakened, still exhausted, and his legs didn't budge.

Brigitte sighed dramatically. "I can see now is not the time to talk sense into you. I believe Henri and I will take some time to explore this New World of yours. I imagine we can have some fun and adventures while we wait for you to accept reality." She smiled, that sweet, innocent smile that didn't belong on her face. "One of the joys of immortality, no? We have all the time in the world." She hooked her arm through Henri's. "I'll check back with you someday, when you've had a chance to get over your little Jezebel. Then maybe you'll be ready to accept your destiny."

A sharp retort rose from Gabriel's throat, but before he managed a single word, his mind went fuzzy from glamour. When he snapped out of it, they were gone.

26

FOR A FULL WEEK after the battle at the warehouse, Gabriel remained in his apartment, nursing his wounds, waiting for everything to heal up. Every night, he would spend several hours trying to reach Jezebel. And every night, he was forced to give up, exhausted mind and body from the effort.

When he was fully healed, his fingers all grown back, he paid a visit to Drake, who explained Eli's new and improved powers. Gabriel told himself he ought to return to Baltimore. There was nothing for him here anymore, not with Jezebel beyond his reach. Not when he could no longer muster even a scrap of enthusiasm at the thought of revenge against his father. And yet somehow, another week slipped by and he was still in Philadelphia, still hoping against hope that Jez would wake from her unnatural sleep. Through Drake, he learned that Eli was force-feeding her, keeping her body alive. But how long would it be before he decided it would be a mercy to let her slip away?

Two weeks stretched to three before Gabriel realized that he couldn't leave the city without Jezebel. Even if he could never reach her, could never speak to her again, she was his fledgling and his responsibility. He had to try everything in his power to get her back. Even if that meant surrendering himself to Eli's questionable mercy.

He didn't bother to mask his presence as he approached Eli's house. Instead, he strode boldly to the gate, wanting to get this over with. He reached for the doorbell, but the gates buzzed and opened before he had a chance to ring. Taking a deep breath, he stepped through those gates and made his way to the front door of the mansion.

When he arrived, Eli opened the door and just stood there, blocking the doorway while he looked Gabriel up and down with expressionless eyes. Gabriel bristled, but tried to tamp down his anger. He forced a mocking smile.

"Well," he said, "I suppose I should be thankful you didn't greet me with drawn sword." He remembered Camille's head rolling on the warehouse floor and had to suppress a shudder.

"Indeed," Eli said, but he opened the door wider to let Gabriel in.

Gabriel accepted the invitation, then stood indecisively in the foyer, half his attention focused on his father, half focused on Jezebel who was so close and yet so far away. His throat tightened. She was upstairs somewhere. He could feel her presence.

Turning his back on Eli, Gabriel took a couple of steps toward the stairs. Of course, Eli wasn't about to let him go that easily.

"There's been no change in her condition," he said, and Gabriel halted in his tracks.

The tightness in his throat turned to a lump, and his fingers curled into fists. He turned toward Eli and found he couldn't speak. Pain burned in his chest, but it wasn't a physical pain. Much though he hated to show weakness in front of Eli, he had to lower his head and close his eyes or he might have embarrassed himself.

"Why are you here, my son?" Eli asked. His voice was conspicuously gentle.

Gabriel forced his eyes open and swallowed past the lump in his throat. "I—" His voice betrayed him, hoarse and raspy. He cleared his throat, but it didn't help much. "I want to go home. To Baltimore. But I can't leave without her." He shook his head, hardly believing his own sentimentality. "I just can't."

Gabriel's defenses snapped to alert when Eli approached, but his father made no move to attack.

"Are you in love with her, then?" Eli asked.

Again, that burning sensation in his chest. *Was* he in love with her? "I don't know," he murmured. "I can't say I know what love is. I only know I've never felt like this about anyone before in five hundred years." He looked up. "Is that love?"

Eli shrugged, a hint of a wry grin on his face. "I'm not the one to ask. I was celibate as a mortal, and I can say with authority that even as a vampire I've never been in love."

Gabriel raised an eyebrow. "Not even with my mother?"

Eli shook his head. "I was fond of her for a long time. But no, I never loved her, nor did she ever love me."

"Or me," Gabriel blurted, then wished he hadn't.

"I don't think she was capable of it."

And what about you? Gabriel wondered, but he didn't have the guts to ask. Jezebel had claimed more than once that Eli loved him, but he still found that hard to believe.

"Are you going to kill me?" he asked instead. Strangely, he didn't feel terribly concerned about Eli's answer. If he was about to die, then he supposed he was ready for it. Just as long as he got to see Jezebel one more time, even if she couldn't see him.

Eli held out his hand, and his sword materialized. Gabriel blinked and shook his head. It was an illusion, he knew. A mysterious and powerful form of glamour. But he'd seen with his own two eyes what that illusory sword could do. He stood up straight and looked his father in the eye, no hint of fear in him.

"Just let me see Jezebel, first," he asked. "I've tried to reach her through our connection, but I haven't been able to do it. Perhaps if I'm here in body as well as spirit, I'll be able to get through. To help her." He swallowed hard as yet another lump formed in his throat. If he didn't watch it, he was going to find himself bawling like a baby.

Eli wove the sword through the air in a complicated pattern, watching Gabriel's face the whole time, a measuring, assessing gaze. The sword came to a stop with the point about an inch from Gabriel's throat, but he didn't flinch.

"Please. Let me try to reach her. Whether I succeed or fail, I won't fight you."

Eli thought about it a moment longer, then nodded briskly. The sword vanished.

"Follow me," he said, and he climbed the stairs. He led the way to a small, comfortably appointed bedroom, opening the door and gesturing Gabriel in before him.

Jezebel lay on her back on the bed, the covers drawn up to her chin and tucked in around her, her hair fanning the pillow beside her head. The covers rose and fell with her steady breathing. Her face was paler than it should have been, her eyes shadowed with dark circles, her cheeks hollow.

Gabriel whirled on his father. "Drake said you'd been feeding her! She looks half-starved!"

"There's only so much I've been able to get her to swallow."

"You haven't been mixing it with that damned milk, have you?"

Eli gave him a dirty look. "I'm not a fool, son. She'll take a few swallows, then she just starts spitting it out. I don't know what else I can do for her. This is unfamiliar territory, to say the least."

Gabriel sat on the bed beside her, touching the back of his hand to the pale skin of her cheek. Why had she had to interfere?

"If I'd had any idea what she was trying to do," he said softly, "I never would have allowed it. How could she possibly do this to herself for my sake?"

"Because she loves you," was Eli's simple answer. "I might not be an expert on romance, but that much I can say with great confidence."

Gabriel fished her hand out from beneath the covers, wrapping his fingers around hers. If only he had some idea how to help her! He took a deep breath for calm, then started to reach out across the connection, but Eli interrupted him.

"If I might make a suggestion?"

Gabriel was open to any suggestion that might make it possible to bring her back, and he let his face convey that message.

"Many legends that exist about vampires have some basis in fact, though often the reality is far removed from the legend. One could assume, for example, that it is the ability of Old Ones to create illusions that has given rise to the idea of vampires dissolving into mist, or turning into bats, or what have you."

Gabriel acknowledged that with a nod.

"It makes me wonder about the myth of a mortal having to drink a vampire's blood to become vampire. Obviously, it's not necessary, but perhaps you could try feeding her some of your own blood. Perhaps she won't spit that out. And perhaps that will strengthen your connection."

Gabriel's thumb stroked over her limp fingers. "I'd let her drain me dry if I thought that would bring her back."

Figuring it was worth a try, he lowered his fangs, then bit his wrist. The wound started closing almost immediately. He thrust his bleeding wrist into Jez's mouth, using his other hand to raise her head.

His blood coated her lips, and she made a feeble sound of protest. A few drops made it into her mouth, and she didn't spit them out. Unfortunately, the wound had sealed over already. Once again, he bit his wrist open and stuck it in her mouth. This time, her lips moved a bit and she visibly swallowed.

He'd bitten himself three times, only to have the wound heal too quickly, when Jezebel's fangs descended. He shared a quick look with Eli.

"Has that happened at all when you've fed her before?"

Eli shook his head. "Hurry up. Give her more before they retract."

Once again, Gabriel bit himself to start the blood flowing. This time, when he put his wrist to her lips, her fangs sank into him. "That's it, my sweet," he crooned as she started to suck. He climbed all the way onto the bed, careful not to dislodge her, then cradled her body against his as she took big, greedy swallows, her eyes still firmly shut.

Closing his own eyes, Gabriel reached across their connection, trying desperately to find her.

At first, there was nothing. Just the same, strange blankness he'd been feeling for three weeks. Not like her mental doors were closed, but like they were hidden behind a billowing sea of fog. But then there was . . . something. A hint of movement behind the fog, a fleeting glimpse of something solid.

Gabriel lunged forward, grabbing at that hint of movement, but his hands passed through emptiness. He groped his way through the fog.

Jezebel! Are you in there?

No answer, but he plunged deeper anyway. He could no longer feel his physical body at all. For a fleeting moment, he wondered if he'd be able to find his way back. Then, he decided he didn't care and continued forward.

He lost all track of time, flailing his way through mist and fog, chasing an elusive feeling that might be nothing but his wishful thinking. Then he heard it, the very faintest of sounds. It sounded like his name. He propelled himself forward.

Jezebel! he shouted, straining his ears for an answer.

There! He heard it. Still faint, still far away, but he felt sure it was his name. He kept reaching, stretching, shouting.

And then the fog cleared, and she was there, a solid presence in his mind.

Jezebel! Relief flooded him, even as he realized he had no idea how to get back into his body.

Gabriel? What are you doing here?

He almost laughed. *Looking for you, of course.*

He couldn't see a thing, but he could swear he *felt* her frown.

But you shouldn't be here, she argued.

Why not? I want to be where you are.

I don't know where I am, she said, sounding mournful. *I've been wandering and wandering, and I can't seem to get anywhere. And unless you've left a trail of breadcrumbs, you really shouldn't have come after me.*

I don't care, he declared. *Wherever you are, that's where I belong.* And he knew at that moment the answer to Eli's question. *I love you, Jezebel. I didn't think it was possible for me to love, but you've proven me wrong.*

The mist surrounded them, thick, impenetrable, disorienting. Even so, he felt something in his core he might almost have described as peace.

You have to go back, Gabriel, Jez said. *Please. I didn't go through all this hell just to have you throw your life away.*

Even if I wanted to go back, I don't know the way. I love you. I'm where I belong.

You're a pig-headed pain in the ass! she told him, and he chuckled.

But you love me anyway.

She breathed a resigned sigh. *Yeah, I love you anyway.*

Something niggled at him, a strange sensation at the back of his metaphysical neck. Almost like a tug. He puzzled over it, then let himself drift in the direction of the tug.

What is it? Jez asked.

Perhaps I've found my trail of breadcrumbs, he said.

Huh?

The tug came a little more strongly. He might almost have described the sensation as pain, though he wasn't sure it was possible to feel pain without a body.

Can you follow me? he asked Jez.

I think so.

He drifted a little farther.

Jezebel followed, but a bit of distance opened up between them.

Come on, Jez! Keep up.

He moved toward the ever-more-urgent tug, but Jez wasn't keeping pace.

Damn it! he shouted. *Keep up!*

I'm trying. I can't.

But he hadn't come this far merely to leave her behind. *I'm bringing you out of here if it kills me.*

He strained against the tugging sensation, reaching out to Jez, wrapping himself around her.

Gabriel, please—

Shut up and come with me.

Again, he moved toward the tug. And this time, she moved with him.

Something's wrong, she said.

Never mind, he soothed, even as he felt the strangeness she had sensed. He continued to move through the mist, but he felt himself growing weaker. It was as if he was leaving little pieces of himself behind as he dragged Jez along with him.

What are you doing? Jez cried.

He had no idea. And he didn't care. He was drawing Jezebel out of the mist, and that was all that mattered.

The almost-pain became a little sharper, a little more like real pain. Gabriel embraced it, moving faster, dragging Jez despite her protests.

The pain grew sharper still, a stinging, burning sensation in his cheek. He hurried toward it. Another slap, harder, rattling his head, jarring his teeth.

And suddenly, Gabriel was back in his body, lying on his back on a soft bed, Eli hovering over him, holding the front of his shirt so tight the collar was practically choking him. Eli pulled back his hand, and Gabriel finally understood the source of the pain in his face.

"Stop it, old man!" he protested. "I'm back!"

Eli's hand dropped, and he let go of Gabriel's shirt, sighing in evident relief. Gabriel wondered briefly why the man who was soon to kill him should feel relieved to have him back. Then he turned to look at the bed beside him.

Blood spotted the coverlet and pillow and stained Jezebel's lips. Her eyes were still closed, but the color had returned to her cheeks. She ran her tongue over her lips, drinking in the last drops of his blood, then turned on her side and snuggled against him, sighing contentedly.

Jezebel? he asked uncertainly.

Mmm?

Are you with me?

Her eyes fluttered open. Never in his life had he felt so close to weeping. She gave him a mournful, reproachful look, then her eyes drifted closed again.

"Tired," she murmured out loud.

"Then sleep," he responded, stroking her hair as his eyes burned and his throat ached.

Eli's hand came down on his shoulder, squeezing lightly in a gesture that seemed almost fatherly.

"You did it," Eli said. He sounded amazed.

Gabriel nodded, unable to trust his voice. He'd brought her back, all right. But something very definitely wasn't right. He felt strangely hollow inside, like somehow he wasn't all there. He sighed. What did it matter when Eli was going to kill him anyway?

What would happen to Jezebel when he was gone? With her fiery temper, he doubted she could ever forgive Eli for killing him. And she was too young a fledgling to survive on her own. He hated to bring her back from the mysterious misty place only to abandon her. But there was no choice. It wasn't like he could defeat Eli in combat, even if he were at full strength.

Eli's hand slid away from his shoulder, and Gabriel took a deep, steadying breath. Better to get this over with before Jez awakened again. Moving gently and carefully so as not to wake her, he slid away from her and tucked the covers under her chin once more. Then he bent and placed a soft kiss on her forehead.

When he stood up and turned around, the sword was back in Eli's hand, and his face was the impassive mask Gabriel had learned to hate over the years. Gabriel held his head high and glared at his father.

"Can we at least move out of her room to do this?" he hissed. The last thing he wanted was for her to awaken and see his head parted from his shoulders.

Eli gestured toward the door. Gabriel strode through, hoping he wouldn't lose his courage before this was over. When he heard the door to Jez's room close, he turned around and faced his father. He certainly didn't want to give Eli the chance to behead him without looking him straight in the face while he did it!

Eli ran a finger along the edge of his blade, drawing a line of blood over his skin. "This is the real sword," he said. "Not an illusion."

"Why the hell should I care?" Gabriel growled in response. When he'd first come here, thinking Jezebel was lost to him for good, he'd felt no fear whatsoever at the thought of his own death. Now, when he had something to live for after all, he found he wasn't quite as resigned to his fate as he'd once been.

Eli shifted his grip on the sword, his hand on the blade while he held the hilt out to Gabriel.

"Because you can kill me with it," he said.

Gabriel's jaw dropped. "What?"

One corner of Eli's mouth twitched upward. "Which word didn't you understand? Take the sword. I wasn't able to kill you two hundred years ago when I thought you were a heartless, soulless Killer. How can I possibly kill you now when I know you are not?"

Gabriel blinked and shook his head. "You can choose not to kill me without handing me the sword."

"True. But that's not what I'm doing. Take the sword, my son."

Warily, Gabriel reached out and took the sword. The hilt felt real and solid in his hand. He hefted the blade experimentally, getting the feel of its balance. He'd rarely used weapons in his life, his glamour being all the weapon he needed, but he was not completely unfamiliar with them either.

"The sword is real," Eli said again. "And I will make no effort to defend myself." He met Gabriel's gaze steadily. "You know I'm not lying to you."

Gabriel nodded. For all Eli's faults, he was not a liar. He could be secretive and deceptive as hell, but for whatever reason, he refused to tell an outright lie.

Here was an unprecedented opportunity, a chance to vent five centuries' worth of wrath. Just a few weeks ago, Gabriel would have separated Eli's head from his neck without a second thought. Now, he stood hesitating.

Where was the hate, the rage that had fueled him for so very long? He tried to call on it, but he couldn't even find it. And then he thought about Jezebel. What would she think of him if he killed Eli when Eli had spared him?

He lowered the sword, hardly believing how much knowing Jezebel had changed him. Hardly believing how many deep, ancient wounds she'd somehow managed to heal. He stared at the floor, trying to absorb it all, as Eli took the sword from his unresisting fingers.

When he raised his head to face Eli again, Eli's eyes widened and his jaw dropped.

"What?" Gabriel asked, looking over his shoulder in case there was something or someone behind him.

"The scar," Eli said.

Gabriel raised his hand to his scarred cheek . . . and found the skin smooth and unmarred. What the . . . ? He checked his other cheek, just in case he was so out of it he'd forgotten which was the scarred one, but of course he hadn't.

"Is it really gone?" he asked, hardly daring to believe.

"So it would seem."

"But how is that possible?"

Eli shrugged. "How was it possible for you to scar in the first place? I can't say I know, but I can venture a guess."

Gabriel gestured for him to continue.

"My guess is it was the vampire equivalent of a psycho-somatic illness. The mind is an amazing instrument, even in a mortal. In a vampire who is capable of glamour . . ."

"Yeah," Gabriel agreed. It was as good an explanation as any. He reached up to his cheek again, just to be sure, but the line of scar tissue was most definitely gone.

Eli smiled at him. "Why don't you go sit with Jezebel? I suspect she'll want you by her side when she wakes again."

And that was exactly where he wanted to be.

Epilogue

JEZ WAS STILL WEAK and shaky after her ordeal, but she was as eager as Gabriel to get back to Baltimore, to home. Some of it was homesickness, a homesickness she hadn't even realized she'd been feeling, but some of it was sheer practicality. Eli and Gabriel were temporarily at peace with each other, but she suspected the peace would be easier to keep if they had at least a hundred miles between them.

Gabriel insisted on carrying her to the rental car, though they both knew she was capable of walking. She decided not to argue with him too much. It was kind of fun to have Gabriel in all his bad-guy glory fussing over her like she was a three-year-old.

They made one stop before heading out of town. When they parked in front of Drake's brownstone, Jez decided to put her foot down—literally—and walk the few steps from the car to the door. Gabriel gave her a darkly disapproving look, but there was no missing the affection in his eyes.

Drake looked distinctly wary when he let them in. Jez smiled at him, even as Gabriel ushered her immediately into a chair as if being on her feet for more than sixty seconds at a time would break her. She would have to have a word with him about that soon. But not yet.

"To what do I owe the pleasure?" Drake asked.

Neither he nor Gabriel sat. Jez hoped they weren't about to get into some kind of pissing match over Drake aiding her in her quest to save Gabriel's life.

"Jez and I are going back to Baltimore," Gabriel said, though of course Drake knew that already.

"So I'd heard."

Gabriel hesitated, and Jez smiled. He wasn't used to relating to others as equals, and for a man who usually exuded confidence, he was looking mighty uncomfortable.

"We've been talking about what to do with the rest of our lives," Jez said for him.

Drake raised an eyebrow and looked at Gabriel. "And that involves something other than creating a flock of fledglings and becoming the Master of Baltimore?"

Gabriel was still capable of a world-class sneer, which he demonstrated now. "I've been Master of Baltimore for months. I don't need an entourage."

"Gabriel . . ." Jez said warningly.

He held himself a little taller and straighter. "Well, I don't!"

That might not be true, however. They hadn't had much time or opportunity to test it out, but it seemed like the effort he'd made to draw Jez back into her body had cost him something. His glamour seemed a tad erratic, not always there at his call, and didn't have as much oomph as it used to.

Apparently, Gabriel's attitude problem was going to make this conversation less than productive—if Jez let him do the talking.

"We're thinking about starting up our own branch of the Guardians in Baltimore," she blurted, trying not to laugh at the sudden tick in Gabriel's jaw. He wasn't a hundred percent comfortable with the idea yet, but he didn't contradict her.

"I see," Drake said, but it was impossible to miss his skepticism.

"You don't think a Killer can be a Guardian?" Jez challenged, before Gabriel could get his back up.

Drake winced. "Touché."

"I don't suppose my methods will exactly match Eli's," Gabriel said dryly, and they all laughed a bit at that. "But I'm through condoning what I know is wrong. I'm going to take a page from your book and try to make the best of my situation." He made a sour face, and it was all Jez could do to stifle another giggle at his expense.

"I see," Drake said again, with less skepticism this time. "But why are you telling me this?"

Jez had the feeling Drake had a good guess already, but Gabriel spelled it out for him.

"Because I'm inviting you to join us," he said. "You and I both know that the Guardians will never fully accept you. In *my* version of the Guardians, you would be an equal partner." Gabriel grinned. "Well, not *equal* exactly, but you wouldn't be the red-headed stepchild, as it were."

Drake's expression was tight and unhappy.

"With Eli's new powers," Jez added, "the Guardians won't be so desperately in need of your strength. Gabriel and I probably will be."

After all, Brigitte and Henri were still out there somewhere. Brigitte would not be happy that her plot to remove Jez as an obstacle had failed. Jez doubted she would give up on her quest to make Gabriel her ally, and she didn't think her methods were going to get any friendlier.

Drake moved over to a chair and sat down, his eyes troubled. "I've worked for Eli for more than a century. And Philadelphia is my home."

"But things have changed," Gabriel pointed out brutally. "I may have reconciled with my father, but we still both know he is not the saint that you and the rest of the Guardians wanted him to be."

Drake laughed without humor. "And you're an improvement?"

Jez held her breath, but Gabriel didn't have a temper tantrum. "I don't have a long history of deceiving you. And I won't treat you like a second-class citizen because you're a Killer."

"I'll think about it," Drake said.

Jez suspected that he meant "no." But she and Gabriel had agreed in advance that they wouldn't push.

Gabriel grabbed a newspaper that was sitting on a side table, scribbling his phone number in the margins. "If you decide you want to join us, give me a call. The offer is open-ended."

Drake nodded, but didn't answer. He stood up and reached out his hand for Gabriel to shake.

"Good luck to you," he said.

Gabriel smiled crookedly as they shook hands. "Thanks. And the same to you."

"You'll take good care of Jezebel, I'm sure."

Jez rolled her eyes. "Oh, puh-lease! I'm perfectly capable of taking care of myself, thank you very much."

Gabriel looked at her and arched a brow. "Care to arm wrestle, my sweet?"

She stuck her tongue out at him. He laughed.

Hardly appropriate behavior for a subordinate, he said in her head.

Subordinate? Who said I was subordinate?

His grin was wicked in the extreme. *It seems I'll need to teach you a lesson.*

Jez giggled, visualizing him bending her over his knee.

He groaned, although she felt the hint of lust the image evoked. "Not *that* again!" he complained out loud.

"What?" Drake asked.

Gabriel's cheeks flushed pink with embarrassment. "Nothing," he muttered.

Amusement sparkled in Drake's eyes. "Jezebel, if you

can make a bad-ass like him blush then you must be just the right woman for him."

"I'm not blushing!" Gabriel protested as his cheeks turned a slightly darker shade of pink.

"Yes, dear," Jez said. "Now let's hit the road, shall we?"

He sighed dramatically and scooped her back into his arms.

Why do I have a feeling this is going to be a very, very long road trip? he asked.

I have no idea! She batted her eyelashes at him innocently.

From the look he gave her then, she gathered he was going to drive like a race car driver with the finish line in sight. But she had her own ideas on how to shorten the wait. After all, that's what rest areas were for!